BRUNCH AT RUBY'S

DL WHITE

 BOOKS
BY DL WHITE

CONTENTS

COPYRIGHT

Brunch at Ruby's
DL White

*For my Mother, Angela with whom I share my "wacky" sense of humor,
my love of books and beautiful writing.*
*For my Father, Marvin, from his "favorite" daughter. *wink* You always
tell me how proud you are of me. Your love and never ending support has
propelled me toward this dream. Thank you.*
*In loving memory of Uncle Edwin "T" and Delois Kennedy, whose long
and loving marriage was an inspiration for this novel.*

PROLOGUE

ebra

I'm packing up my office to leave for the day when he saunters in, unexpected but not unwelcome. My heart skips a beat, and my belly quivers like I'm a teenager in love and not an adult in a forbidden relationship.

"Is that your equipment inventory? How are we looking?"

I gesture to the stack of papers folded in his hand. He bypasses me, dropping the form into the IN basket on my desk. His scent is a mix of cologne and manly sweat and freshly cut grass from working on the football field most of the day.

"All there," he says with a confident nod. "All good. We're ready."

I smile at him, my arms full of folders and a heavy bag hanging from my shoulder. School begins in a few weeks, and as Principal at Morningside Middle School, I still have hours of work before my day is complete.

David Loren, my Athletics Director, moves across the office slowly, taking his time.

"So, I was just leaving," I hint. "Was there anything you needed?"

"Just... one thing."

Swift and smooth, like an eagle dipping to pluck its prey from the river, he moves in and drops his lips to mine. My heartbeat quickens with panic... then I relax. It's the end of the day. The building is empty; the halls are quiet. I drop the armful of folders onto the nearest chair and let my bag slide from my shoulder. It lands at our feet with a thud.

I lean into him. Into the kiss. Into the moment.

A noise sounds above the quiet moans between us, ripping my lips from his. We leap apart, each taking a few steps back. At the faint sound of a door closing, we rush into the hallway in time to catch a fleeting figure dart past the window and down a darkened hall.

"Hey. HEY!" David takes off, bellowing into the shadows. Whoever it is, they move quickly enough to get away from a former football player. Too soon, he's back in my office, leaning heavily on one leg more than the other, wrinkles of pain across his forehead.

"Could you see who it was?"

He shakes his head. "Moved too fast. I'm pretty sure it was a kid. It was dark." He drops into a chair. I can't breathe suddenly. My knees buckle. I collapse into the chair next to him.

"Don't panic, Debra. Maybe they didn't see anything."

My glare is pointed and severe. "Maybe they didn't see your tongue halfway down my throat? Are you serious?"

David pouts, shrugging a bulky shoulder. "Okay, but it's our word against theirs. Who's going to believe a kid that says they saw you and me kissing in your office? Sounds made up to me."

"You mean no one would believe the young PE Teacher would be interested in the old married Principal?"

He sighs. "That's not how I meant it, Debra."

"You know what, never mind. It doesn't even matter. The

rumor is enough to make my life hell. I told you we needed to end this!"

"Don't overthink it. That's how people make mistakes—"

"Mistakes?" I cough out a sarcastic chuckle. "I think this is way bigger than a mistake right now. Do me a favor, David. Shut up. You have no idea what you're talking about."

I drop my face into my hands as my world swirls around me. The hallways of a middle school are lined with gasoline. Gossip spreads like wildfire around this place, especially during the first few weeks of the new school year. The thought of my fate being in someone else's hands or someone having something to hold over me makes my stomach roll.

"This is a nightmare. I'm going to have to tell Willard. And maybe Bernice..."

"The Superintendent? Over a kiss that somebody says they saw? You don't have to tell anybody anything. You didn't tell them about it before—"

"No one else knew before!"

"No one else knows now! Stop and think, Debra! All we have to do is deny it. Maybe we just lie low and—"

"No." I hop up from the chair, grabbing the handles of my bag and tossing it over my shoulder. "I can get another job, and so can you, but I can't risk my marriage anymore."

I shake my head, my resolve stronger every moment. "Willard cannot find out about this when whoever..." I point toward the window. "Whoever that was decides to play their hand."

David stands and limps toward the door. The knee injury that destroyed his dreams of being drafted to a pro football team is flaring up. "At least wait before you tell anybody but him. Let's see how things play out before you get us both fired."

CHAPTER ONE

ebra

Love fades.

Wait… that's not right. Passion fades. Love changes. It shifts, it breathes, it adapts. Passion burns bright and hot but, over time, grows dim. Bit by bit, so slowly that you don't even notice until you look for that spark, and it's gone.

Passion is the kind of thing you have to keep feeding because if you don't and it dies, there's no guarantee of bringing it back. When the passion is gone, but you're desperate to feel it, you might do anything to find it again.

I mean… anything.

On Saturday mornings, I pay the bills. It's more out of habit than a necessity but rain or shine, I'm at the kitchen table sorting through envelopes and writing checks for the bills we don't like to pay online.

This table is older than I am. A rectangular slab of wood, nine feet by twelve feet, worn soft by Wednesday night dinner and Sunday afternoon dessert, and so many years of homework and books and bags piled on top of it. It belonged to my parents, who bought it brand new when they bought their house in 1970. When my husband, Willard, and I moved my aging parents to a smaller home, we took the kitchen table that I've been staring at my whole life.

Twelve hours ago, this table was witness to a dramatic change in my life. Willard's life too, and by extension, our daughter Kendra, though she doesn't know it yet. I should feel relieved, like a load has been lifted from my shoulders, but I can't help but recognize a sense of dread and foreboding. I'm bracing for impact.

My coffee, once hot with curls of steam rising from the lip of my favorite mug, is lukewarm as I pick it up and slurp down a mouthful. I grimace at the bitter taste. I can't get used to this stuff without sugar, but I'm trying to cut my sugar intake. That's something I'm known for. Debra, the Health Nut. I'm also Debra, Suzy Homemaker and Debra, The One with the Answers. I find that last one particularly ironic. I'm drowning in questions, and I have no answers for any of them.

"Ma, can you pick me up from band practice?"

Kendra is twelve going on thirty. Tall like her father and thin like me with big doe eyes, long lashes and skin the color of caramel. Kendra is a beautiful child. Smart, social, sweet and loving. Also spoiled. We've been fighting all summer about how short her shorts are and how midriff-baring her shirts are. I like letting her buy her own clothes, but not to let her waltz around town with all of her skin showing. Today, she's dressed like she knows I'm watching. Her shorts fall at mid-thigh, and her tank top covers her belly. That's all I ask.

Her expression betrays impatience with my delay in responding to her haughty request. One hand rests on her hip; the other clutches the handle of a rectangular black case. Homecoming is fast approaching, and the band is rehearsing a whole new routine, the Band Director tells me. She's having the kids come in before school even starts to get a leg up on the material.

Kendra is in the seventh grade at Morningside Middle School. I'm the Principal — something that should have stopped me in my tracks, but... well, you know that song by Cher, If I Could Turn Back Time? That could be my theme song right now.

"Why can't you get home the same way you're getting there?"

"Because it's going to be hot when I get out of practice. Please, mom?" Her thin arms flail around her. Desperate and dramatic, she is nearly faint at the thought of having to walk an entire six blocks in the Georgia heat.

"I don't think I can. I have plans with Aunt Max and Aunt Renee today, and I don't want to be rushed."

"But Ma, it's supposed to get over ninety today!"

"Kendra, I said no!"

I don't mean to snap, but it's like she can't remember what the word 'no' means anymore. "We live six blocks from the school. You won't melt."

She sucks her teeth, heaves a tortured teenage sigh and slowly exits the kitchen, dragging her feet across the tile floor. I feel guilty now for snapping at her. It's not her fault I didn't sleep.

Because my husband isn't talking to me.

Because last night I confessed to having an affair.

I jumped in front of the proverbial train and spilled everything, not out of a need to save my marriage, to be honest with my husband of fourteen years, to repair what was broken between us. Not even out of a sense of loyalty and full disclosure. I told my husband about my affair because I got caught with another man, and some shit was about to hit the fan.

"Well..." I sigh. She halts her slow, morose exit from the kitchen. I'm such a sucker. "Call me when practice is over. If I'm on my way, I'll come to get you."

Her disposition brightens considerably. The brat. "Thanks, Ma!"

She bounds out of the side door that leads through the garage, leaving the door open in her wake. She and a friend meet up at the end of the driveway, and they take off in the direction of Morningside.

Morning sun streams into the space where Willard's Lexus is usually parked. He's been gone since early this morning. That isn't unusual, but most Saturdays, he would at least hang around for breakfast before going into the office.

I stack the bills together, stuff them into my purse, take one last gulp of coffee and head out of the same door Kendra went through, pulling it closed behind me. I slip into the Benz that Willard bought for me two years ago. I'd been driving a ten-year-old E-class and was happy with it. He knew I had been eyeing the S550, though, and when I was promoted to Principal at Morningside, he got me the car. It was the biggest surprise of my life. Even Kendra was in on it.

Our home looks happy from the outside–a professionally manicured lawn, a trellis on either side of the porch covered in roses, and dots of brightly colored flowers in the flower beds. We hung a vintage wooden swing off of the beams, and in the summer, we like to sit outside and drink sweet tea, watch the fireflies buzz through sunset and call to the neighbors as they take their evening walks.

One would think the Macklin family lived a life of easy, suburban bliss.

One could not be more wrong.

CHAPTER TWO

enee

"It's your turn, Daddy."

"I thought it was your turn. I was waitin' on you."

Bony fingers pluck a card and slowly transfer it to the stack in the center of the table. After he plays, Daddy fans his cards out and brings his elbows in, hunching forward. As if his failing memory isn't enough, his eyesight is going downhill, too. He looks so much older than his sixty-seven years.

We play cards every day. Every single day. He might forget my name, what street we live on, his own birthday or that he doesn't work at the Ford plant anymore, but he never forgets to rifle through the top right-hand drawer in my mother's mahogany China hutch, pull out the bundle of cards banded together and take his seat at the table across from me. We play until Jessie, his caregiver, arrives. I let him think he whips my butt.

The cards we play with are thin and tattered, so old you can barely see the photos of the Jazz greats printed on the back of them —Duke Ellington, Dizzy Gillespie, Eartha Kitt. Daddy refuses to play with the new set I bought him. He and my mother played cards together with his set.

Memory is a funny thing. It has belongings, smells and sights and sounds and things. The cards belong to a time that he barely remembers anymore. Maybe that's why his grasp on them is so tight.

He squints as he peruses his hand, his brows pushed closer together by the creases between his eyes.

"Daddy." He grunts. "Where are your glasses? You're going to give yourself a headache, all that squinting and staring."

"Don't know," he mumbles, shuffling his cards around. The last time he lost his glasses, I found them in the microwave. There's no telling where they are now.

I lay down my next card. "Jessie is going to have your hide if you don't find them before she gets here."

"Jessie comin' today?"

"Yes, sir. I'm going to see Maxine and Debra today. You remember them, Daddy? My friends, that used to live down the street from us?"

"'Course I remember," he says, grunting again. "Why's Jessie coming? I told you I don't need no babysitter. Old enough to babysit you."

"Good, because she's not a babysitter. She'll make you some lunch, maybe take you for a walk—"

"Babysitter," he interrupts, slapping a card onto the table.

In his more lucid moments, my father knows that there are long periods of time that he can't remember. Flashes of memory pulsing in and out. He's insistent that he's fine. It's just a few spells, old age, it'll blow over. He protests having Jessie here, and they bicker like siblings, but without Jessie, it doesn't work.

Debra and Maxine, my oldest and dearest friends, love Atlanta. The city, the people, the sweet gentility, the slow pace and southern tradition. Born and raised here, I couldn't wait to get out of this place. I took my Business degree from Georgia State as far north as New York and as far west as Los Angeles, looking for anything to keep me away from Atlanta.

I ended up in Philly, where I got hired on at SimCore, a pharmaceutical manufacturer. That's where I met Marcus — six foot two, lean and muscular, dark brown eyes, velvety skin the hue of a coconut husk. Quiet when necessary. A beast when I needed him to be. I had a good job, a nice apartment, a man I was falling hard for.

My mother taught elementary school when I was young. When I was in high school, she quit that job and opened a small bookstore in downtown Decatur. Gladwell Books was the perfect second life for her, a cute little shop that made just enough money to keep it afloat and Mama's hands busy. After her death, Daddy kept it open as an honor to her memory. I really think he couldn't let it go.

Between the bookstore and taking care of the house and his card club (a bunch of old men sitting around talking about old women), he seemed busy. Like always, he said he was fine; he didn't need my help, don't bother him.

One of our neighbors took it upon herself to watch over Daddy and the house, water my mother's roses, check the mail—basically be a busybody, but she was my lifeline. One evening, I'd just come home from work, was changing out of my business suit to meet Marcus for dinner when I heard my cell phone ringing. I thought it was Marcus, egging me on to hurry since I was already late. I let it go to voice mail.

In the shower, something niggled at me. I felt like I needed to check my messages. I wrapped a towel around myself and found my phone plugged into the charger on the kitchen counter.

Four missed calls read the display on my Blackberry. I dialed into voice mail and was greeted with urgent messages from the neighbor. I knew it was about Daddy.

Around dusk, she'd said, he was marching down the street in his Ford uniform—dark blue slacks, light blue shirt with the Ford emblem over the right front pocket. He wore socks but no shoes, and he was shouting for Lorraine. Lorraine, my mother, had been dead for four years.

I flew home and checked him into a hospital. At first glance, the doctors thought it could be stress. Repressed grief, maybe. Daddy thought everybody was crazy. He said he was fine, worrying about him was a waste of time, and he didn't need anyone watching over him. He didn't want to stay at the hospital, and he didn't appreciate nurses poking and prodding him.

"Go on back to Philly," he'd said when I brought him home. "I don't need you here. Get on back to your life."

I went back to Philly, back to my job, my apartment, my handsome boyfriend. I was looking forward to introducing him to Daddy, and we were talking about moving in together.

A few months later, I called for our regular Wednesday night chat. He didn't recognize my voice. He was distant and slow to answer questions and confused about my reminder to set the garbage out for pickup. The garbage has been picked up every Thursday morning next to the driveway for as long as I've been alive.

I called the neighbor for a report. Daddy was not fine. He didn't know where he was half the time and where he was going the other half. Worst of all, Gladwell Books, the biggest Lorraine Gladwell keepsake possible, was on the verge of collapse. Daddy hadn't opened the store in weeks.

I flew home and took him back to Dr. Crawford. I've been here ever since.

A knock at the kitchen door interrupts a spirited session of bickering about who is losing. Jessie is wearing her usual uniform of khaki slacks and a faded short-sleeved polo with the Atlanta Rehabilitation Services logo over the left breast. Wisps of gray hair peek out from under a short curly wig, brushed and fluffed to a brilliant shine and impressive height. She carries a black leather bag with her, which holds games, music and anything she feels she might need for the day.

The first year with Daddy, I tried to make it on my own, but I realized, quickly, that if I didn't get some help, I might kill him. Accidentally or otherwise. His illness and general, obstinate nature make him grumpy and argumentative. Because his decline has been so markedly slow, he knows that he's sick, that his condition is incurable, his symptoms uncontrollable. That doesn't make accepting his Alzheimer's diagnosis any easier. It is a violent internal struggle that presents itself in the habit of throwing things. Or disappearing.

The first four nurses, my father chased away. The last one, I fired myself. Jessie has been with us for the last two years. She is an old school nurse who doesn't take much of anything from anyone, including Bernard Gladwell. She's all business from the minute she walks in the door until she leaves for the day. Daddy is on a schedule, and she keeps him active. They play games, go for walks, and she takes him to his appointments when I can't. He grumbles and argues and calls her his babysitter, but she has a way of being bossy and direct in a motherly way. She's a lot like Mama, actually. I suspect that this is why they get along.

I tip my head at Jessie. Daddy doesn't acknowledge her, but he never does. She drops her bag onto the couch and, propping her hands on ample hips, takes in the scene like we aren't always in this spot, doing this very thing every morning.

"Well, who's winning?" I nod my head across the table to Daddy, who is squinting at the cards he's holding close to his face. "How's he winning, and he can't even see?"

She taps him on the shoulder, and he nearly jumps out of his skin. "Mistah Gladwell! Where your glasses at, old man?"

Daddy shakes his head, grunts a little, plucks a card from the stack and plays it. She heads for the flight of steps that lead to the second floor. "They're probably on his nightstand. You know how he gets those headaches without them."

A few minutes later, silver wire-framed glasses appear at

Daddy's elbow as she passes the table on the way into the kitchen. He glances at them, picks them up and puts them on.

"I'm headed out in a few minutes," I tell her. "So, it'll be just the two of you for lunch."

"How romantic." Sounds of cabinets opening and closing and items being taken out of the refrigerator waft from the kitchen. "Bernard! You want a hot ham and cheese sandwich? You got some potatoes about to go bad in here. I can fry them up like potato chips."

"I don't care," he mumbles.

I swallow back a little guilt, watching them fall into their daily routine.

My Corolla sedan shares garage space with a slowly rusting Ford Mustang, kept under an enormous tarp. The '66 raven black hardtop, restored from the ground up by his own two hands, was Daddy's pride and joy. He named it Lorraine, and when he would talk about Lorraine, we were never sure if he meant the car or his wife. Sometimes when Daddy disappears, I find the indigo blue plastic unceremoniously dumped on the cement floor and him in the driver's seat, his fingers roving the five gauge instrument panel, gripping the gear shift, caressing the leather seats. I wish we could take her for a spin, but she hasn't run in years.

I was sure I would be excommunicated when I parked my Toyota in a Ford man's garage. Daddy didn't even refer to it by name. "That foreign junk you drive," he called it.

I slide into my foreign junk and back out of the garage, watching the wide mouth close before pulling into the street. I reach for the radio dial and flip through the FM stations. It has been a long and stressful month, and I need to be around people that understand me. And remember my name.

Debra and her family lived a few houses down the street. Maxine and her mother, Inell, lived a few blocks away. Max intimidated me, mostly. She was easily the prettiest girl in our third-grade class. She had long hair that she religiously washed and pressed every Saturday night. Her skin was the tone of light brown sugar, her eyes almond-shaped and hazel, in sharp contrast to Debra and me with cocoa skin and dark brown eyes. Max always had lip gloss that smelled like strawberries. Debra and I could only wear Vaseline on our lips.

Once, while my mother was twisting my hair into braids, I told her I wanted to get my hair pressed and wear it straight like Maxine. She clicked her tongue and rolled her eyes at me in the mirror. "Don't compete with Maxine. She will always win that game."

Debra, her high school sweetheart, Willard, and I went to Georgia State University. Max decided not to go. "It's boring," she said when asked why she wasn't applying to colleges. She flipped her hair and sashayed away in one of her new designer outfits. She had a job at the uppity, rich people mall, and her whole check seemed to go to her hair and wardrobe. Maxine already had everything she needed: a job, a car, money, and endless attention from men—and I don't mean the boys we went to school with. I mean grown men.

Maxine went to school, though. Real Estate school. When she earned her first commission check, she knew exactly what she wanted to do with her life.

A stark white streak zooms past me as I get out of my car at Ruby's. I don't even have to look up to know that it's Maxine in her brilliantly bright white Maserati. She's a self-made woman, owns her own real estate firm and sells big houses to rich people. Debra is a middle school principal, married to a high-profile accountant with a perfect child and a house in the suburbs and a Mercedes Benz.

Then there's me, in a dusty piece of foreign junk, trying my hardest to keep a neighborhood bookstore afloat and my father from wandering into the street in his underwear.

CHAPTER THREE

*M*axine

I coast into the parking lot at Ruby's slowly, so as not to kick up rocks and mar the paint on my car and honk as I pass Renee. She waves without even looking, pulling at the jacket of that purple Juicy Couture sweatsuit she wears all the time. The one she thinks hides those ten pounds she's picked up.

Ruby's Soul Food café is a neighborhood staple, the perfect spot for after- church gatherings on Sunday and the occasional weekday evening when a plate of hot catfish and hush puppies would hit you just right. Back in the day, it was where we went for sodas after school, for group outings on Friday nights and post-movie, pre-make out point Saturday night dates. We spent so much time there that Ruby, the restaurant's founder, is practically an adopted grandmother. We don't see her much, but when we do, it's an event. It's only fitting that Ruby's is where Debra, Renee and I have met for brunch every month for the last four years.

I brush the wrinkles from my dress as I step out of the car and pick my way through the gravel parking lot, cursing Richard, the

General Manager of Ruby's like I do every month when I have to trudge through dust and rocks just for brunch.

Stepping inside Ruby's is like a step into the past. Silver stools still line the front counter; the old-style cash register still sits on the counter next to the front door, over which a small bell still tinkles to announce new arrivals. The linoleum floors are dull; the shine buffed out of them after so many years of being mopped twice a day.

Ruby's holds twenty tables indoors, another ten outside, another eight at the front counter, so a busy day is a madhouse. Today the place is packed.

Four men seated at the front counter lean back and give me the once-over, head to toe. I nod to each of them as I pass, a leather bag on my arm, designer shades clutched in my palm.

"Gentlemen," I greet them, nodding before spotting Renee and Debra seated on a bench that resembles an old church pew painted yellow to match the sunny décor. I sit next to Renee, who is on the phone, and reach across her to tap Debra on the knee. She's staring into space and hasn't even noticed I've arrived. "What's up, Deb?"

Her head pops up, and she sucks in a breath as if I'd crept up behind her. "Hey, Max. I didn't see you come in."

"I can see how you missed her," says Renee, ending her call and tucking away her phone. "You've been studying that crack in the floor pretty hard."

Debra half-smiles, drawing lines around her mouth. "I guess I have some things on my mind. Ready?"

After so many years of faithful patronage, we always get the same table when we come for brunch—the big booth in the back corner with the tall sides. Loyalty has its privileges.

Our waitress is a former student of Debra's. I half listen to their animated chatter as we are led to our table and take our usual seats. Debra sits on the outside, Renee and I on the inside, as close as we can get without elbowing each other.

We always order the same thing at Ruby's. Renee gets the shrimp and grits with sausage. Debra is our health nut, so her usual is an egg white omelet with roasted vegetables, chicken apple sausage and her splurge–fried potatoes. As for me, when it comes to comfort food, I like it fried. Serve it up with lots of whatever I order on the side with a knife and fork. I don't eat with my hands. My usual is chicken and waffles with butter and so much syrup, my food practically does the backstroke.

Our waitress knows the drill and bounces away to place our orders. A busboy arrives with glasses of water for the other two and a bottle of Perrier water for me. I break the seal and pour myself a glass.

"Renee, how's Bernard doing?"

She grimaces as if the topic is distasteful while dropping a lemon into her glass. "He's about the same."

"The same is good, right? He's not getting worse?"

"I guess. But even the good days are hard to manage."

"It's that bad?" Debra asks, coming out of her stupor.

"I don't know if it's that bad. I'm that tired." She relaxes against the cushion of the booth, playing with the zipper on her jacket. "Half the time, he doesn't know who I am. The other half, he's yelling at me. If I leave him alone for five minutes, he turns a room upside down. Stuff turned over, drawers emptied, things everywhere."

"Maybe he's looking for something," I suggest.

"Apparently, he doesn't remember what he's looking for. Guess that's why he hasn't found it."

"Is Jessie still there?"

"Yeah," she answers, but with a weary sigh. "She'll be retiring soon. What if he gets really bad, really fast? What if he forgets how to use the toilet? I don't think I can change my dad's diapers."

Renee holds the wide-eyed stare of panic. I reach out to give her a reassuring pat on the shoulder but pull back with a frown at the texture of the cheap crushed velvet jacket. "I thought I told you to throw this purple thing away."

Renee laughs, but I sense tension and frustration melting away.

"You're not the boss of me, Maxine. It's comfortable, and it's what I want to wear. I'm not you."

"You sure aren't," I mumble. I don't even care that she heard me. She ignores me anyway. "Debra?" I lightly kick her under the table, bringing her out of another stare into space. "What's up with you today?"

"I'm fine," she says, brightening. "Just work, you know. School starts up again in a few weeks and Kendra has so much going on with the band and Willard is…" Her arms move back and forth as she rubs her palms over her thighs. "Willard is busy. The business tax deadline is coming up, and he's working long hours."

"When isn't Willard working long hours?" Renee asks, a rhetorical question because we all know the answer. Working to provide is one thing. Working yourself to death is another.

"I know; it's the same every year, but now my workload is heavy. I worry about Kendra being raised by the Internet. Or her friends. You know how grown some of these little rich girls can be."

Renee and I nod. Our eighth-grade class had two girls in a close race between labor and graduation.

Three plates land on our table. My chicken is still sizzling from the fryer. I cut my food into bite-sized pieces. "Is that all? You seem real quiet today, Deb. It's not like you."

"Things could be better but I'm alright," Debra mumbles, around a mouthful of omelet. "How are you doing?"

"Well, you remember last month, I was trying to unload that place up in Sugarloaf? Next to some football player, what's his name?" I stop cutting and try to remember, but my mind is blank. If I go to a football game, it's not to watch the game, it's to meet the players and I've already had my picks off of the Atlanta Falcons team. "Anyway, I finally sold it to some pro golfer."

"Tiger?" Renee asks, a spoonful of grits and shrimp halfway to her mouth.

"Wouldn't I have called you if I was selling a house to Tiger Woods?" Renee shrugs and goes back to her lunch. "So, after I sold that house, he started sending his friends to my office. If it's not golfers buying homes, it's football players selling them. Property up is being snapped up like hotcakes at a church breakfast and going for millions." I spear a piece of chicken and waffle and quickly chew and swallow.

"So Donovan is selling all of them?" Renee asks.

I nod, proud. "My agents have showings scheduled every day this week." I sigh, smiling into my plate. Men, money and food— my three favorite subjects.

"Sounds like business is good," says Debra. "You've done really well for yourself, Max."

"And did I tell you girls that I dumped James last week?"

"You know you didn't." Renee stifles a laugh. "What was it this time? Was he only worth a billion dollars? Did he only have one Ferrari?"

"You joke, but those things tell a lot about a man."

"Sure," Debra interjects. "That he has a lot of money that he likes to waste on things he can't take with him when he dies."

"Well, you might as well have fun while you're here. I swear, Debra. You're so morose today." I turn toward Renee so I can share the story with the both of them. "There were a few things. First, he's old. James is in his mid-50's so night out for us ends with him snoring at ten o'clock. And that wouldn't even be so bad if it wasn't for the other stuff. Like his height."

"His height?" Renee and Debra squeal in unison.

"Wasn't he going to take you to Italy next summer?" Renee asks, spooning more grits into her mouth. "Maybe you'd better run after Mister Short Man."

"The man is five foot ten on lifts. I wear heels, tall heels. If I'm looking at your bald spot when we walk to the car, it's just not going to work. I'm not even that tall–"

"You're almost six feet tall in heels!" Debra sputters, not even trying to hold in her laughter.

"That's exactly my point! But... it's not just that. He was short in other places." I twist a lock of my hair around my index finger, looking at first Debra, then Renee, and back to Debra.

Renee sucks in a sharp breath and sinks back into the worn fabric of the booth. "Noooo," she whispers.

"And he was self-conscious about it."

"He had a little dick complex? Ugh, that's the worst." Debra huffs and crosses her arms.

"How would you even know what a little dick looks like?" Renee asks. "You have had one frame of reference since you were fifteen and not to pry, but I'm sure you wouldn't still be with Willard if that was a problem."

Debra's jaw falls open and hangs there, slack. "Whatever," she finally shoots back, trying not to laugh. "I watch Oprah."

"I don't think Oprah has ever done a show about little dick complex, but okay." Renee turns back to me. "So how do you date someone for three months and never know this important... bit of information?"

"I knew it, I just..." I shrug, picking at the remnants of chicken and waffle on my plate. "I wanted it to work. I thought we were falling in love. I was picking out China and monogramming hand towels." I wave my hand in the air, reciting, "Mrs. James Rubineaux. Maxine Donovan-Rubineaux." I lower my hands and come back to Earth. "Doesn't that sound classy? I was going to hyphenate my name."

Renee is laughing so hard, tears cascade down her cheeks. Debra's face is buried in her hands. I'm always good for a funny dating story. They always seem funny to everyone but me.

At least I'm trying to find someone and not sitting alone on the couch in my condo, watching reality show trash, or sitting out on my balcony with a glass of wine watching the sunset alone. The last three men I have dated should have led to proposals: Derek, the Investment Banker (he lasted all of six months before he 'wasn't ready for anything serious'), Robert the Real Estate Broker (he felt like he was always in competition with me and he wasn't a gracious loser), and now James, who owns several auto dealerships. I don't drive American and he loves Ford. He hated the Maserati. Add his height and other shortcomings to the mix, plus his belief that he — cheap, short, impotent and opinionated, was the catch and I should bend over backward for him and he hit the chopping block faster than anyone in recent history.

Maxine Donovan bends over backwards for no man. Unless it feels really good to do so.

"I tried to make it work, you know? I'm not getting any younger. He's almost sixty. But the first time he 'forgot his credit card'," I say, with finger quotes, "I told him I could get this kind of treatment from a poor, tall brother with a big dick, so he wasn't giving me anything I couldn't do without."

"You did not!" Debra practically screams.

"Yes, I did. Anyway, I heard he found himself a new one already. I hope she enjoys those four inches he's offering. I should have known from that enormous truck he drives. Overcompensation." I refresh myself with some water and rant on. "He was probably cheating on me with her. Men can't stand to be alone, always overlapping. I hope she's a welfare case and spends all of his money."

"Maxine," Renee chides.

"Well." I pout, tossing my napkin onto my decimated plate. "It would serve him right." I wave at the waitress and make a motion for the check. The girl reaches for the folder in the pocket of her apron and I reach for my purse.

"I hate to eat and run, but I've got to head to the office for an appointment this afternoon. He's a referral from the owner of that security firm—remember that enormous house I sold with the gates and everything? His partner just moved to town, and Brent wants me to find him a nice place in Buckhead that he probably won't take. I love wasting my Saturday afternoon on a wild goose chase, but Brent sends me lots of referrals."

"What's wrong with Buckhead?" asks Renee.

I shrug, drop my wallet onto the table and pull out my compact. I check my makeup, blend a spot with powder and slather on a layer of lip gloss before putting it away. "Not a damn thing. Brent said something about how his new partner wasn't interested in living in the city. He would probably want something in the suburbs but to humor him and show him around. I hope he's cute. I hate being stuck in a car with an ugly man. I don't want anyone thinking I would settle for that."

"Max!" Renee is laughing this time. So am I.

"And I hate being in my car with someone who obviously has no money. Sometimes they're way too impressed with the car."

"Well now, wait," says Debra, her lecturing finger in the air. "You bought an expensive car because you like how it makes you look. You cannot complain when people notice and are impressed by it."

"I sure as hell can. Whose turn is it to pay?" I open the folder and stare at the total, though it's the same every month.

"You always ask whose turn it is when it's your turn," says Debra. I slide a platinum credit card into the slot and hand it to the waitress as she walks by. A few minutes later, she is back. "Was nice seein' y'all! See you next month!"

"That girl has too much energy," Debra comments, picking up her purse. "That reminds me I haven't heard from Kendra. I don't know if I'm picking her up from band practice or if she's catching a ride–"

A muffled chime rings from inside the bag. "Speaking of my angel. I'll see y'all." She frowns. "Y'all? Listen to me now. Thanks, Max."

Debra tucks the phone between her shoulder and ear while heading toward the door. I grab my receipt and my purse and Renee and I follow Debra out. My phone rings as soon as we get outside, so I wave to Renee as we head in opposite directions.

A car passes with what looks to be high-school-age kids hanging out of the passenger window, yelling comments, whistling and catcalling. "Hey! Hey, Ma! Nice ride!"

With a swipe of my thumb on the handle, I slide inside the car and close the door, shutting them out. I pull my Prada shades from my bag and slip them over my eyes, press the start button and grin with the thrill of hearing the engine roar to life.

Debra is right. She's always right. I bought the Maserati because I love how it looks and how I look in it. I refuse to be ashamed about that.

I have always had an eye for things that set themselves apart. The car is expensive; I can admit that. She's something not just anyone can get. She's an investment. As anyone in real estate can tell you, appearance is everything. If you don't look like you can sell million dollar homes, you won't.

Look the Part is my mantra and not a hard one to believe in. If I can afford to shop at the organic grocer and have my orchids flown in from Japan and wear the latest in designer fashion, why shouldn't I?

Why should I pretend to be meek and humble to ease your discomfort with my lifestyle?

CHAPTER FOUR

ebra

If I could think of a reason to not go home, any reason at all, I wouldn't. I wouldn't sit in an empty house, waiting for Willard to decide my fate and map out how we'll work this out. I never thought I would be here. It's so unlike me. I've been unlike myself for a long time.

I wish I could claim that don't know how it started, that I just woke up one day in the middle of an affair, but that would be a lie. I know exactly how it began. And how and why it ended.

I've been with Willard since we were in high school, over twenty years. That's a long time. Long enough for us to be comfortable with each other, which is a good and a bad thing. Good, because I don't have to win him over every day. After so many years together, I couldn't wake up next to him every day, live with him, raise a family with him without that level of comfort, that freedom to be ourselves.

Comfort, though, can make a person lazy. It can make someone take things and people and promises like 'till death do us part' for granted. Comfort makes people passive. Comfort made me unsatisfied and lonely.

Willard and I have jobs with a lot of responsibility, which means long hours. He's on track to be the youngest partner at Hyatt and Willoughby, a prestigious CPA firm in Atlanta. Their client list is practically the Hollywood Walk of Fame. Most people think tax professionals are only busy from January to April, but that's just personal income tax. There are quarterly taxes, franchise taxes and annual business taxes, which are due in September. That's what Willard is working on now.

I went to Georgia State University and got a BA in Secondary Education, started teaching and loved it. I earned a Master's Degree, stumbled into Administration and loved it. Now I'm Principal at Morningside Middle School and most of the time I love it.

Of course, I could do without the teachers that think they know everything about teaching because they've been doing it for twenty years. Or the very involved mothers who join the PTA as some sort of community status symbol, wielding a very limited amount of power over a small organization. The PTA President, Charlotte Rogers, is all the way up my ass right now and the school year hasn't even started.

When I took over this job, it was to her dismay and disappointment. She'd been campaigning for another candidate, and when I won the assignment, she went on the warpath. She's been watching my every move, complaining about every little thing since my first day.

David Loren runs my Phys Ed and sports programs. College football took his knee and with it, his chances of being drafted into the NFL. There's a saying that those who can't do, teach. Well, those who can't play, coach. David brought his degree in Secondary Physical Education and his summers running community sports programs to Morningside. For a young man that is not yet thirty, David is doing pretty well for himself.

Since it was his first year teaching, I took him under my wing and let him know that he could talk to me anytime. It wasn't long before he took me up on it. I saw myself as a mentor to him, but I can't deny that he is attractive — broad, bulky, thick linebacker build, arms I couldn't even wrap both hands around. Skin so smooth, it looked sprayed on and a close, nicely edged haircut. Clean shaven, bright brown eyes, and wide nose. A specimen.

I looked forward to seeing him come into my office, take a seat in one chair across from my desk and pour his heart out about frustrations with the job, fellow staff, his assistant coaches, district politics. Our conversations moved from my office to a coffee shop in the strip mall down the street from the school.

They also moved quickly from business to personal. My loneliness was palpable. He was sympathetic to it, fed off of it. He didn't understand why I had a husband that paid so little attention to me. His words were music to my ears and exactly what I wanted to hear.

I was beautiful.

I was sexy.

He thought about me constantly.

He wanted to make love to me.

He wanted to show me how a real man treats a woman.

Willard works six days a week, comes home well after sunset, rolls into bed and snores through late night TV. I wanted attention. David gave it to me.

The first time I followed David to his apartment, I had no intention of doing anything with him.

That's what I told myself back then. What I tell myself now is that I knew good and well what I was walking into and my flesh was more than willing to ignore every signal screaming 'No!'

I blush at the scenes that flash through my memory. Naked on his leather couch, his face between my legs, his lips on my breasts, his hands… everywhere. Limbs tangled in satin sheets, David hovering over me, whispering beautiful, sinful, dirty, lovely words in my ear, words Willard probably doesn't even know. David, hunching, shuddering and letting go so passionately, so vocally, with so much abandon.

I was drunk with the idea that someone wanted me.

The guilt hit me full force, like a bucket of ice water. I blamed myself, punished myself, chided myself. I stayed away from David. I wouldn't go on anymore coffee breaks and referred him to an Assistant Principal if he needed guidance. I refused to go to his apartment, take his calls, read his emails. The end of the school year was coming up, and I was grateful to have not only some time off from work, but some space from David.

As if he could sense that we were in trouble, Willard was great over the summer. We took Kendra on weekend trips. We even took a few brief vacations alone. I rededicated myself to my husband and my marriage. No young buck was going to take away what I'd worked so hard for so long to build.

Then the summer was over. Willard went back to working long hours. The school year was kicking up again. Books, supplies and food arrived and the hallways, after lying dormant for months, would soon crawl with students again.

Some nights, I'd drive home by the sliver of light on the horizon and try to grasp that feeling that I had during the summer. Those days with Willard and Kendra didn't fill a storage bin of satisfaction and feelings, something I could dip into when I needed a hug or someone to sit and talk with, swing on the porch with, be silly with. I was, once again, lonely.

David made sure I knew he was around, though he wasn't supposed to be. With fall sports starting up, he had plenty of work to do in his office, downstairs near the gym. Whenever I left or returned to my office, David was in the hallway, talking with this teacher, joking with that one. Female teachers. Younger female teachers.

I got the hint. Even laughed at it a little. After a week of blatant flirtation with every skirt on staff, I summoned David to my office. We would calmly and rationally discuss the "issue" and put the affair to bed, no pun intended. I couldn't go through the entire year at odds with him because we'd shared some intimate moments.

He strolled into my office, as cool and calm as ever. His

broad, sun darkened shoulders shone with sweat that matched the beads gathered around his thin hairline. He dropped into a chair across from my desk, his legs splayed open. "You sent for me?"

I glanced up from the stack of papers I had been systematically shifting from one side of my desk to the other. New bus routes and schedules, purchase orders for the cafeteria, last-minute textbook requests—all issues that would have to be sorted before the first day of school.

"I did," I said, closing one folder and sliding another off of the stack to the right. "I wanted to tell you you didn't have to work so hard, you know. To make me jealous."

David blinked once, slowly and said, "What do you mean, work so hard? Why do you think I'm trying to make you jealous?"

"David…" I slid the folder to the left, the pile that I'd let my assistant take care of. "I've seen you. All week. Talking with Lisa Flores and Marcia James and Jennifer Potter."

"You're sure up in my business."

"Because you conduct your business in the hallways outside my office. What we had was what we had, but it's over. I need you to have some professionalism about this situation."

"It's over because you decide it's over? What happens when the old man forgets you exist again? What happens when you miss this-" He gestured toward himself.

"You will respect me in this office." My lip curled in that way that I know scares Willard. David wasn't moved.

"And if I don't?"

I planted my palms on my desk and pushed myself up from my chair. "You might find yourself out of a job, Mr. Loren, if you don't."

I stepped around my desk to the door and flung it open. The secretaries and office staff had all gone home for the day. The hallways were dark and quiet.

David took his time standing, stretching and flexing as he made his way around the two guest chairs in front of my desk, but he didn't walk out. Instead, he came behind me, gripped my waist with both hands and squeezed.

His voice was low, his tone non-threatening as he leaned in to whisper into my ear. "You used me and dumped me and I'm supposed to pretend like nothing happened? Like we didn't have something between us and that something wasn't real, real good?"

The scent of his cologne tickled my nose and dredged up not-so-distant memories. His breath fell on my neck, causing the hairs to rise and stand on end, sending an avalanche of the same down my arms. His lips, wet and cool, landed just below my earlobe. I might have let out a tiny sigh.

"Are you sure you're done with me?"

"I don't think this is a good–" My words were cut short by full lips, a warm tongue, sensuous moaning and a bit of a whimper, but that might have come from me. The door slammed shut, and I was gently edged backward until I was sandwiched between it and David's muscular form.

"You didn't think you could get away from me so easily, did you?"

Words breathed between stolen, hungry kisses were accompanied by groping and squeezing and pressing. My mind was a blur. I'd spent the last few nights in bed alone with a trashy romance novel or late night talk shows. I was already needy, but rekindling the affair with David was not part of the plan.

A moan escaped my lips while David's rough, calloused hands explored beneath my blouse, creeping further and further until they slipped under the band of my bra, His hands cupped my breasts, kneading them, eliciting feelings I hadn't felt since the last time I was with him. Willard never made me feel that way. My legs turned to soup and my will turned to mush and there, in my office, it began again.

CHAPTER FIVE

$\mathcal{M}$ axine

I like peace when I drive– no music or talk radio, no phone calls from my spaz of an assistant, just me and the sound of the car. She's a white panther, stalking and purring, the rumble of the engine like a lullaby. So I'm a little ridiculous about the car, but I feel like it says something about me, about my level of accomplishment. I'm living my dream.

Sometimes after leaving Ruby's, I can't help driving a few blocks away to a familiar place full of memories: 1844 Castlerock Drive, in the heart of Decatur, Georgia. The Maserati no doubt looks out-of-place sitting in front of the house is more of a shack that barely stands on its own. The lawn, maintained monthly by the least expensive lawn service in the area, is mostly weeds. The paint is chipping, windows cracked, sills warped and misshapen.

Inell, who didn't like to be called mother or anything resembling the maternal, did the best she could with what she had. What she had wasn't much. We made good use of handouts and thrift stores. I had faded My Little Pony bedding set for years and when

I outgrew that, she bought fabric and made bedding and curtains. She picked up cotton batting from the craft store and sewed a rudimentary comforter. Somewhere in storage, I still have them, once bright white, now dingy and threadbare.

My father, Isaac, was not a father in any sense of the word. He didn't want a kid, and I didn't want a dad. He came around every few months or so, mostly to get on Inell's nerves. He might give her a few dollars here and there, but Inell was proud and rarely would take it. I had no such feelings of pride and would take money from Isaac in a heartbeat. I wanted things Inell couldn't buy me. I learned early on that my light skin and pretty eyes could get me those things.

I heard what girls at school said about Inell, words usually repeated from their mothers. "Don't worry about me," she would say, a tendril of smoke curling from the joint dangling limply from between two fingers. She always held a glass of something brown that smelled putrid. "You worry about yourself. Finish school and get the hell out of here."

I followed her instruction to the letter. Except I got us both the hell out of that house.

"Call from Donovan Luxury Realty."

The Bluetooth system plucks me from a frequent trip down memory lane. I put the car in reverse and pull out of the driveway. I press 'accept' on the touch screen and hear the click that means the call has connected. "Maxine Donovan."

The voice of my assistant, Virgil Hartington, fills the interior of the car. "Maxine, you are late. Your two o'clock is waiting."

"I'm on my way, Virgil. Keep your pants on."

"I'll try. I hope you're looking your usual smashing self because FYI, he's gorgeous." My heart skips a beat at this news. I could handle an afternoon driving around the city with a good-looking man.

"Details."

The echo in the background means he's in the kitchen, hopefully brewing a mug of tea like a good little assistant. "Tall, dark, handsome– check, check, check. Six-four at least, shoulders for miles, nice goatee. Deep voice, pretty brown eyes."

"What's he wearing?" Maybe I wouldn't even bill Brent for the time.

"Short sleeved Dolce & Gabbana shirt in a gorgeous baby blue, open collar. Gucci dark rinse blue jeans. No jewelry except a watch."

"Brand?"

"Movado," he answers.

I shudder, though he can't see me. "Do your thing. I'm on my way." I hang up without listening for a response. That he called to fill me in on my appointment tells me he is already on the job.

I met Virgil five years ago at a star-studded open house. He was inarguably the best dressed man in the room and took an immediate liking to my Louboutin pumps. He handed me a glass of champagne and dragged me to a quiet corner where we drank until we'd both spilled our stories. I'd just launched Donovan and was still getting the hang of luxury real estate. I'd come to the open house to spy. Virgil was an agent who was more enthusiastic about the guests and the decor than the home he was supposed to be showing. He hated sales and confessed that he was looking for a way out.

Virgil's father was an entertainment lawyer, his mother an interior designer to the stars. His uncle had been active in politics for the last twenty years and loved to entertain. Having grown up on the fringes of government and entertainment, Virgil had more connections than I could ever dream of cultivating.

I stole him from his former firm, and I'll never regret it — he's the closest thing to a soul mate I've ever had. His critical eye spots a designer bag, shoe, watch, or scarf from miles away. He knows instinctively what makes me tick and caters to it, keeping the Donovan Luxury Realty staff in fine linen paper, delicate china, gourmet teas and decadent European chocolates. A thick Rolodex full of high-powered names makes him indispensable. I couldn't run Donovan without him. And he knows it.

I check my makeup and lipstick, smooth down my hair, and make sure the car is impressive—no folders or papers or gravel from the parking lot marring the interior. Appearance is everything.

I breeze through the double doors of the office suite. It's a busy Saturday at Donovan. All of my agents are on the phone or on the computer. I nod at each of them as I walk by until I get to my office at the back of the suite.

Virgil is seated at his desk, still wearing his telephone headset. The wire cuts into his spiky, upswept hairdo. If it wasn't for his classic button-down shirt and crisp slacks, he would almost be too hip for Donovan.

He moves the microphone from his mouth and stands as I approach. "He's in your office, flipping through some pictures. I started him off with the Buckhead condo set."

"Great," I answer, passing the desk and turning around again. "Why are you here? Don't you have a life?"

Virgil rolls his eyes. "This is my life, Maxine." I snicker. "I knew you would be late. Someone has to keep this place together."

I smile my thanks and step back. "How do I look?"

"Flawless as usual," he offers after a cursory glance at my knee-length Prada shift dress and strappy sandals. He's partial to my shoe collection. "Nice. Those really bring the look together."

"Thanks. We'll be leaving soon to look at some places. When I leave, you get out of here, you hear me?"

He nods. "See you Monday. Staff meeting at 8:30. Sharp."

I open the door to my office to find a delicious hunk of man waiting for me. "Mr. Brooks." I extend a hand, walking toward him.

"Ms. Donovan. Please call me Malcolm," he replies, the bulk of him towering over me.

"Maxine. It's a pleasure to finally meet you."

His hand swallows mine, giving it a hearty squeeze before releasing it. He waits until I make my way around the desk. Only then does he take a seat and pick up the sampler book that I always offer to people new to town.

In a city like Atlanta, with so many neighborhoods and suburbs, it's hard to decide where you want to live. People are afraid of traffic and like to be close to work. The more that factors like price, privacy, and expanse of land figure into the equation, the further away from the city the choices land. I always start the search in Buckhead because it offers luxurious living spaces in the most convenient area of the city with the most amazing views. And the highest prices. When you work on commission, high prices matter.

"So Brent said you're relocating. Where from?"

"DC," he answers, his voice as low as a drum. "Well, Maryland, but I worked in DC. I'm in a hotel right now. I'd like to have a place squared away soon."

"I understand. Millennium Security has a suite at Lenox Over-look Towers, right?" I turn to my computer and pull up a map, plotting the office location and several housing options surrounding it. "That area has nice condos and upscale town homes. Luxury living spaces, close to work, shopping, and churches... do you attend church?"

"That's not as important to me as security and quality of life. Traffic in Buckhead is a mess, and I don't want to live anywhere near a mall. I told Brent that I wasn't interested in looking at places close to the office."

I smile, hiding my frustration. I'm definitely billing Brent for my time. "We can expand the search if we need to. I'd like to give you a tour though, at least to look at some places in relation to the office. It might surprise you how calm the neighborhoods are a few streets away from the main drag. What do you say? Humor me?" I turn on the charm, batting my eyes and tilting my head just so.

Malcolm shrugs his shoulders, his lips forming a nonchalant pout. "I'm open."

"Great." I push back from the desk, grabbing the booklet from his hands and my purse. "I live in the area. I'll show you my favorite haunts. Wine shops, great places for coffee and dessert, some nice venues for date nights."

If he catches my hint, he doesn't let on. He waits near the door for me to walk through it. He's nothing if not a gentleman. A polite gentleman. How annoying.

～

I drop Malcolm back at Donovan and watch him climb into a black Denali. What a waste of an afternoon.

In my hurry to get Malcolm out on the road, I forgot what time it was. Atlanta has a rush hour every day and traffic on Peachtree is often backed up. My go-to shortcuts were just as packed with cars trying to get around the bottleneck. I watched Malcolm become tense, the longer we sat through red light after red light.

"This isn't normal," I said, over Jill Scott crooning from the six speaker audio system.

"Excuse me?" He leaned over onto the armrest, tilting his head so I could speak into his ear.

I turned the music down. "I said, this isn't normal. There must be an event or something, blocking traffic somewhere."

"So when there's an event in a city this big, it causes a headache?"

"Not always. More than one event at the same time in the same location would cripple any metropolitan area. There's probably a Braves game and a concert or something."

When we finally got moving, I took him to a few high rise complexes I thought he should see, specifically the ones with a manned front desk, valet parking for residents and 24 hour security patrol. Malcolm was quiet during the tours, keeping his thoughts to himself. He nodded and listened while I rambled about amenities, but he didn't have much to say. Maybe he was the strong, silent type. Also annoying.

I swung into a parallel space in front of Sip, one of my favorite coffee houses. The beat of tribal drums and strumming of a guitar poured out of the door as he held it open for me. I strolled in past him and headed straight for the front counter. The décor at Sip is modern and contemporary. They serve the best French press coffee I've ever tasted, and their wine selection isn't bad either. It's a nice place for a casual meet and greet. I would waste none of my wine bar recommendations on Malcolm unless he started giving me some good, healthy signs of interest.

Sometimes men that I would absolutely be interested in figure that I wouldn't agree to a date with them if they were the last man on earth. Invariably, the men I wouldn't touch with a ten-foot pole are always trying to get my attention. I stopped noticing them after a while. If I want you, I'll let you know.

"So you're still a solid no on taking something in the area."

Malcolm sat in the straight back wooden chair and lifted his glass of micro-brew. He smiled as he brought it to his lips and said, "Correct." He swallowed a sip and set the glass back down. "I appreciate the tour, though. This is a nice place. How far is this from our office?"

I gave him a quick geography lesson, complete with shortcut hints on getting from the Lenox area to Lindbergh quickly. He seemed to actually be listening, nodding, mapping the areas out in his head.

"You know your way around."

"It's my job," I said, smiling as I sipped my iced coffee. "I quiz my agents at the drop of a hat. I throw out an address and ask them what city, what neighborhood it's in, give me directions and at least one shortcut."

Malcolm laughed. "That's serious."

"My clients expect us to know this city like the back of our hands. It comes naturally to me, though. I was born and raised not far from here. Decatur, do you know it?"

"Where it's greater." He grinned, repeating the unofficial saying of my hometown. "I've heard a lot about it actually, the downtown area. Do you have anything out there that you could show me?"

I could have kicked myself. Downtown Decatur is rustic and

small town neighborhood chic, not luxuriously upscale. I hoped to get him into something gated.

"Stumped you, did I?" A dimple showed itself, indenting his cheek like an invisible poker.

"Not at all. Let me do some research and I can have some places lined up next week. Early, since I know you have a deadline."

"That sounds great," he said, fully smiling now. "If you don't mind though, I'd like to go back to my truck. I drove down yesterday and I'm beat."

"Of course." I scrambled to finish my coffee, tossed the cup away and met him at the front door. We strolled down the street to the car.

He fit nicely in the buttery smooth, white leather seat. "Nice wheels," he commented, his first mention of the car. I was thinking he hadn't noticed it. I pressed the ignition button and grinned as she roared to life. "New?"

"About two years old. Straight off the assembly line."

I put the car into gear and eased into traffic, heading back toward the office. He nodded in what I assumed was appreciation, but I couldn't really tell.

Malcolm is too... something. Quiet, cagey, polite. I like men that I can read easily.

But when I want you, I'll let you know. Malcolm was about to know something.

CHAPTER SIX

ebra

"What are you and Daddy fighting about?"

I glance up from reviewing Kendra's homework–Intro to Algebra. I just barely remember basic math.

"Just some stuff."

"What kind of stuff?"

I consider ignoring her, but think better of it. Kids- teenagers especially, hate to be ignored. "Stuff between me and your dad," I answer.

"But what kind of stuff? It seems serious. I'm a part of the family. I should know."

"You should know things that involve you. This doesn't."

"Can I know anyway?"

"Don't worry about it," I tell her, in the gentlest voice I can muster up. I even work up a small smile. "How was band practice today?"

"You asked me that already. I said it was fine. Are you okay, Ma? Is Daddy okay?"

I nod. She didn't seem satisfied with my nod. I don't blame her, but I sense more questions coming. I glare at her, hoping my expression tells her to let it go.

Hearing the light rumble of the garage door makes my stomach twist itself inside out. I'm suddenly ill and I know I don't want to see Willard. I don't want to watch him stomp past me like I'm not here, grab a plate of leftovers from the microwave or a frozen dinner, even worse, pour a drink from the bar and head upstairs.

I shuffle the pages of Kendra's homework together, sign off on the parent-teacher check-off sheet and hand the stack to her with a smile. "Sounds like Daddy's home. Why don't you say hi and hop in the shower? It's almost bedtime."

She takes the stack from me and shoves it into a purple plastic folder and slides the folder into her book bag. The interior door opens and I hear Willard's heavy footsteps on the kitchen tile. Kendra gets up to greet him.

I escape via the back stairwell and head upstairs to our bedroom. I spend a long time in the shower. I wash my hair, then rub cocoa butter lotion into my skin and brush my teeth. I rub a towel over the mirror to wipe the steam away and get a glimpse of my face.

I look old. Tired. My eyes are dull, and there are crow's feet creeping up around them. My cheeks are sunken; my mouth framed by long lines. Every day I pluck another wiry, stiff gray hair from my scalp.

Is there any wonder my husband wasn't paying attention to me?

I wrap a bath sheet around myself, tucking the end in between my breasts and open the door to the bedroom. To my surprise, Willard is in our bedroom, lying on the bed fully clothed except for his shoes. One ankle is crossed over another and he holds the remote to the TV in one hand. At my appearance from the bathroom, he presses a button to mute the canned laughter of a sitcom.

"Did you save me any hot water?"

I'm so surprised that he's speaking to me, I stand mute for a few moments. When he tilts his head toward me, I snap back. "Uh, yeah. There should be enough hot water for another shower."

He sits up, drops his feet from the bed to the floor and stalks toward the bathroom. "Great. I'll hop in before I head to my room." My heart sinks. He still plans to sleep in the guest room.

Slowly, I drift through the motions of getting ready for bed. I put on a nightgown, an emerald green, shimmery number–Willard's favorite color, with spaghetti straps that hits me mid-thigh. Just in case he decides to sleep in our bed, I don't want to be wearing something my grandmother would wear. I consider tying my hair back in a scarf but opt not to and slip into bed with the lamp on to wait for him.

I hear the water turn off, the door to the glassed-in shower click shut, the linen closet door open and close. Sounds of a soft cotton towel rubbing against skin. The bathroom door opens, spilling steam and the manly scent of Willard's body wash into the room.

His nightly routine is painful to watch while I'm waiting to see if he's going to keep treating me like I'm not here. With a towel wrapped around his torso, Willard moves through the room without acknowledging me. At the bureau he slides open a drawer, picks out a pair of white briefs and pulls them on, tossing the towel into the pile of laundry in the closet. He slaps some lotion onto his arms, legs and chest. Brushes his hair, applies deodorant to his underarms.

Finally, he turns to face me. I'm in bed, on my side, the sheets and comforter gathered around my waist so he can see the night-gown I wore. He smiles, but the smile is... off.

"You wear that for him, too?"

Blink. "What?"

"I said, did you wear that for him too? Does he like you in green, Debra? What's his favorite color?"

He turns, opens a drawer and rifles through my stash of silky, slinky fabrics. He pulls out a black lacy thing that I only wore once because it made me itch. I remember Willard laughed when he took it off me and I was so grateful, not because he was being romantic but because I was about to go crazy from the itching.

"Did he like this one? Did you wear this one for him?"

"Don't do this, please."

"Don't do what? Don't ask my wife if the other man she's fucking likes her in the lingerie that I bought her? You know what we call that in accounting? Cost of Use. When you buy something that's expensive, but you get so much use out of it, it's cost effective. So this..." He tosses the gown to the floor. "Has a low cost of use."

"I think we should talk—"

"About what?" His laughter nears maniacal. "About how you looked me in my face every damn day while you were fucking some other man—"

"Lower your voice, please."

"Lower my voice? Lower my–don't tell me to lower my voice in my own house! Are you afraid your twelve-year-old might hear about how Mrs. Macklin is doing one of her teachers?"

"Willard—"

"Just tell me how. How you came home every day after being with him? Tell me, because it seems to me that cheating is a choice you make. And you were doing this for almost a year? That's a lot of choices. Him over us. Him over me."

He shakes his head, stomps toward the bed, and snatches the pillow from his side of the bed. "I have nothing to say to you. And there's not a damn thing you have to say to me."

He leaves the bedroom, slamming the door behind him.

I am stupefied, staring at the closed door. My vision blurs, my eyes fill with tears.

He's not going to forgive me.

CHAPTER SEVEN

enee

The autumn sun bears down, shining furiously through the windshield. The air is an odd mix of warmth and early fall crisp, typical for the Atlanta change of seasons—cool in the morning, blazing hot at midday, cold at night. I let go of the steering wheel for a few seconds and reach for the visor to shield my eyes from the visual assault.

I return to meandering my way through the few streets that separate us from Broad Street and Gladwell Books. A drive-thru Starbucks opened just down the block, so on this near-chilly morning, I'm holding a piping hot caramel latte in one hand and steering with the other.

By the time I make it to the bookstore each day, I've already had a full day with Daddy. He's an early riser, up at five o'clock most mornings. I get him showered and dressed for the day and we head downstairs for our morning card game. It doesn't matter what day it is—Christmas, his birthday, a random Tuesday in June, we play cards. Some mornings I don't feel like it. Most mornings I don't feel like it. My mother loved it.

Between hands, I make us breakfast. Daddy likes scrambled eggs with cheese, wheat toast with butter and strawberry jam. He'll tell you he wants grape jam, but he doesn't like grape jam. He doesn't remember that he doesn't like grape jam.

Daddy and I eat breakfast, play cards, and listen to the news until Jessie arrives. Once Jessie takes over, I get dressed for work.

Running a bookstore is not what I intended to do with my business degree, but I have to admit, I'm not bad at it. Picking up where Mama left off hasn't been that difficult.

Gladwell Books does okay, if okay means we can stay open another month. Running a bookstore is like going off to war every day. Fighting to stay afloat, pushing my old-fashioned hardbacks and paperbacks when everyone is turning to a device for their latest reads. Some days it's so slow that I give my staff the day off. Then it's just me, alone in the store with nothing but the muffled sounds of traffic to keep me company.

A bookstore has to evolve; it has to be more than a bookstore to survive in this new era. It's a coffee shop, a magazine rack, a study nook, a music store and a meeting place. It's a neighborhood hangout. At least that's what I've tried to turn Gladwell into.

I pull into my parking spot behind the building, juggle my purse, my coffee and my keys and unlock the back door to the shop. It's cool and dark as I walk through, snapping on lights and turning on machines. I keep a break room with a coffeepot and a dorm fridge, a table and chairs and a set of lockers for my employees to keep their things when they are on shift. I start a pot of coffee and slide the chairs under the round table, arranging them just so.

My office is in a corner, to the right. My mother picked it because it was a private space with a large window. The view isn't much to write home about, just the stone walls of the building next door but there's enough sun to brighten the room. There's a desk, a printer, a few filing cabinets and a chair that doesn't match any of the other furniture in this place. I have no idea where it came from, but it's been here since I took over.

I drop my purse at my desk, flip the switch on the desktop PC and listen to it grind and beep as it comes to life. Taking my usual spot in the leather desk chair, I sip my coffee and take in the sounds of industry coming from my surroundings. Outside, cars and pedestrians pass by. Customers laugh and talk loudly on the patio over at Sam's Grille next door.

Once the computer boots, I log into QuickBooks, the bank website, email and the storefront management software that I implemented when I took over Gladwell. My mother did everything by hand—inventory, product management, even the accounting and when he took over for her, Daddy did everything exactly as she had. He never changed a thing, never moved anything and never updated anything. While he was declining, he often forgot to open the bookstore. He forgot to restock items. He forgot to order special requests. Business was limping and on life support.

Daddy used to insist on having Jessie bring him to the store to check up on me. He'd stand around with a sour frown, disapproving of all the changes I made to keep the place alive. I had the hardwoods stripped, stained and buffed to a brilliant shine, moved the cases around and hung signs to label different book categories. I dedicated a space for patrons to not only study but socialize. Plush couches in dark, comforting colors, antique coffee tables spread with magazines and music softly playing overhead invite patrons to sit and relax. I even carved out room for a vendor to sell her wares — sweets, coffee, juice, those soy shakes all the kids drink.

Gladwell Books may not be in the black, but we're not in the red either. After payroll, rent and utilities and product buys, we're treading water. Not bad, for a person who knew nothing about running a bookstore.

At five minutes to ten, the back door swings open and Lexie, my manager, bounces in. She's the young, energetic type, full of hopes and dreams and doesn't know the meaning of the word 'no'. She graduated from Georgia State and is currently earning an MFA in Creative Writing. I was managing the shop myself until I realized I can't do it all, sun up to sundown, six days a week. In my halfhearted search for a manager, I stumbled upon Lexie and she practically begged me for the job. She's been with Gladwell for a year.

Lexie is singing loudly and badly as she steps into my office. Her micro braids are swept up into a high ponytail, making her look much younger than her twenty-six years. She pulls her ear buds from her ears and waves in my direction, though I'm looking right at her and she's looking right at me.

"Morning, Renee. How you doin' today?"

"I'm fine, Lex. And you?"

"I almost missed my bus this morning," she answers, fiddling with her phone to turn off the music pouring from the ear buds. "My son was playing with my phone and turned down the alarm." She rolls her eyes, tucking the phone away. "I see you stopped and got yourself a cup of jump start. Daddy got you running on fumes already?"

I gulp the last of the now cold latte and drop the cup into the desk side waste basket. "I had to get something. These early mornings are killing me."

"Well, it's good you finished it before Mona comes in. You know she don't like Starbucks."

Mona, the woman that runs the cafe inside the shop, is five foot nothing with a six-foot personality. She's a little—okay, a lot pushy. She does indeed hate Starbucks. And Dunkin' Donuts and any place that sells anything remotely similar to her wares. Never mind that she buys her beans from the internet and grinds them to make the gourmet coffee, for which she charges nearly four dollars a cup.

I once made the mistake of walking into the shop with a Starbucks cup. The lecture that I had to hear about how the Big Box is destroying the Mom and Pop business model and how I should know better because I'm a small business owner... I escaped to my office and shut the door. Her patronage is older women who love to gossip over a cup of coffee. And if they'll buy a slice of cake and the new Danielle Steel on the way out, Mona and I both win.

"Anything exciting on the schedule today?"

I lean over to check the monthly calendar that I keep next to the keyboard. "We have a book signing today, so we need to get the display up in the window. The box of books from the publisher came in the other day. They're in the storage room."

"That's that Ruth Ann Paul gal? She writes all those romances set in Georgia?"

"Uh huh."

"I wonder why she wanted to do her signing here. She sells enough to book a big store."

I shrug. "She's from the area. I heard she knew my mother. I also heard that her last book didn't sell well. Maybe she's hoping for some nostalgia sales."

Lexie sighs and turns toward the door. "Guess I'll open up shop and get to work on that display. Holler if you need me."

I spend the morning reviewing the previous week's numbers, placing orders for product and fulfilling our digital orders. I get about ten orders a day for used and new books. I process payments, pick the books from the shelves and stuff them into padded envelopes for shipping. I weigh the envelopes, create labels and postage and stick them on each package, seal them up and drop them into a box to take up front. They'll go out in the day's mail.

"Lexie, this looks nice," I say, admiring the book display in the window. Ruth Ann Paul's newest release, 'Sin in Savannah' looks like a steamy one. I pick up a book and flip it over, reading the back blurb and turn it over again. The cover image is the stereotypical lovers in embrace in the shadow of the setting sun. The man is shirtless, his muscular back practically rippling before my eyes. The woman is beautiful—mysterious eyes, dark wavy hair, a tight bodice revealing dress.

I make a mental note to grab a few copies for Debra and Maxine. It'll be the closest I've come to Sin in Savannah in about four years.

I shouldn't still miss Marcus. He did me dirty and I'm not over it yet. When I left Philly, he was helpful. He packed up my apartment and helped me get down here, and we had decided to play things by ear. I found out from a friend we had, apparently, broken up. How embarrassing to find out you're single when your friend calls to offer her condolences on your breakup.

Marcus said I should have expected it. After all, he said, if I didn't make it back to Philly, he didn't see how things were going to work out. He didn't want to transfer to Atlanta, and I couldn't very well leave my father and the bookstore.

All this melancholy makes me hungry, so I head back to my office and grab my purse. I don't want anything greasy from Sam's so I decide to drive up to Buckhead and grab Max for a quick bite. I yell up front to let Lexie know that I'm leaving and wave at Mona, who is busy setting out her sugar laden goodies for the day. She waves back without missing so much as a beat of her conversation.

I climb back in the car and flip on the radio. A familiar song plays and I smile, despite myself. One of our last dates was a concert in our firm's box seats at Wells Fargo Center in Philly. It was a great night, full of good music, good drinks and great company. I was so in love with him that night.

My move to Atlanta should have been a short stint. I was going to put Daddy in a nice retirement home, sell the house and the bookstore, and get back to the life was in progress before it was so rudely interrupted. But when I got here, Daddy wasn't sick enough for a home. He wouldn't hear of selling the house, and the bookstore was in bad shape. Now I'm in limbo, four years into a temporary relocation.

I start the car and dial Max's office. After two rings, her assistant Virgil picks up. He always sounds annoyed. I'm assured that it's not just me, he always sounds like that.

"Donovan Luxury Real Estate, Maxine Donovan's office."

"Hi, Virgil. It's Renee, Max's friend?"

"Yes. Can I help you?"

I pause. Well, it's not like I want to buy a house. What does he think I want? I put on my sweet tone and ask, "Is Maxine in the office today? I'd like to see if she's free for lunch."

"She's very busy. I'll check with her." I roll my eyes as I listen to the faint, classical hold music for what feels like an eternity before the line picks up again. "Hold for Maxine," he says, and I go back to classical music for a few seconds.

"Hey, girl! Virgil said you wanted to go to lunch. Do you want to meet me at Pricci? I love it there lately."

"What I want is for you to tell your assistant that I have known you since you wore pigtails, so don't treat me like belly button lint when I call your office. And you know my stomach can't handle that fancy food and I'm wearing jeans. Can't we just go to Piccadilly or something?"

I can hear her scrunch up her nose at the mention of the cafeteria like restaurant. "Let's see if we can get in at Ruby's. I want some chicken and I'm not in the mood for fast food."

"I'm headed there now. I'll grab a table."

Max and I beat the lunch rush, grabbing a table in a sunny corner. She is resplendent in white, from her cowl neck sweater to her pencil skirt and stark white pumps. The diamonds around her wrist and in her watch twinkle and glint in the sunlight. She's wearing white feather earrings and a cute white headband holds her hair back from her face. I feel like a scrub sitting across from her.

"You look like Lisa Ray McCoy," I tell her, flicking my eyes up to silently thank the bus boy who drops two glasses of water at our table. "You know, that actress that only wears white, no matter the season? And whatever happened to not wearing white after Labor Day?"

"Oh no, no," she says, picking up the glass of water in front of her and handing it back to him. "Perrier in the bottle, please. And a glass of ice."

I feel sorry for the kid as he slinks away from the table. "You couldn't just drink the water, Max?"

"The water here is nasty. Tastes like it comes straight from the river." She makes a face as I unwrap my straw, dunk it into my glass and take a sip. "And when you're wearing Dolce & Gabbana, you can wear white whenever you damn well please. If you wore couture, you would know that."

"Well, I guess I'll continue being unfashionable and not wearing white after Labor Day."

"That's a good lemming. What's with the bags under your eyes?"

"Why are you already insulting me?"

"You just told me I look like Lisa Raye."

"That wasn't an insult. It was an observation."

"I didn't like your observation. You're grumpy and you look exhausted."

I sigh, shaking my head, stirring the ice in my glass with my straw. "I couldn't get Daddy down last night. He was up twice after midnight and up for the day at five o'clock."

"Why doesn't he sleep?"

I shrug. "I'm wondering if it's his medication. I'm going to call his doctor and ask, because the man does not sleep."

"Well, I remember him always doing something." He always had the Mustang and a long list of household projects. He was head of several organizations post retirement and he also had his card club. Now he has nothing.

"You know, you're right. He doesn't have anything to occupy his time. I just wish he could be restless during the day with Jessie. Not at night with me."

"What if you hired a night nurse?"

"I can't afford it. And I can't imagine how many nurses it would take to find one that he could get along with."

"He's just sleeping. Why do they need to get along?"

I laugh. "Because he doesn't sleep!"

A waitress brings a bottle of Perrier and a glass of ice for Maxine and announces the lunch specials for the day. Two wings and fries for $3.99 sounds like a winner, and Max agrees.

"How was your appointment last weekend? That referral you said you had? Did he work out?"

Maxine waves a hand in the air as she delicately sips her water. "Sort of. Good news first. Brother is fine." Her eyes roll upward and I already know she's halfway in love with him. "Tall, handsome, brooding and mysterious. Quiet. I showed him a lot of places in Buckhead that aren't far from his office. He didn't want any of them."

"Aww."

"But guess where he wants to look?" My blank stare prods her on. "Decatur."

"For real?"

"Yeah. But he reads like he wants something cheap. I can find him something nice for a low price, but Brent needs to hand out some huge favors for this. I'm not Re/MAX, dammit."

Our lunch arrives straight from the fryer, so both dishes are sizzling. Maxine asks for a knife and fork and while she waits, spreads several napkins over herself. "You would want to eat out on the day I'm wearing white D&G."

"Coulda said no," I offer, picking up a fry and blowing on it before dipping it in the provided cup of ketchup.

"I wanted to get out of the office. Have you heard from Debra?"

I shake my head, my brows suddenly furrowed in concern. "It's odd to not hear from her at least a couple of times a week."

"Maybe she's real busy with school?"

"Maybe." I shrug. "She seemed distracted at brunch. Like something was wrong, but she didn't want to talk about it."

"I noticed that too. She blamed it on Willard's schedule." The waitress brings a fork and knife for Maxine, wrapped in a napkin. She unwraps the utensils and gets to work, slicing meat off of the chicken bone.

"You could just order chicken strips, you know."

"It's not the same," she says, deftly working her way around the plate. "I'm used to it. Doesn't take but a minute. Anyway, I'll give her a call tonight. See what's up."

"Yeah, okay. And let me know if she says anything. I'll try her tomorrow."

After lunch, I watch Maxine head to her car and I get into mine. The drive back to Gladwell is a short mile, but I like to make it last as long as possible. It's not that I don't want to go back to work, but having time to myself is priceless. It gives me pause, peace and quiet to think about the plans I hope to put into action sooner rather than later.

I open my bag and dig out a brochure I'd picked up a few weeks ago. I've been meaning to call, but I feel so guilty. I flip the brochure over and dial the number on the back.

"Golden Rays Memory Center," answers a cheerful voice with a thick country accent. "How may I direct ya call?"

"Hi. I wanted to schedule a tour of your facility. And talk about possibly placing my father there."

"Does he have Alzheimer's, Dementia or a memory disorder?"

"Alzheimer's. Yes, ma'am."

"When was he diagnosed?"

"Four years ago."

"And how old is he?"

"He's sixty seven."

"Mmmhmmm," she hums. "Early Onset then?" Early Onset means that a patient is symptomatic before the age of sixty-five.

"Yes, ma'am."

"Mkay," she drawls. "You'll want to speak with Ron Williamson. He's our intake physician. He'll show you the facility and answer questions you might have about our care. He's pretty booked up the next few weeks, but I could do a Saturday in the first week in October."

I check my calendar. "That's fine. An afternoon, if that's okay."

"I'll put you down for three o'clock with Ron on Saturday, October third. He'll call you a few days prior and y'all will talk about your father, his symptoms and stage, and whether Golden Rays is a good fit. Mkay?" Her accent is so comforting and disarming.

"That's perfect. Thank you."

"Uh huh, darlin'. See you then."

The line disconnects and I drop my phone back into my bag. I immediately feel better knowing I've made the appointment. Like I'm pushing this thing forward. Taking control.

Now I just have to make it a few more weeks with Daddy before I know if there is hope.

CHAPTER EIGHT

$\mathcal{M}$axine

After lunch with Renee, I head back to my office for the afternoon. Malcolm is on my mind. I've called him several times to chat him up about available places. I'd love to get him into something higher class than a Decatur condo, but he's dead set against anything within city limits. I've given up the fight and directed Virgil to research locations in Decatur, but slightly more upscale than your average condo.

I called Brent and tried to pump him for information on his partner, but he's as closed mouthed as Malcolm. I need details! Is he a confirmed bachelor, or looking for someone new? What are his tastes? Do we both like Neo-soul, Japanese food and the sunset over Curacao? Malcolm's answers to my questions are too short, too guarded. What's going on with this man?

I walk past Virgil and into my office. Like a loyal puppy, he pads into the room behind me, wearing a pair of Prada slippers that don't go with his pinstripe slacks.

Virgil drops into a chair across from my desk and flings one leg over the other. "Ready for your messages?"

I drop my bag in the space between my chair and my desk and give him a wilting glance. "Just give me the Cliff's Notes."

He consults his note pad and runs a finger down the page. "Judge Mason is looking for a starter home for his daughter and new son-in-law. About two million." He looks up at me and blinks. Only at Donovan could a two million dollar home be considered a starter.

"The Falcons rep called. They have a new quarterback, or something. He's looking for a place here. Married, three kids, the works. Something in the mini mansion category, about three million, gated. Very south or very north."

I'm listening, already rifling through listings in my head for a perfect fit.

"Just give me a few windows of time and I'll add them to your schedule." I nod. He continues. "Atlanta Women magazine wants to do a feature on you for next month's Women in Power issue."

I shrug a shoulder. I've been featured before and we have nothing print worthy to highlight. "Let's hold on that until we sell something to a big name. I want to have something to talk about."

"Mkay, that's a 'not right now'." Virgil runs a line through that item on his list. "Next, we're going to have to do something about the Newman situation. I know you don't want to talk about it, but Maxine—"

"I know. I know." I lean forward, prop my elbows on the desk and drop my forehead into my palms.

The Newman situation is a recurring nightmare. Braxton Newman, a prominent Atlanta attorney, nicknamed Mouth of the South, snagged himself a trophy wife and moved her into his home. The culture shock must have been too much for her, because she didn't mesh- not with his children, his house staff, his office staff or the neighbors. The marriage fell apart relatively quickly and Braxton moved on. He and the soon to be new Mrs. Newman have already purchased another home. All that's left is to sell the old house.

The problem? The current Mrs. Newman refuses to move out. Braxton gave her sixty days to move herself and her things. Today is day sixty-three. Not a single item has been packed. It could take six months to kick her out.

The Newman home sits on five acres of prime real estate located at holes five and six of the Marlow Country Club Golf Course. The chef's kitchen features granite counter tops and pristine stainless steel appliances. The rest of the house boasts a custom stone fireplace, five bedrooms, eight full baths, heated pool, hot tub and guest house. Braxton wants to unload it quickly. I could have a bidding war, driving up the cost and my commission. But Adora— yes, Adora won't move out.

"I am so tired of that twit. What's her problem?"

"She dropped out of school to marry this rich guy that promised to take care of her. She's twenty-five, he's fifty. Word is that the pre-nup he had her sign is iron clad. She has no degree, no skills, and she's empty in the head. What did he expect?"

"Well, I'm not about to be in the middle of it. Set up a meeting with Fletch and Braxton. Tell him to invite his counsel and let's find out what the options are. This house was supposed to be on the market months ago. I can't show it with the stripper still living there."

Virgil makes a note to contact our attorney, Fletcher Callahan. I already have a headache and that meeting isn't even scheduled. You know how doctors are the worst patients? Attorneys are the worst clients.

Braxton will puff up his chest and tout his knowledge of the law, which has been limited to corporate litigation for the past twenty years. Fletcher will pace the room in his plaid bow tie and matching seersucker suit jacket and utter phrases like 'that dog won't hunt!' Fletcher, however, knows real estate law. If anyone can find a way out of this mess, it's Fletch.

"Okay, moving on. Brent from Millennium Security called to

make sure you got the invite to his party next month. Oh, and his partner Malcolm said he looked through the listings we sent and he's ready to tour some spaces."

I snap to attention at this last item on the list. "A party? Thrown by Millennium?" At which Malcolm is sure to be in attendance?

"You got the invite," he says, pointing to a stack of mail on my desk I've been ignoring. "I thought you'd want to go, so I accepted for you."

Virgil's brows lift, and he smirks. He's exactly like me, which means my thoughts are his. "I'll call Malcolm," he says, getting up from the chair and flapping his way to the door.

"Thanks." The door closes with a soft snick and I turn my chair toward the window and an amazing view of downtown Atlanta. I reach for my D&B satchel and pull out my mobile phone, sliding my thumb across the screen to unlock it and pull up Debra's number. I said I'd call her this evening, but she's on my mind right now.

After a few rings, the line picks up, and a tired voice greets me. "Hey, Max. How are you?"

"Debra?"

"Yeah, it's me. What's up?"

"You don't sound like you. Are you okay?"

"I'm fine. Are you okay? You don't usually call in the middle of the day."

"I just had lunch with Renee." I lean back in my chair and swivel it back and forth, watching SunTrust Tower move from right to left and back to right again. "We realized we haven't heard from you in a while. It's my duty as a best friend to call and check up on you."

"Oh. I've just been busy. This school year is already crazy and Kendra has so much going on. I'd lose track of my head if it wasn't attached." Debra sounds strange. Distracted and hesitant and entirely too quiet. She always has something to say.

"Deb... you know if something was going on, that you could talk to me and Renee, right?"

"I know that."

"And so... clearly there's something going on. It's turned you into a different person. You don't want to talk about it?"

Debra hesitates. I know she wants to spill what's on her mind, but she won't let herself. "I'm going through some things," she admits, her voice barely above a whisper. Tears are on the horizon, about to break at any moment. "I'll talk to you guys soon. I will. I can't right now."

"Are you sure? I'm discreet and so is Renee."

"I'm sure. I just need a little more time. I uh..." Debra sniffles. "I have so much work to do. I'm sorry to cut this short. I love you for calling. I'll see you girls at brunch in a couple of weeks. We'll talk."

I see I have no choice but to let her brush me off. But not for long. "Alright. But you give me a call if you need anything."

"Okay. I sure will. Thanks Max." The line goes dead before I can respond. I hold the phone in my hand and stare at it.

The phone on my desk beeps and Virgil's voice scratches through the speaker. "I've reached Malcolm. He'd like to stop by in an hour and look at a few places on the list you sent him."

It's the kind of day I love spending in the city, zipping through the streets with the top down and the music up. Clear blue skies, warm air blowing through my hair, people taking advantage of the good weather to eat and shop outdoors, each neighborhood emitting a palpable aura of happiness.

I'm pleased to be sharing the day with Malcolm, my tall, dark and handsome client who smells amazing and looks even better in creased slacks and a dark shirt that stretches across his broad shoulders. A few undone buttons hint at a well-formed chest. His massive forearms fill out his short sleeves nicely.

I smile when I greet him, something that normally makes men melt and stammer, but he's playing the usual hard to get. I've made a decision about Malcolm, recently. I've decided that he's big into the professional relationship. He's probably holding off on showing any interest until after our business has concluded. I will close this deal.

And then pounce.

I pull into the parking lot at Haynes Street Lofts, a brightly colored building on a busy downtown corner, and take a space close to the front door. Standing in front of the building, Malcolm tips his head up, blocking the sun with a hand to view the four stories of the building's facade.

"These are about ten years old. You'll see a lot of businesses along the block here. My friend Renee has a bookstore a few blocks over. There's a lot of foot traffic and people around. Pretty great community."

Malcolm listens while following me through the front door. My voice echoes in the empty lobby. Lining the walls are vending machines, a coffee and snack food stand that is closed, and rows upon rows of mailboxes down one long hallway.

"There are ninety units in this building. Pool out back. Granite counter tops, wood floors, spacious bedrooms and living spaces, a fireplace in every unit. There are only a few available—a one bedroom with a den and a two bedroom."

"I'd like to have two bedrooms. I won't be spending all my time at the office if I can help it."

I consult my map of available units and locate the two-bedroom loft. I push the call button for the elevator and the doors open right away. We climb to an upper floor bathed in sunlight from a window at the end of the hallway and quietly plod down the hall, our footsteps cushioned by springy carpet. I stop at #427 and slip my key card into the lockbox. A small door pops open and I retrieve the key from inside. I twist the key in the lock and swing the door open.

The scent of paint and cleanser hit my nose as we cross the threshold. "Walk around, get a feel for the place."

Malcolm has decidedly less expensive taste to which I'm accustomed to catering. Where most of my clients won't look at anything that doesn't have marble and Italian stone tiles, Malcolm's flooring preferences stop short at dark hardwood over carpeting. He's more interested in a large bedroom and living area than an updated, state-of-the-art kitchen with modern touch screen, stainless steel appliances.

Malcolm sets off through the open space of the living room and dining room toward the bedrooms and bathrooms. I sign the guest book and pick up a few flyers from the only piece of furniture in the room, a small round coffee table. I like an empty unit to be staged, to give prospective buyers an idea of how the space can be used. A welcoming, warm set-up helps a client feel at home as soon as they step inside. Donovan keeps a warehouse of spare furniture and design elements, enough to furnish a home several times over.

I walk through the kitchen, noting that it's spotless. The appliances seem new. I hum lightly, nodding my approval as I make my way down the hall. For a foreclosure, it's clean and presentable. Often, that's all you can ask for.

"Thoughts?" I join Malcolm in the master bedroom. He stands in the center of the room, the top of his head almost brushing the overhead ceiling fan.

"Nice area. Seems quiet. Close to town. About eight miles, you said?"

"Give or take."

"It'll do. I don't need anything fancy. A comfortable place to rest my head is more than enough."

"It'll do? So you don't want to look at any of the places on your list? We have…" I consult the printout I'd received from Virgil. "At least four more places in this area alone."

"This fulfills all of my needs. How much do they want for it?"

I consult the list again. "One-ninety. But it's a foreclosure, so–"

"Sounds fair." He walks past me, out of the room and into the hallway and ducks his head into the other bedroom, opens and closes the closet door, glances into the bathroom and ends up in the living room. "What do we do now?"

We breathe. This is an easy sale, I tell myself. But it wasn't supposed to happen this quickly! I argue back.

"Malcolm..." I start, but stop. What am I supposed to say? I expected to drag this out much longer? "Are you sure you don't want to look at a few more places?"

"Maxine," he says softly, turning slowly and offering me a full smile. "I know you're not used to people moving this quickly, but I'm sure. You showed me some nice places a few weeks ago, but I don't need that much. I want to get settled, and this seems like a nice place. Let's go for it."

He heads toward the door and opens it. In a daze, I walk through it, lock the key in the lockbox, and follow him back to the elevator.

Back in the car, we are headed back to town. The top is up, enclosing us in a cocoon of soft leather and low, soulful crooning coming from the sound system. I tap my fingers on the steering wheel and chew the inside of my lip. I've never not known what to say to a man.

"So, are you attending the party Brent is throwing?"

Malcolm frowns in my direction. "I'm not a party person, really."

"Oh? Well, that's too bad."

"Why is it too bad?"

"Because I was hoping to see you there." I flash him another bright smile. To my surprise, he smiles back.

"Were you?"

"Sure. By that time you'll have closed on your place and maybe we could celebrate."

He's relaxed, slouching into the seat, a finger mindlessly tapping his thigh. I slow down a bit. I'm not ready for him to go back to the strong, silent type just yet.

"How long have you known Brent?"

"Years. He was one of my first clients, a friend of a friend."

Brett McClure is short, pale with ruddy cheeks and reddish brown hair with a goatee to match. Stocky, always well dressed, drives an enormous Lincoln Navigator and has a Bluetooth earpiece attached to an ear at all times. "Have you been to his place?"

"No, but I hear it's practically a palace."

"He wanted a huge house."

"He got one."

Brent's five million dollar home sits on nine acres of prime Buckhead real estate, behind both a wall and a gate. It features high ceilings, natural light, a theater, wine cellar, a billiards room and no such thing as a bad view from any window. He loves to throw parties and galas that last until sunrise. When guests travel from out of town, they're swaddled in comfort in one of five taste-fully appointed suite bedrooms. Summers are spent partying around the pool, winters around the fire pit. Brent's home is the type I love to sell. Top end finishes, contemporary furnishings–an example of living in style.

"He got his money's worth. It was a great deal." Malcolm bobs his head to the beat of a new song. "How about you? How did you meet Brent? And how did you come to move down here?"

"He's a buddy from high school. He was always playing with computers, trying to break into them." He chuckles. "He almost got expelled for breaking into the grading system. He didn't do anything; he just wanted to see if he could get in. And then..."

Malcolm laughs, exposing two rows of straight white teeth. "He sent them a report about their security flaws. That's how they caught him."

"And now he runs a corporate security firm."

"Irony, right? That's always been his passion, breaking into things and teaching people how to make their systems impenetra-ble. He could have gone to work for the government, but I guess that wasn't his speed. He stays busy keeping Atlanta safe."

"And you?"

"And me... I uh..." He shifts uncomfortably. I sense a story. "I was in a situation I needed to get out of. I'd been working security for VIP types and celebrities. I was talking to Brent one day and mentioned that I was looking to move on. We hammered out an expansion to Millennium Security to let me do my deal down here and..."

He shrugs, glancing over at me. "Here I am."

Malcolm is all kinds of mysterious. A situation? What kind of situation would make someone move to an entirely new city?

While we talked, I'd crept my way back to Donovan and parked in my spot.

"So, you're going to this party Brent is throwing?" I nod. "I guess I might go. Provided we have something to celebrate."

I grin, with no attempt to mask my happiness at this change of heart. "Let's go make sure we have something to celebrate."

CHAPTER NINE

 enee

"Lorraine!"

I snap from deep slumber to confused awake in seconds. The room is dark. The sun isn't even up. I sit bolt upright and listen for the sound again.

"Lorraaaaaiiiinnneee!"

This time the voice cracks, as if on the verge of tears. Accompanying the voice is something like the pitter-patter of raindrops or a fast leak or… no. No, he didn't.

I toss the light comforter across the bed, not bothering to throw on a robe over the shorts and over-sized t-shirt I wear to bed and yank open my bedroom door. Standing in the hallway, looking more lost and confused than I've ever seen him, is my father. His face is thin, his eyes blank. He's mostly bones jutting out at appropriate junctures—elbows, pelvis, knees. His V-neck white t-shirt is dingy. His boxers are dark in the crotch. At his feet, a puddle grows, floating on the surface of the wood floor.

I groan, not caring if he hears it until my eyes make it back to his face. He looks so ashamed; it breaks my heart.

"Daddy, what happened? Are you okay? Did you forget to go?"

"I'm sorry, Noodle. I couldn't find the bathroom. Where is the bathroom?" Noodle was his nickname for me growing up because my hair used to curl up like a bowl of cooked spaghetti noodles. I smile because he remembered.

Alzheimer's is a humiliating disease. A thief, too. It isn't just stealing his memory, but also his self-respect and sheer manliness. What was a virile, athletic, healthy man is now a frail shell, standing in the hallway of a home he owns, trying to remember where we keep the bathroom in this place.

"It's okay, Daddy. Let's get you cleaned up."

I side step the puddle and tuck my hand in the crook of his elbow, ushering him back down the hallway toward his bedroom. I find his robe hanging on a hook in the closet, fold the soft terry cloth over my arm, grab a towel from the hallway linen closet and walk him to the bathroom, right next to his bedroom.

"Do you need my help in the shower?"

He shakes his head, pursing his lips in a pout, and shuffles into the bathroom. I step out but make a note to myself to check on him in a few minutes.

The puddle of urine is soaking into the hardwood, seeping in between the cracks. It won't evaporate on its own, so I get to work. I run downstairs and grab a bottle of spray cleaner, a few towels and a mop and head back upstairs.

I never imagined I'd be on my hands and knees on a Saturday morning, cleaning up a puddle of my father's urine because he can't remember where the bathroom is.

I sop up most of the liquid with a towel, spray the area down with cleanser and mop. By the time I am finished, the shower is off and he's humming a song.

I tap on the door. "You okay in there?"

"I'm fine," he answers, opening the door and stepping out. His robe is on, cinched tightly around the waist. He smells like body wash. Steam billows around him, enveloping me in a warm embrace and dissipating in the coolness of the air. "Is my babysitter coming today?"

He walks past me, chuckling under his breath. A half hour ago, he was about to cry. Now he's alert and laughing. And I'm confused and disoriented.

I grab the pile of discarded clothing and the towel from the bathroom floor and add it to a white plastic laundry basket. "Any more laundry?" I ask as I pass his bedroom.

"Nope." He rifles through drawers, pulling out clothes for the day. "You hear me, girl? Jessie coming today?"

I lean against the doorjamb, the basket propped on my hip. "Yes sir, but not for a while." I take a long glance at the twilight peeking from behind the blinds. "It's five in the morning."

"Time to get moving. Can't waste the day."

I yawn. "I wouldn't have minded a few more minutes of sleep. Do you want some breakfast?"

He chuckles. "Does a bear shit in the woods? Make me some eggs. With cheese. And toast. And grape jelly. We never have grape jelly anymore."

"You don't like grape jelly, Daddy. Are you going to say please?"

"I ain't sayin' please." He turns around, tosses a few articles of clothing on the bed and grabs the ends of the tie to his robe. "You best get out of here before you see some things you don't want to see."

"You are getting rude in your old age." I take his please as implied and leave, closing the door behind me. I listen to him whistle and hum the same tune he'd been humming in the shower.

I wish this version of my father could stick around, but I know better. I've had fewer and fewer days with the real Bernard Gladwell.

~

I feel guilty about the sense of relief that washes over me when I see Jessie walk in. Daddy requires so much work and concentration that I am tired by ten am. When he develops a new behavior, I worry that he's declining and that I'm losing him and I'm still not over the loss of my mother. By the time Jessie gets here, I need a break. I turn the reins over to her and escape upstairs to my room.

My old bedroom was a place where I'd spent so much of my life, growing up. I was shy and I thought I was plain, compared to Debra and Max. I preferred the company of books and TV to people, especially since no one ever wanted to talk to me unless they wanted me to do something for them.

I wanted to feel good about being dependable, but I didn't. Five dozen cookies for the bake sale? Call Renee, she can probably do that. Babysitting this Saturday? Only person I can think would be free is Renee. It's no wonder I was on the first train to anywhere but here.

I never thought I'd be back in this room. In fact, I remember telling my mother to turn it into an exercise room or a sewing room or something like that, because I wouldn't be coming back. My mother, while helping me pack, laughed and said, "Don't say what you won't do. You never know when you'll have to eat those words."

Wouldn't you know it? A few years later, here I am in my childhood bedroom, less the posters of Prince and New Edition adorning the walls, eating the hell out of those words.

I have brunch with the girls today and a tour of Golden Rays. I spoke with the intake doctor a few days ago. He seemed optimistic and said it would be a good idea for me to come down and take a look.

If this plan works, it'll benefit me and Daddy. At least I hope so, because I'm not sure how long I can hold up. I'm not cut out for being the sole caretaker of a man in the throes of a disease that makes him irritable, confused, and unable to care for himself. I'm not going to be able to take many more puddles in the hallway.

CHAPTER TEN

ebra

I've been in a daze for the last month. Just going through the motions, doing things that need to be done from the time I get up until it's time to go to bed. I collapse and sleep fitfully, and get up the next morning and do it all again.

Outside of anything to do with Kendra, Willard hasn't said more than a few words to me since that night in our bedroom. If I try to bring up the "situation", he shuts down and walks out of the room like I never said a word.

He's angry. I get it. I would be, too. But his anger is festering and growing, feeding off of itself, becoming a beast I don't think I can tame.

The only thing saving my sanity is getting dressed and out of this house. I'm going to see my girls today. They know something is wrong and Maxine made it clear that I won't get out of Ruby's without telling them what's going on. They see me as a model of a successful life. I dread saying the words I know will disappoint them.

I pull my twists back into an unruly puff with one of Kendra's hair ties. I throw on an old t-shirt, jeans and a pair of sneakers and grab my new eyeglasses off of the bureau. Bifocals. I frown at my reflection, pick up my purse and keys and walk out to the garage.

I've had a lot of time for thinking since I told my husband I'd been unfaithful. I think about things like my new car. Like the diamond studs I wear every day that were an anniversary gift or the African painting hanging in the living room that Willard got from an estate sale because he knew that I would love it.

I think about how Willard must feel like loving me was a waste of his time. I wonder how long he's going to punish me by keeping us in limbo. Will he leave? Or would he ask me to leave?

I pull into Ruby's and park next to Renee's Corolla. Maxine's car, a stark white piece of Italian design that is never dirty, is parked all by its lonesome at the edge of the lot, far from cars or trees or anything that might drop a speck of dust on it.

The two of them are seated on the bench. They're laughing, watching a video on Maxine's phone. I plaster a smile on my face and sit next to Renee.

"What are y'all watching?"

"This little girl is trying to sing this song, but she keeps messing up, and when she does, she screams. It's hysterical!" Just then, a tiny scream comes from the speakers on the phone and Renee and Maxine burst into laughter.

"You two ready? I'm hungry." I wave to Bethany, who points toward our usual table.

"Guess we seat ourselves now," mumbles Renee. I follow her and Maxine. Renee, for once, isn't wearing her signature purple sweat suit, but a dark blue button-down shirt, sleeves rolled up to her elbows and a white camisole underneath with a pair of dark jeans and boots.

Maxine looks smart and sophisticated in a simple short-sleeved dress with ruffles along the deep cut V-neck. I don't have to ask her what brand it is. Prada is her favorite designer and her closet is bursting with it.

As we sit, Maxine takes in my t-shirt and jeans and glances at Renee in the most put-together attire we've seen in a while. "At the risk of sounding like an asshole," Max begins, spreading a napkin over her lap. "It's like Invasion of the Body Snatchers in here. Why does Renee look so nice? And Debra, why do you look like Renee usually looks?"

Renee laughs. I don't. "Fuck you, Maxine. I've been going through some things. Looking suitable to be in your company wasn't top of mind today."

I often wonder how we're still friends. After Renee moved back and we started having these brunches, it wasn't my idea to invite Maxine. If I hadn't known her for so long, I'd hate her.

I have to admit, though, that I look a little torn up.

Our waitress arrives and in an entirely too cheerful manner, asks if we want our usual orders. I change mine without thinking about it. "I'll have chicken and waffles. And a glass of sweet tea, please."

I feel the stares from the other side of the table. Renee and Max gawk at me like I've grown a second head. I'm our healthy eater, always pushing egg whites and whole grains. I never drink sweet tea, but today I don't give a damn. I need comfort food.

"Going through some things?" Max leans in, laces her fingers together, props her chin on them and waits patiently for me to respond. I inhale deeply and for the second time ever, say the words.

"Look, uhm... So, I'm having an affair. Was having an affair." I swallow. And swallow again. I can't decide if I am hungry or if I'm going to throw up.

Renee speaks first, practically whispering across the table. "Did you... sorry, I thought I heard you say you're having an affair."

I can barely lift my head to face them. "Had. It's over. With one of my teachers."

"Girl. No, you didn't." Max sits back against the booth and covers her mouth.

"Does Willard know?" Renee asks. "And uhm... I mean, are you still together?"

I feel strangely like a little piece of the weight that had been bearing down on me has lifted from my shoulders. "He hasn't spoken to me since I told him."

"And how long ago was that?" Renee asks.

I roll my eyes to the ceiling and pretend to count the days and weeks since I had a meaningful conversation with my husband. "About a month ago."

"I knew it!" Maxine squeals. "I knew something was wrong last month!"

Renee reaches across the table and grips my hand. I hold on tight and notice that I'm shaking. "You could have told us. We could have talked about it."

"But I couldn't. I couldn't tell you. I've been giving out relationship advice like I know what I'm talking about." I give her my helpless look. "And now I'm here and I had no idea what was happening with us. I'd just told Willard about it and everything was up in the air."

"So who is this man? He's one of your teachers, you said? How long has that been going on? What did Willard say? And Kendra must not know—"

Maxine is interrupted by three hot plates of shrimp and grits with sausage and fried chicken and waffles. I cannot believe I'm about to eat this food.

When the waitress is gone and it's just the three of us discussing my affair in hushed tones over fatty food, I answer Maxine. "He's my Athletics Director. And it's over. It's been over since I told Willard."

I pause, not for drama but to take a breath and busy myself arranging my plate. I douse the waffles in butter and syrup and start cutting the long strips of chicken still sizzling from the fryer.

"Is Willard angry?" Renee asks, her voice small and timid. She doesn't like conflict. This qualifies as conflict.

"Willard is not talking to me. If Kendra knows, she's doing a bang-up job of hiding it. We haven't discussed it, but I don't want to tell her until we have to." I spear a portion of waffle, add a chunk of chicken to it and chew. It takes everything in me not to roll my eyes and moan at the delicious indulgence.

"You should not bring her into this," Max declares, her knife and fork working their way through her waffles and chicken strips. "There's no reason she needs to know."

"I agree." Renee nods. "Why would you need to tell her something like that?"

"Because we got caught," I blurt. The knife and fork I'm holding slip through my fingers and fall to the cheap porcelain plate with a clatter. The few bites I took roll around in my stomach and this part of the story especially makes me feel a little sick. "We were in my office. He kissed me and I let it go longer than it should have. We heard someone in the hallway. David tried to find them but…" I shake my head.

"Who was it?" Max asks.

I shrug. "We don't know. We just know it was probably a student."

"So whoever that was could say something to someone, and it could be a big thing. Or they could keep it quiet and it could be nothing," Renee muses.

"Exactly. So I'm just waiting for some arbitrary shoe to drop and the waiting is killing me. It's been a month! What are they waiting for? Maybe nothing will happen. Maybe I jumped the gun, telling Willard. I could have just ended it and let the whole thing blow over."

Max chuckles, but it comes out like a snort. "That's sure how it works on TV."

"People have affairs all the time, Max, then cut them off and go back to living their lives, and no one is the wiser."

"Not in the real world, Debra. Out here, people have to pay for their mistakes. But you know what? It's your marriage. Whatever." She dismisses me with a wave of her knife.

"Don't whatever me, Maxine. I would think you of all people would understand what I'm going through right now."

Maxine tosses her silverware onto her plate. Her pouty lips purse and pinch into a tight bud. Her eyes, framed by thick, bushy lashes and well-manicured brows close and open, revealing two light brown orbs of fire.

"What do you mean me of all people?"

"Max–" Renee reaches out for her, but Maxine flinches as if Renee's hands are red hot.

"No, I'm curious. I want to know what Debra means by me, of all people. I want know what this whore thinks she has on me."

"Let's not say things we don't mean," pleads Renee.

"A little too late for that, I think." I stare at Maxine, the word whore hurtling through my brain.

"You know what you are, Debra? You are an ungrateful simpleton. And that has nothing to do with me." Maxine hisses, leaning forward, a manicured finger in my face. "I have never cheated on a man. You've known Willard for more than half your life. You've sat at this very table–"

She taps the surface of the table, her nail clicking on each syllable. "And bragged about all the things he's done for you. Some young thing with a big dick swaggers into your life and shows you a few things. Now you see that you've fucked up and you're looking for some kind of alliance to make you feel better."

She sits back slowly, shakes her head, her eyes never leaving mine, her bottom lip trembling. "You may have ruined your life, but you did that all by yourself, honey. Me, of all people? No, ma'am. You don't have a partner in this one."

"Maxine, I'm sorry."

"You sure are."

"Look… there's a lot happening in my world. Home is miserable, and with this lingering black cloud over my job, I've not been sleeping well. I just…"

Max is wearing a tight-lipped frown and attacking her lunch

with fervor. My throat narrows so quickly that I'm close to choking. My eyes burn with unshed tears.

"I guess I thought my friends would understand." I push my chair back from the table and toss the strap of my purse over my shoulder. "I have to go," I squeak out before I walk away. Away from the table, from them, from judgment, from shame and embarrassment.

How could I have thought they would understand? Neither of them has ever been where I am.

I hear Renee call after me, but I'm too intent on getting out before the first tear falls. I almost make it, heaving and sobbing by the time I get into the car. I crank the ignition so hard that the motor squawks and peel out of the parking lot, spitting gravel in the air.

And drive. Just drive, with no actual destination in mind, but I suppose if I think hard enough about it, I know where I'm going.

CHAPTER ELEVEN

enee

"Well. That was… dramatic."

I drop heavily into the booth and scoot back into place, in front of my bowl of shrimp and grits. I tried to run after Debra but she'd reached her car and squealed out of the parking lot before I got to the door.

Maxine doesn't even look up. Her knife and fork pound through her meal and she systematically shoves chicken and waffles into her mouth. She angrily chews, breathing hard through her nose.

"You called her a whore. You realize that, right?"

"Mmmhmmm."

"You're okay with that? We can just say those things to each other?"

Maxine forces out a quick breath and lays down her knife and fork. "She hurt my feelings with that me of all people shit. I don't know the first thing about cheating on a man."

"Surely you have heard worse about yourself. Remember high school?"

"I didn't care about those bitches. Debra is supposed to be my friend. How does she even form her lips to insinuate that I know what the hell she's going through?"

"You know this is not about you, right? That she's been with Willard for more than half her life, which, as she knows it, is probably over?"

"And whose fault is that? I have to be insulted because she has a wandering puss—"

"Maxine Elise Donovan. Don't you go there."

Only Inell ever calls her that. It's the one way to quickly get her attention, because she hates her middle name. She thinks it makes her sound like an old lady, and considering her middle name came from her grandmother, she's right.

Maxine pouts, crosses her arms and sits back. "Well. She shouldn't have said that."

"I'm sure she knows that by now. How long are you going to stay mad about it?"

"As long as I want to." She lifts a hand to wave at the waitress, our signal that we're ready for the check. "And she was supposed to pay today. She just ran out of here like the dramatic lead in some Lifetime movie."

I sift through my grits, picking out pieces of shrimp and sausage. "Probably because her best friend just called her a whore." Max glares at me. "I'm just saying."

"Well, Debra needs some time to sort things out. I think I'll just let that sit awhile."

"But Debra's the dramatic one."

"And here I was going to invite you both to a party in a couple of weeks. Humph."

"What party?"

"Oh, it's just this thing." She reaches for the leather folder that holds our bill, then produces a credit card, slides it into the plastic pouch and hands it back to the waitress. "Millennium Security is throwing a soiree out at Brent's house. His partner is my client, the one that only wanted to look at places in Decatur. He's buying a place at Haynes Street. We close in two weeks."

My eyebrows lift in surprise. "Wow, that was fast. And cheap."

Maxine's lip curls. "I know. That's why I told Brent he was going to be making things worth my while for a long time. I said I was bringing my two best girlfriends to his party, and he said fine, the more the merrier. So, go shopping. Pick up something fancy."

She eyes me up and down and points at my head full of springy, dark brown curls– only dark brown because I recently had a session with a box of Dark & Lovely. "Get your hair done. Or... do something else with it. Try an updo."

I frown. "You know I hate shopping. I'll just wear one of the dresses I have–,"

"No. You won't. This is an upscale, black-tie affair. You wear the same two dresses all the time and I'm sick of looking at them. We'll go shopping. I'll get you something."

She waves away my protests as the waitress brings back the folder. Max plucks her card from the slot and puts it away, signs the receipt and leaves it on the table. "I need to run. I'm meeting Reginald Mayberry and his wife this afternoon to look at some houses."

I grab her arm and squeeze. "Wait. Falcons quarterback, Reginald Mayberry?"

"You know who he is?"

"Duh," I answer, laughing a little, then a lot at her blank expression. Maxine doesn't follow football. Neither do I, but I know about Motorin' Mayberry. "The Falcons about broke the bank, stealing him from the Eagles."

"I hope they gave him some of that money so he can buy a big, expensive house." Max shrugs, looking bored, and hooks a supple black leather bag over her shoulder. The gold zipper pull says Chanel. I bought my black canvas bag at Target.

"So what's he buying? And where?"

"I was told to dig up something around $3 million." She shrugs again, so nonchalant about selling homes worth millions to celebrities. "You never said why you look so nice."

I blush and tug at the hem of my shirt. "I'm going on a home tour today, too. For Daddy." I steal a glance at Maxine with a wry twist to my lips.

She knows exactly what I mean. "Oh. Is it time?"

I sigh. "He peed in the hallway this morning. He got turned around looking for the bathroom." My eyes rise to the scalloped ceiling. "Maxine, I love my Daddy but... if it gets to a point where he can't control his bowels, I will freak. I'm not even kidding."

"I'm so sorry." She strokes my arm, softly rubbing. "I know this is hard. Just do the thing you think is best."

"I'm trying. I just know he'll hate being in a home."

"He might. But it's not like that will be any different from normal. Bernard Gladwell hasn't liked anything since 1960."

I snort a short laugh. "Isn't that the truth?"

CHAPTER TWELVE

ebra

A cobalt blue Acura RSX sits parked in its usual spot, the bright sun glinting off of a spotless shine. David loves that car like it's his first. For all I know, it is his first real adult purchase. He babies the car, washing it weekly, using Armor All on the dashboard and leather protectant on the seats, constantly vacuuming the floor mats and carpeted interior and forbidding people from eating in it.

I hear the creak of a door on a squeaky hinge and look up. David stands in the doorway of his apartment in knee-length jean shorts and a sleeveless white t-shirt. The muscles in his arms ripple when he jams his fists deep into his pockets. After a few seconds of mutual staring, he steps back into the apartment, but leaves the door open.

As Willard so eloquently put it, I make a choice every time I see David. I want to do the right thing, back up and pull away and go home. Maybe it was a mistake to tell Max and Renee. Maybe it was a mistake to tell Willard. As long as I am making mistakes, I may as well make some that give me pleasure.

I turn off the ignition and get out of the car, push my feet to move, one in front of the other all the way to the door. I step over the threshold and close the door behind me.

David sits on the black leather sofa that I remember well. We had a few teenage-level make out sessions there. And on the matching chair and on the floor, in front of the fireplace on the cheap, scratchy rug. He's barefoot, his legs stretched out. He gestures to the cushion beside him. I cross the room and sit on the sofa, but at the other end of it.

"What brings you by?"

I open my mouth to answer but nothing comes to mind. I don't have a reason for being there. It's the first place I thought to go. David is the only other person who knows everything.

Shyly, I admit, "I have had the worst day. The worst month actually."

"Oh yeah? What's going on?"

I let it out. All of it. Willard, my friends, work, Kendra. That weight that had lifted from my shoulders when I felt relieved to tell Max and Renee about my affair had replanted itself and added a few friends. Talking to David didn't make that load feel any lighter, but I didn't expect it to.

"I feel like I'm losing my mind. How can so much be going so wrong, right now? All I did was…"

All I did was disregard marriage vows and a firm district policy. I have no excuse. I breathe a lung emptying sigh and sit forward, grasping my head in my hands. "I know I brought this on myself. But I'm miserable."

David appears in front of me, on his knees. "Do you want my advice?" I don't answer, but I lift my head. "You should let me help you forget all of this for a little while."

"David…"

"Listen. You're tired. You're hurt, and everybody is against you right now. Take a break from it. When's the last time you and Willard had sex? Do you remember?"

I think back, searching my recent memories. It's been an embarrassingly long time. I dip my head to hide, but he catches my chin in his palm.

"You been doin' for yourself?" I blush, my face red-hot. Is he asking me if I've masturbated? "I guess not?"

David scoots closer and tips his head toward mine. I can make the choice to move back, to rebuff him... but I don't. I haven't been kissed in so long and I miss it so much. My head sinks forward until our lips meet.

Gently, he presses soft lips against mine. Again and again until I've relaxed enough to open my mouth, accept his warm tongue and let the kiss deepen. My body remembers this surge of emotion and hormones and reacts as per usual. Nipples harden. Breathing quickens. Body trembles. And just when I can't stand it anymore, I feel his hands, soft and smooth as a baby's bottom, creeping underneath my t-shirt.

A sensation ripples through me, creating goose bumps along my arms, my thighs, up the back of my neck. I scoot toward the edge of the couch and make room for him. David moves even closer, pressing himself to me. I feel him through his jeans and mine as he pumps his hips in slow circles. He unhooks my bra and brings his hands around to my breasts. He kneads them, squeezing and releasing.

It feels amazing to be touched again.

His thumbs find my nipples. This is my weak spot, and he knows it. I convulse, my pelvis rocking forward, riding against him undulating against me.

He stands and offers me a hand. I take it.

David's bedroom is a study in young black men. The art on his walls are images of women in various stages of undress. The room is black on black—shiny lacquer bureau, dresser and framed mirror, lazy boy chair in the corner by the window, matching bed frame and half-moon headboard. The comforter is goose down inside of a black duvet. The sheets are black satin. The whole room smells like him.

Willard wears a musk scent. Like an old man.

It's a familiar place for me, so I'm not at all uncomfortable as David leads me across the room to the bed, sits me down on the edge and undresses me from the feet up. He unties my sneakers, removes my socks, unsnaps and unzips my jeans and I lay back so he can pull them off. Last, he rolls my shirt up from the hem and I lift my arms so he can pull it off. The bra comes with it. I'm naked, except for a pair of panties.

Having far fewer clothes to remove, David joins me in my near nudity, throwing off the shirt and pulling his shorts and boxers down in one tug. As he steps out of them, I watch him, stiff and at attention, bounce with his movements. I'm ashamed at how my mouth waters.

I move back on the bed. David pulls the comforter and top sheet down, and I slide inside the cocoon of darkness. He follows, scooting every inch of his muscled body up against me. I shiver at the feeling of being so close to him.

"You cold? Come here." He wraps both arms around me and I snuggle as close to him as possible, bury my face in his chest and breathe in the scent of him. So familiar. So forbidden.

We lie there awhile, breathing and holding each other until eventually David moves again, rolling us so he hovers over me. I feel my panties being tugged down my legs and soon I'm naked, sliding around on satin sheets.

"Relax and have a good time." He says this as his hands travel my body, from my belly to my warm, wet core. His thumb finds my clit, and he begins a gentle stroke, then a circular rub. My hips know what to do, rocking against the rhythm he's set. As if it were possible, my nipples harden even more. I feel my body flush with pending orgasm.

Moaning, whimpering, I call out his name. "David…"

I rarely have to say much more. The tone and tenor of my voice always betrays where I am in the throes of ecstasy. He enters smoothly, in one stroke. My body receives him, welcomes him in. My legs lift and lock around him. My hands land where they always do, on either side of his thick neck.

"I need this so badly." My eyes meet his. My voice shakes even in my whisper.

"Me too, baby. Me too."

David is a slow and steady sexer. He's not a jackhammer, he's not a rammer. There's no irregularity in his stroke. He sets his rhythm and like old reliable; he keeps pumping. Building, building, building until my toes curl, my body explodes, my pelvis jerks in convulsions and I spasm around him.

His eyes snap shut. His head rocks back. He grunts loudly and pumps a few times before I feel him release.

"Fuck... Debra." He glistens with sweat, his breaths coming in heavy gasps of air. "You should take time off of sex more often. You feel good."

I laugh. "I have a feeling that there will be more breaks than sex in my future."

"It doesn't have to be like that. Not as long as I'm around."

"It doesn't have to be like that and you know it."

He pulls out and rolls to his side, gathering me to him. "It's too bad, though," he mumbles. His cheek rests against my temple. "We're good together."

The faint sound of a ringing bell breaks through a heavy fog. A pause and ringing again. Then a pain in my side as the sharp point of an elbow makes its mark.

"Debra," I hear, but the voice isn't Willard. I force my eyes open and sit up, glance around the room, slowly coming to the realization that I'm in a bed that isn't mine. The rosy glow of sunset peeks around the drawn blinds and curtains over the windows. Sunset! I've been gone all day without a word to anyone.

"Oh my God." I toss back the covers and slip out of bed, head back out to the living room and grab my mobile phone from the couch, where I'd left it. I scroll through missed calls and texts. Two from Renee- are you ok? And call me! Missed calls and a slew of text messages from my daughter. I sense her panic level rising with every message and each passing hour.

Shaking, I press a button to return the last call from Kendra. She picks up in half a ring. "Ma? Are you okay? Where are you?"

"Hi, baby. I'm so sorry to make you worry. I... I forgot my phone in the car." I wince at the lie as I make my way back to the bedroom and gather up pieces of that day's outfit. David's eyes follow my every move. "I had to do a little bit of work and I lost track of time. Where are you?"

"I'm at home. Aunt Renee said you left brunch early, and she hadn't heard from you. Daddy didn't know where you were either."

A lightning bolt shoots straight through my chest. "You... you called your dad?"

"Uhm... yeah." She pauses. "I didn't know I wasn't supposed to."

"Oh, of course you should have." I sit on the edge of the bed and wedge the phone between my shoulder and ear so I could put on my panties, socks and jeans. "He's just so busy this time of year. I hate to bother him."

"Well, he said he didn't know where you were and said he'd see me later tonight and hung up. He's so grumpy lately."

I slip my arms through the holes in my bra and adjust the cups. Behind me, David grabs both ends of the bra strap and hooks them together. I give him a tight smile over my shoulder.

"He's under a lot of stress," I tell her, while wrestling with the t-shirt I'd worn that day. "So, yeah, he's been kind of weird."

"I don't like it. So where are you? When are you coming home? Can we have pizza for dinner? I mean real pizza, not that frozen stuff. It gets soggy."

I pull the shirt over my head and down over my bra, stand and slip my feet into my sneakers. Without a word of goodbye to David, who sits naked and cross-legged in the middle of the bed, I grab my purse from the living room and walk out of his apartment, careful to close the door softly so Kendra won't hear.

"I'm heading home now. I'll be there soon and we'll talk about it."

I drive the few streets between David's place and my house slowly, putting the day together in my head. If Kendra caught onto anything strange, she didn't make it apparent. And Kendra would. She hasn't yet learned the art of subtlety.

I'm dreading a conversation with Willard, though. He'll have no trouble guessing where I was when Kendra called looking for me.

Arriving home, I pull into my spot in the garage. Willard's spot is empty, as usual. The kitchen is deserted, but I hear the TV blaring in the family room. I dump the armful of materials I'd dragged into the house and head toward the noise.

Kendra is on the couch, her legs curled beneath her, fingers moving wildly across the touch screen of her phone. I pat the top of her head, smoothing down the soft kinks at the crown. Her eyes roll up to meet mine and she smiles before going back to the screen. I perch on the arm of the couch, halfway watching the TV, halfway eavesdropping on her text conversation.

"Did you get all your work done?"

"Hm?" I realize that she still thought I had been at work all afternoon. "Oh, yeah. Enough of it, I guess. There's always a lot of work to do."

"Yeah, when you're everyone's boss."

"Yep," I answer, letting a laugh slip out. "It can be tough. Anyone give you a hard time because your mom is the Principal?"

Kendra shakes her head, her mouth turning down a bit. "The kids I know think you're cool. My friends, anyway. What's up with Dad?"

The sudden left turn in the conversation startles me. "What about Dad?"

"Remember, I said he was grumpy."

"He's just busy and stressed out."

"But Ma, there's always stress." She sits up, twisting her body around to face me. "He's never been like this. I asked him if he knew where you were, because I wanted a ride home and he got all quiet, and then his voice got all low and mean. And he said, 'I don't know, Kendra. I don't keep track of that woman'. He didn't want to talk. He didn't care where you were when I couldn't find you. It was..." She shook her head slowly, her eyes almost pleading for the truth. "Just weird."

I tuck a finger under her chin and lift her head, look her in the eye and tell her as much of the truth as I can at the moment. "Remember, we talked a while ago about your dad and I having some problems? But that it's not something for you to worry about? This is adult stuff between him and me. I know there's some weirdness, but that's how he gets when he's got things on his mind. We just have to hope it will pass."

Or not. Or he'll hate me and want to end our marriage, want me to move out of the home we worked two or three jobs each to build, and later ate peanut butter sandwiches for every meal to keep.

Or maybe he'll move out. He'll get a nice bachelor pad with an extra bedroom so Kendra would have a place to sleep. We'll shuffle her back and forth to make sure she gets equal time with the both of us. He'll come to pick her up and awkwardly stand in the driveway and wait for his daughter to come out of his wife's house, the house he lost in the divorce that he will ask for.

Kendra heaves a heavy, dramatic sigh and scoots down on the couch to lay her head on my lap. I run my fingers through her kinky shoulder length twists and let my mind drift, trying not to sift through the TV room and figure out what Willard would take with him if he left. Or what I would take if he made me leave. Or if we split and sell the house entirely.

I close my eyes against all of that. It's not over yet. In order for it to be over, we would have to talk and we hadn't been able to accomplish that.

Kendra sniffs. "You smell like my gym teacher."

CHAPTER THIRTEEN

enee

I pull out of Ruby's parking lot and unlock the iPhone that Max and Debra pressured me into buying. I didn't need a smart phone and didn't think I would use it, but darn it if all these apps aren't useful. Daddy is on medication to help his cognitive brain function and other medications to battle the side effects of those medications. I started making notes and keeping a schedule of what, and how much, he was taking, what it was supposed to do, and if it was doing what it said it would do. So far, they aren't doing much.

Aside from all my notes and games, I love my GPS app. I've lived here all my life but I still need the comfort of an electronic map. So much has changed in the last ten years that I hardly recognize this city anymore. I open the application and type in the address I'd written down on a scrap of paper and shoved into my purse.

I head for the interstate and indulge in a daydream about what life might be like after my father is comfortably settled at Golden Rays. I hate to think about selling the house. It's the only home I've ever known, but it would seem so empty without my father and the overwhelmingly heavy blanket of memories of my mother.

Before I can even worry about selling the house, I have to think about the bookstore. Could it survive another few years? I couldn't afford to be stuck in Atlanta with an unusable space.

The GPS directs me to take Interstate 285, a belt around the city that forms a perimeter between Atlanta proper and the suburbs. One of the ways that snobs like Maxine judge people is which side of 285 you live on. The most preferable, desired location is inside the perimeter.

My moment of peace is interrupted by the warble of an incoming call. I pick up the phone and glance at the display: Marcus Evans. My heart leaps a little.

"Marcus."

"Renee?"

"You don't know who you dialed?"

A chuckle wafts over the line, one that fills my mind with memories and my heart with emotions. I use to lay awake thinking about what my life would be like, had I just taken care of business and ran back into his arms. Maybe we'd be married by now, have a few children.

"You sound different."

"I'm not different. How are you?"

"I'm good," he answers, and begins telling me about how things are going at work. I miss the old job, where Marcus was just one floor away. He's moved up several times since I left and now manages a sales team. I can tell he's proud of himself.

"That's good. Really great. I'm happy for you. So, what's up with... what's her name? Lisa?" You know, the woman you were dating after we supposedly broke up, but you neglected to inform me that we'd broken up?

"Lise'," He corrects, adding the arrogance that goes along with pronouncing her name correctly. I bet her name is actually Lisa and she invented that pretentious pronunciation, like when Debra tried to go by Debi for a few weeks. "It's French."

I roll my eyes at his correction. Who cares? "Lise'. Are you still dating her?"

"Nah. She wasn't a long term thing. Just something to do."

"Humph," I mutter, shaking my head and watching the road at the same time. "Does she know that? That she was something to do?"

"I didn't call you to talk about her."

"Why did you call, then?"

"To see what's going on with you. I miss you."

"Was I not something to do?"

"Would I be calling you if you were?"

"I don't know, Marcus. I don't even really know you anymore."

"And that's my fault, Renee? I'm not the one that left."

I turn on my blinker as my exit approaches, making my way over to the far right lane. "Yeah, you like to remind me that this is my fault. I could have everything I ever wanted, if only I wasn't such a saint. Let's not talk about the ultimatum that you knew I could never accept."

"I can't believe we're about to have this argument again. It wasn't an ultimatum."

"The hell it wasn't! 'Come back to Philly or I don't know what's going to happen to us' isn't an ultimatum? Sounds like one to me."

"If you weren't coming back, I needed to know. What was I supposed to do? Hang out up here while you play savior down there?"

It takes every fiber of strength and will to not scream at glass-breaking pitch, toss the phone into the street and run it over. Play savior? What was he supposed to do?

"You know what Marcus? My bad. I thought I was in a relationship with someone I loved that loved me back. I thought I had something real with someone real. We hit one bump and all you care about is how it affects you. Did you give a shit that my heart was breaking? Did you come to see me, come meet my dad or offer any kind of help? And after you knew I couldn't leave, where was your offer to come down to Atlanta?"

"I don't want to live in Atlanta."

"Like I do? You act like I'm down here having a good time."

He laughs, which is infuriating. "Look, Renee. I really just called to say hi and to see how you and your dad were doing. I didn't mean to start a fight."

"Bullshit. You start the same fight every time you call. And you wonder why I didn't run right back up there."

"Okay, okay." He inhales a breath and slowly exhales it out. "I know I didn't make myself or my point clear but all I wanted to know was if you wanted me to hang on or let go. You told me in not so many words where I could go. So I went. And you're mad that I went instead of hanging on."

"I'm not..." I force myself to stop talking and breathe before I have an aneurysm. Deep breaths in and out. In. Out. In. Out. "I can't keep having this conversation. It's not healthy for me, okay? Let's just move on."

"Fine by me. Really."

"Me too."

"So how are you," he asks, before I can cut him off. "I mean really."

I suck in a breath of cool air from the air conditioner blowing in my face, in battle with the warm autumn afternoon sun.

"I'm..." I try to force some of the words rolling around in my head to come out of my mouth. Truth is, I go to the bookstore or I make up errands to get away from Daddy because I don't know him anymore. "I don't think about me, really."

"You see, Renee? That's you. I knew you'd get wrapped up in being everything to everyone and not giving a shit about what's good for you and what's important to you. You did build a life up here with someone that loved you, but someone else cries out for you and you run to them. You left that life you built here... here."

His words cut like a knife and the worst part about it? He's right. And were my mother alive and my father coherent, they'd never stand for it. They'd love me enough to not let me give up so much.

I swallow back tears, lean forward to turn off the ignition and toss my keys into my purse. Since the air is off, the heat of the day is cloying and sticky.

"You have a point, I guess. I don't bear all of the blame, though."

"I'm not saying it's your entire fault. You assume that's what I mean, but it isn't. I just... I couldn't figure out where I fit, so I stepped out."

I refuse to let myself cry, but I swear, cross my heart, wish on a star, that if I ever get another chance with Marcus, I won't let him go.

"I have an appointment to look at this place for Daddy, so I need to go. Thanks for calling, Marcus."

"Sure. Can I call again? Just to check on you? I won't bring that other thing up again. I promise."

I hear his smile through the phone line. "That would be nice."

I grab my purse, my phone and a notepad and get out of the car. Showtime.

Golden Rays Memory Care Center is one of Atlanta's premier Senior Care facilities for patients who suffer from Alzheimer's, Dementia, and other cognitive brain diseases. At first glance, it resembles an upscale apartment complex except instead of yuppies in Brooks Brothers and Kathie Lee suits rushing in from work to get in a few sets of tennis at the courts, there are older people, aged fifty-five and older, milling about the campus.

The administrative office looks like a leasing office. A receptionist is seated in front of a set of closed doors. She wears a pair of scrubs, pink with white flowers all over, reminiscent of Kathy Bates in Fried Green Tomatoes, except her hair is fire engine red and sprayed to within an inch of its life. She's probably significantly contributed to the hole in the ozone layer all on her own–there's no way that football helmet of hair is moving.

She wears a name tag that reads Norma and her smile is bright and friendly. Like one of those people who is annoyingly cheerful all the time.

"Did you have an appointment, honey?" She croons at me with a sweet, southern country drawl that I recognize from our phone conversation weeks ago.

"I do." I step up to the counter to dig out the slip of paper I'd buried in my purse. "Renee Gladwell for doctor... Williamson?"

"Oh hello, Renee. Ron will be right with you." She picks up a clipboard, already loaded with a stack of pages. "Fill this out for me, honey? It's standard information we have to keep on file."

"Even if I haven't decided that I—"

"I can't let you tour the facility without this information." She blinks once, a long and slow blink that said she had an answer to every question and protest I had, so just take the clipboard and fill out the damn sheets and stop wasting her time. "Won't take long. I'll let the doctor know you're here."

She rises from her seat and waddles to the closed door, opens it and edges her way through an unnecessarily small opening. I take the clipboard to a set of burgundy, cloth covered chairs. They look comfortable, but in fact are not. The seat cushion is flat and missing any foam or padding. I feel like I'm sinking through the bottom of the chair.

I scoot up so I'm sitting on the edge of the chair and balance the clip board on my knees. The forms attached look like standard intake forms at a hospital or a clinic—name, age, address, condition, stage of illness, medications, etc. I fill out the information as asked, including any medical history that I could remember and insurance information. Daddy is still covered under his separation package and pension from Ford, thank goodness. He never would have made it this far, if it wasn't for that coverage.

Norma comes back from her clandestine trip behind the closed door, accompanied by a tall, balding man. His brown and white checkered shirt is tucked into brown pants. He's not wearing a lab coat. He would be drab, were he not so tall. At well over 6 feet, he towers over everyone in the office and lobby area. He walks toward me, hand extended.

I stand and accept his gesture, a good hard shake, ending with a knowing squeeze. "Nice to meet you, Doctor."

"Ron," he corrects. "I'm not into titles. You must be Renee? We talked the other day about your father."

He remembered me. His eyes are warm and he's still holding my hand in a gentle, reassuring squeeze. I had hoped it would be this way, when I finally met him. When we spoke on the phone, he made me feel like he knew exactly what I was going through. He had to have talked to hundreds of caregivers of Dementia patients who were at their wit's end. I felt like I was almost there, like if one more thing happened, I was going to lose my mind.

"Come on back to my office. We'll talk before we take a tour." He finally releases my hand, only to take the clipboard from my arm. He flips through the pages as he walks, mumbling as he leads. I follow closely behind him to an understated office. It isn't much more than a desk, a lamp, some chairs and a filing cabinet. He isn't into decoration, either.

He drops into a chair and pulls the pages from the clipboard. "Okay, so... Bernard, right?" He continues when I nod. "Diagnosed at sixty-two, thus the Early Onset qualifier. You mentioned the loss of your mother—"

"She had been gone a few years when he started getting bad."

Ron sits back, grabbing a pencil to play with as he crosses an ankle over a knee. "Often we see that symptoms will be intermittent before anyone notices an illness. It could have been the trauma of losing his wife that started the ball rolling. It's likely he's been declining for some time and since you weren't living with him, you weren't alarmed until he started showing more severe symptoms."

I nod, listening. I do a lot of nodding when experts talk.

"He can feed himself, dress himself, he's not immobile?"

"Correct."

"He still retains motor function, cognitive ability?"

I hesitate to agree. "Around the house, he's okay. He needs help on the stairs. Walking outside is a disaster."

"Right. He can't see depth, so things like steps are a challenge."

"He can't read. He doesn't remember my name. He knows his nurse. One minute he's fine and the next minute he thinks it's time to go to work the Ford plant. And…"

I stop to take a breath. I'm doing a lot of complaining, but one look in Ron's eyes tells me he needs to know this information. "This morning, he didn't know where the bathroom was. I put him in the shower and between then and when he was done showering, he was fine again. I feel like I'm going crazy, like maybe he's not as bad as I think he is. Is this normal?"

He tosses the pencil onto the desk and sits forward, dropping his leg to the floor. "Listen… yes, completely. Don't think of it as a bulb that blows out suddenly. Think of it as a dimmer bulb. It's just very, slowly losing light. Some days, the bulb is darker than others. Talk to me about his medications."

We have a long discussion about his vitamin and prescription regimen, none of which I feel really helps but I'm afraid to take him off of anything, for fear that it's somehow slowing down an even more rapid decline. Ron nods and adds an 'mmm hmmm' occasionally but lets me talk. More importantly, he doesn't make me feel crazy.

"Let's take a trip around the property and I'll show you our living areas."

I follow him out of his office, but instead of going through the front office, he turns the opposite way and we leave the building through a side door where a fleet of golf carts waits. He picks one and slides in, smiles at me and offers the passenger seat to me.

I get in and brace myself, but he's a skilled driver, rolling along the pavement past several sets of buildings. "We house our residents based on stage. Every stage offers in-home care, just like you get with Jessie. The later stage patients have constant care."

Ron guides the golf cart to another path and stops in front of a doorway, turns off the cart and gets out. "This is our model apartment. Most every unit looks like this one." He digs a set of keys out of his pocket and unlocks the door, opens it and steps aside.

It looks like a regular apartment. Nice sized living room, a wall of windows for natural light, a kitchen with plain white appliances and tile floor and a muted, cream colored carpet.

"Most residents have a hard time adjusting to an apartment after having their own homes but eventually they acclimate."

"So would he be with a roommate?" Ron nods. "That'll be interesting. He's stubborn and likes to argue."

"We try to blend temperaments. That's not to say we don't have to move some residents, but sometimes knowing that someone is here who knows exactly how he feels and what he's going through is a comfort."

"So, if I admit my father here, how often does someone come to check on him? He can't be alone right now."

"That would be according to the care plan that you and I set up for him. We can talk about it more at the office, but basically as often as you have Jessie come in is how often a staffer will be here to take care of him and his roommate every day. If he'd like to eat here in the apartment, a staffer will prepare meals. Some families like to buy the groceries and stock the cabinets. I've got a guy whose mother is a resident. He visits every day and cooks for her as if she was living in her own home."

He flips the keys from hand to hand while we walk through the apartment. The bedrooms are a nice size, as are the windows. There's a bathroom off of each bedroom and a walk-in closet in each room, plus a hall closet and a storage room.

"Once he needs more one-on-one care, he'll move to another unit that works more like a group home where there is always someone around on a revolving schedule."

"I hate to admit it, but I think my father is probably somewhere between this place-" I wave my hand around to indicate the apart- ment we're standing in. "And the group home. He'd be mad if I put him there, though. And I'd be mad at myself if I let him stay somewhere like here and something happened to him."

"The stages can overlap." Ron's face clouds and he hesitates to add, "It could also be that it's just not time for a home for your father."

He winces as if he knows that isn't what I want to hear. It isn't, but I am impressed that he isn't trying to sell me on the place. "He's doing well, considering. Some minor, minor issues, but he's healthy and functioning. That's saying a lot for an Alzheimer's patient, four years after diagnosis. I know it seems like a lot because he's so different from the Bernard you know, but... he's not bad off right now."

I'm lost, standing in the middle of the model unit. I had hoped that Golden Rays would be the answer for me—for him, but it just doesn't feel right. I'm disappointed. I feel so selfish, wanting to put him here.

He shows me out of the apartment, locks the door behind us, and joins me in the golf cart. He points out different areas of the property—the Commons, where they eat meals, have dances and social functions; the Gardens, where all the ladies and gentlemen with hobbies gather. There is a sewing circle and knitting klatch and arts and crafts twice a week. I'm sure my father doesn't want any part of glue and string and paper towel rolls.

"You're handling an awful lot," Ron says, as we settle back in his office with bottles of cold water. "Even with help, taking care of Bernard night and day and worrying about him is probably giving you gray hair."

I absentmindedly run my hands through my hair. I don't mention the Dark & Lovely session to Ron. Maxine will surely let me know that it's time to color.

"I wish I could just put him somewhere," I admit. "I feel guilty for thinking that and tell myself that I can handle it. And then he screams at me because he can't find something or can't remember something, and I want to run away. But I can't. I'm all he has. It's hard to handle, but I can't break down. I have to keep going."

Ron reaches for a post-it note and a pen. He scribbles some information on it and hands it to me. I take it and read the amazingly legible doctor's handwriting. Alz-Connect, it reads, with a web address listed underneath. "It's a support group, completely made up of people like you, people who understand where you're coming from. It might help you handle this period where your dad is pretty much okay, but you're not."

I thank him and tuck the piece of paper into my purse, already knowing that I will not sit in front of some group and complain about taking care of my father. That would be too much like therapy, and I'm not crazy. I'm just tired.

I head back to my car after promising to think it over and give Ron a call. I pass a few people out for an afternoon walk. One of them, a woman who seems entirely too young to be a resident, sees me and gives me the biggest, brightest smile.

"Are you Jenny?" She asks.

"No ma'am," I answer. "I'm Renee. Who are you?"

"I'm Gloria." Her smile fades, replaced by a confused half frown. "Jenny was going to come see me. I don't know when she's coming."

"Come on, Glo." One of the Resident Assistants, dressed in scrubs with a name tag, slides an arm around her shoulder. "Sorry," she says, giving me a small smile.

"It's no bother," I tell her, watching the small group shuffle along the sidewalk. I wonder if that was what it would be like for my father, wandering around this place, asking everyone if they're Lorraine.

I feel like I am being punished for wanting some relief. Is this what karma feels like?

CHAPTER FOURTEEN

ebra

To the outsider, my life hasn't changed. I appear to do the same things I did before. I still have to show up at school every day, be a leader, a boss, an administrator, a mentor. I still have budgets to review and purchases to approve, skirmishes to settle and disciplinary problems to handle. And those are just the daylight hours. That's the biggest misconception of the job, one that didn't take long to impress itself upon me. This is a twenty-four-hour-a-day job. I solve school problems in my sleep.

The momentum has kept me going.

By 8am, the day is in full swing. I try to stay in the hallway and greet students, teachers and staff to avoid having a throng of people in my office. The secretaries have been in since 7am and the phones are ringing off the hook. I've already worked with the custodian on an urgent plumbing issue in the east wing boy's restroom. Once the bell has rung, I head to my office and address the blinking phone, the stack of pink While You Were Out message slips and the towering pile of paper in my inbox.

At 8:15, I pick up the voicemail messages. "Debra, this is Bernice. Call me in my office this morning, please. I'll be in all day. Thanks." The recording makes her silky voice rich, but I hear the stiff professional tone.

Bernice Johnson is the Superintendent of Public Schools for Gwinnett County. She's also a friend, so her messages normally have a conversational tone, like "girl, I need to talk!" Following would be a two-minute description of what she needs to talk about, ending with "call my cell!" To hear her use a tone she might reserve for strangers and people she doesn't like strikes a dagger through my heart.

Come on, Debra. It could be nothing. She could have just been busy. It was early for her to be calling. I reach for the phone and punch in the numbers I know by heart. I've made many a call to the Superintendent's office in the past two years.

"Superintendent Johnson's office."

"Hi, Sandy. It's Debra Macklin at Morningside. Bernice left me a message to call her. Is she in?"

"One moment." A few seconds later, the hold music is interrupted by the familiar voice of my friend.

"Debra, thanks for calling."

"Hi Bernice," I'm hoping she'll pick up on my light tone. "How are you? Your boys aren't already crazy this morning, are they?"

Her twin boys, Jordan and Jason are Kendra's age. They're cute with wide-set brown eyes and lanky frames. They're on the basketball team at Tucker Junior High—Morningside's rivals. They are also holy terrors. Identical twins with wicked senses of humor, they like to gang up on teachers, pretend to be each other and switch.

"They are going to have me in an insane asylum. If they're this bad at twelve, imagine when they're fully fledged teenagers! I won't survive it."

"Kendra will be thirteen in March and she is already emotional. When the hormones kick in? I'm not ready, Bernice. Why can't they stay little?"

"This is what we get for wanting to bring something beautiful into the world."

We both laugh though, because as much heartache as our children give us, we wouldn't trade them for the world.

"Well, I know you're busy, so I'll get down to the reason I called you." Here we go. "I think you might already know what's going on."

I nod my head, though she can't see me, and bite down on my bottom lip. "I have an idea."

"So it's true?"

"What... exactly are you asking about?" I'm not willing to fall on my sword. If she's only heard part of the story, I'm not going to confess to all of it.

"I had a visit last week from one of the parents, who heard from one of your students that... well, that you were in your office, shall we say... behaving inappropriately with another member of your staff. Does that ring any bells?"

"It does."

"How long has this been going on? Is it still going on?"

"It's over. It's been over. It was off and on during the last school year and I ended it and…"

"And?"

"And he wanted to rekindle. And I… I didn't fight him on that. But the incident that was reported happened after hours. No one was in the building."

"Except your witness. And you. And…" I hear paper shuffling. "David Loren. He's Director of Athletics, isn't he?" She clicks her tongue. I feel her eyebrows rise over the phone line. Had we not been discussing my affair and the possible ending of my career, she would have a lot more to say about David.

"Can I ask who made the report?"

"That's confidential, I'm sorry."

I attempt to unclench my fist before I crush the receiver in my hand. "Okay. So, what happens now?"

Bernice breathes an audible sigh. "I'm trying to keep this in-house, because I know you, Debra. I know this job means a lot to you and you're doing great. Be that as it may, this is expressly forbidden, something we stress during the kickoff meeting every year. That you signed the agreement acknowledging these policies and blatantly disregarded them — for two years — disappoints me. You know what's going on in Atlanta. Gwinnett doesn't want that kind of attention, Debra."

The Atlanta School District has been under scrutiny for years, most recently because of a cheating scandal that has been splashed all over the front page of the Atlanta Journal Constitution. Principals and teachers have been fired, and the Superintendent is facing charges. Gwinnett has been quietly smug about its spotless reputation. The school board won't like being compared to Atlanta. Not one bit.

"I know, Bernice. I'm sorry to disappoint you. I really am."

"Do Willard and Kendra know?"

"Willard knows. I told him after we got caught because I wasn't sure how fast it would hit the wires. I don't think Kendra knows."

"Well..." She hesitates. "I'd want Kendra to get it from me. And from what I hear, she's going to know about it sooner rather than later."

My heart skips a beat and I'm having trouble getting in enough air. The space in my skull seems to expand until I feel like my head might pop off my neck and float to the ceiling. I drum up enough courage to ask, "What do you hear? What's going on?"

"My guess is that a concerned parent has locked arms with the PTA, who we know don't like you and would be happy to see you removed."

"Makes sense."

"I can almost guarantee that this is racing through the halls at Morningside like wildfire. Forget about Kendra finding out. If things get out of control, the school board will have to step in. You don't want that."

"I sure don't." I shove a thumbnail into my mouth and nervously chew on it. My leg bounces incessantly, knocking against the desk and creating a staccato rhythm in the otherwise quiet of my office.

"I want to see what I can do to keep this quiet, but I'll be honest. I've already received a follow-up call asking when you're going to face disciplinary action. Watch your back."

My lung capacity drops, as does my stomach. I must have made a noise, because I faintly hear Bernice asking if I'm alright.

"No. I am not alright!" I bite out. "My life is a mess. My husband isn't talking to me, someone wants to destroy my career and now I have to sit my twelve-year-old down and tell her about how I love her dad but I made a mistake and she might hear some things about her mother and to not get caught up in defending me! No… I'm not okay, Bernice."

"This has got to be tough, but stand strong, Debra. I know people make mistakes, and I'm not inclined to level any kind of punishment. Like I said, though, it's not just up to me."

"You'll let me know if you hear anything?"

"You'll be the first to know. Hang in there."

"I'll try," I choke out before I hang up. I immediately drop my head onto my folded arms and stop trying to fight back tears.

A little after 5pm, I swing into the driveway and press the button to lift the garage door. I am surprised to find Willard's Lexus parked in his spot. My mind races with reasons why Willard might be home before six o'clock. Hell, before sunset.

I try to hide my shaking hands and questioning eyes as I walk into the house, lugging my work bag, my purse and a few books. The house is quiet as I unload onto the kitchen table, kick off my shoes and pad through the living room, my pointy Nine West hanging from my fingertips. The den is empty, the 52-inch TV that I bought Willard a few Father's Days ago a yawning dark hole in a corner of the room.

Willard and I share an office on the main floor of the house. I hear the irregular rhythm of Willard's fingers pounding on a keyboard. Give him an adding machine and his fingers fly so fast, you can't see them move. A keyboard is another beast. He is a 'hunt and peck' typist, so even a short, two paragraph letter would take him an hour to type.

Two desks are wedged into the room and butted up against each other so that Willard and I are staring right at one another if we're both in the office. I use a laptop; Willard prefers an old IBM desktop that, despite grinding noises from the fan, still works. My side is a study in ordered chaos, with files and papers and check stubs everywhere. Willard's side is neat and utilitarian. Not a speck of dust out of place.

He sits in his office chair, a burnt orange number covered in vinyl so old that the arms are cracked and the stuffing is stained from years of exposure. He's in his normal typing stance—glasses perched on the edge of his nose, two forefingers out and banging letter keys, his head intermittently rising to view the flickering monitor in front of him.

I duck my head in and paste a smile on my face. "Anything I can help you with? You know you get frustrated trying to type things yourself."

Willard tips his head up, stares at me over the rims of his eyeglasses, and drops his eyes back to the handwritten page. "No," he grunts eventually, before his fingers tap out another word. "I think you've done quite enough."

I step into the room and lean against the doorjamb. "Are we going to talk, eventually? Or just keep moving around each other, communicating through email and post-it notes? Our daughter is asking me what's going on, what's wrong with Dad—"

"Oh?" Willard straightens and pulls his glasses away from his face. "Is she really? Asking what's wrong with Dad? And did you tell her, Debra? Did you tell her what you did, so she would know what was wrong with Dad?"

I don't answer. Willard glares for a moment, puts his glasses back on and goes back to his document. "I have something I'd like to complete this evening, so if you'll excuse me."

I had thought about offering to make him some dinner, but with his attitude, I don't care if he starves. I walk back down the hall, past the den and the living room to the kitchen where I pick up my bags and books to take them upstairs.

The front door opens and closes as I make my way to the rear staircase. "Kendra?"

"Yeah." I hear her bounding through the living room, her nylon backpack swishing against her light jacket. I come around the corner to meet her before she can go upstairs.

"Hey, baby. How was your day?"

"Fine," she answers with a shrug. "I got an 'A' on my algebra quiz and my science project, and Mrs. Locke said if I continued to do good—"

"Do well."

"Do well... in my science classes, she would consider letting me join the Science Team. Isn't that cool?"

The Science Team is a special interest group at Morningside, created to target those students gifted at mathematics and science and put them on a track to success. The group meets weekly to put together projects and hold friendly competitions. At year end, there is an exhibition.

"That's wonderful, sweetheart! I'm proud of you. That's using the old noggin, isn't it?" I playfully tap her temple with the tips of my fingers. She beams and leans into my hand.

"I need to talk to you," she whispers. My heart drops to my feet. Has she already heard? Is this the moment I don't want to have with my daughter?

"Okay," I whisper back. "Right now?"

"I'll come up later," she says, letting her bag slide from her shoulder. "I saw Daddy's car."

I watch her walk away and turn the corner, hear her say hi to Willard. Get jealous over how happy he is to see her. Hear his accolades and kind words over her math test and her science team possibilities. I sigh, my heart heavy, and turn to climb the stairs to my bedroom, which has become my new prison.

Willard moved out of the bedroom a few weeks ago. His clothes, shoes, toiletries, cologne have been moved to the smallest bedroom and bathroom in the house, just to not have to share with me. He leaves for work early in the morning and comes home late at night. He goes straight to his room and if I don't try to see him, I won't.

I change out of my suit into comfortable yoga pants and a t-shirt. Pull my twists back, remove my jewelry, and wash my face. I settle on the bed or the wingback chair with some paperwork or, on rare occasion, a recent novel.

Having a best friend that owns a bookstore has the best of privileges. Anything I want to read, Renee will loan to me for a few weeks, so long as I don't damage the book or crack the spine. Usually I buy it from her with our unofficial friends and family discount. It's been awhile since I felt carefree enough to kick back with a trashy novel.

Tonight, I can't focus on anything. My conversation with Bernice rolls through my mind over and over. I can't imagine what I could have done to make someone so angry that they would attempt to ruin my career. I don't have the best relationship with everyone, but I can't think of anyone who would dislike me this much.

My eyes flicker open, blinking and squinting from the sudden burst of light. The fog of sleep rolls away as I realize the overhead light is on. A shadow stands over me and an envelope drops into my lap.

"That's for you. Read it. Let me know what you want to do." Willard stalks out of the room and nearly slams the door behind him.

I pick up the plain white envelope with my name scrawled across the front. I flip it over, pull the flap open and draw out a single page. Unfolding it, my eyes skip down the page.

Separation. Custody. Alimony. Divorce.

What?

'Debra,' the letter reads. I half expect him to refer to me as Ms. Macklin or even worse, Ms. Reid, my maiden name.

'Some time ago you made me aware of your infidelity. While I was angry and hurt, I believe that I could have eventually come around to realize that this was a problem between us and with our marriage and not just me and not just you. All I needed was some time to think.

You're obviously still seeing this man. You have continued to choose him over me, over our daughter, over our marriage. You have continued to show me where your priorities lie, so I'm forced to take this step.

I feel that we have one option, and that is to make our separation quiet and painless for Kendra. I need to know if you plan to move out or if you would like me to obtain other housing for Kendra and me.'

Kendra and–what? I sit up. "You are not taking my daughter anywhere," I mutter aloud.

'If you are leaving, I think it would be best for you to be gone by Thanksgiving. That way we don't have to pretend to be a family for either set of parents. Once you are settled we can discuss a parenting plan and divorce. I have no intention of leaving my daughter to be raised by a woman who stepped out on every promise she made to this family. I will not consider joint custody, however we can discuss visitation.'

Just who does this man think he is? He can tell me to get out of a house I designed and helped build with my own two hands? He can tell me that if I don't move out, he's going to take our daughter —my daughter, the only child I can ever have, and keep her from me because I made a mistake? Granted, a huge mistake. Then he can tell me I can't have joint custody of a child I bore and nursed and raised and have been so careful to have not damaged in any way?

I disregard the cold, cordial sign off and fold the letter, shoving it back into the envelope. My head pulses. I hear blood rushing in my ears and my heartbeat is erratic. I angle myself to get up out of the chair and give that man a piece of my mind when I hear a light tap-tap at the door.

CHAPTER FIFTEEN

$\mathcal{M}$axine

"I mean just the nerve, you know? The gall of that woman…me, of all people? She was lashing out and taking everyone with her, and I'm not going down like that."

"But if you know she was just lashing out, how can you still be mad?"

"Easy. You don't understand because she didn't link arms with you and call you a whore."

"She didn't call you a whore, Max. If you remember, it was the other way around. And if you really think about her, then—"

"Well, I don't. But she made me mad, acting like we have something in common."

Perched at my vanity table, running through my regimented morning routine: moisturize, pluck, conceal and reveal. Renee's voice sounds tinny through the speakers of my phone, but I need both hands to do this delicate work so I can leave on time. Virgil takes his job seriously and if I'm not there to begin the staff meeting at 8:30 am sharp, he's testy with me all morning. As if I wouldn't fire him and throw his stylish, snappily dressed behind out in the street.

I guess I wouldn't. Virgil knows that, which is why he's so damn bossy.

"I'll make up with Debra when I'm good and ready. I can't just let this blow over, you know."

"No, I don't know," says Renee. I hear shuffling in the background and what sounds like Bernard asking her something. Her voice is muffled as she answers him and after a moment, she comes back to the phone. "Sorry. We're running late this morning and he's mad about it. I'd better get some breakfast on before I head to the shop."

"Isn't that what Jessie is for?"

"She's not the maid. And I want him to know I'm doing things for him. I don't want him to wake up one day and think I've shoved him off onto someone else."

"I'm sure he knows, Renee." It sounds funny because my mouth is open while I apply mascara. I flick the wand from root to tip, expertly darkening each lash and separating the lashes with a miniature comb. I bat my eyes at myself in the mirror and smile, pleased.

"I don't know about that. But just in case, I want to do it while I can. I don't know how much longer I'll be doing it."

I pluck a tube of lipstick from my collection of designer shades and smooth a deep crimson onto my top and bottom lips, rub them together and blot them with a Kleenex. "Did you check into that retirement home? How did it look?"

"Yeah, I went up there." She fills me in on her tour of the facility. Sounds cushy, a nice place to spend your twilight years. Renee sounds skeptical. "It's an option. I don't think now is the time, if there's ever a time to put him in a home."

"If ever?" I stop fluffing my hair just out of heated rollers. The curls are gorgeous, big and bouncy, but I know as soon as I hit the humid Georgia air that they'll fall like a rock. "You can't take care of him forever. You know that, right? What if he falls or something?"

"He falls all the time. He's going to break something soon." I hear a crash in the background and a male voice cries out. "Daddy!" Renee yells, without bothering to pull the phone away from her mouth. "I'm making your eggs right now! Stop it!" More grumbling, more yelling, more noise. "I heard you! I'm doing it. Go watch the news or something. Getting on my nerves."

The doorbell chimes over the din. "That's Jessie. Thank God. This man has lost his mind, throwing around mama's pans." She blows an impatient puff of air into the phone. "Look, I've got to go before he sets something on fire. Call Debra, alright? She really needs us right now."

"I'll think about it."

"Maxine."

"Fine! I will call her. Later."

"Okay. Just make sure you get in touch with her soon. I don't want this… whatever… to go on too long. She needs us."

"You said that, Renee. I'll do it. I need to go—you're making me late."

I push myself back from the vanity table and pad into my favorite spot in my condo–a spacious walk-in closet, an entire room unto itself. It makes me happy to step inside and be enveloped by rows upon rows of fine fabrics and classic materials that stand the test of time and fashion. I designed the closet, from the glass topped shoe drawers to ample space to hang dresses, skirts, slacks, coats- whatever I feel like storing. I always hang my favorites in the section closest to the door. While I love to try new couture, luxury lines and styles and be a little daring, my daily wardrobe is more classic cuts and I wear some selections more than others.

I thumb through my choices until I find something that speaks to me, a beautiful Prada dress and pair it with black leather four inch heel slouch boots to match. I practically skip out of the closet and rush back to the bedroom to dress.

I toss off my thick terrycloth robe and drape it across the edge of the already made bed, step into the dress and the boots. They zip easily and fit just right, hugging my feet in decadent leather.

I check my reflection in the full-length mirror that hangs on the closet door, smoothing the dress over my hips and smile at my perfect size four frame. From the jewelry box, I select an understated diamond solitaire and clasp it around my neck; insert matching diamond studs in my ears and pick up a platinum Gucci watch. Last, I drip a few drops of Dolce & Gabbana, The One, around my neck. Satisfied, I pick up my purse from a table in the hall, toss the phone into the bag and walk out, locking the door behind me.

My Maserati sits safe and sound in her spot in the secure parking garage. A swipe of a finger unlocks the door and I climb in, press the ignition button and pull out of the garage.

I don't live far from the office, a detail that I didn't , but it worked out for me. I bought the condo at a steal from a client who was trying to unload it. Renovations took months, but when it was complete, it was everything I ever dreamt a home could be. The original construction was sound—high ceilings, thick noise-canceling walls between units. I had real hardwood floors installed in the entryway, living room and dining room and marble tile laid in the kitchen and bathrooms. I tore out walls and built new ones, had the entire place wired for surround sound and high definition, and generously coated the place in a brilliant white paint.

Debra says she feels uncomfortable in my place because it's so pristine—white walls, white leather furniture, stainless steel appliances and fixtures.

When I could get what I wanted, I went for it. It's just another thing she doesn't understand about me.

Despite what I said to Renee, I have been thinking about Debra. It's been weeks since I heard from her. In the past, she's always been quick to reach out and make up. She's good at offering the olive branch. I'm good at taking it. Granted, we both have apologies to make and I guess I'm waiting to see how long she's going to hold out, but I'm probably the last thing on her mind. It's unlike her to be so emotional, such a live wire, so reactionary. Debra is our even keel, cool and calculated. She's the calm to our storm. If Debra falls apart, Renee and I have no hope.

I flash my badge at the security gate, park in my reserved spot, and catch the elevator going up just as the doors are closing. I press the button for the top floor and squeeze in.

Donovan Luxury Realty leases space in one of Atlanta's most prestigious high rises. From my desk, my view is midtown, downtown and beyond, from the bustling metropolis to suburban eclectic to exclusive gated upper crust real estate.

My fellow passengers are three men in finely tailored Italian suits, anxiously checking watches or tapping touch screens, trying to appear as if they aren't taking sidelong glances in my direction. I'm used to it but that doesn't mean I don't notice it. I also notice wedding bands or, in the case of one man, the telltale indent where a ring usually sits. He's the one staring the hardest.

One by one, they step off of at their respective floors. At thirty-three, the doors soundlessly slide open. The elevator lobby, also Virgil's domain, is in its usual elegant state, with morning sun warming delicate white orchids and vacuum stripes in the deep pile carpet.

Appearance is everything. If you don't make a good first impression, you've already lost the client.

I throw open the double doors to the Donovan suite and step inside, ready to conquer the day.

The Monday sales meeting has become an episode of The Young and the Restless—or more appropriately the Rich and the Spoiled. My agents, seated around the oblong cherry wood table, offer updates on open, stale properties. These go on a list that I call the Trouble List, reviewed weekly. Virgil and I determine action items to move them to closing. Virgil begins with an update on the Newman listing.

"Last week, we met with Fletcher Callahan, Braxton Newman, and his attorney. Adora Newman signed a prenuptial agreement. She's surprised to find herself tossed out on her ass at only two years into a marriage that she expected to last much longer. So long as she refuses to sign the divorce papers, Braxton is legally obligated to take care of her.

"We agreed that Braxton would approach Adora with a cash offer, to include moving her to one of his other properties where she will live rent free for six months. This will give her funds to live on and get back on her feet..."

Virgil stops to drop a sardonic chuckle. Adora is an exotic dancer. With a name like Adora, I don't think she could do anything else.

"When was Braxton going to offer her the money? And how soon can he move her out? The place needs to be cleaned and staged."

"He was supposed to have met with her over the weekend. I'll call him as soon as we're out of this meeting and get an update." I nod; Virgil tips forward and bends his head over his notebook. He scratches a few lines, dots the last sentence with a flourish, and drops his pen. "Jonathon, tell us about the Stone Mountain property."

At 6'3", 350lbs, deep bronze skin and honey-brown eyes, Jonathon looks more like a pro linebacker than a seasoned real estate professional, but he's been with me the longest. He and I worked for Coldwell Realty before I flew the coop to start my firm. Jonathon showed up on my doorstep two weeks after I launched Donovan with a vision for serving Atlanta's elite population with delectable properties. He agreed to a trial run on nothing but a handshake and sold his first home for Donovan a week later. We've been in business ever since.

His property is a $1.6 million home within a gated community, perfect for an up-and-coming doctor, well-to- do attorney, or even a junior politician. The surrounding neighborhood lands it on the trouble list—for a mile on either side of the gates, the homes are rundown with peeling paint, boarded-up windows, unkempt yards with broken-down cars parked in full view and on prominent display.

"There was a break-in last week, which I discovered when I went to prep the place for a showing. Pretty much cleaned the place out of copper pipes and wires, took a few appliances. The property owners filed a police report. Thankfully, everything is covered under insurance. My problem is that they now want to sell 'as-is'. They don't want to buy new appliances."

"What about the pipes and the wiring?"

"The electrician and plumbers will be out this week to do an estimate of what it will cost to replace it. They're talking about pulling the house off the market."

"For how long? Until they replace everything?'

"Presumably. It's that or lower the price to under a million and let the new owners worry about a dishwasher."

My expression likely reveals my thoughts on this situation. I glance at Virgil, knowing he can read my mind. He clears his throat and leans forward, fiddling with his pen as he speaks.

"Donovan isn't selling a mini mansion as-is like a foreclosure. If they have to pull it off the market to get it fixed, fine. But stay on them. We need to close this sale."

"That's my plan. I've pulled it down from the listing service and as soon as I hear from the owners, I'll update you with an ETA when it will be available again."

"If there's no new business, let's wrap this up."

I close my notebook and twist my Mont Blanc pen closed. A flurry of activity and indistinct murmurs follow as my staff–four agents and Virgil push away from the conference room table and file out of the room. I linger for a few moments, lost in thought as I scan the Atlanta skyline through the floor to ceiling window. I have to get this Debra thing out of the way. I'm not good at groveling, which is why I always make her come to me first. It doesn't seem like she's going to come this time. May as well get it over with.

In my office, behind the closed door, I take a seat and dig out my mobile phone, scrolling to the M's in the address book. When I reach Debra Macklin, I hold my finger over the number. I used to think nothing of bothering her in the middle of the morning, especially a Monday. Before I can change my mind, I press the icon to call Debra's desk.

"Debra Macklin."

I toy with pretending to be angry, but lose all resolve once I hear her voice. She sounds so tired.

"Debra, it's Max."

She's quiet for a moment, then breathes a sigh of relief. Honestly, I feel relieved too. "Max. Hi. I'm so glad you called. Hang on a second." I hear her put the phone down, the muffled sound of a door closing, and she's back. "Okay. I needed a little privacy."

"A little privacy would have probably been a good idea when you were doing the PE teacher."

She chuckles, despite her morose tone. "I'm gonna let you have that one, because I owe you an apology."

Surprised, my eyebrows lift. "Do you now?"

"I know you've been waiting for me to come around. I just..." She forces out a heavy breath. I feel its weight across the line. "I don't know what I'm doing, you know? I didn't mean for what I said to hurt you and I'm so sorry I said it. I'm sorry for what it meant to you to hear that. I didn't mean that you and I were alike, not in that way. Just..."

"Just?" I prod.

"I've never had man problems before," she admits quietly. Little does she know how jealous this makes me. "You have men eating out of the palm of your hand. Haven't you been caught between the affections of two men? Haven't you been bored with one and sought excitement with another? My affair, my marriage... they're a big, huge deal, but on a very basic level, I guess I thought you might have some advice for me."

"That would make sense, if you would have–" I pause, remembering Renee's words. This isn't about me. "First, I'm sorry for calling you a whore. I don't think that about you, and I never did. It was just the worst thing I could think of to call you and it fell out of my mouth and it never should have. Okay?"

"Okay." I hear the small smile in her voice. Debra is so easy to please. "Secondly... honey, have you talked to Willard"

She sighs. "Yeah. Some."

"Yeah? And?"

"And... well... it looks like I might be moving out."

I grip the phone so it doesn't slide through my fingers. Debra and Willard have the most stable relationship I've ever seen. Or so I thought.

"You're kidding."

"No. That day that I left brunch, I uh... ended up in bed with David." She ends the sentence in a whisper and I feel my eyes roll. I can't help it.

"Really, Debra."

"I know. I know. I fell asleep and woke up late. I'd missed calls from Renee and Kendra. Kendra had called Willard looking for me. I knew he'd be able to guess where I was. He didn't say anything to me all week, but last night he came home early and he was typing something up in his office. Later on he dropped it on me, laid it out."

"Dropped what? Laid what out?"

"A letter. He said he'd been giving me some time to sort things out, but that I'd made it clear where my priorities are. He said either I go before the holidays so we don't have to pretend for family, or he goes and he takes Kendra." A sob caught in her throat. "Can he do that? Can he take my baby? I don't even know what to say. I'm so ashamed of myself."

"Damn, girl. I think you need to stop feeling sorry for yourself and call a lawyer."

"I guess maybe I do. I was hoping..."

"You're not really going to leave, are you? Like, move out of your own house?"

"He expects me to. Or he leaves with Kendra and I don't want her uprooted like that. "

"I know it doesn't help, but if you need anything–a place to stay, or someone to be there while you cry into a glass of wine, you know my number."

"Thanks," she says, through sniffles. A long, protracted bell sounds in the background. "Oh, that's me. Gotta go. I feel like I haven't done any work today and I have so much of it to do."

"You stay away from that PE teacher, you hear me? He's nothing but trouble."

She chuckles, a sad little patter of laughter. "I think it's a little late for that. The Superintendent knows."

I gasp. "How did she find out?"

"Somebody's big mouth. There's so much going on. I also had to talk to Kendra..."

My jaw drops. "Girl! You've been keeping all of this to yourself?"

"I know. It's bad."

"Well, one of my clients is having a big party in a couple of weeks and I told Renee that we three were going. You should come shopping with us this weekend. You need your girls right now."

"Oh, Max." She sighs, sounding dejected. "I don't think I'm up for a party."

"It's a cocktail party. You stand around with a drink in your hand and eat and gossip. You can do that for two hours. Think about it?"

She sighs, mumbles something about having to get to work, and hangs up without saying goodbye.

CHAPTER SIXTEEN

enee

Daddy has what Jessie and I call a rough temperament. I've never known him to be a happy go lucky person. I don't know what a 'good mood' looks like for him. I never have. Mama learned to ignore his grumblings. "He doesn't mean it," she would say, smoothing a hand down my back to comfort me after he'd uttered something particularly hurtful. "He's doing his best." I disagreed.

He's been an unbearable, irrational person to be around for the last week. Even Jessie remarked on it, to which he advised her where she could shove her opinion of his behavior. It's a good thing she's not easily offended, or we'd have lost the last nurse in Atlanta that would care for him. Today, he's worked himself into such a fury that he had to lie down for a few hours.

Last week, I was flipping through an old calendar that my mother kept in her office. In January of each year she'd sit down with an old calendar and a new one, transferring birthdays, anniversaries and other dates of note. I'd forgotten my Aunt's birthday and though it was seven years old, I knew I could find it on this calendar, the last one my mother updated. I recognized certain events like retirement parties and guest speakers at the bookstore. Mama loved to host city officials, really anyone important that need a space to give a speech. I smiled at her classy, slanted handwriting and flipped a few pages forward, finding all the dates that Mother thought important enough to remember. She even noted Maxine and Debra's birthdays. Daddy's birthday. My birthday. And hers. October ninth.

At some point, an 'X" had been drawn through November seventeenth. I'd guess it was daddy, since he ran the bookstore after she was gone. He could never bring himself to throw away anything that belonged to her, so he would have kept this calendar. I glanced up at the current calendar on the wall.

November ninth.

Jessie wanders through the house, picking up things Daddy had thrown or knocked over mid-fit. Embarrassed, I join her in setting the house straight again.

"It's the disease, baby," Jessie finally says, breaking a long, thick silence. "It's not him."

"I know," I mumble, on the verge of tears.

"It's frustratin' for him too."

"I guess. But he gets to forget it."

She laughs, picking up two throw pillows and arranging them on the couch just so.

"It's not just the illness." I sit on the couch where she'd placed the pillows. I gesture that she should sit, too. She eases her large frame onto the cushion next to me.

"I know. It's your mama, too. He always gets bad around the middle of November. She died about… when?"

"The seventeenth."

Jessie hums and nods, clasping her hands together. "Yeah. That'll be it. He's missin' your mama."

"Also, when… when she was sick, he refused to believe there was nothing more that could be done. He felt like she gave up. He thought she should have kept fighting. Joined another med trial. Took another round of chemo. Something more."

"Mmm hm. But sometimes, there's nothing you can do but enjoy the time you have left."

"By the time he finally got that, she was in decline. He wasn't ready." I shake my head. "He still isn't. And I think he's angry with himself for wasting so much time that he could have spent with her."

"Sometimes when he's having a real good day, he gets to talking." She nods, as if reassuring herself. "He talks about your mama. He loved Lorraine more than anything."

I turn toward her and draw my feet up onto the couch. "What else does he say?"

"He talks about you and about how he would do things different. He knows he wasn't the best daddy, but he did what he could. He always thought your mama would be around, you know, to be a buffer between y'all. He says he don't think you know him, and he for sure don't know you. All he knows is that you look like Lorraine. You remind him of her."

"So that's why he's so crabby when I'm around."

"No, no baby. You make him feel like Lorraine is here with him. He's crabby because he's a grumpy old man." This makes me laugh longer and harder than I've laughed in a long time. "What you got planned to mark your mama's passin'?"

"We rarely do anything for it." It's not like it's an anniversary we like to celebrate.

"I think it would help for y'all to do something that would remind him of Lorraine. You ever take him to visit her?"

I shudder. I haven't been to the cemetery in years, not since the headstone came in and I went out there to make sure everything looked fine. Daddy hasn't been there since the day we buried her. "No. I can't bring myself to go there."

Jessie pats me on the shoulder before she wrestles herself up from the couch. "It's not about you, baby girl. That man up there?"

She points upward through the ceiling to Daddy's room where he lay slumbering. "He's hurtin'. It's not about you."

~

The eighth anniversary of my mother's death arrives in an explosion of sun. It's the warmest I can remember it being in November. The hardiest of birds are in the bare trees that surround our house, chirping away as Daddy and I step out of the side door into the driveway. I'd pulled my car out of the garage and left it idling, then gone inside to get him.

He's dressed in a button down white shirt, black slacks, socks and shoes I helped him shine earlier. We even shaved the grey, matted beard that he would never let me or Jessie touch. Mama liked him clean shaven.

Daddy stops at the passenger side door and steps back. "You 'spect me to ride in this piece of foreign junk?"

I laugh and shake my head and reach for the door, swinging it open. He's mumbling something about Toyota, but lowers himself into the car. I pull the safety belt across him tightly and snap the buckle. "You think I don't know how to put on a seat belt? I used to build cars, you know."

I smirk. He's feisty today. At least he's playful and not mean. I drop a kiss on his forehead and I can tell this gesture surprises him. "I just have to make sure we get you there safely, Daddy." I shut the door gently and walk around to the driver's side and slip in beside him.

We say nothing, reveling in quiet moments on the drive. He watches the scenery pass by; I'm tamping down my anxiety at seeing my mother's name etched into stone, the dates of her life and death memorialized until the end of time.

I turn into Resthaven Memorial Gardens and drive through two stately, white stone columns. I follow the path that I haven't traveled in years but still somehow know by heart, passing rows upon rows of white crosses and grey headstones. So many people gone. So many lives to be remembered.

I slow, then pull over so as not to block the path for anyone else and put the car in park. Before I cut the ignition, I look over at Daddy. His mouth is slack, not a taut line across his face. There are no wrinkles of worry or agitation across his forehead. There are no darts of anger between his brows. He's at peace.

That brings me peace.

"Let's go see your mama." He unbuckles his seatbelt and opens his door, meeting me on my side of the car. Together we walk the natural path between the plots. Ten rows up. Six plots over.

"There she is," he says, stopping in front of the headstone we had designed together, the placement of which I'd supervised. Except for the stems of long-dead roses in the built in metal vases on each side of the headstone, the area looks good. Free of weeds, not overgrown in the least. In fact, it looks as if the lawn has been freshly mowed. The grass is damp either from morning dew or a fresh watering.

I toss away the stems and brush away bits of grass and dirt that had gathered in crevices. Daddy stares at the headstone, more so at the photo of her that we'd had encased behind a pane of glass. She wore a bright, indigo blue short-sleeved sundress. Her hair was lovely as always, a bob that fell just above her shoulders that layered in graying waves. It was one of those over-the shoulder poses we'd captured at a family picnic. We called it her glamour shot, and she loved that photo. It was the last one we took before we learned of her cancer, its advanced stage and her prognosis. She seemed to age almost immediately after that.

The photo captures her spirit and holds it in limbo forever. She wanted to be remembered this way.

Above the photo is her name, Lorraine Jeanette Simms Gladwell. I'd paid a small fortune to have an engraver etch her name, mimicking her signature. Her dates of birth and death are below the photo, and seeing today's date eight years ago doesn't stab me in the heart like I thought it would.

"She was a good woman," Daddy says. "I sure miss her. You're a lot like her, my Lorraine."

I squint into the sunlight but smile at Daddy. "Really? You think so?"

"Mmmm," is his response. He taps the top of the headstone with a note of finality and turns away, walking back to the car. I guess we're done here.

"Come on. You said we was going to lunch. I ain't been there in a long time."

As I help Daddy over the threshold and through the front door at Ruby's, a short stump of a woman lumbers down the hallway behind the cash register that leads to the back offices.

Ruby won't give up ownership, but she hasn't done the day-to-day management of the restaurant in many years. This falls to her Richard, her son and General Manager. He follows closely behind her, bewilderment all over his face.

"I'm not gonna tell you again, Richard!"

"Mama, I'm working on it. You didn't like the last three quotes I got for the work."

She stops short and turns to him, balls a pudgy fist on a generous hip and arches her neck back so she can look her son, who stands at well over six feet, in the eye. "Then get more quotes. The place looks like shit. Y'all fry in too much lard if it's splattering the walls like that. The place needs a good cleaning up and I don't care what excuse you give me that you can't get it done."

"I can get it done, Mama. But you realize it means we have to close up shop for that?"

"Well, whatever it takes," she bellows, turning just in time to see me and Daddy walk past her. "That ain't Bernard Gladwell, is it?"

Upon hearing his name, Daddy stops and looks around. "I hear a little loudmouth in here. Where is she?"

She marches into the lobby where others are waiting to be seated for lunch and walks right up to Daddy, her head angled up toward him. "Down here, you fool! How you been?"

Daddy smiles—his first smile in a long time. "Some days bad. Some days good. I'm doing alright today. Ain't I, Noodle?" He turns to me for confirmation that he's been on his best behavior.

I smile at Ruby as she glances toward me with a scowl. "He's been good today, Miss Ruby. Don't be too hard on him."

"Well, alright. Long as he's not giving you any problems. I know how he can be." Daddy chuckles and I laugh along. "Where you was, all gussied up on a Thursday mornin'?"

"Been to visit my dear Lorraine."

Ruby's face instantly falls from a wicked grin to a sympathetic smile. "Oh, Bernard. That's right. It's been—"

"Eight years," he finishes. I'm surprised he remembers this.

Ruby is solemn in her nodding. "Yes. Eight years. I loved her so, that Lorraine. She brought little Renee in here all the time. One of my favorite customers." She clicks her tongue and sighs, shaking her head slowly.

"She was my favorite everything," Daddy says, his smile wistful but tinged with sadness. A moment later, he brightens. "My daughter promised me lunch, so why don't you get in the kitchen and fix us up somethin'?"

Ruby laughs, her melancholy crashing into giggles. "I ought to smack you, Bernard, but I know Lorraine is watching from above. I'd be happy to make y'all something. How about my special?"

We both nod, grinning. Ruby's special is two pieces of hot fried chicken, gooey macaroni and cheese, collard greens (made with pork, but you could get them with turkey if you like) and fluffy sweet cornbread muffins. Ruby's special also comes with a wide slice of her sweet potato pie. She still bakes the pies for the restaurant, and they are always delicious.

I feel bad about it, but we're seated right away. Ruby won't hear of us waiting in line, shoehorning us into a table near the window.

"Now you just give me a little bit. I got to fry the chicken special."

"Take your time, Miss Ruby." I watch her diminutive figure speed away. At eighty-five, she moves like a woman twenty years her junior. It doesn't seem as if Ruby will go quietly into retirement. Much to Richard's chagrin, she'll probably hang on for another twenty years, just to spite him.

"Her family is from Memphis. Same as your mama. That's how your mama knew her."

"Oh?" A busboy sets glasses of water and silverware for our table. I wait for him to leave again before I press Daddy for details. He unwraps a straw and dunks it into his glass.

"I met your mama in Memphis. I played short stop for the Atlanta Wildcats in a regional baseball league. All negroes."

"Not the Negro Baseball League?"

"Naw, girl." He waves a pale, bony hand at me. "The Negro Baseball League disbanded when I was nine years old. The south was slow to integrate sports, so we put together our own teams. We would travel and play different teams around the area — Alabama, Tennessee, Florida, Carolinas."

He sips water and a small smile crosses his lips. "Lorraine was sitting with a bunch of girls on the Memphis Tigers' side. Prettiest one in the bunch. Wearing a blue dress, like the one in the picture."

I leaned in, intrigued. Like Jessie said, he needed to get the memories out so someone else could remember them, too.

"After the game, everybody got together at this juke joint over on Beale Street. She was watching me from across the room, so I got up the nerve to speak. She was sitting next to Ruby's daughter, Yolanda. They were friends their whole lives."

I remembered Yolanda—I called her Aunt Yoli–and her mother and father staying with us when they'd finally moved from Memphis to Atlanta. Ruby and George bought a neighborhood café on the brink of closure and before long, a star was born.

"Anyway, we talked for a while. She flirted with me. I played it cool." Daddy stops to wink in my direction before continuing his story. "I knew that day that I would marry her. Didn't matter that she lived in Memphis. I would drive up there when I got the chance. We wrote letters, talked on the phone. Got to know each other real slow, like it's meant to go."

I marvel at how dating has changed since my mom and dad met. These days, you meet somebody and they practically want to be in bed before they know your full name. Short, misspelled emails or Facebook messages or texts that used letters for numbers have replaced letter writing. Phone calls? Maybe a rushed voice-mail on his way to one thing or from another. My parents were from the time of real courting.

"After a year, I was tired of all that driving to see her. I already knew what was gon' happen, so I talked her mama and daddy into letting her move to Atlanta, promised I'd take care of her. Only way they'd let her do it is if she stayed with my folks."

"Mama lived with Grandma and Grandpa when she first moved here?"

"Sure did. For six months before we married. By then I was working at Ford. It was hard work, but good money. Lorraine was going to school for teachin'. Didn't take long at all to get us set up in a nice little place. We were real cozy for a while. Then you come along. Life been crazy ever since."

I giggle, seeing the glint in his eye. I'm really enjoying this time with my dad.

"Why did Mama stop teaching? I never understood that."

"She said she fell out of love with teachin'. Negro schools got the books the white schools threw away. Old and outdated. Written in. Like the kids knew the books would go to Hoover— that's the school in the black neighborhood where Lorraine taught —so they'd write messages in the pages. 'Die, nigger', stuff like that. Got so she'd go through every book erasing stuff that was scribbled in 'em. Got too hard for her to handle. She'd cry herself to sleep every night.

"I asked her why she kept going back. She says she don't know. What else is there to do? I said she could do whatever she wanted to. 'What do you want to do?' I ask her. She rolls over, and she says, 'you know how Yoli's mama opened Ruby's? I want to do something like that. Except I want to open a bookstore'. She asked me what I thought. And I told her, like I said, you can do whatever you want to do."

He shrugged, then relaxed against the seat. "She was real happy with Gladwell. She felt like it made a positive mark in the community."

"It did. And it still does."

He pauses before his gaze meets mine. "Gladwell still doing alright?"

"Gladwell is fine, Daddy." He seems pleased.

Ruby delivers our lunch herself, balancing two full dinner plates and two small dessert plates on her arms while maneuvering through the packed restaurant. "Here ya'll go now. Take your time, eat up, and don't leave a lick of nothin' on these plates. I want 'em clean, you hear?"

She turns to me especially, with a hand on her hip. "I know how you young ladies are about calories. Ain't no calories in this food today. You follow?"

I laugh and pick up my fork, ready to dig in. Maxine would just have to pick on me about gaining weight, because I planned to follow Ruby's instruction to the letter.

CHAPTER SEVENTEEN

ebra

The room is teeming with people in tuxes, dark suits, floor length gowns and smart little party dresses, each coddling a glass of wine or champagne or a plastic cup of juice. Elevator music wafts through the air above us, just loud enough to dim the sounds of boring conversation. Maxine claims this house isn't a mansion, but I swear it spans a city block. If your bathroom is the size of my bedroom, I call that a mansion.

A few people try to talk to me, but I literally only know Maxine and Renee at this party. Throw me in a room full of teachers and administrators, and I'm the belle of the ball. I've attended Willard's CPA firm Christmas Gala each year, and we're the life of the party. Tonight, I can't focus on anything anyone is saying. I'm selfishly, obsessively thinking about my situation.

I moved out last weekend. I didn't take a lot of things, just a few bags since didn't plan on being gone for long. I needed a few days, a little space between Willard and me. Then, I thought, he'd come to his senses and tell me to come home. It's been ten days.

Ten days of sleeping in Maxine's guest room, which might be worse than living with an angry Willard, because had it not been for me staying with Maxine, I would not have been dragged to this party tonight.

At least I look nice. I've lost a lot of weight in the last month, so Max and I are the same size. I borrowed a dress from her closet, a metallic lace mesh dress that she had never even worn. I glanced at the tag before I snipped it off—$450 from Neiman Marcus. It had to have been one of those items she bought on a whim and decided wasn't really her style and never took it back. She'd never let me wear one of her "regulars". The mid-thigh length hugs my body but doesn't make me feel like I'm naked. I like it, and I'm not one for designer fashion.

I thought Maxine's eyebrows would lift clear off of her face when I stepped out of her closet with it on. She swiveled around, wand in one hand, tube of mascara in the other.

"What do you think? Is it too short?"

It moved her enough to recap the mascara and stand up. "It's perfect. See now, this is why that young pup was running after you." She circled me, smoothing the fabric over my hips, and tapped my behind. I snickered, but appreciated the compliment.

"What I don't understand is what crawled up your husband's ass. The nerve of asking you to move out of your own house."

I stepped to the full-length mirror and turned to one side, then the other. Despite my mood, I smiled. "I told you, it's just a phase. He's mad. He's trying to punish me. I bet I'll be home again by the end of the week."

She frowned and let out a light humph. "You realize today is day ten and you've been saying that since day three?" She bypassed me and walked into the closet. "Let's find you some shoes to go with that dress. And I'll do your makeup."

She came out of the room sized closet holding a pair of tan, four inch high pumps. "And is there anything you can do about your hair on such short notice? I should have predicted this mess and made you an appointment."

She tried to hand me the shoes, but I frowned at them, running my fingers through my puffy twists. She was right. My hair needed attention. "I can't even walk around the living room in those. Don't you have any sensible shoes?"

She groaned, rolling her eyes, and stalked back into the closet. "What are sensible shoes? Those Nine West you wear? They make your feet look like boats. I don't get how you and Renee are so plain." She poked her head out of the closet so she could emphasize the word plain and ducked back inside. She re-emerged with a pair of nude peep-toe pumps that were an inch lower. She handed them to me with one hand while pushing me out of her bedroom with the other.

"Best I can do, I like my heels high. Don't whine. Don't put them on, yet. You don't want your feet to swell. Try to do something to your hair. Renee will be here in a few minutes."

The last sentence was yelled through the closing door. I eyed the shoes with a wary look, knowing my feet were going to be cold and my toes cramped. Giving up, I shuffled down the hall to my temporary home.

Renee showed up a few minutes later, toting a garment bag from one of Max's favorite designer boutiques. When she unzipped the bag to reveal her dress, I had to do a double take. I wasn't sure how it would look on her body, but Renee filled out the off-the- shoulder floor length sequined gown like it was made for her. The shade was slightly lighter than pewter and offset her caramel skin beautifully. Renee glowed, excited to have a nice dress to wear, with shoes and a clutch to match. If Donovan ever tanks, Maxine would make a killing shopping for other people.

Max turned on the TV and the surround sound speakers and tuned into VH-1 Soul. We swayed to the music of our childhood-Shai, Jodeci, KC & JoJo, all the slow jam hits. We talked and laughed while waiting for one of the others to get dressed or have her makeup done. Renee's fingers worked her magic with my hair and Maxine crafted perfect faces for us, doing what she knew how to do best—make a great impression.

We hadn't done this in so long; get ready for a party together. Hanging out with my best friends, listening to music, laughing and playfully critiquing each other took me back to Decatur High, the three of us crowded in Max's bedroom with the bright bulb of a shadeless lamp burning spots into my vision while Max bent over me and swiped all kinds of crazy stuff all over my face. Renee would be in Max's closet, trying things on, asking to keep things, stomping around in her heels. It was the best of times.

Having all of us together seemed to ease my pain, if only for a little while. But standing at this party in a room full of strangers, I'm not feeling the sister-like camaraderie.

I spot Maxine and Renee, coming at me from different ends of the room. Maxine, wearing a strapless black sequined Chanel gown, is dragging a tall, dark and handsome man by the hand. The grin plastered across her face tells me that this is the Malcolm that she can't stop talking about. Renee sidles up next to me, holding a plate of assorted hors d'oeuvres and a glass of punch.

"Ladies," Maxine gushes. "I'd like you to meet one of my VIP clients, Malcolm Brooks. Malcolm, these are my dearest friends, Debra and Renee."

I nod at Malcolm and mumble something about it being nice to meet him. Renee does the same, after she swallows the bite of tea cake she's just shoved into her mouth.

"It's a pleasure to meet you ladies," he says, in a baritone so deep, the floor seems to vibrate. He is broad shouldered, smooth, his even toned skin the hue of a walnut. His hands are mammoth sized, a detail I notice when my hand becomes lost in his for a moment. He's also wearing a tuxedo, one that seems cut specifically for him. It fit him like a glove. An expensive glove. I see why Max is head over heels.

"Maxine is a force in real estate. I've enjoyed my experience with Donovan."

"He's been my easiest sale all year. We found a place and closed in four weeks!" Maxine is practically hanging off of Malcolm, standing close to him, her arm twisted around his.

"Oh, that's right. You're in Decatur, aren't you? How do you like your new neighborhood?" Renee asks.

"Nice, just what I wanted. It's walkable and quaint. Nothing like DC or Maryland, though those areas have their benefits."

She nods like she's ever been to DC or Maryland, agreeing in pleasant tones. "My bookstore is just a few blocks from you. Gladwell Books. You should stop in sometime."

Somehow, Malcolm unravels himself from Maxine and moves a few steps forward to stand next to Renee. The room is loud, and it's hard to hear, but I didn't think it was necessary to stand so closely. I glance at Max, who looks like she's suddenly lost something.

"Maxine mentioned that. I had planned to come in to meet you. I'm an avid reader, in my spare time."

"I could special order something for you, sort of as a welcome to the neighborhood."

Malcolm grins widely, showing off sparkling white teeth. "Let's refill our punch glasses and discuss. I have a few choices in mind." He and Renee wander off to the food and drinks table in the next room, chattering away at each other about books and authors and other nerdy things.

Maxine's expression is sour. She stomps a well-heeled foot, one hand on her hip. "What the hell just happened? That's not how that was supposed to go."

"How long are we going to hang out? These shoes are killing my feet and I don't feel much like partying."

"Let's find some seats. I want to stay just a little while longer, in case I can get a hold of Malcolm again."

She leads me outside, through the patio that has been transformed into a tented, heated reception area to the stone pit that is spitting sparks into the night sky. We take two seats on the couch nearest the heat and kick off our shoes. I sigh, sinking into the fabric, wiggling my numb toes.

"Have you even spoken to Kendra lately?"

"I see her every day at school, so that's nice. Willard gives me one night a week and one weekend day to spend with her." I roll my eyes at this. I helped create that child and I'm relegated to four hours on a weeknight. She spends two of those hours doing homework. "I would have been with her today, but there was a sleepover, so she went there instead. I'll see her tomorrow."

"So she knows..." I nod, once. "You never said how that went."

The last thing I want to do right now is to go through my mistakes over the last year. Again. But not talking about it hasn't made it go away. "She'd told me she needed to talk to me. Kendra is so sensitive to my emotions. She's such a good kid, you know? She came right to me and wanted to make sure I knew what was going around.

"She started talking about all these things she was hearing about me and a teacher." I swig a sip of wine. "I had to break it down to her, tell her what was absolutely not true—"

"Like what?"

"Like we were not having sex in my office. And I was not pregnant with his baby." I huff a frustrated breath and roll my eyes hard. Max giggles. "I had to tell her what was true. I did mess around with that teacher and I might be in a lot of trouble and daddy is very angry. And..."

I heave a long, loud breath that feels like my lungs are emptying. "I tried to explain to her what might happen between me and her dad."

"And how did she take all of that?"

"She said it broke her heart. She wanted to know how I could do that to..." I click my tongue against the roof of my mouth and roll my eyes upward to stop the swell that comes, anyway. My eyes fill up, then overflow. "How I could do that to her dad," I finish, warbling through a sob. "How do I even have tears left? I'm so tired of crying."

Maxine scoots close to me and draws me to her. She is warm and soft and I can't help it...I fall apart on her shoulder. She strokes my head with one hand, holding me tightly with the other, and whispers to me about how everything's going to be alright.

I feel someone slide onto the cushion next to me and more arms around me. The flowery scent of Renee's perfume is calming. I'm reduced to sniffles and hiccups and sit up, swiping my cheeks with the back of my hand.

"Stop that," Max chides, flipping open her clutch and handing me a handkerchief. "You'll smear makeup all over your face. Dab, dab, dab." I take the dainty white cloth and follow her instructions, dabbing my face until it's dry.

"Kendra?" Renee asks. I nod. I'd already broken down with her on the phone earlier that week. It's my tender spot. I can't stand that I've disappointed her. "Everything is going to work out. I just know it is."

I shake my head, feeling for the first time that they might both be wrong. "I just don't see how, right now."

Sitting back, I tip my head back so I can stare at the night sky. Maybe I'll wish on a star. It has just as much of a chance of working as anything else. Max and Renee snuggle close and join me in my slouched position, staring upward.

"Deb, can I ask you something?" Renee asks.

"Yeah."

"Was the gym teacher... good?"

I don't think she meant for the question to be funny, but I can't help the giggle that bubbles up. Maxine snorts, which makes my laughter bust forth like water through a crack in a dam.

"What?" Renee asks, laughing along, which makes me laugh even harder. My stomach hurts and I can't breathe and we're practically rolling around on a couch in front of the fire pit. We're a sight, I'm sure, but I don't care. I instantly feel better.

"Oh, Renee." I tousle her hair, fighting back residual giggles. She smacks my hand away, like she always does. "He was alright. Different."

"Younger, for one," offers Max.

"And, you know, more sexually experienced," adds Renee.

"And uh... probably..." Max hints, an evil grin on her lips. "Had more to offer?"

"Oh, boy. Here we go."

I sit up and grab the empty wineglass, then stand and straighten my dress, which had bunched up from our bout of laughter. I hesitate, looking down at my girls who are waiting with bated breath for me to offer some minute detail. I lean in, so I can lower my voice. "I still don't know nothin' 'bout no little dick complex. Now, if you'll excuse me, I'm parched."

I escape our little circle before more questions are hurled at me, a chorus of 'oooooooh's following me into the house.

CHAPTER EIGHTEEN

M axine

I love Sunday mornings, no matter the season. It's the one day a week I reserve for myself. On warm mornings, I like to sit on the patio, the downtown Atlanta skyline over my shoulder and city sounds twelve stories below. Once the temperature cools, I sit at the island in my kitchen and enjoy the morning sun with my coffee and breakfast and newspapers.

It's still early and I don't want to wake Debra, so I tiptoe around my condo, humming lightly while putting things away from last night's festivities. Two empty wine bottles clank together as I toss them into the recycling bin. I close the open box of crackers and throw away the dry, hardened slices of cheese.

It was so nice to have the girls here yesterday. We hung out like old times, reminiscing about when life was as simple as worrying if James Thomas liked me enough to dump Kyra Parker, who thought she was better than me because her father was a doctor.

The plates, silverware and glasses are loaded into the dishwasher. I wipe down the counter and open a cabinet to pull down two ceramic mugs and a plastic pouch of private label coffee beans. I dump a few handfuls into the grinder and wince as I push the button. The grinder is loud, and normally Debra is up and around when I do this.

I tamper and tap, then install the porta filter into its slot on the Rancilio brewing system. I slide the two mugs under the dual spouts and press the button to brew. The air fills with the aroma of a specialized hazelnut blend. I would normally steam milk for a latte, but I'm feeling lazy, so I grab a bottle of flavored from the refrigerator and set it on the island, along with a bowl for sugar.

A door slowly creaks open and a quiet yawn comes from down the hall. I crane my neck around enough to see Debra in what used to be a fluffy robe, but is now threadbare and thinning in spots, and I imagine at some point, was pink. A few of her twists peek out from under a satin scarf tied haphazardly around her head.

She pulls the robe closed over a long t-shirt and ties it shut before shuffling toward the kitchen. "Morning. Sorry if I woke you with the grinder."

Debra shakes her head, stifling another yawn as she slides into a chair on the other side of the island. I set a cup of coffee in front of her and point to the cream and sugar.

"I was awake," she croaks. "I didn't sleep well last night. All that wine upset my stomach."

"I'm sorry to hear that." I spoon cream and sugar into my coffee and stir until the color is perfect. "What you need is some grease. You want to drop in some place for breakfast?"

"I'm having lunch with Kendra today," she answers, propping her elbow on the counter, and drops her head into one palm.

"Oh, well, that'll be nice."

I set my coffee cup in the space next to her and go the door to pick up the three papers that are delivered on the weekend- The Atlanta Journal Constitution, the New York Times and USA Today. The three publications are lying in wait, neatly stacked. I grab them up and duck back inside, perusing the front page of each. I offer Debra the USA Today, since I usually read it last. She declines and takes another sip of coffee.

"Didn't your mother ever tell you that if you did something funny with your face, it would stay like that?" I take the seat next to her and flip open the front page of the Times. I have a digital subscription to all three newspapers, but something about Sunday morning demands that I get ink smudges on my fingertips. "That's what's going to happen to the lines across your forehead."

"I'm not concerned about the lines across my forehead."

I click my tongue while lifting my mug of coffee to my lips and scanning the day's headlines. "You should be. Did you have any fun last night?"

"Yeah," she says. "It was a nice time, breakdown notwithstanding." I know she's thinking about those few minutes when she actually let herself be human and show some emotion. That's the most I've ever seen Debra cry. "How about you? Did you hook up with Malcolm again?"

After Debra left to refill her wineglass, Renee and I re-entered the party. I spent the next hour making the rounds, introducing myself to Brent's clients and friends. I made a few connections, handed out a few cards, met a few very nice—and nice looking gentlemen, but I only had eyes for Malcolm.

"I think he left early. I looked everywhere for him." I pout, but only briefly. I have his phone number, his email address, I know where he lives and where he works. He won't get away.

"I saw you talking to someone for quite a while," says Debra, leaning back in her chair, crossing one leg over the other. "About six-two, nice cut, black suit, red tie. Looked a little like Morris Chestnut?"

My eyebrows lift at the memory of the man Debra describes. "Oh yes. John? Joe? Joseph. Yes, Joseph. He was nice."

"He seemed a little more than nice. He sure was smiling in your face." Debra sips, her eyes smiling over the mug. I smirk, because of course he was smiling in my face. Most men do.

"He's an Investment Banker. I guess he does well, but he talks like his money is new."

"So? Your money is new."

I scoff. "You know what I mean. He's easily impressed. Anyway, yes, we talked for a long time. He's a nice man, good looking, a gentleman but…"

"But he's not high enough on the food chain for you?"

I set my mug down and turn the page. "I already know where this is going."

"Oh really? Where is this going?"

"This is the part where Debra gets down on Maxine for wanting someone of a certain stature in life, someone established, who makes his own money—"

"For wanting someone rich so y'all can be elite together." She gives a humph and sips, then slides the USA Today out from the stack of newspapers. She flips to the Lifestyle section and scans the first page.

"Well, whatever. No one tells men that they should want less. They all want a Beyonce body with a Halle Berry haircut and a Kerry Washington attitude. Nobody tells them they're unreasonable. Excuse me for knowing what I want."

"I'm not saying you're unreasonable. I'm saying you should expand your horizons. You know, live a little. Slum it in the hundred thousand a year range."

I hear the near laughter in Debra's voice. This is her and Renee's favorite pastime. It's not my fault I have always drawn wealthy men.

"Says she who recently bedded a man ten years her junior."

"We have already determined that you and I are nothing alike."

"Got that right."

"You are so judgmental, Maxine. Why not give Mister Regular Joe a chance? You seemed to enjoy the conversation, and he looked interested."

Again, this is not a surprise. That a man is interested is not one a tenet upon which I base my interest. I have standards and while

Joseph is a handsome, charming man, blessed with a stocky physique and attractive features, he's not quite what I'm looking for.

"Maybe he'd be interested in Renee."

Debra snickers. "He'll have some competition."

"What do you mean? Who's after Renee? What have I missed?"

"You didn't miss the flirt fest when you introduced Renee and Malcolm. They practically skipped off into the sunset."

I snatch the pages from Debra's fingers, grab the other papers and shove them all under my arm, pick up my coffee cup and dismount from the bar height chairs at the island.

"Look, I know your life is miserable, but that doesn't mean you can just say mean shit to me. You know good and well that I have a thing going with Malcolm. How dare you insinuate–"

"Maybe Malcolm doesn't have a thing going with you."

I refuse to dignify her comments with a response. Instead, I stomp to my bedroom, my slippers slapping against my heels. I slam the door shut and toss the papers onto the jumbled sheets and duvet and join them as I sprawl across the bed.

"I have had about enough of her," I mumble, just loud enough to be said aloud. Reaching for my cell phone on the bedstand, I unlock it and scroll to Malcolm's number. It's early yet, but knowing him, he's awake. The line rings twice before it picks up.

"Hello, Maxine." That man's voice is so smooth, like silk; so deep vibrations roll through me when he speaks. I feel all shaken up after a conversation with him.

I smile and put on my brightest voice. "Hi, Malcolm. I apologize for calling so early, but I figured you would be awake."

"You know me well. I'm up with the sun. I've already had my workout and now I'm enjoying some breakfast and coffee at my new dining room table."

I know that's a special message for me. I helped him pick it out. Actually, I purchased it and had it delivered as a gift from Donovan. Take that, free book offer from Renee. He said it was perfect. Well, he agreed when I said it.

"Oh, you're already eating. I was going to see if you were free for breakfast this morning." I make sure my pout comes through loud and clear.

"I'm just about finished, actually. But thank you for thinking of me." I wait for an offer to dine together another time, but it doesn't come. "Was... there anything else I could do for you?"

Make an effort, I think to myself. But out loud, I suggest, "Perhaps we could do lunch or dinner sometime this week?"

The line crackles with his hesitation. I almost feel him squirm and my heart sinks. "This week is going to be busy. Brent and I will be training new employees on our security systems, and I have two events that I need to work on. But I'm sure we will see each other again soon."

I'm disappointed but not defeated. One decline is not enough to throw me off my game. "Sure. I'll reach out to you next week and we'll get together. It'll be fun."

"Sounds great, Maxine. Take care." The line disconnects before I have the chance to respond. I frown at the display, tossing the phone aside.

Debra really thinks Malcolm would be interested in Renee? The thought makes me laugh aloud. She looked great in that dress that I picked out for her, sure. But wait until he sees that ugly purple sweat suit she insists on wearing all the time. I shudder, then chuckle, reaching for my coffee and the discarded New York Times.

I have nothing to worry about. I sip coffee and peruse the front page of the Times. Renee is not my competition.

I wait for Debra to finish her coffee and retreat to the guest bedroom before I come out again. At least she washed her mug and put everything away and wiped down the counter. She's a quiet and courteous roommate. No matter how big of a pain in my ass she's been today.

The melodic lilt of chimes sound from my bedroom. Maybe Malcolm changed his mind? I rush back and snatch the phone from its hiding place between the sheets, but frown when I see the name on the display– Joseph Glass.

Not the tall, dark and handsome man that I wanted to be on the other end of the line. I must have been halfway drunk when I gave him my number. In the light of day and fully sober, I don't know if I'm interested in getting to know Joseph. Although, he is very handsome. And he does have some money.

"Ugh," I grunt, debating with myself—should I pick it up? Or let it ring? At the last minute, I slide my thumb across the screen to pick up the call.

"This is Maxine."

"Oh… hi. Hi, Maxine. This is uh… this is Joseph. From last night." His voice is slightly rough, just enough rasp to ride down the nerve endings in my back. I smile, congratulating myself on taking his call. Maybe it will be fruitful.

I sit on the bed and lean back against the headboard, settling in. "Joseph from last night. This is how you introduce yourself on our first phone conversation?"

He chuckles. "I apologize. Let me start over. Good morning, Maxine. This is Joseph Glass. We met last night at Brent's party. I was the devastatingly handsome man that made you laugh, then forced you to give me your number so I could call you today. Does this information ring any bells?"

I'm giggling at his effort. He is cute. "Good morning, Joseph. How are you?"

"After all the wine I had last night, I expected to be feeling worse, but I'm doing very well. And you?"

"The same, feeling good. My friend must have been drinking the cheap stuff, though." I roll my eyes toward the guest room. "She's not much of a drinker and she's feeling it."

"I'm sorry to hear that. But I'm happy to hear you're not feeling the same."

"So, what can I do for you? When we spoke last night, you said you weren't interested in upgrading from your condo. Change your mind?"

Our conversation touched on several subjects, one of which being his real estate situation. Joseph owns a two-bedroom condo in an aging downtown high rise. I know the building, and given what he brags that he paid for the place, I know it's lacking in luxury finishes and if he has a view, it's of a parking lot or the building across the street. As an Investment Banker for J.M. Porter, one of Atlanta's premier capital management firms, I'm interested in moving him up to a property in the half million dollar range. For starters.

When I mentioned this figure, he laughed until he choked on his wine, then drained the glass, trying to get his bearings. "That's way out of my range," he said, still laughing. "I'm still a Junior Banker, for the next year or two at least. If I were to move to something—which I'm not interested in, but if I were, I'd max out at around three hundred thousand."

I wilted at that low number. Donovan would never turn a profit if I sold in that range. "I know your type, Joseph. You're ambitious. A hard worker. You'll be a Senior Banker in no time, living in a plain condo in an old building, rushing to upgrade your lifestyle. And I know Randall Porter wants his bankers to enjoy the profits from the hefty fees they bill."

I happen to know Randall. The home he purchased two years ago bought me the Maserati.

"No, no. Still not interested in another condo. You are tenacious, though. I can appreciate that. Uh…" He pauses, clears his throat. "What's up is that uh… and I realize this is short notice, but I was hoping you might be available for lunch today."

I flick my wrist to check my watch, my eyebrows rising. Sensing my hesitation, his words come rushing out in a flood.

"I know I should call today for dinner tomorrow, but I realized that I don't want to wait until tomorrow to see you—"

"Joseph—"

"So if you're free for lunch, I hope you'll consider forgiving the last minute invitation—"

"Joseph!" I finally breakthrough, it seems, because he stops talking. "Normally, I would decline on such short notice. I typi-cally already have plans by this point. However, my plans for today have changed and I need to leave the condo before eleven thirty, anyway."

The cleaning service and the caretaker from Atlanta Flora & Fauna come on Sundays. I hate being here while they're working. It makes me nitpick. "I'd planned to go the Ritz Carlton for their Sunday Brunch. Perhaps you could join me. Have you ever been?"

He pauses. I wait, patiently. "The Ritz? No... but I look forward to experiencing it with you. Eleven-thirty?"

"Parking is valet only."

"Yeah... okay." I hear him mentally checking his bank account balance. I almost feel bad for him. Almost. He seems to think he can handle me.

Let's see you work, Mr. Glass.

CHAPTER NINETEEN

enee

Sunday is inventory day at Gladwell Books. It used to be something I hated. I can think of nothing more boring than counting books. Lately, I don't mind it. The store is usually empty and if we get customers at all, they just want to sit on the couches and flip through magazines, drinking coffee and staring into their electronic devices. I cherish the time I get to myself, away from Daddy and Jessie. Even Maxine and Debra can get to be a bit much.

Inventory day has become a puzzle, and it's my job to figure out how the pieces fit together; how the number of books I have in the stacks matches up with the number of books that my software program tells me I've sold. It works like an equation in my head. From there, I make strategic decisions– what to order more of, what to order less of and what I have to send back unsold.

It's a beautiful day, cool but bright and not a cloud in the sky. Beams of sunlight stream through the front windows, illuminating the dust that I'm kicking up by moving the books around. Next to the register at the front counter, an 80s era boom box crackles, sending static and tunes to mix with the dust swirling in the air.

I bounce between rows of mahogany book-filled cases, singing along to the Sunday afternoon Old School Show on 107.9FM. My inventory sheet is soon full of hash marks and scribbles. I bump my shoulders to the beat of Will Smith's Gettin' Jiggy Wit It as I migrate from self-help to travel. These are my smallest sections, so I like to get them out of the way first.

"Looking great in here."

It's not the sound of his voice, full of barely concealed laughter that makes me nearly leap out of my skin as I whip around to face Malcolm, the beautiful man with an affinity for books that I met last night. It's the knowledge of how I looked as he crept into the store and came behind me. My back was to the door, the music was loud and, thinking I was alone, I was having a good time. My mind's eye runs an instant replay of shoulder bouncing and hip shaking and so much… jiggling.

I suppress a cringe, but can't stop the nervous, embarrassed giggle. I inhale a calming, steadying breath and push it out. It sounds like I'm in labor.

"Hi, Malcolm. I didn't hear you come in. It's nice to see you."

He graces me with a wide, gorgeous smile and it's like the sun came out all over again. "I was pretty sure I walked into a book-store, but it seemed more like a dance club a minute ago." His shoulders shimmy in imitation. My breath catches in my throat and my heart flops around in my chest like a fish out of water.

Malcolm is a handsome drink of café mocha. His wide shoulders and stocky build fill a dark blue, short-sleeved shirt collared very well. I'm sure Maxine could name its designer on sight, but I'm not educated on such things. All I know is it looks good, laying open at the neck and tucked into well-fitting blue jeans. I watch a muscle ripple down his arm as he chuckles and leans against the nearest bookcase.

Inventory day calls for crawling on the floor, climbing ladders and hauling boxes from the storeroom. I'm wearing a t-shirt and sweats, thankfully a pair that doesn't have JUICY spelled out across the backside.

I reach across the counter to flip the power switch on the boom box to OFF. The sudden silence fills the empty store to the rafters. "Sorry about that. Did you decide what you'd like me to order for you? Or would you like to look around the shop?" I smile, hoping he'll move past the recent sight of my shaking rump.

No such luck. "I was hoping to see more of your moves."

Were it possible for me to blush deeply, my skin would resemble a tomato. My gaze drops to the worn wood of the front counter. "You know... it's just that... it's inventory day, and I wasn't expecting company."

He smiles, his eyes crinkling in the corners, which somehow both excites and calms me. "This is a great little place. I've passed by a few times, peeked in the windows. I'm glad I stopped in this evening."

"Well, I'm open for another hour. Unless I can help you find something, I need to finish the... um..." I gesture, waving my sheets around.

"Inventory," he finishes, nodding. "And dance party." He laughs.

"I'd offer you some coffee, but..." I angle my head toward a darkened corner of the store where a few tables and chairs sit empty. "The lady who runs it is off on Sundays. If you like that sort of thing, she usually has coffee, tea, juice and homemade pastries."

"You bake, too? As well as you dance?"

"Worse, actually. That's why I sublet the space to a nice lady that sells her product here."

"Okay. I see." Malcolm nods as if he's completely interested in the inner workings of Gladwell Books. His eyes rove the stacks near him, but eventually make their way back to me.

Something inside me pushes me to keep him here, not to let him get away. Damn that Maxine, rubbing off on me! "It's great to see you exploring the neighborhood, finally. Especially on such a pretty day."

"I bring the sunshine, I like to say." He laughs again. It's a nice sound, a baritone rumble from deep in his chest.

"Well, except about five years, I've lived here all my life. If you have questions about the neighborhood–or the city for that matter, or if you want someone to show you around a little, just let me know."

One hand slides into a pocket of his jeans while the palm of the other smoothes over a closely cut head of hair. "I appreciate the offer. I didn't mean to interrupt your work. I should let you get back to your inventory."

I know a gentle letdown when I hear one. I'll see him walk by the store and he might even come in a time or two, but he's way more Maxine's speed. I'm just Renee, the nice girl next door that could do things for you because she has nothing better to do. Of course he wouldn't want to spend time with a frumpy bookstore owner that lives in jeans, sweats and t-shirts.

I pick up my inventory sheets and turn back toward the stacks. The warmth of his hand covering mine stops me in my tracks.

"You live around here, right? Do you know a spot where we could grab a bite to eat?"

Frozen in place, my mouth forms a perfect circle of surprise. "I... well, sure. But..." I glance at myself, mindlessly brushing away dust and dirt from my t-shirt.

Those broad shoulders effortlessly lift and lower in a shrug. "We don't have to eat at a five star joint. I just want something besides Fat Burger."

Just say yes and see where it takes you.

"I've made you uncomfortable," he says, misreading the long pause between his suggestion and my answer. He withdraws his hand and backs away. "Please forgive me. I don't know what's too forward down here. Sorry to bother you–"

"Malcolm." He pauses, so still he could be a mannequin. "I know a place."

The bright, wide smile returns to his face. "Yeah?"

I nod. "I have to finish this." I wave a few pages around in the air. "But give me an hour, hour and a half tops. If you like fried chicken, macaroni and cheese, collard greens and hush puppies–,"

"About as much as I like breathing air." Bless him, he seems excited. "I'll see you in an hour, then." With one hand on the door handle, he turns back and adds, "Can't wait."

I watch him saunter across the sidewalk and climb into a jet black Denali. The truck rumbles to life, Malcolm pulls into traffic and disappears down the street. "Brother," I mutter under my breath. "Neither can I."

I don't have to say anything more than 'dinner with this guy I just met' to get Jessie to stay for a few hours. She and Daddy are in the middle of a puzzle that takes up half of the dining room table.

"I don't have nothin' else to do but help him put pieces in this puzzle," she says, flapping an arm at me. "Go on, child. Have a good time."

I rush upstairs to my room, throwing off clothes as I go. A quick shower, a few minutes of fussing with my hair, a frantic ten minutes picking out jeans, a sweater and a pair of low heels and I'm grabbing my purse and flying out the door again, offering profuse thanks to Jessie just as Daddy notices I'm home.

"Where's she going?" I hear him ask as the door slams shut.

"So you took over the store from your father?"

I nod over a steaming plate of the Sunday special at Ruby's. I'd met Malcolm back at the bookstore right on time, climbed into the passenger seat of the Denali and guided him a few blocks away.

"I don't run a bookstore because I'm crazy about books. I moved back to Atlanta about…" I tilt my head up at the ceiling while my mind counts the years since I'd returned to Georgia. "Four years ago, now. The bookstore was my mother's dream. My father took it over when she died. Her death hit him hard, and running the bookstore was his way of keeping her memory alive."

"Sorry to hear about your mother."

I stop stabbing my fork through pasta and cheese long enough to smile my thanks. "When my dad started showing signs of Dementia, I moved back and started taking care of him. I thought he'd be back on his feet in no time. Stress. Aging."

I shake my head, dipping my fork into the greens. "I never thought I would be back here for good. And I never thought I'd be taking care of Daddy. Out of all the people I know, he was the most self-sufficient. It just doesn't seem right." I pause before admitting, "I might have to put him in a home. I've been looking. I know he won't want that, but…"

"I know the feeling. I had to consider the same for my mother."

My eyes flick up from my plate at the tenderness in his voice. He's not even looking at me, just staring into his half eaten dinner plate, fork poised over the cooling mounds of soul food.

"Pop is in his 80s. Mom had heart failure. It took her pretty slowly. He wanted to take care of her, but he had his own issues to deal with. High blood pressure, cataracts, the like. We couldn't risk him giving her the wrong medications because he couldn't see what he was doing. Or feeling poorly himself so he couldn't give her the attention she needed. So my sister took in my dad, and I took mom. She died two years ago."

I'm suddenly and oddly thankful that Daddy was relatively well when Mama was sick. Though he was in denial about how much time she had left, he could care for her. "I'm so sorry. You know I know what you're going through."

"That I do," he says quietly, digging into his dinner again. A forkful of macaroni and cheese disappears into his mouth and I watch him chew at a slow, deliberate pace. He swallows and continues. "Pop is giving my sister a run for her money, though. He can't see and he needs blood pressure meds every day, but he's showing no signs of slowing down."

He chuckles, wistful as he fiddles with the corner of a folded napkin next to his plate. "I didn't mean to take over the conversation. Please… continue." He picks up his fork again and loads it up with greens and a corner of cornbread. I watch him eat, completely mesmerized. I never realized how sexy eating could be. Marcus was not a sexy eater. He practically poured food down his throat.

I blink and avert my gaze. I can't concentrate when I'm watching him. "Yeah, so I took over the store. It was something to do, and we needed the income. I worked there in high school and college, stocking shelves and working the register for my mom. I knew nothing about the back end."

"That's the best place to start."

""I suppose. I struggled through the first six months, trying to get a grip on everything. I figured that if Gladwell was going to survive, we had to at least come into this century. Daddy never owned a computer. If it didn't put a car together, he'd never touch one. I couldn't keep us open that way, so I used some savings and a small business loan and added an inventory system.

"Then the space next to us became available. I expanded the store and added the café. Business picked up once I had space for poetry nights and book club meetings and started carrying a lot of specialty genres. Kids are reading this vampire stuff now."

I shrug, picking up my glass of water and taking a few sips from the straw. "I don't have to love it; I just have to make it available. I'm happy with what I could accomplish."

"It's a great little place. Like home. Welcoming. Smells like old books, like it should." He takes a bite, chews and smiles. "Seriously, you should be proud of yourself. It looks like it took a lot of time and work to put together."

"It did. Thank you for recognizing that."

"And not only for that, but for being here for your dad, too. So many kids dump their parents in a home and go back to their lives. When I was coming up, they taught us that family takes care of each other. We took in my grandparents. They lived with us until they died. An elderly aunt, down-and-out uncle—family helps family."

I feel a twinge of guilt at Malcolm's impassioned diatribe on family. I'm planning to dump my father in a home and go back to life as I know it. But maybe I believe in his philosophy more than I want to let on, which is why I'm having such a hard time deciding what to do with Daddy.

"So, did your man help you out with the shop?"

I smirk, biting into a piece of catfish. "I don't have a man, since you're asking."

I sense his blush. "Never hurts to ask."

He and I finish the last few bites of dinner and push our plates toward the edge of the table. This is a sign at Ruby's that we're finished eating. And we're ready for dessert.

Malcolm watches the busboy pick up our plates and shuffle toward the kitchen. "I've been to Atlanta several times, but I mostly stayed in Buckhead. That's a big reason I didn't want to buy a place there. I know there's more to this city than Buckhead and the six square blocks around my apartment. I'd like to take you up on that offer of showing me around. My schedule is tight and I know you're busy taking care of your dad and the store, but..."

He pauses, leaning in, his muscular forearms resting on the table. "I think you and I have a lot in common. And I think we'd have some fun together. What do you say?"

Something tells me he's not talking about riding a roller coaster at Six Flags over Georgia or exploring the Fernbank Museum of Natural History. He means fun in the biblical sense. And everything in me says yes. Yes, tall bottle of dark chocolate milk... yes.

Except for one thing.

"So, remember five seconds ago you were talking about why you didn't want to buy a place in Buckhead? The woman that sold you your condo is one of my best friends. I've known her forever. And you and I both know she has a thing for you and I'd feel awful for even attempting to be inappropriate where Maxine is concerned."

"Okay, but—"

"Maxine talks a big game and she acts really bad ass, but she's actually very sensitive and she can hold a grudge forever. I think she's still mad at me about something from high school—"

"Renee." His big, heavy hand grips my wrist so gently that I'm shocked into silence. "I'm not dating Maxine. I'm not interested in Maxine. She's a beautiful woman, classy and accomplished, and I'm sure the toast of the town. And lucky to have a loyal friend. But I don't have interest in her. And she knows that." He releases my wrist and gently settles my arm back on to the table.

I might regret it, but I'm not about to turn down a chance to spend more time with Malcolm. "Well, when you put it that way, I guess I don't have a reason to refuse."

Malcolm smiles. It must be my reward for saying yes. "This week is going to be crazy, but I could call you. We could do dinner again. Maybe go on a little tour. Whatever you have in mind."

I'm nodding and grinning and I feel like an idiot, but I don't care. Dinner? With a man that knows my name? Absolutely.

Malcolm drives slowly, inching his way back to the shop. I know the feeling; I'm not ready for our evening to end, either.

"So you work in security? What exactly does that mean?"

"Millennium is a boutique agency. Brent and I both have a specialty. He's great with systems. People pay him millions to make sure even the smallest location is secure—financial firms, law offices... places where people have to keep things confidential and secure. It's great peace of mind."

"And your specialty?"

"I'm the muscle." I reach over and grab his bicep and squeeze. He flexes, showing off the rock hard muscle there. "I worked my way up from security guard to manager, to owning a security company. Years ago I wanted to do something a little bit more professional." He flicks the turn signal and, when it's clear, hangs a right onto Broad Street. Gladwell is a few blocks away.

"I was more interested in personal security. I took business courses, some self-defense and personal security training, and farmed myself out as a bodyguard. I found that high-profile people feel more secure having a big, black dude walking in front of them. I opened a firm, added some staff, trained them myself. Contracted some regular clients."

He pulls over in front of Gladwell. The shop is dark, but I keep a single lamp lit behind the register so the neighborhood patrol can see the shadows of anyone skulking around at night. He puts the truck in park, but keeps it running and directs a heat vent my way.

"Then my mom got sick, and I had to back away from doing so much, especially out-of-town work. I still ran the agency, though. I liked the managerial role. I could do it from anywhere, even my house, while my mother was being cared for."

"Sounds like everything was going okay."

"Then my mother died. And I was in a situation that got ugly quickly. The quality of my clientele was dropping. I was getting more so-called musicians that want to look important than high-powered executives and heads of state. I much prefer heads of state." He glances at me.

I nod, understanding.

"I needed to get out of Maryland. I'd lived there my whole life. What seems more exciting to you is the underbelly of the city to me. I wasn't interested in being a part of that." He slouches in his seat, leaning an elbow on the armrest between us. He's so close I can feel his breath on my shoulder, smell his decadent, spicy cologne.

"I hit up Brent, who's a buddy from high school. He said he'd been doing well with Millennium, but his clients were asking for recommends for personal security. He threw me a bone to see if it interested me to join forces, expand that side of the business. It took a year to put it together, but..."

He shrugs. "Here I am."

"So you do the same thing here that you did in DC?"

He nods. "Essentially. I do some gigs personally—consulting with the Governor, the Mayor's office. Mostly, I run the organization. Hire and train staff, attract clients, maintain those relationships. I schedule all my guys and I work with the office staff on their role. We do background checks on all of our clients. A lot of what we do is research."

"Sure. You need to know what you're getting into. There's a reason people need personal security right?"

"Right. I do a fair bit of work with musicians, but it's a little different down here. I don't work concerts or autograph signings– you need a ten dollar an hour kind of guy for that. But say a record label needed a security team for a platinum recording artist's upcoming tour? He'd come through me. I'd train his chief of security and the guys that work for him."

"Interesting." I'm riveted by his breakdown of his job. I never imagined so much would be involved in walking a famous person from the car into a building. "Is your work dangerous? Do you carry a gun?"

"It can be," he responds, his tone solemn. "But rarely. We train hand to hand and weapons. I'm licensed to carry and I always have my piece on me if I'm working. At home, I keep it in a safe."

My heart thumps at the mental image of sexy Malcolm wielding a gun. Like 007 on steroids. "Wow. Do you wear a bullet-proof vest, too?"

"If necessary. I always keep one in the vehicle I'm working in. But…" He shrugs. "Not to scare you, but most shooters will aim at body parts not protected by a vest."

"Right," I say, nodding like I know. "They'll assume you're wearing one, anyway."

"In a few weeks there's some kind of high level political convention. My guys will be on-site, working hand in hand with each representative's forward security agent. Scoping out the place, providing around the clock protection."

"Sounds exciting."

"And you thought only DC could be this exciting."

I blush and laugh. "I guess you've shown me where I was wrong." My head turns toward the darkened windows of Glad-well. "You'd roll your eyes at my security system. I have old locks and an alarm on a single entry."

He chuckles, leaning around me to glance at the shop through the window. "Ever had any trouble here?"

"When my mother first opened her shop, yes." I glance at him, my expression full of meaning. He nods in response. "I haven't had any trouble."

"I'll take a look, if you like, and pass along some suggestions. Especially if you provide Wi-Fi. Internet security is cheap but necessary."

"That would be nice. I'm not using you for your connections, though."

He laughs, sitting up again. "Even if you were, I don't mind making sure people are secure. Better safe than sorry, right?"

I hold back a yawn and stretch without seeming like I'm yawning and stretching. I'm not ready for our date to be over, but I've been up since 5am, worked most of the day and did inventory. And that cranky old man will be up before sunrise.

"Where's your car?"

"I park around back."

Malcolm turns the key in the ignition and twists the knob that turns the headlights off. "I'll walk you."

I hop down from the truck and walk with him around the side of the building to the gravel covered lot at the back of the strip mall that holds Gladwell's, Sam's Grille and a few other stores. The crowd at Sam's is loud, voices and laughter carrying over from the guests out on the deck behind the restaurant.

"Awful dark back here. You need a light on a motion sensor."

"I'll make a note of it."

I stand next to my car, not ready to get inside. Malcolm walks across the parking lot, his head moving back and forth. Surveying, I suppose. It's sexy. He makes his way to me and my car and holds out his hands. Once again, I slide my palms across his. I love the softness and warmth of them as they close around mine. I tip my head up and smile.

"I had a really nice time with you. The best evening I've had since I moved to Georgia." This makes me laugh, because except for the company, the evening seemed ordinary to me. "I'm serious. I'm looking forward to more time with you. I hope the feeling is mutual."

I feel like my heart stops beating for a second and picks back up, but in double time. I might faint. "Oh... it is."

"Great. Then I'll let you go. You've suppressed about five or six yawns and I'm taking it personally."

I would have been embarrassed, but he didn't give me time to feel anything but a rush of warmth spreading through my body as he leaned in to brush his thick, soft lips against mine. Once. And again. He steps back, dropping my hand and reaching for the door handle. It opens. I hadn't locked it.

He looks back at me and shakes his head. Sheepish, I slide into the driver's seat. He pushes the door closed and steps back a few inches. I back out of the space into an arc and point the nose of my car toward the alleyway that leads to the street. Malcolm walks around the building. I make sure he sees me wave as I drive by.

I wish I worked further from home because I would have a long drive, during which I could muse about my dinner date and our conversations and the things I've learned about him. He seems gentle, so quiet and calm. Maxine said he seemed cold, not forthcoming with her. He wasn't that way with me.

I guess that's why he's going out with me and not with her.

I quietly step into the house in case Daddy is still up, but the kitchen is dark except for the hood light over the stove. Jessie reclines on the couch, flipping through a magazine by the light of a single lamp.

She sits up when she sees me tip toe in and pats the cushion she'd been lying on. "He's been out like a light for a couple of hours. I tried to wear him out so he wouldn't wake you up so early."

"I fully expect him to be awake at five, like usual. But thank you." I flop down onto the couch and lean my head back against the cushion. I kick off my shoes and sigh.

"Well, now. How was the date?"

"Great." I grin, rolling my head toward her. "Really, really great. He's new in town. He wants an um... personal tour of Atlanta." I wink.

She snickers. "Unh huh. That's not all he wants a personal tour of."

"Jessie!" I feign shock but giggle. "He's handsome and tall and dark and smart, a business owner, like me." I sigh again, grinning like a fool. "It was a great night."

"That smile on your face tells me that." She grunts, pushing herself up from the couch. "I'd best be heading home. My cat has probably decided I've left for good. I'll have to reclaim my bedroom."

"Thanks for staying longer. I really appreciate it."

She stuffs a few things into the big bag she carries and rolls it onto her shoulder. "Anytime, child. Me and Bernard got a good thing going. I'm happy to sit with him. Now that you met a nice man and all." She grins, taps my knee and shuffles past me, heading toward the front door. "See you in the morning, baby."

The door closes, bringing a comfortable silence to the house. I love this time of night, after Daddy is down and there's nothing left to the day. I squish my toes into the throw rug under the coffee table and check the time. I'd better get to bed. This house runs on Bernard time.

CHAPTER TWENTY

ebra

It's stupid, but I'm nervous, driving to meet Kendra for lunch. So far we've avoided talking about what's going on but I don't want to keep dancing around it. Now that she knows the story, I want her kept as much in the loop as she can handle. I suppose it's selfish to want to talk this out with Kendra. It's like I want her to be in my corner. I'm sure her dad wants her to be in his. I'm trying hard not to put her in the middle.

Kendra's favorite place to eat, for reasons only God knows is Bojangles, It's one of those places that serves fried chicken sandwiched between halves of fresh biscuits. There's a location within walking distance of the house, so I agreed to meet her there at noon. I arrive first and grab a seat near the window, so I can watch for her to come around the corner.

Willard's car turns into the parking lot. Kendra's long legs hang out of the open door as she leans over to peck him on the cheek. She watches him drive away before turning around and bounding into the restaurant.

I stand to greet her, closing her up in my arms. She wraps her thin limbs around my waist and lays her head on my shoulder. She squeezes me, so tightly. In that moment I feel so loved by her.

I hand her my debit card so she can place our order. In a few minutes she is back, setting a numbered placard on the edge of the table. "It'll be a few minutes. They gotta cook some more chicken."

I nod. "So, catch me up. How are things going?"

Kendra dives into details, most of which I know because I've been speaking with her teachers. I don't want her grades affected by this mess. There are great opportunities in store for her if she can keep up with math and science. She's telling a story about how Bobby Carter almost set the Experiments Lab on fire when a red plastic tray bearing two boxed meals slides onto our table. The employee smiles at Kendra. He's a cute kid with dimples and light brown eyes, a nice clean edge to his haircut. His uniform shirt is clean and pressed and tucked into pants that don't sag.

Still, I've only got an hour with my baby girl. They can flirt any time. I clear my throat rather loudly and, I admit, rudely. He jumps as if I pointed a loaded gun at him and rushes back toward the counter.

"Ma," she whines, rolling her eyes. "Way to embarrass me."

"He had to get back to work, anyway. Do I know that kid? He doesn't look familiar."

She shakes her head. "He goes to Tucker Prep." Tucker Preparatory High is a private high school. "His dad like... works for the mayor or something."

"Hmm," I muse. "I don't like a high school boy sniffing around you."

"He's only two grades above me. And he wasn't sniffing. Geez."

I've become the uncool parent. Frankly, I don't care. I see too many pregnant children to care about being cool.

"Are you still at Aunt Maxine's?"

"Yep," I unwrap the chicken biscuit that Kendra ordered for me, take a small bite and chew, then slide it away. It's not that it

159

tastes bad; I'm just not much for eating these days. Besides, I rarely eat fried food and my stomach is still a mess from that party last night.

"How is she?"

"She's the same old Maxine. Hasn't changed a bit."

"So y'all are fighting."

"No, not really. We have our disagreements but we always make up."

"Are you going to stay there? Like... forever?"

"For a little while, baby. I want to give Daddy some space, you know? I hurt him pretty badly and I think he needs time." I hesitate before asking but I'm wildly curious about what life is like with Willard. "Is he... okay? He's not leaving you alone for long periods of time, is he? You know how he gets, always buried in work."

Kendra squirms, chewing on a huge bite of chicken and biscuit. "Actually, he's been fine. He stays home until I go to school. He comes home around six and does work in his office. He makes me make my lunch and pick out my clothes for the next day, like you used to. Then he works more. Sometimes I get up around midnight and he's still up."

"Doing what?"

"Work. Using the computer. Watching TV." She shrugs. "What old people do at night, I guess." It's hard, but I hold in my laughter. I called him Old Man when I was with David.

"What about school? Things behind the scenes, I mean."

Rumors have been rampant at Morningside. First I was pregnant, then I'd dumped David for another member of the staff who was happily married, so that rumor had to be squashed quickly. The Teacher's Lounge is a tense, quiet place now. When I walk into a room, people stop talking and stare. The secretaries eye me like I'm some kind of Jezebel. I sense the thoughts beaming through their foreheads. Slut. Whore. Power Trip.

I'd endure all of it if it meant I could save Kendra from the cruelty of children. Surely they've picked on her, made comments to her about me. Maybe she's had to defend me a time or two. I feel a sharp pang of guilt as I realize the cost of a few moments of pleasure.

"Things are okay," she answers, hesitant and calculating. This tells me that things are far from okay. I prod her to talk. "The kids are still saying stuff in the halls, but it's not the kids that keep it going. The teachers talk about it way more. In front of the kids. And kids with parents on the PTA say they're going to talk about it at the next meeting. They're saying you're going to get fired, you never should have got the job, you weren't ready to lead. Stuff like that."

I push the chicken biscuit even further away and prop my elbows up onto the table, burying my face in my hands. I just barely hear Kendra asking if I'm okay. I nod. I say yes, but I'm really not. If they discuss this at the PTA, it won't be long before the school board finds out. I wish I could stop the constant forward motion of this train, but I can't. This means my career and possibly David's are in jeopardy.

For right now, though, I need to act like I've got this under control. I don't, but I am going to win an Oscar pretending that I do.

"I'm so sorry that you have to hear things like that at school. I'm going to put a stop to that. And I'm happy to hear that Daddy is taking good care of you. Where was he headed when he dropped you off?"

"A date."

I choke on my breath and cough furiously.

She giggles. "I'm kidding, Ma. He went back home to work for a couple of hours. But… if you were with Mr. Loren, why do you care if daddy has a date? You had dates."

There are so many answers to this question, I don't know where to begin. I turn my eyes on my daughter, who is the perfect mix of me and Willard, both of us personified in a beautiful human being.

"It's not that I don't love him. I've loved him for a long, long time. It's like... let's say you wrote a piece for your clarinet, a new song. You love that song and you play it all the time. That song means the world to you. But can you imagine playing that song all day, every day of your life?"

Her lip curls on one side. "I'm never getting married if it's that boring."

"Well, it doesn't have to be," I protest. "But when you add in all the other things that Daddy and I do all day, playing that song every day becomes so much less important. You still love the song, but it's not at the top of your list of songs to play anymore."

"And then one day you hear a new song?"

I nod. "And playing that song reminds you of the first time you played that old song, but it's different. And you love how different the new song is."

I dip my head and fold my arms, leaning onto the table. "I still love the old song. Your dad and I... we just have to make playing the song every day fun and important and the thing we love to do more than anything."

"I understand," she says, chewing on her straw.

"And unfortunately because Mr. New Song works at our school– and I was dumb about that, I know–you have to be involved. But please know that I am trying hard to keep you out of this."

"Yeah. I know." She's quiet for a minute, then admits, "I miss you."

My heart cracks right in two. "I miss you too. I really, really do."

"Daddy does a good job, but it's not the same as having you there. He doesn't care about healthy stuff like you."

I groan. "Oh, no. What does he have you eating?"

"Sugary cereal," she responds, smirking because she knows I'm going to cringe. "Two percent milk and not almond milk. Pork sausage. Pizza from Domino's, not that healthy, gluten-free crust, veggie stuff you make us eat."

Lord, I've got to get home. He's going to turn my baby into a pillar of preservatives.

I drop Kendra at home, lingering to take in the view of my house before I pull away. I don't think I'm made for mid-city living. It's so loud, especially on the weekend. It's impossible to get out of Max's complex, with all the traffic zipping back and forth on Peachtree. Everything is expensive and impersonal. Not like this sweet house in a Tucker subdivision, friendly neighbors and low prices on everything from food to gas. We've got no one to impress but ourselves.

I chuckle out loud, thinking of Max as I head back to Buckhead. I've had the same argument with Max so many times I can't count. Maxine is looking for someone exactly like her– as in love with money and the elite experience as she is. It's just that not even Maxine is like Maxine. All those airs she puts on, the rich, exotic, elite experience stuff she claims to enjoy… it's a facade.

That girl grew up around the corner from me and Renee in Decatur, Georgia in a two-bedroom shack. She gives the impression that she was born with a silver spoon in her mouth, but I have it on good authority that the spoon was wooden. And it's now inserted some place else.

I use the garage key fob and door key that Maxine lent me and let myself into her condo. It's empty, cool and sparkling clean, which means the maid service has been in. Fresh flowers in the crystal vases throughout also mean the plant caretaker was in. Max's place runs with an efficiency that would rival a factory.

I plop myself on the couch with a few piles of work that I picked up at the office and sift through them. But my mind isn't on budget forms and orders for next semester.

I'm going to have to call Bernice and see if she can put a stop to this PTA nonsense. Those people do not understand how many lives they're about to destroy with their gossip and Pitchfork Mafia. I want to keep my job. But if I can't, I want to able to get a job elsewhere.

I hear the lock turn, and Maxine sweeps into the room, as

Maxine does. Her jeans, a perfect shade of dark indigo blue, ride low on her slim hips. A white button-down shirt flutters open to reveal a white cable knit tank top. For a change of pace, she's wearing loafers, but I am sure the shiny, sturdy black shoes are some brand I can neither pronounce nor afford.

"Hey," I call to her when she walks past the living room. She stops when I speak and turns to face me. "You weren't going to even say hello?"

"It's my house. I don't have to greet you."

"Well, since it is your house, I'll greet you. Hi. How was your day?"

Maxine clears her throat and plays with the interconnected links around the strap of her purse. "It was fine. I ran some errands. Grabbed some brunch." She dips her head and barely audibly mutters, "With Joseph."

My eyebrows shoot up in open surprise. "Excuse me? You had brunch with Joseph? Regular Joseph? Run of the mill, not a millionaire, Joseph?"

"Shut up, Debra."

She paces from one end of the living room to the other while telling me about her date. I don't let on that I know Malcolm turned down her invitation to breakfast. Even more so, I don't let on that his denial of her invitation was the reason she agreed to go to out with Joseph. Maxine juggles men like no one I've ever seen.

"We went to the Ritz Carlton. You know I love their brunch." I nod, as I know this. I refuse to go with her unless she's offering to pay. Willard would have a fit if he saw that charge come through on the bank statement. She finally sits, perching on the edge of an upholstered chair. "I had poached eggs and wheat toast with that peach preserve they make fresh every—"

"I'm not interested in the menu, Max. What did you talk about? Did you like him better than you did last night?"

She shrugs one shoulder. The right side of her top lip curls slightly. In Max speak, this doesn't bode well. "I'm not saying he's not a great guy..."

"He just isn't Malcolm."

"Don't start that again. Did you ask me all these questions just so you could lecture me some more? Because I'm not interested."

"No." I pause for a few moments to let Maxine breathe and settle down. "I was going to apologize."

"Oh?" She pouts, her eyes cast downward. "Well, no one's stopping you."

I try hard not to roll my eyes at Maxine too much, otherwise they might roll out of my head. "Alright. I'm sorry. I was picking on you like I always do. I didn't know you were so sensitive about Malcolm. Okay?"

"Okay. If you forgive me for bringing up how sorry your life is."

"You mean earlier today, or just now?"

She raises her gaze to mine. "Both. Sorry."

"Girl, whatever." I reach for my piles of paperwork and continue sifting through it. "My life is sorry. You spoke the truth." In reality, so did I but Maxine believes enough of her own hype to define what truth is.

"So, how long do you think you're going to be here?" She asks, fidgeting with the zipper on her purse. "Not that I don't enjoy having you here..."

"Let's be honest. I'm totally cramping your style."

"Yeah. So..."

I shuffle some pages together and lay them in my lap, cross my arms and lean my elbows on my knees. "I didn't think Willard would let me leave the house. Then I thought he wouldn't let me stay a night in a house that wasn't ours. Then I thought he wouldn't last the week without me, but..."

I shake my head, suck my teeth in frustration. "I talked to Kendra today. They get along. He goes grocery shopping. He checks her homework. He sees her off to school. He's home by six o'clock. Six!"

"When is he usually home?"

"During peak tax season?" A hand flails through the air as I shake my head. "Sometimes midnight, depending on the month. Six o'clock, Max. He'll bring work home and sit in his office until midnight, but for Kendra, he's home before sunset."

She leans forward, her brows furrowed. "Debra... what do you expect him to do? There's no one to take care of Kendra."

"Thanks to him." Max doesn't speak the words I know she wants to, but her eyes tell me, anyway. I sigh, defeated. "I know. I know, thanks to me."

"So Willard isn't going to ask you to move back soon?"

The edges of my mouth seem to drag my entire face down. I don't want to cry. I give myself just one time a day to break down. "I guess I need to find a place. I can't keep living out of a suitcase."

I lean back, indicating the stack of papers in my lap, poking out of my bag, across the cushions of the couch. "My personal life is a shambles. I can't let my work life go down the same drain. Some mess might be going down soon and I need to be ready."

"What kind of mess?"

"Kendra says all the teachers are talking about it, and some parents are taking it to the PTA. If the school board gets wind of this, not even Bernice can help me."

"Can you stop them? Can you cancel the meeting?"

"I don't know. But tomorrow I'm going to find out."

CHAPTER TWENTY-ONE

$\mathcal{M}$axine

I can't wait until Debra is out of my place. It's not that I don't love her. I do, I guess. Sometimes I feel like we're just friends for history's sake, like you know a person for so long, you just consider them a friend. It's been a long time since Debra and I had anything in common, since we saw eye to eye on anything. Honestly, it takes a lot out of me to be there for her. I know it shouldn't, but I can't help how I feel.

This situation with Willard and Kendra and the gym teacher and her job? I feel like she brought this on herself. She lies in bed at night and cries herself to sleep. She thinks I can't hear her, and I let her think that. I also let her go to work with red-rimmed eyes, but that's beside the point. What did Debra think was going to happen when people found out about her affair? Did she think everything would be alright? Did she think Willard was going to be his usual easygoing self, forgive her and move on? Maybe Debra didn't think. Maybe she should have.

I'm trying not to be selfish. I have the room and she's my oldest friend. She couldn't stay with Renee, not with Bernard up and down at all hours of the night, forgetting where the bathroom is and Jessie there most days.

I have to be there for her, but I have a life, too. And that life is being severely impacted by her irresponsibility and unwillingness to accept that she created this situation and now needs to get herself out of it. All this Good Samaritan stuff is really chapping my hide, but the sooner I get Debra out, the sooner I can resume my life, which now includes two men— one I want, that's playing hard to get and one that wants me and I'm willing to play with until the one I want comes around.

Joseph is a nice man. Good looking, tall, broad shouldered, nicely built. He's from New York and still has a hint of an accent when he gets excited. We've found a lot to talk about. He had me laughing like my previous companions never have. When he called me out of the blue to go to brunch, that was just what I needed. I was happy to get out of the house, have some place to go, enjoy the company of a handsome man.

He just…isn't the Maxine standard. He doesn't own a business. I like men that work for themselves. He drives American. He wears JC Penney, for goodness sake! If there's one thing I've learned from Inell, it's that I have to have some kind of standard about myself. If I don't put myself first, no one else will.

So, while Joseph is a nice guy, he's not quite 'it' for me. Malcolm, though… he could be it. If only he would open his eyes and see it.

Monday morning just feels like a Monday. Pellets of rain beat against the windowpane, and it's dark and moody outside. It's hard to get going, but I pull myself out of bed. Debra got up early and figured out the coffee grinder and the brewer. While I sit at my vanity and apply my makeup, she brings me a cup of coffee and leans against the doorjamb.

I take a dainty gulp of hot, sweet coffee and set the cup back down, checking out her workday fashion, a peridot blue Jaclyn Smith skirt and jacket with a white silk blouse. Shoes to match.

Maybe I am rubbing off on her. Except that she probably bought that get-up at Wal-Mart.

Debra chuckles, sipping her coffee. "You have a comment on what I'm wearing today?"

"Not at all. That's a pretty blue."

"Uh huh."

I swirl a delicate feather brush into a container of powder and lightly dust my face and neck. "Don't start stuff, Debra." I pause my routine to cut my eyes at her. "It's too damn early on a Monday morning for that smug nonsense. What do you want?"

"Nothing. Why do I have to want something?"

"You're standing there like you want something."

"I'm watching you put your face on. Remember, I always used to watch."

Back in high school, we had slumber parties almost every weekend. Since Inell was never home, the girls were usually at my house. We'd rent movies—VHS back then, we didn't have cable and there was no such thing as DVD or Blu-Ray. We'd bake frozen pizza and cookies, have ice cream and makeup parties. I talked about all the boys that had crushes on me. Debra talked about Willard. All the time. Renee was quiet and shy and we were almost seniors before she had a boy to talk about. Until then, she would sit between us, her gaze bouncing back and forth while Debra and I swooned and gossiped and swapped stories.

Renee and Debra couldn't wear makeup until the tenth grade, but that didn't stop them from sneaking it at my house before we went to dances and parties. I gave lessons and Debra asked a hundred questions. What does that do? Why do you do that? What is this for?

I smile at the memory and sip more coffee. "And you are just as clueless today as you were back then."

"Cheap shot," she says, but she laughs then pushes herself off of the wall. "I guess I'll head out. I want to call Bernice before her day gets busy."

"Oh yeah. Good luck."

Debra hums a thanks and walks down the hall to the guest room. A few minutes later she is back, her coat hanging over her arm and her bag over her shoulder.

"I'm going to look at a few places after work today. Maybe a studio or something. You know, the kind you pay for by the week."

I stop poking my eyelashes to look up at her. "You cannot stay at a seedy weekly motel. Let me help you find something."

"Not right now. I don't know how this thing…" She pauses and licks her lips. "This thing being my marriage… I don't know how it's going to pan out. I don't want anything permanent right now. If I get divorced…." She bows her head and closes her eyes.

"Okay," I whisper, letting her off the hook. "If you need any help…"

She backs away, then hurries down the hall. I hear the door open and close. I rise from my chair at the vanity and head into the bathroom to brush my teeth.

With five minutes to spare, I blow into the Donovan suite. As I pass his desk, Virgil sweeps his eyes down my profile, nodding at my mid-thigh length, heather gray Armani jacket over a high waist pencil skirt and silk blouse. My pumps are the most supple leather I've ever slipped onto my feet. His eyebrows wiggle when he sees them.

"Nice," he murmurs. "I guess if you're going to be late, look good doing it."

He picks up a leather folio that holds his notepad, a stack of printed pages, and his Mont Blanc pen. I take off my jacket, grab my pen and a notebook and follow him to the conference room where all of my agents chatter quietly around the oval table.

"Let's get started," says Virgil, slipping into his usual seat to my right. I pour myself a cup of coffee, snap off a vine of green grapes from the fruit tray and a mini muffin from the pastry selection to snack on. Porcelain cups and saucers, silver spoons and butter knives dot the table. Virgil's only acquiescence to convenience is paper napkins, but at least they are thick and don't shred in my hands. I spread a napkin across my lap and sip my coffee.

"Somebody tell me some good news."

The agents go around the table and update the group on their sales numbers and prospective buyer's lists. I'm slightly disappointed in the sales report. Donovan has been fortunate in the past, riding the economic downturn well. This year, however, sales have dipped alarmingly low. We're not in danger of closing, but we'll need a busy spring housing market to make up for the slump. I'm crossing my fingers that some millionaires want to give their trophy wives a home for Christmas.

Virgil's pen scratches across the yellow legal pad as he dutifully takes notes. He opens his folio and pulls out the dreaded Trouble List.

"Maxine, why don't you update everyone on the Newman situation?"

I perk, hands clasped in front of me. At least there is some good news. "It looks like Adora Newman took the bait. Braxton wrote her a check, and she's moved into one of his condos in the city. Near to me, unfortunately." I roll my eyes. The room titters in light amusement. "She appears to have taken everything she plans to take. Braxton is having the house emptied and cleaned, which means it'll be ready for staging and listing soon."

I turn to Virgil. "I'd like to put together an open house. Schedule a photographer to take some attractive shots of the place for the listing and to include in the invitation to some VIP clients that might be interested. I'm thinking a cocktail party, late afternoon—champagne, wine, hors d'oeuvres and a few agents around to give tours as needed."

He nods, his pen scratching again. "That goes for everyone. If any of you have a client that might be interested in a golf course estate, please let Virgil know. We'll do a commission split if it sells to your client."

The announcement sets everyone on edge, as I'd hoped. Though I never split commission evenly, even thirty percent of what I make on a sale is enticing. I feel like I've set out a challenge, one to which I hope each of them will rise.

"Jonathon, is the Stone Mountain property ready yet?"

"Not yet," he answers after swallowing a mouthful of coffee. "I have convinced the owners to replace the appliances, pipes and wiring. They won't get the full value of the house if they sell it as-is and they see that. The plumbers and electricians were on site last week. I haven't received an update on the replacement appliances. That's on my list today."

"Good." I nod. Today is looking better. If we can get this house sold, it will help Donovan's bottom line at year end. "Stay on it. Offer as much help as you can, even if it seems unreasonable. I want that property sold at high value."

Jonathon smiles, gathering his papers and tapping the stack against the table. "That's the goal, Max. You know I do good business."

"I do. So live up to your reputation."

I search the eyes around the table, looking for anyone that has more to add. My gaze settles on my newest agent. Vanessa Jackson came highly recommended from another firm when I felt I needed a young, fresh mind to appeal to the 'new money' wealthy—the singers, actors and wanna-be music moguls that flock to Atlanta because of the "Hollywood of the South" reputation. Before they spend their million dollar advances and their first album sales, I want Vanessa in their faces with her Donovan business card and a smile. A home is an investment that will outlast short-lived fame. So what if it'll be in foreclosure in five years? We've made our money.

Need to unload your place in a hurry? We'll sell it for you, too.

Vanessa has yet to make a sale. She's not new to real estate, and I expected her to be a firecracker, so I'm concerned about my investment in her. She gazes at me, fear in those doe eyes. I decide against saying anything to her in an open meeting, but make a mental note to speak to Virgil about her.

Virgil gathers his notes and twists his pen closed, stands and announces, "Have a great day, everyone," before leaving the room, his slippers flapping softly against argyle socks. Vanessa and I are the last to file out of the room. She turns to me as we enter the hallway and slows, so we walk together.

"I sensed that you wanted to say something to me earlier." Her voice nears a whisper in the empty hallway. "I know I haven't made a sale yet, but I have some things in the pipeline and some really good meetings on tap. It's just…"

She lowers her gaze to the carpet under our feet. My eyes follow and I frown at the well-worn toes of her heels. The leather around the toe box has puckered and they are dusty, like she pulled them out of storage and put them right on this morning.

"It's almost impossible to get meetings," she says. "At Carlyle Realty, I didn't sell to VIP clients. I'm trying to break into the wall that people keep around themselves, but I'm nobody."

I lay a hand on her slight shoulder, almost grimacing at the scratchy wool of her jacket. "First, Ms. Jackson, you're not nobody. You're Vanessa Jackson with Donovan Luxury Real Estate. I want you to wake up every day and tell yourself that. VIP clients are like your regular clients, only they have more money. I'd like you to meet with Virgil and see if we can grease some pathways for you, make things a little easier. He'll set up an appointment. Okay?"

I smile. She smiles. I feel the tension leaving her body as she does.

"One other thing," I tell her, my eye slipping down her slim frame, upon which her clothes appear to listlessly hang, then back up to her shoulder length hair which is pressed but seems frizzy, probably from the rain. "I'm approving a wardrobe advance for you. I'll send you a list of affordable consignment shops where you can buy quality pieces. You'll pay it back from your first commission. You sell million dollar luxury estates, not cookie cutter clapboard town homes. You work for Donovan Luxury Real Estate. People know our name. My name. You need to look the part."

I leave her in the hallway, staring down at her ill-fitting skirt, wool jacket and polyester blouse with the button hanging by a single thread. I head into my office and close the door. Logging into my computer, I check my email and almost smile when I see a message from Joseph. He wants to have lunch again today.

I ponder declining, but then figure… why not? I enjoy his company and he enjoys mine. I click the reply button and answer back, suggesting a restaurant within walking distance.

I respond to email and make a few phone calls before I receive a response from Joseph. Counter offer, he replies. City Grille. Great steaks.

I groan at the thought of a pedestrian steak restaurant, but agree to meet him. He asks if he can pick me up and I agree to that too.

A lunch date should excite me, but I can't help but think about Malcolm and wonder why I can't get this kind of attention from him. I'm used to getting the man I want. As far as I'm concerned, though, I haven't failed with my attempts to snag Malcolm. I'm just not working hard enough.

Jumping back into my workday, I leave my office to sit with Virgil at his desk. Donovan needs Vanessa to make a sale. He and I are going to make that happen.

CHAPTER TWENTY-TWO

enee

Nothing seems out of the ordinary when my eyes pop open. The steady drip of rain and the scent of water fills the air as I roll my head toward the digital clock on my nightstand. 4:54AM shines into the pre-dawn darkness. I sit up, pushing the covers back and swing my feet to the floor.

I like to get up a few minutes early, just so I don't feel like I'm at Daddy's beck and call, like I operate at his whim. I hop in the shower and take a quick one, hoping that the sound of water rushing through fifty-year-old pipes doesn't wake him. He's always disoriented in the morning and I have to make sure he doesn't go places he isn't supposed to be going.

I get out of the shower, my body wrapped in a bath sheet, my sopping wet curls dripping onto towel draped shoulders. I open my bedroom door and listen for the pitter patter of geriatric feet. Hearing none, I close the door and go back to getting dressed.

My phone buzzes against the wood of the nightstand. I stare at it from across the room. Who would send me a message at 5:15 AM?

Hope I'm not waking you. You said your dad gets up around this time.

Malcolm! Still in my towel, I sit on the edge of the bed and tap out a message in reply.

He just slept in today, but I'll forgive you. :)

I stare at my phone, waiting for a return text. Willing it to come. After a few seconds, I see he's typing a response.

Apologies, then. I'm glad you're so forgiving. I just wanted to say good morning to you.

I grin at the phone, then feel stupid, so I stop. Then I realize he can't see me, so why do I feel stupid?

Thank you, and good morning to you! I'd better get him up. He's just as grumpy when he gets too much sleep as when he doesn't get enough.

I need to get moving. Have a good day. I hope to speak with you later.

I set the phone back on the table and finish getting dressed. There is a noticeable pep to my step as I tiptoe past daddy's room and head downstairs to start breakfast. I notice the time when I finish his eggs—nearly six am. He's normally halfway to kicking my tail at a game of cards by now.

I climb the stairs and stop in front of the door to Daddy's room. It's not the room he and Mama shared. After she went into the hospital and never came home again, he never slept in that room, in their bed again. He's been in a guest room for over eight years now. I've thought about moving into their old room, but Daddy would probably have a fit.

I tap on the door a few times, softly. I don't hear anything in response, so I turn the knob and inch the door open. The room is slowly brightening with the hint of sun breaking over the horizon. Daddy is in the bed, sitting straight up. The strong punch of urine hits my nose.

"Hello?" He calls out, in a voice that I know is his but I don't recognize. "Lorraine? Is that you?"

I cross the room and snap on the lamp next to the bed. His eyes are wild and wide open, the little hair he has left jutting out at all angles around his head. He sleeps in a t-shirt and boxer shorts. Both are soaking wet.

"Daddy, it's Renee. Let's get you up and cleaned up, okay?" I reach for him but he cowers, shrinking away from me.

"Who are you? Where is Lorraine?"

"It's Renee, Daddy. Your daughter."

"I don't have a daughter!"

I sigh. I'm really not in the mood to bring my father thirty-six years forward. "Can I help you get cleaned up? You can't sit in that mess."

"Are you the nurse?"

"Sure." I roll my eyes and push the blankets back. Then I realize there is more than urine in the bed. My shoulders sag and, resolute, I mumble, "Yeah, I'm the nurse. Let's get moving."

I hate to do it but I leave the sheets for Jessie to take care of. She swears she doesn't mind, that it's part of her job and she's used to it. She's been a Dementia Care Assistant for most of her career, but I still hate to that to her.

It takes most of an hour to get Daddy to the shower, cleaned up, dried off and dressed. He would normally shower and dress himself, but today he's so disoriented that he lets me do it for him, standing silently and every so often asking for his wife. I don't answer.

I help him down the stairs and to the dining room table. I expect him to ask about the cards, but he doesn't. He's watching the morning news—well, staring at the TV when Jessie knocks, then walks in the front door.

"Who's that?" He shouts. "Lorraine? Lorraine!"

I poke my head around the corner and give Jessie the look that means we're in for it, today.

"Good mornin', Mistah Gladwell. I'm Jessie, your nurse."

Even more confused, his head whips around to me. "You said you was the nurse!"

Jessie looks at me and frowns. I shrug my shoulders and go

back to making a plate of toast and eggs with strawberry jelly. I set it on the table in front of him. He stares at it, then looks at me. Then looks at Jessie.

She sinks into the chair next to him, grabs a napkin and tucks it into the neck of his clean shirt, grabs his fork and begins to feed him. I can't watch.

On Mondays I go into the bookstore late. We stock shelves and set up displays, load the system with new inventory and adjust prices based on existing product. Normally Jessie would work a split shift and come back in the evening for a few hours so I can go in on Monday nights, but with Daddy needing assistance to do everything all day and Jessie taking care of the mess upstairs, she doesn't leave at her normal time.

I call in to work and Lexie answers. "Hey, Lex." I'm on the phone in the kitchen. Daddy is napping on the couch in the living room. "I'm not going to make it in tonight."

"Alright," she says, always a good sport. "I can stay and do the stocking. But can I have someone stay with me to help? I'll be here all night if not."

I agree to let her call in help. Before I hang up, she asks, "Are you okay? You sound…"

"Worn out?"

She chuckles. "I wasn't going to say it, but yeah. Is your dad okay?"

I nod, then realize she can't see me nodding. "He's okay. He's just…"

"Sick. I know. My grandma, remember?" I did vaguely remember Lexie telling me about her grandmother's bout with Dementia. She was older, though. I feel like this is different. Daddy is too young to act so old.

"He's not having a good day. I'm going to lose my help and I can't leave him alone."

"I get it. No problem. I'll cover you."

"Thanks, Lex." I breathe a small sigh of relief that I at least have a dependable manager. "I'll make it up to you."

"You sure will," she responds with light laughter. I know she'll collect on it, probably before Christmas. And I know I won't mind.

I hang up with Lexie and almost run into Jessie. She motions me into the laundry room, away from Daddy snoring on the couch. She looks serious and for a moment my worst fears surface. I'm so afraid she's going to quit that I start to cry and openly beg her to stay.

She stares at me, her pudgy face not unlike a grandmother who can't fathom why her grandchild is misbehaving. "Hush that up," she orders, tapping my shoulder. "You're in over your head. You got to do a few things differently around here, making some changes to help you and Bernard.

"He doesn't know who you are. He doesn't know where he is, that he's in his own house. He doesn't recognize his daughter, except to know that you look like his wife. The accidents are getting more frequent and now the man can't feed himself. He's moving stages and you act like you can't see it."

"I see it. I just don't know what to do about it."

One fist planted firmly on a hip, Jessie paces, which isn't easy because her hips are wide and the room is narrow. "He needs to be in a bedroom on the ground floor. He'll get more restless and he could start wandering and you're not going to contain him with a baby gate. You got a room down here with nothing but boxes in it."

My mother's things. He never let me get rid of them, so they've been sitting in a back room for eight years.

"Let's clean out that room and we'll move his bed into it." Jessie waves off my arguments about her hours. She's more concerned about her patient than about her pay, and that's why I love her.

We work through the stacks of boxes, transferring them to the garage. After Daddy wakes up, we take turns sitting with him, playing cards and watching TV while the other moves boxes, dusts surfaces and creates space.

In a few hours, we empty the room, wash and re-hang the curtains, dust the windowsills, vacuum the carpet. Together, we disassemble the bed upstairs and, piece by piece, cart the frame down the stairs. Daddy sits in his La Z Boy lounger and watches us like he's watching the most interesting show on TV.

We take the mattress from a bed in another room and set the old one out to go to the dump. The sheets from Daddy's bed go into the trash. They're too far gone and not worth the effort to wash.

Jessie puts clean sheets on the newly constructed bed. She makes her way around, tucking in all the sides and smoothing down the handmade quilt.

"So, if he has another accident, tonight…"

She straightens, anchoring a hand in the small of her back. "He has had no accidents today, so I think he just had a bad night. But just in case, you'll want to run to the store and get some adult diapers, a size medium should be fine. And see if you can find rubber sheets or a mattress pad."

A fog settles over my brain. I respond with appropriate phrases and head movements; I even grab my keys and my purse and walk out to the garage, but I sit in my car and stare at the wall, frozen.

This is the level of sickness that I have been dreading since I moved back to Atlanta. Going to the store to buy adult diapers. Monitoring when they need to be changed. Rubber sheets? I don't even know what those are.

This disease is taking my father, and not so slowly anymore. He's rapidly becoming less Bernard Gladwell and more a frightened, sixty-seven-year-old Alzheimer's patient. His personality is fading along with his memory. He doesn't even know me, so what little relationship we had is a blip in his past. Only I hold the memory.

And now I might have to put him in diapers. I can't change my father's diapers.

~

I'm hurting like I moved an entire house instead of a single room. Jessie and I got all of my father's clothes, shoes and a five drawer bureau out of his bedroom, down the steps and into the room on the main floor. While I was at the store, where I couldn't make myself buy adult diapers, let alone look for rubber sheets, I bought a baby monitor. I brought that home and plugged it in, put one end in his room and one end in mine, so I can hear him if he needs me.

Jessie leaves at seven. Daddy is in his pajamas and resting, watching an old black and white movie in the living room. I assure her I'll be fine until the morning and watch her pull out of the driveway.

I'm on edge all evening, like I'm expecting my father to lose his mind, go running around the house or something, but he's fine. Talking to the TV. Asking me if I'm Lorraine and where is the nurse that was here? When he yawns, I get him settled into bed in his new room. He doesn't seem to notice that it isn't the same room, and within a few minutes he's snoring.

I'm hoping I can snore soon, too. I turn off the lights in the house except near Daddy's room and the bathroom. At moderate to advanced stages of Dementia, the eyes play tricks, makes him think he's seeing things. Light removes hallucinations and imaginary holes. It also eliminates him not knowing where the bathroom is.

I trudge my way up the stairs, feeling every pound of my body weight as I climb to the top. I go straight to my room, close the door, and collapse onto the bed. The monitor is on and working. I hear Daddy snoring loud and clear. I reach over to turn the volume down and notice a missed text on my phone.

Hope I'm not disturbing you. Wanted to say hello.

I smile, and this time I don't feel stupid about it. A minor distraction is just what I need right now. I check the time and find that the message is a half hour old. I knew he was up early, so the chances of him still being awake are... well, as great as the chances I'm still awake.

Hello. Sorry to respond so late. It was a tough day with my dad.

Before I can change my mind, I hit 'send'.

A moment later, my screen shows the dots that mean he's responding. My heartbeat thumps in my ears as I realize he's awake. Or I woke him. Either way, he's answering my text.

It's no bother. I don't sleep much. Sorry to hear about your day. Is your dad okay?

He's okay. He's just oblivious. It's hard to watch.

Do you want to talk about it? I could call you.

I hesitate to answer yes. I'm so exhausted that I'm punchy and so emotional I might cry. But that voice... I would love to hear that deep, smooth baritone in my ear.

Okay. For a few minutes.

Within seconds, the phone rings in my hand. I slide my thumb across the screen to answer. "Hello."

"Hello," he says. "Thank you for letting me call. I don't type so well. Siri is the only reason my texts are legible."

I chuckle and lay back, kick off my shoes and point my toes to stretch my feet. They ache from climbing the stairs and standing all day. I don't get this much exercise at the bookstore. "I don't use it. I can't figure it out."

"What's to figure out? You press the button and talk into the phone."

"I guess. I just feel stupid, talking to the phone. So why are you awake right now?"

"Speaking with you. And a few minutes of paperwork I brought home from the office."

"Ah, you're one of those types?"

He laughs, his voice so deep the line vibrates. "I try not to be, but sometimes I can't help it. There's a lot to do, and until Brent and I hire some folks, there's no one else to do it. But never mind that..."

I hear some shuffling in the background and his breathing changes, like he stood up or sat down or something. "Tell me about your day. What's going on with your father?"

CHAPTER TWENTY-THREE

ebra

The first thing I do when I get to my office, after the kids are in classes and the front office is clear of students and the secretaries are tapping away at their computers, is sit down at my desk and pick up the phone.

"Superintendent Johnson's office. Sandy speaking."

"Hi, Sandy. This is Debra Macklin, over at Morningside. Is Bernice in? I just need a minute of her time."

"One moment, Ms. Macklin." Sandy puts me on hold and light rock music fills the space until the line picks up again.

"Debra? I'm surprised to hear from you. What's going on?"

"Hi, Bernice. I think there's been a development, and I hope you can help."

I speak with Bernice for a half hour, explaining the things I'd spoken with Kendra about over the weekend. My concerns are myriad—my staff undermining my authority in front of the students, the students talking to their parents about it; the parents planning an airing of grievances at the PTA meeting scheduled for Wednesday.

"I understand your concern, Debra. I'd be concerned, too. Is there any way that you could call the PTA President and request that—"

I'm laughing before she even finishes her sentence. "You know Charlotte Rogers doesn't like me. She's probably so giddy about this, she can't see straight. If I ask her to cancel the meeting, she'll laugh in my face. But… what if you called her?"

"Oh, Debra, I'm trying not to get involved here. People know that we are friends, personal friends. I feel like they'd think I'm taking your side."

"Aren't you? Aren't you supposed to take up for the teachers, for the staff?"

"My job is to look out for the children," she responds, adding coldness and a terse edge that she's never used with me before. "I sympathize with your situation. I truly do and I can use what powers I have to straighten this situation out, but you cannot run to your friend the Superintendent to fix your problems. If you want that meeting canceled or postponed, you're going to have to make the request. I don't care who doesn't like you. You're the Principal and that carries some weight."

I sigh as my shoulders drop. My head feels heavy and I'm suddenly so tired. I haven't slept soundly in such a long time, especially at Maxine's. All I want is to go to my house and get in my bed and sleep for days and days. And maybe if I just never woke up, everyone would be happy.

"Debra? Debra. Are you there?"

"Yeah." I sit up, snapping to attention. "I'm here. And I hear you. Thank you for speaking with me, Bernice."

"Sure. And if you need anything…" I don't hear the rest of the sentence because I hang up. What good does it do me to be friends with the Superintendent if she can't help me? Frustrated, I pound my fist against the desktop, just as my office door opens.

"Mrs. Macklin?" Phyllis Andrews, one of my Assistant Principals, is standing in the doorway with a uniformed member of the security team. "We have a situation."

I walk with them to Ms. Andrew's office a few doors down the hall. Seated in one of two chairs is a girl that looks like she should be over at the high school. Her face is mature, more womanly than child-like. The bangs of a badly sewn in weave hang over her face, but I can see her dark eyes glaring at me.

"Hello," I greet her, taking a seat in the chair near her. Her skirt is short—a dress code violation, but I'm not going to nitpick right now. Her thick, shapely legs are crossed at the knee. She's wearing ankle socks and platform Mary Jane's. Her blouse is a short-sleeved white button-up, but she's left enough buttons open to reveal ample cleavage. "I'm Mrs. Macklin–"

"I know who you are," she hurls at me. "You the one that's been fuckin' the Coach."

"Anetra!" Ms. Andrews barks sharply. "Language. And sit up. You're talking to the Principal of this school. If you want to remain a student here, she's the one that's going to save your hide."

The girl sits up, uncrosses her legs, then crosses them again the other way. She folds her arms over her chest and glares in my direction. She sighs loudly and rolls her eyes to the ceiling.

I turn to Phyllis. "What's going on? Why is she in your office and not in class?"

"Mr. Loren called me down to his office to retrieve her," the security officer explains. "He found her there waiting for him and she wouldn't leave."

I turn to the girl, Anetra, and ask her, "Did you need to speak with Mr. Loren about something?"

A hint of a smile crosses her lips. "I went down there to see if he wanted to have a little fun. Seemed like he was into breaking rules. If he'd fu–" She pauses, then starts again. "If he'd do it with you, then why wouldn't he do it with me?"

"Well, you're a student, for one."

"So? I'm more woman than these babies walking through these halls. Shit."

"Anetra–"

"Look, whatever, y'all!" She jumps from her seat, hovering over me. "I went down there to see if he wanted to have some fun. He ain't want to. He called you to come get me. You kickin' me outta here or what?"

I lift a hand in a show of surrender and as calmly as possible, tell her, "Sit down, Anetra. Let's just talk." She plops back into her chair and tosses one leg over the other. I glance at Phyllis and nod my head toward the door. She and the security guard step out, pulling the door shut behind them.

"Okay. Now that it's just us, I hope you can lose the attitude and the language. How old are you?"

"Fourteen," she mumbles.

"And what grade are you in?"

"Eighth, but I supposed to be at the high school."

"Okay, so why are you here?"

"'Cause I keep quittin'. My mama say I'm running with a bad crowd, skipping school and whatever. She send me up here to my Auntie's house, because the schools are better. Kids is the same everywhere though."

"And you went down to see Mr. Loren because you heard about what was going on between him and I. And you thought he would be interested in you because of that?"

Her soft expression retreats and the glare returns. "Don't act like you can't imagine it. I'm younger and prettier." I disagree with the prettier part, but on the youth angle, she has me beat.

She sucks her teeth and shrugs a shoulder. "Anyway. My boyfriend don't have no car and ain't no metro train up here. It take him all day to come up and see me and he real lazy, so I ain't seen him in a while. I be lonely and stuff. And Mr. Loren, he kinda reminds me of Duke, you know? That's my man's name."

"Duke?"

"Yeah. His daddy name him Ducati, after that motorbike." She shakes her head. "I think that's a girl's name, but..." Anetra sucks her teeth again and levels her gaze at me.

"You know that it's wrong to approach a teacher for sex, correct? And it would be wrong for him to agree to it?"

"Yeah. But—"

"But nothing. What happened between Mr. Loren and me is our business. And it has no bearing on the laws of this state and the regulations at this school. Now tell me, if you get kicked out of Morningside, where do you go next?"

She stares at the floor before she mumbles an answer. "Mama say she gonna send me away to some youth camp for bad kids. They wear prison uniforms and work all day and don't get to see nobody until they're cured of bad behavior."

"Do you really think she'd send you there?"

She shakes her head slightly, then shrugs a shoulder. "I don't know. I didn't think she'd send me up here and she did, so I guess she carry out her threats."

"Do you want to stay at Morningside, Anetra? Or are you trying to get kicked out so you can drop out and be with your boyfriend? Because as much as I care about your education, I won't fight you. If you don't want to be here, I don't want you here. We can find an alternative school. I can talk to your Aunt and your mom…"

"Naw," she interrupts. "I don't want you talking to nobody, saying nothing. I got to finish out this year. When I can get a job, maybe I quit."

Well, it's a start, I think. And then I think how crazy it is that I consider an intention to stay in school until one is old enough to work instead to be a good start.

Anetra and I come to a tenuous agreement. She'll stay out of trouble and away from Mr. Loren, and I won't kick her out. And we won't tell her Aunt or her mother about today's episode if she keeps her nose clean.

"Think about it," I tell her, as we're walking out of Ms. Andrews' office. "It's just a couple of weeks until Christmas. You get two weeks off and you can see Duke. And only five months until you're out of Morningside and done with us. You can hang in that long, can't you?"

Anetra nods, heaving her book bag onto her shoulder. "I can do that. Thanks, Mrs. Macklin."

"You're welcome. Now button that blouse and pull that skirt down. Tomorrow I want to see you in clothes that don't violate my dress code."

She makes her way down the hall and out of the office. I turn to Phyllis and the security guard, nod, and walk back to my office.

Back at my desk, I pick up the phone and ring one of the secretaries. "Hi, could you get me the PTA President's phone number? Yes, Charlotte. Email it to me? Thanks."

I hang up and sit back in my chair. I feel so much pressure in my chest, it's like an elephant is sitting on me. The PTA discussing this issue is going to be like a room full of Anetra's, people who think they can get away with anything because I did it first. I broke the rules. I disregarded policy. I put people's careers in jeopardy.

My computer dings; a new email has arrived. Charlotte Rogers' phone number is staring at me, taunting me. Daring me to call her.

I pick up the phone, dial half of the number, but set the handset back down as the bell rings, reverberating through the walls. The loud sounds of children and lockers and teachers fill the air. My door opens and another Assistant Principal has a question. A teacher drops off a form and stays to chat for a minute. The janitor stops in to chit chat and by the way, have I thought about ordering such and so for the boy's bathroom?

I decide to call her after lunch. Maybe.

CHAPTER TWENTY-FOUR

enee

Daddy adjusted so well to being downstairs. I hate that it took us this long to make the change. He still wakes up early, but now he shuffles to the bathroom and sits in the living room in his lounger until I come downstairs and make him some breakfast. Sometimes he can turn on the TV and change the channel. Sometimes I find him just staring at the TV, then he seems surprised when it comes on, suddenly. He turns around and I'm standing there, remote in hand.

He still doesn't know me. He thinks I'm the nurse, The Small One. He calls Jessie the Big One. About once a day he calls me Lorraine and when I tell him I'm her daughter, he says that's nice.

Things with Malcolm are heating up nicely. We text each other a few times a day. We've talked a few times on the phone. He sent over some recommendations for security features I could add to the shop, so we've spent some time discussing that.

And last night, we had another date.

I wasn't planning on going out. I've been such a hermit since the change with Daddy. Malcolm's event ended early, and he stopped by the bookstore on his way home and asked if I was up for a tour. I chuckled and told him it depended on what kind of tour he was looking for. I surprised myself, being so coy. It's not really my personality. Maybe Maxine is rubbing off on me in a good way.

I went home after my shift, talked Jessie into staying a few hours and changed into jeans, a soft sweater and boots. I met Malcolm at his building and we drove to a tiny hole-in-the-wall Ethiopian restaurant off of Buford Highway, arguably Atlanta's home for ethnic eats. The atmosphere inside was charming and traditional. Rhythmic music wafted from speakers above; bold, red colors covered the walls and decadent silk draperies hung over the windows. Malcolm and I shared a cozy table in a quiet corner.

"I haven't had Ethiopian since I left D.C." He handed me a few folds of flat bread. I took them, tore off a small piece to taste, surprised to find it toasty and flavorful. "I've really missed it. One of my recruits was telling me about this place. He said I should try it."

"I have never had Ethiopian. And you've dragged me here to eat things called..." I squinted at the menu. "Tibs?"

He laughed at my plain pronunciation. "It's beef, lean. Cooked with spices, served with garlic, tomato and onion."

"Interesting." I then flipped the menu over. "I'll trust you on this one."

We had a great time, talking and laughing, swapping stories about the week. Malcolm's event went really well, everything fell into place as it should. Gladwell is doing just fine. With the Christmas season approaching, book sales are up and I have more requests to hold events in our space than I think I've ever had before. And Daddy is stable, for the moment.

"You think you'll be able to keep him at home?" Malcolm asked, on the way back to his place.

"I don't know. Things seem okay for now. I made myself buy

adult diapers. I really don't want to have to use them. When it gets to that point, I'll have to reconsider."

"Do you want to keep him at home?"

Now that's the million dollar question. A few months ago I would have told anyone that my goal was to put my father in a home, sell the bookstore and the house and hightail it back to Philly, but... something funny happened along the way. I started enjoying owning a bookstore. My best friends became my best friends again. And I met this very nice man who, against all odds and beyond my understanding, enjoys my company. My previous goals aren't my goals anymore, so I don't know what I want. Not anymore.

"Most days I'm just trying to make it to the next day."

"I understand that." Malcolm pulled into his condo parking garage and eased the Denali into its usual spot. "You should come up for a few minutes. I have a great bottle of wine I've been waiting to open."

I checked my watch, noting the time. It was only eight thirty, but Jessie was waiting. "It's not that I don't want to. It's just... I should really get back–"

My words fell away when he leaned over the center console and his lips brushed over mine, ever so briefly. They were as soft and plump as I remembered from our first brief kiss.

"I'd like to spend a few more minutes with you."

I gulped back any argument I might have tried to come up with and nodded. He got out of the truck and met me on my side, tucked my hand into his as he walked through the garage to the interior elevator. We stepped inside and he pressed the number '4'. The doors closed, and the cube climbed for a few seconds before the bell sounded and the doors opened again.

"Wow, almost door-to-door service," I remarked as I followed him down a brightly lit hallway dotted with closed doors. It seemed quiet, and then I remembered. It's Friday night in down-town Decatur. Most people are out for the evening.

"Yes, that's a nice perk. I don't have to see the lobby unless I want to." He inserted a brushed gold key into one lock and then another.

I rubbed my palms together, watching him unlock his door. "I can't wait to see what kind of system a security expert has in his own home."

He laughed. "Well, remember though, I'm the muscle. Brent is the systems man." He swung the door open and waved me inside ahead of him. "Aside from a deadbolt and the standard ADT system, I have nothing impressive here."

I feigned disappointment. "Aw, I thought I was going to see something like Mission: Impossible in here."

"Maybe my next place," he said, still laughing. "Come on in. Make yourself at home." The front door opened into a small entryway which led to the kitchen and just past that, the open space of the dining room and living room.

Most of his furniture was eclectic and urban–a deep red microfiber couch and a mustard yellow sitting chair and end tables painted a glossy black. The prints on the wall were framed posters or African Art pieces. Then there was this... oversized dark wood behemoth with white cushioned chairs.

"Did you bring this table with you?"

I heard rustling in the kitchen—drawers opening and closing, the sound of glass tinkling against glass. Malcolm came around the corner holding an open bottle of wine in one hand and two stemless wine glasses nestled in the other. He nodded us over to the living room where he set the drinks on the table. I settled in next to him and let him pour.

He handed me a glass. I took it, and after waiting for him to pour himself a glass, lifted mine in toast and took a sip. I have never been much of a wine drinker, let alone red wine, but the taste wasn't too bad. A hint of sweet, but not overpowering. It was fragrant and a deep, bold red.

"That table was a gift from Maxine," he said, just as I took a second sip. I laughed but forgot I was swallowing, so I inhaled and coughed, then panicked because I couldn't breathe. He took the glass from me and rubbed and pat my back until the coughing fit subsided.

"You couldn't wait until after I'd swallowed to tell me that? Why on earth did Maxine give you a table?"

He sipped his glass of wine, sinking into the couch, his long legs stretched under the coffee table, the collar of his dress shirt unbuttoned enough to reveal a hint of curly chest hair.

"I woke up one morning to a phone call from this guy. He said he had a delivery for me. I tried to convince him it was a mistake, but he had my name and address. I called the store and checked on it; they said it was paid for by Maxine Donovan. When I called her about it, she sounded so excited."

He paused, took another sip, then let his eyes wander over to the table and back to mine. "So, I let them in and they put it together."

"It's a big table," I said, glancing at the table again and back to him. "A really big table."

"I think of it as a metaphor."

"For?"

"Maxine. How she likes to throw her weight around. Make herself noticeable. Larger than life, too big for a room. Like the table."

I nodded. Truer words have never been spoken about my friend Maxine. "She's always been that way."

"She likes for people, especially men, to know her power. What she can do with her name or her money. She tries hard."

"Mmmm." I mused, sipping more wine. I'm feeling loose, so I relaxed against the soft fibers of the couch. We were close, so close that felt the heat radiating from his thigh, which lightly brushed mine. "She has a big heart, though."

Malcolm lifted an arm and dropped it around my shoulder. I leaned in so I was up against him. He felt solid, like a wall. It was a comfort to be wrapped in so much strength. "How about you?" He asked. "Is your heart big?"

"My heart is big. It's my wallet that isn't. That's the difference between me and Max."

"I think there are a few more differences between you and Maxine."

The tone of his voice, the softness and tenderness in his words made me lift my face to his. "You're right. There are vast differences between us. She's New York stylish and I'm homegrown comfortable. She's a well off business owner and I'm just trying to make ends meet. She's–"

"Not someone I'm interested in," he said, cutting me off. "I'm impressed by her business acumen, but I'm interested in homegrown Renee. What makes her tick?"

"I don't know why you'd be interested in me when you could have someone like Max. In fact, you could have Max."

"I don't doubt that. If I wanted Max, I would be with her. What if I want you?"

I was tempted to pinch myself to see if I was having one of those vivid dreams, or was I living in this moment? Before I could wake myself, Malcolm dipped his head and brushed his lips across mine, gently at first. And then again with more pressure, lingering, pressing. He inhaled deeply. The most beautiful groan rolled from his lips.

"You taste good," he mumbled against my lips. I could only hum and murmur in response. And hope he wanted to kiss me some more. My heartbeat pounded in my ears when his lips landed on mine again, this time his tongue gently teasing and prodding my mouth open. I succumbed; the kiss deepened as our tongues swirled around each other. Malcolm tipped his head one way and another, changing his method of attack every few moments, sending me spinning higher each time. For the first time in a very long time, my body was responding to a man—his touch, his sounds, and the way he made me feel, like an itch was being scratched and I couldn't get enough.

Malcolm moved closer to me, then tucked his hand behind my head and gently pushed. I willingly tipped over, sprawling over the wide cushion. He hovered above me, then lowered, fitting between my legs and nestling his body weight top of me. My arms circled his neck, then rested on his broad shoulders as my fingers rubbed the back of his head, smoothing down the thin layer of hair.

He made the most pleasured, enjoyable sounds as he kissed me, then tipped his head to dot kisses along my chin, down my neck. His breath was hot, but his lips were cool against my skin as he licked the open area around the collar of my sweater.

"I wish you were wearing something more accessible."

"Malcolm…."

Again, he moaned. I felt the rumble in his chest. And the growing lump against my thigh. It took every bit of will in my body to not buck my hips.

"Malcolm," I tried again. "I can't. I want to. I really want to. But…"

He lifted his head and gazed at me with an expression that I expected to be frustration but was instead understanding. "I'll stop if you really want me to. Do you really want me to?"

I almost laughed at the absurdity of that question, because what I wanted was for him to pick me up, throw me over his shoulder and cart me to his bedroom, where I hoped there was an enormous bed that we could explore together. What I wanted was to be naked and under him. What I wanted was my first orgasm that wasn't self-induced in four years. What I wanted most of all was to have my back blown all the way out.

Did I really want him to stop? Hell no.

But Daddy. And Jessie. And I hardly knew him. And to be honest, I was still stinging from Marcus. I wanted no regrets.

I sat up, pushing against him. He didn't offer resistance, instead moving to the side to help me sit up. "I should go. Thank you for the wine. It really was great."

Malcolm seemed to pout, sitting nearly a cushion away, his elbows on his knees, fingers woven together. "You don't have to go. We can just talk. I won't try anything else."

I laughed, then grabbed the strap of my purse and stood. I was shaky, a little uneasy on my feet. "See, that's the problem. If I stay, I'll want to do more than talk. And I'll want you to try everything else."

He smiled, nodding as he stood. "I guess I hope that means we'll get together again soon. And do more than talk."

"I hope so," I said, then stretched up onto my toes to hug him. I took a chance and kissed him on the lips. He responded with a moan that made me cut the kiss off, step back and practically run to the door.

"I'll walk you to your car," he said, grabbing his keys from the counter where he'd left them.

"No, no. It's unnecessary. I'm parked right out front."

"Renee, it's no trouble, I want to—"

"Malcolm." I paused, kissed him again, and stepped into the hallway. "I find you very attractive. And I really, really want to stay here with you. I am making myself leave because I need to see about my dad. His nurse needs to go home. I cannot be selfish though I really want to be. The least you can do is stay here and don't tempt me. Okay?"

I turned on my heels and walked down the hall to the elevator, pressed the down button and waited for the doors to open.

"Renee." I turned my head to see Malcolm standing in the hallway outside his apartment. "I learned, when taking care of my mother that I didn't have to sacrifice being happy to be a good son. You, making yourself happy, doing something you want to do isn't a sacrifice you have to make. You're not selfish if you give in to pleasure. I know enough about you to know that you could never be a bad daughter."

The elevator arrived, the door opened, but I was rooted in place. I didn't move until he said, "You'd better catch that elevator. It's popular at night," and went back inside his apartment. I pushed the strap of my purse onto my shoulder and caught the doors just as they were closing.

I slept like a baby, dreaming of Malcolm all night long. That smooth, dark skin. Those big, soft lips. His deep brown eyes, how the flecks in them seem to change depending on what he's talking about. His body—oh, man, is he a man! There's not an inch of him that is scrawny or slight. He's built solidly thick. Manly. I hated to wake up. I'd sleep all the time except that in the waking world, he exists.

And if last night was any indication, I'll be seeing him again soon.

I'm in an excellent mood, moving around the kitchen, making Daddy's breakfast. He watches a movie from his lounger while I work. When breakfast is ready and on the table, I lead him to his chair.

I grab two cloth napkins from the stack I've been keeping in the drawer in Mama's china hutch, tuck one into the collar of his shirt and spread one across his lap, then sit next to him and pick up his fork.

Daddy can handle bacon and toast and most finger food. Holding a fork, wielding a spoon or a knife is a skill he can't seem to manage anymore. I've gotten used to feeding him his eggs and letting him feed the rest to himself.

"Alright, Daddy. You ready to eat?" I scoop some eggs onto the fork and guide them to his mouth. His mouth opens and closes around the fork. He chews, watching me.

"Where's the big nurse?" He asks, his mouth full of food.

"Jessie will be here in about an hour." He grunts, nodding. I scoop more eggs into his mouth. He chews slowly and quietly, staring into space. "What are you thinking about Daddy?"

His head turns ever so slowly and the look in his eye changes. "Are you Lorraine?"

I give him a warm smile, but shake my head. "Lorraine was my mother."

"You look like Lorraine."

I laugh, loading up another forkful of eggs. "You say that every day."

"Lorraine was your mother?" He asks, a near mouthful of egg

dropping onto the napkin in his lap- the exact reason I started using two napkins.

"Mmm hm. You've got bacon." I point to his plate, where he seems to have just noticed that there is bacon and toast there. He picks up a piece of bacon and guides it to his mouth while I grab the napkin from his lap and shake off the discarded egg and spread it over his lap again.

"Lorraine was my wife."

"I know. You've told me. She was a good woman." I gaze at him, wondering if he's going to make the connection.

"Lorraine died." He takes another bite of bacon and chews it, his eyes moving back to that faraway place. He doesn't quite seem with me today. But he remembers that his wife died. "She had a daughter?"

"Yes, she did." I smile at him, then reach over to brush my fingers through the bush of gray hair atop his head. I watch him, content in his own world of bacon and toast and whatever thoughts happen to be rolling through his mind.

At ten, Jessie walks through the front door, lugging her ever-present giant black leather bag and wearing her usual uniform of khaki slacks and a short-sleeved polo shirt. She drops the bag near the front door and greets Daddy, who has moved back to his lounger and is watching Guess Who's Coming to Dinner with Sidney Poitier.

"Hello there, Mistah Gladwell," Jessie says, giving his arm a pat as she passes him. He grunts in response, which is normal for him. I'm seated at the table, going over the bills and monitoring Daddy. "How's he doing today?"

"Good, so far. He remembers that Lorraine had a daughter. And he knows Lorraine was my mother. I don't think he's made the connection from me to him."

"It might come to him. What time you leavin' for brunch with your girlfriends?"

I check my watch, then jump in surprise, gather the bills and slide them into the folder where I keep the current payables. I shove them back into the drawer and grab my purse, which I'd hung on the back of my chair. "Five minutes ago. He's already had breakfast and his morning meds. He could use some water, I'm sure. Everything's on schedule. Have fun."

She waves me off and as I close the door; I hear her say something to Daddy about the movie.

It only takes me a few minutes to get to Ruby's. Debra's car is front and center and Maxine's car is in its usual spot in the corner of the lot, far away from anyone else. The December morning is chilly, so I slide my arms into a sweater as I walk through the gravel covered parking lot to the front door of Ruby's.

Inside, the place is packed. Scents of waffles and pancakes, sausage and fried chicken mix in the air. The din of patrons talking and laughing, waitresses shouting orders to the cooks and the cooks responding, plus the soul music coming through the speakers overhead makes the small café loud.

I don't see Debra and Maxine waiting for me at the bench, so I walk through the restaurant to our usual table and find them there, already seated, water already poured and silverware already set.

"Speak of the angel," says Debra, sliding her phone into her purse. "I was just about to call you. I thought maybe Daddy was giving you fits today."

I bend to tap her cheek with mine, circle the table and do the same to Maxine, then slide into the booth in front of the spot set for me. "I'm so sorry I'm late. Daddy is fine, today. I was going through the bills and lost track of time." It's hot in the café, so I peel off the sweater again. "How are you ladies? Anything new? Debra?"

Debra lifts her glass of water and takes a long sip through the straw and sets it back into place. "I'm okay," she answers. I'm not convinced. She's trying to be peppy, our usual upbeat Debra, but she looks tired. Wrung out.

"You don't look okay."

Debra's eyes drop to her lap and her shoulders sag. It must be something terrible.

"The PTA is trying to get Debra fired," Maxine volunteers. Debra's head jerks up and after a moment of those two shooting fire at each other, her expression softens. Maxine continues, "Debra tried to have the meeting canceled last week, but the PTA President is a heinous bitch that hates Debra and wants nothing more than to publicly humiliate her. So they had the meeting anyway and brought up the situation with the gym teacher. Blew things all out of proportion, I felt. Then they opened the floor to comments and all these parents got up to give speeches about how they give a rip what the Principal does in her free time." She rolls her eyes and reaches for her glass of water, taking a dainty sip.

"I had a few people in my corner, but overwhelmingly that room was angry with me. They've always had it out for me. I wasn't the candidate they wanted to take the job at Morningside."

"I remember you said something about that. They expected the job to go to someone else."

Maxine hums, her lips pursed. "Somebody they could control. They're so pissed that Debra got the job and that the school is flourishing since she took over. Test scores are up, kids are well adjusted and seem happy to be there, teachers are… teaching."

Debra nods. "I can't do a good enough job. This is exactly what they needed to get rid of me."

"Can they do that, though? Can they get rid of you?"

"They can try," Debra answers, with a sad expression. "And they are trying. They have summoned me to appear before the school board."

"You didn't tell me that!" Maxine exclaims, a little too loudly. "You're going before the school board? When?"

"I don't have a date yet. The district will be on winter break through the end of December, then it's the new semester, so I am guessing mid- January."

"Man, they really have it in for you," I tell Debra. "Can the school board fire you?"

"They can make Bernice fire me." She sucks in her lips in like she's trying not to cry.

"Of course, we aren't just going to assume that. We're going to hope for the best and fight. Right?" Maxine reaches across the table, palm up. Debra slides her palm across Max's and tightens her grip. At our last brunch, Max called Debra a whore and Debra ran out crying. They sure seem to be close now.

"So what else is up? Are you still staying with Max?"

Debra shakes her head and sighs, long and loud. "I'm moving tomorrow. I found a room to rent; it's furnished, month to month. Not that I haven't appreciated Maxine–" She squeezed Max's hand again. "But I need to be close to work and my daughter. And until I know what's going on with Willard, I don't want to make any permanent changes."

Our waitress, an unfamiliar girl, comes to take our order, but frowns that we don't have menus. About every six months we have to train a new waiter or waitress or busboy. We come here often. We always sit at this table. We always order the same thing. Maxine always gets a Perrier and ice. We always get one tab and we take turns paying.

Once the waitress is up to speed and has taken our orders, I pick up the conversation again. "Has he filed for divorce? Separation? Anything?"

Debra shakes her head, no. "We don't speak. I email him about seeing Kendra and remind him of anything important coming up. He does the same. If I call the house, I get Kendra or the voicemail."

"How is Kendra doing?"

"She's alright," Debra says, after a few thoughtful moments. "It's nice that I'm there at the school, with her teachers. I can see her grades and her progress, and she's still doing well. I'm sure the kids are talking about the... situation... but she seems to do alright."

She sips more water. "The problem is the teachers. Gossiping old bats with nothing better to do than talk shit about me. Kendra hears it and that stuff bothers her."

"It's a shame she has to be subjected to that, like they don't know she's your daughter."

"It's despicable behavior. I don't know how to address it, so I haven't. I hope it's died down some. I don't want her in the middle of this. I wish–" Debra bites her bottom lip, rubs the back of her neck with one hand and clutches a small silver chain at her throat. It was a gift from Willard a few years ago. "If I could go back in time..."

"Would you still have the affair?" asks Maxine.

Much to my surprise, she shrugs a shoulder and shyly admits, "I would love to say no, knowing what I know now. I wish my job and my kid wasn't all wrapped up in this. I think I wish I could go back in time and cut it off before we got caught. I don't know that I'd wish I'd never had an affair. David showed me some things."

Maxine snorts and says, "I bet he did."

"I don't mean that the way you're taking it," says Debra, but she's laughing. "I figured out a lot of things by being with someone else. And no matter what happens with me and Willard, I know I can't go back to the same marriage I had before. I'm at fault here. The mistake was mine. But our marriage, its safekeeping, was our responsibility, and we failed it, Willard and me."

"But I always thought you guys had a great marriage, a good relationship," I tell Debra. "You've always talked about how good you guys are together."

Debra hunches her shoulders, bringing her hands up in a helpless gesture. "And yet I had an affair. On the surface, it was good, but a marriage is so much more than what you see. It's like an iceberg—what you need to be concerned about is the stuff no one else can see. Statistically, women cheat for emotional reasons. I love my husband. I'm sure he loves me. But he wasn't there. And eventually neither was I."

Brunch arrives, and we're back to our usual orders—shrimp and grits for me, chicken and waffles for Max and an omelet for Debra. We dig into our food and eat in silence for a few minutes, both savoring the food and reviewing the current conversation.

"Daddy and I saw Ruby here a few weeks ago."

Max's eyebrows shoot up, but her eyes don't leave her plate where she is busily dicing chicken into bite-sized pieces. "The Ruby?"

"The Ruby. She was here yelling at Richard, as usual. It was the day I took Daddy up to the cemetery. I brought him here for lunch; she even cooked for us."

"That's nice that he got to see Ruby before…" Debra's sentence trails off, but I know what she's almost saying. Before he got worse and most of his memory seems to have been wiped clean.

"Yeah, it was nice. His long-term memory seems more reliable. He remembers his wife. We've been going over the fact that Lorraine was my mother, and Lorraine was his wife. It's like he's trying to make the connection in his mind. I'm hoping his brain will let him remember that he has a daughter. I haven't heard…"

I'm suddenly choked up and struggle to finish my sentence. "I haven't heard him say my name in a really long time."

I'm surprisingly emotional. I thought I had a handle on these changes, but the hurt in my heart, the tears rolling down my cheeks and the sobs that sit at the back of my throat tell me differently. I've just been shoving it down. Doing what I have to do, because I have to do it.

I'm surrounded on both sides in the booth. Maxine smells classy and decadent like always, the soft cashmere of her sweater so comforting when she wraps her arms around me. Debra smells like coconut oil and everything about way she rubs my back and tells me things are going to be alright makes me a little jealous of Kendra.

Sometimes… sometimes I really miss Mama. She made everything seem like it was going to be alright. I need to feel her warm hand on my back and her voice in my ear, telling me that everything will be alright.

When my moment passes, I'm mildly embarrassed and thankful that we're tucked away from most of the restaurant. I sniffle and wipe my face, erase the tear tracks. And try to laugh about it. "Is there some new rule that one of us has to break down at brunch, now?"

Both Debra and Max slide back to their seats and go back to their meals like I didn't just fall apart for five minutes. They laugh and joke, lightening the mood as we finish our time together. We talk about Christmas plans—Daddy and I will celebrate with Jessie, likely. She loves to cook for us on Christmas, and Daddy and I love to eat it. Maxine will be with Inell and her new husband.

Debra mumbles something about spending Christmas Eve with Kendra, then Willard was taking her to visit his parents, who live two hours north in Chattanooga. Kendra spent Thanksgiving with Debra at her parent's home in Stone Mountain, about twenty minutes south of town. She won't talk about it, but I got the impression that it was awkward.

"You're more than welcome to come over for dinner on Christmas," I tell her. "You know Jessie goes off on Christmas dinner. There will be plenty, and she'd love to see you. And Daddy, too. He might recognize your face, just not know your name."

Debra laughs. "Thanks, I appreciate the offer, but I'll probably end up at my folks' place again. My brothers and sisters come home for Christmas. I'm not looking forward to updating them about my marriage, but..." She shrugs. "Things are just how they are. I can't make them any better. Not on my own."

"Amen," Maxine and I agree and laugh. The check comes, and it's my turn to pay. I slide my debit card into the slot and hand it to the waitress. When she brings it back, I sign the slip and we file out of the restaurant, waving to staff we've known for many years.

Debra stops at her car and gets in, starts it up and backs out of the parking lot. Maxine is tip toeing through the gravel lot in four-inch stiletto boots. She's smiling and I recognize the tone she uses when she's talking to a man—sultry but trying hard to be nonchalant.

I get into my car, slip on my shades and start it up. I have to go by the bookstore for a few minutes and pick up the bank deposit and, since I have Jessie for a few more hours, maybe I can stop and see Malcolm.

Maxine passes me in the Maserati. The sun roof is open and I can hear her laughing. She waves as the engine whines and she is gone. She is definitely talking to a man.

"Okay, then. I don't feel bad about liking Malcolm. Not bad at all."

CHAPTER TWENTY-FIVE

ebra

My home-for-the-moment is cute, as far as rooms go. It's spacious and bright, with its own full bathroom. My landlord is a woman who I'd guess to be in her sixties, looking to make a little extra money so she rents out her guest bedroom on a short term, month-to-month basis. I met her at Fresh Market. She was posting a notice on the Bulletin Board.

I hadn't been looking for a place, not since that nightmarish tour of weekly rentals that looked like some place that Jason guy from Friday the 13th might frequent. Dirty carpets, smelly refrigerators, curtains that stank like cigarette smoke and bedding... I don't even want to think about the bedding. I met Roberta at just the right time; right when I'd resigned myself to living with Max for at least a few weeks.

She is tall, her dancer's body lithe, graceful and elegant, her silver hair a batch of spun silk against olive skin. She's Italian, a grandmother, and a retired schoolteacher. When I told her who I was and where I work, she smiled so brightly I thought she might burst. She insisted that we sit down and have a cup of tea and a chat. The next evening, she invited me to stop by her home, where we had more tea. And we had more chats.

I ended up telling her everything. I can't help myself. I want to confess to everyone all the time, about the things I've done, the lives I'm ruining at right this very moment. When people laud me and tell me what a superb job I'm doing at Morningside, I want to argue with them. "But there were budget shortfalls last year. And we almost had no food on the first day of school this year. And I slept with my Athletics Director and now my husband hates me and they might fire me over it."

I expected Roberta to shrink back, maybe withdraw her offer of a place to stay, but she didn't. Her eyes slid closed; she pursed her lips and inhaled deeply. Then opened her eyes and said, "Well then, you'll need a place of quiet and comfort while you work through your ordeal. Let me know when you want to move in and I'll have an agreement drawn up and a key ready for you when you arrive."

In my temporary bedroom, I am perched on the edge of a queen sized bed with crisp white linens and a colorful quilt. Long draperies cover the windows and pool on the floor, giving the room a regal touch. There's a mirrored dresser, a chest of drawers and a walk-in closet. I'm only carting a few things around with me; most of my belongings are still at home. I refuse to pack everything up and move it out. Willard hasn't brought up the fact that I haven't. When I see Kendra on Wednesdays, I bring a few things and switch a few things out, but I leave everything in its place. As far as I can tell, Willard still doesn't sleep in our bedroom.

The thought of Kendra makes me glance at my watch. She's supposed to stop by and we're going to lunch. I have a few minutes, though, so I pinch off my shoes, lean back against the firm pillows and sink into the firm gentility of the bed.

I have never felt so tired. Worn down. Beat up. I'm trying my hardest to keep it together, to look like I've got everything under control, but I feel my life beginning to twist like a tornado, spiraling out of control into an area that is unknown and scary as hell. A place where no one can tell me what happens, when it happens, how long it will last. My greatest fear is that unknown place. I'm underwater, drowning, kicking like mad but still sinking.

I'm scared. Of everything. Of losing everything.

Willard's ears must have been burning yesterday, when Renee asked if he'd filed for divorce or separation. I received an email yesterday that answered that question. He'd printed out paperwork and filled it in. But we both have to sign it and we have to come to an agreement about the care of our child. The body of the email was short, to the point. Willard was never one to linger over email, since he didn't type well, but this note seemed terse and clipped.

Georgia law dictates that we must be legally separated for sixty days before they can grant a divorce. I have attached the forms necessary to file for legal separation. Sign them, then scan and email them to me so I can file it.

-Willard

I was tempted to delete the email and pretend I never received it. It would be childish and unnecessarily drag this situation past civil and into ugly. Instead of downloading, printing and signing the forms, I pressed the arrow to reply.

Willard,

I understand your desire to process this situation with speed and without drama. However, I think 22 years deserves more than an email. Do you not even want to talk to me? Yell at me? Ask me why? Do you even wonder why? Do you think any of this is possibly your fault?

Are you ready to throw away something you've been a part of since we were 14?

I'm not signing these. Not until we talk.

-*Debra*

This morning, Willard tossed the ball back to me.

As far as I'm concerned, this marriage was over the moment you consid-ered sleeping next to another man. I'm tying up loose ends. Our daughter will bring hard copies of the agreement with her this afternoon. I advise you to sign them and let her and I get on with our lives, and you can resume the life you seem to crave.

-*Willard*

I laughed aloud when I read it. He must sit up at night thinking of snide comments and witty retorts. When I ask to talk to him, he insists that we have nothing to talk about, that I have made all the decisions for us. I've never seen him so bitter, so cutting, so... angry. I don't think I've ever seen Willard so angry.

There's a light tap-tap at the bedroom door. I shoot up, smoothing the wrinkles out of the quilt before moving across the room to open it. Roberta stands in the door frame, an arm around Kendra.

"I didn't even need her to tell me she was your daughter," says Roberta, beaming down at Kendra. "She looks so much like you, I imagined that you planted her in the yard and she grew like a delightful sunflower."

"Something like that," I say, reaching for Kendra and gathering her into my arms when she steps forward. "Thank you so much, Roberta. I must not have heard the door."

She gives a little three fingered wave to Kendra and walks away, her steps quiet. I hear her bedroom door close with a snick, the blare of the TV behind it betraying her afternoon habit of watching The Golden Girls.

"Weird lady, mom." Kendra hands me a manila envelope. It is

sealed, with my name scrawled across the front in Willard's chicken scratch. "Dad said to give this to you. He said you know what it is and I am to bring the finished product home."

I roll my eyes at his instruction, then regret doing so in front of Kendra. It's hard staying impartial when he's being such a dick. I toss the envelope on the bed. "Thank you. I'll talk to him about those separately. There are some things we need to talk about before I sign them."

"Are they... are they divorce papers?" She ends her question in a whisper, like someone might stand around, listening.

"No, honey. They aren't divorce papers." The sag of relief in her shoulders breaks my heart. I grab my purse from its spot on the dresser and try to brighten up. "So this is my room. It's cute, isn't it?"

Kendra glances around and nods, then shrugs a shoulder. "Not like your room at home. But it's okay. For now."

I nod in agreement, toss my arm over her shoulder and guide her out of the room. "Yeah. For now."

I can't take another meal at Bojangles, so I spring for Burger Palace, opting for the turkey burger and sweet potato fries. Kendra orders a thick, juicy cheeseburger with bacon and a side of chili cheese fries. How she maintains her lithe figure is beyond me. Kendra eats more than Willard and I combined some days.

"Some of my friends said the PTA meeting was turned up," says Kendra, her mouth full of chili and fried potato. She shoves in another French fry.

"Don't talk with your mouth full. And are you not eating at home? Why are you so hungry?" Kendra downs another chili covered French fry, then picks up her burger and takes a bite. "What does turned up mean? Swallow, then tell me."

She chews a mouth full of food and swallows before answering. "Means a lot was happening. It was wild. I heard parents yelled at you and stuff."

"I wish you didn't have to hear those things."

"Me too, Ma. But I do. So are you in trouble?"

I don't want to admit it but I can't really lie. I mean, I could, but I just don't have the strength anymore. "I might be. The school board wants to talk to me, but probably not until the next semester starts."

"Is Morningside going to get a new Principal?"

I frown, pick up my turkey burger and take a bite. I chew a mouthful of dry, unseasoned ground turkey, swallow and suck down a mouthful of iced tea. "That's terrible."

"I could have told you that. They don't make turkey burgers like you do."

"Obviously not." I drink more tea to erase the taste of turkey from my mouth. "I don't want to get too far ahead of things, but if something were to happen to me one of the assistant principals would fill in, like Miss Sanders."

"She's mean," Kendra remarks.

"I know," I respond with a wink. "That's why I hired her."

"So what if the school board decides—"

"Kendra… honey. I don't want to speculate right now. And besides, this isn't something that you should concern yourself with. You should be—"

"Yeah, right," she mutters, tossing her burger down, wiping her mouth with the napkin.

"Excuse me? Do you have something to say?"

Her head shoots up, eyes full of fire, lip curled. "Does it matter? No one's listening to me. No one's telling me anything. You're not talking. Daddy's not talking. All I hear is the stuff at school, and if what people are saying is true, you're in some deep crap, Ma."

"Okay. Okay, Kendra, I—"

"And you and Daddy not talking to each other isn't helping anything. It's like you don't even want to be with Daddy anymore. You rented a room in some lady's house? Why didn't you just come home and make Daddy talk to you?"

"It's not a simple as you're making it sound. Just move home and make him talk to me." I have to stop myself before I get in too deep with a twelve-year-old. I can't confess all of my sins and mistakes and missteps to my daughter. "These issues— the thing with Mr. Loren, this situation with your dad—these are not your problems. You can't solve them and I apologize that you're in the middle, but I'm trying so hard not to put you there. Can't you see that?"

"No," she bites out. "All I see is my parents acting stupid and my mom getting talked about like a dog and my teachers looking at me like I'm some charity case. I can't say anything. I can't do anything. I feel helpless and I don't like it."

"Now you know how I feel."

For a few moments we stare at each other, then go back to our dinners. I choke down another bite of the turkey burger before I give up and push it away. Kendra seems to be mindlessly inserting fry after fry into her mouth while staring out of the window at the cars passing by.

"I know that you don't understand what's happening, and why there's not much I can do to fix it right now. But please trust me, baby." I reach across the table and grasp her chin between my thumb and forefinger, turning her face toward mine. "If I could fix this, right this very second, I would. But there's more to this than just me, and we have to see how this plays out. What I need for you to do is to be strong, keep up your grades and take care of yourself."

I eye her nearly empty plate and for the first time notice her rounding face. "Are you okay at home? Is Daddy taking care of things?"

She shrugs a shoulder. "He does fine. Just...." She sighs. "I got my... you know, my time."

"Oh." I sit up straight. Why did I not see this coming? I've counseled so many girls on the same issue, but I feel blindsided by my daughter's budding maturity. "Did Daddy get you what you needed?"

"I didn't tell him."

"Kendra—"

"That's not a conversation I'm having with my dad," she says, glowering at me. "I got some stuff from a friend and the school nurse. I'm surprised she didn't race to your office and tell you."

"She's not allowed to. Did you need me to take you to the store?"

Head bowed, Kendra doesn't say anything, but she gives me a slight nod. Finally, something Willard can't do for her. Only I can guide and direct her in this moment. It's sort of... reverent.

On the way back to the house, we stop by the store and I get Kendra the things she needs. She's too embarrassed to stand in the checkout line, so she dashes back to the car while I buy her items. I sneak in two bags of M&M's and hand the plastic sack to her when I get in the car. No matter how much of a health nut I am, M&M's will cure what ails me.

I pull into the driveway at the house. The garage door is open and Willard's Lexus sits in its usual spot. He hasn't moved over to the spot where I used to park. I guess old habits die hard. Or maybe deep in his heart he hasn't let go of me.

Oh, get over yourself, Debra.

A figure appears at the door as Kendra drops a kiss on my cheek and climbs out. Willard, dressed in his usual Sunday relaxation attire — ratty jeans and an oversized t-shirt, holds the screen door open as she bounds through it. He says something to her as she passes him. At her response, his shoulders sag and he looks right at me and shakes his head.

And closes the door.

It's so ridiculous that it makes me laugh, and I chuckle all the way back to Roberta's.

CHAPTER TWENTY-SIX

$\mathcal{M}$axine

"Finally, a spot where I can pronounce the name of the food."

Joseph holds the door open for me as we step into Ruby's. We have plans to see a movie and Ruby's is close, so I suggested we grab a quick bite and walk over to the theater. It's chilly but not too cold to walk a few blocks. Besides, that's what wool and cashmere are made for.

Joseph, I must admit, is looking ruggedly handsome in one of two Theory cashmere sweaters that I gave him for Christmas. He made a lot of noise about the expense—and yes they were expensive, but if he's going to be seen with me, I want him looking right. And he does, from his molded chest and strong shoulders to his muscular arms and slim waistline. The sweater hangs to just the right length over the band of his jeans and I'm pleased to see he chooses a quality brand of denim. First impressions, you know.

It's a slow Thursday evening, just after Christmas. Decatur Square, which was bustling with activity just a few days ago, is now quiet and serene; sitting back, taking a breather before the

New Year starts with its sales and celebrations. We are shown to a table right away and slide into either side of a booth.

"So what's good, here?" Joseph asks. He looks up from his already open menu and smiles, showing off two rows of gleaming white teeth and a shallow set of dimples. "You said you eat here a lot. I trust your judgment."

"Everything's good here. That's why I have to limit how many times I come to eat. A girl has to watch her figure."

"Don't worry about that, baby. I'll watch your figure for you." He winks, slowly, to match the sultry undertones to his voice.

I playfully smack his hand, then rub the spot I tapped. "Would you behave?"

"Nope," he answers, then laughs and goes back to perusing the menu. Despite myself, I'm having a great time with Joseph. We lack for nothing to talk about, or laugh about. He's a stickler for showing up on time and no matter what I want to do, he always pays. I've received flowers at the office twice, which really got tongues wagging. And thank God Debra moved out a few weeks ago because he spends at least two nights a week at my place. I've had to get used to being with someone so focused on me and my needs, making sure I get my bite of pleasure before he takes his. I normally have to fight to get an orgasm before the flavor of the month grunts an, 'oh yeah!' and collapses in a heap on top of me. I've never met anyone who insists I come first.

Joseph has differed from any man I've ever dated. In almost every way, especially the way that matters the most. Despite his innate need to take care of everything every time we go out, he can't afford me. And while he's been nice to play with, I feel like he's getting attached and that could mean trouble.

Especially since I'm still working on Malcolm.

He's been playing very hard to get. We play phone tag about twice a week, try to make tentative plans to hook up, but something always arises that keeps him from agreeing to meet me—he has dinner or an event or some paperwork. He's a nice enough guy, but he works a lot. I value a man that's on his grind, as long as he makes time for me. So far, Malcolm doesn't seem like the type to make time. But people change.

Joseph decides on the chicken fried steak with potatoes, gravy and green beans. I order the fried catfish basket with collard greens and hush puppies and hand my menu to the waiter as I remind him about my Perrier and glass of ice. Joseph chuckles as his head drops into his palm.

"Don't start. My friends laugh at me all the time about it. I can't help that I don't like how the water tastes here."

"I'm sorry for laughing at you, baby." He reaches across the table and takes my hands in his. They are large, warm, soft. My hands feel like they're nestled in a cocoon. "You're just amusing to me. I find you fascinating. I want to know everything about you. Inside and out."

"Yeah, well." I swallow. "There's a lot to know. There's a lot to me. There might be some things underneath that you don't care for."

"Such as?"

I shrug. "Such as... well... I mean, I don't know—"

"Such as the Maxine Standard? The one I don't meet?"

"I wasn't... I didn't mean—"

"It's okay. We can talk about it. Because I know I can beat that standard."

My eyes narrow, focusing on his eyes, the darkest brown eyes I've ever seen. "Is that so, Joseph?"

"That is so, Maxine." His grin is broad and bright, and I hate to admit how warm I feel inside when he smiles at me. "And my goal is to show you that."

"Sounds like you have your work cut out for you, then."

"I wouldn't be here if I wasn't up to the challenge. I heard a lot about you before I met you."

"You were warned."

He chuckles. "I'm not trying to put it that way, but yeah. You have a reputation."

"On purpose."

He nods, deeply. "It seems that way. Designed to keep the riffraff away?"

I sit back to let the waiter place a bottle of water and a glass of ice on the table. When he leaves, I admit, "Not really for the riffraff because they know they have no chance. It's more for the average Joe–" My eyes flick up from the glass that is filling with water. "Present Joe excepted, that thinks he's my type. I hand pick my men."

"Is present Joe still excepted? Because I'm sure I picked you up."

I giggle. "See, that's the Maxine magic. I let you think that."

"Is that so, Maxine?"

I nod. "That is so, Joseph. So what is this movie you're dragging me to? You know I rarely go to movies. Am I going to like it?"

"You might. It's a new Phil Walters joint. It's about a guy being accused of murder, so he pleads his case and ends up taking a bunch of people hostage until people will listen to him."

I frown, feeling my forehead wrinkle with confusion. "I feel like I saw that with Kevin Spacey and Sam Jackson."

"The Negotiator," he throws out with a nod. "Similar. But different."

"How is it different?"

Joseph is still, quiet for a few moments before his eyes grow wide, and he laughs. "This movie is set in New York. They set the other movie in Chicago." He raises both fists in the air in a victory pose while I laugh.

"That's the only difference?"

"What other difference do you need? Don't pick it apart before you've even seen it."

"Alright, Alright." My eyes roll, but I'm not entirely serious. Joseph makes pretty much everything a good time. A waitress swings by and drops two plates in front of us, pulling a bottle of hot sauce from her apron pocket before we even ask. She disappears as quickly as she came. I rescue my silverware from the tightly rolled napkin and spread the napkin over my jeans.

"I'll give it a fair shot. But if anyone dies in the first five minutes—"

"Oh, that's guaranteed. They've got to get your hopes up that no one else dies. That's how they rope you in."

My fish is still sizzling when I break off a piece with a fork, douse it in hot sauce and pop it in my mouth. Delicious—well seasoned, crispy, flaky. Just how I like it. "Well," I continue, "he can't kill everyone. What's the sense in taking hostages if you kill everyone?"

"He doesn't kill everyone. Just enough people so that the negotiators know he means business. It's a delicate balance."

"Delicate balance. Listen to you, film critic."

"I've seen my share, for sure. I have an opinion on what makes a good movie. It's like a mathematic equation. You take a movie, right? Separate it into four parts, but the parts aren't equal. You've got your script, your direction, your setting..."

I'm hearing Joseph's voice, but I'm not listening to him. My attention is otherwise occupied by the couple just seated in the dining room on the other side of the restaurant. In fact, I'm so surprised—and a little upset to see them, that I drop my fork. Bits of catfish, juice from collard greens and cheese sauce from the macaroni end up all over my sweater and my jeans. My Alpaca wool sweater and $90 jeans.

"What... the fuck."

"Maxine?"

Joseph's voice sounds faded and distant. I can barely hear him as I stare at Renee and Malcolm across the restaurant. They're sitting close together, on the same side of a booth, sharing a menu. Much too close to just have seen each other on the street, at the bookstore, around town and caught a meal.

They are talking. Renee is smiling that big wide smile up in into his face. I can almost hear her laughter bubble up over the noise in the restaurant. Malcolm's body language doesn't say that he's being held hostage. His forearms rest on the table, then he lifts one arm and drops it around her shoulders. And then he leans in.

And they kiss.

"Holy shit!" I grab my napkin and throw it onto the table, then scoot to the edge of the booth and slide out.

"Maxine! Where are you going?"

Renee must have heard Joseph call after me, because that little heifer's head popped up at the sound of my name. The look on her face when I came around that bend—I wish I had a camera, I'd snap that photo and frame it. Malcolm doesn't move, except to squeeze Renee closer to him.

"Hello, Maxine. Nice to see you again."

"Fuck you and your pleasantries, Malcolm. This is why you're never free to do anything?"

"If by this, you mean prior plans, then yes. But—"

"But nothing. I have nothing to say to you. But you..." I point to Renee and try to control the anger that makes me furiously tremble. "You are supposed to be my friend. Are you taking lessons from Debra on how to be sneaky and a liar?"

Renee's eyes are enormous, her cheeks a ruddy red, her nose bulbous, which means she's about to cry. She's shaking her head so vigorously that her curls toss back and forth. "I didn't know...he said you two weren't dating, and I thought—"

"Why didn't you talk to me? Why didn't you ask me?"

"Because I thought—"

"You thought, but you didn't know. Because you didn't ask. Because you didn't want to know. You just wanted to get your fuck on with my man."

"Your man?" I twist around and notice that Joseph has followed me to the table. "I thought I was your man."

"Joseph, this does not pertain to you. Go back to our table. I'll be there in a second." I turn to continue my onslaught, but Joseph has other ideas. He grips my arm so tightly that I can't yank myself out of his grasp.

"Let's let them have their dinner. Maybe continue this when we're not in public."

"I don't care about doing this in public. They didn't care

about being in public. Just waltzing up in here like they belong together or something. Both of them ought to be ashamed of themselves."

"Yeah, yeah. Let's go. C'mon. Let's go."

Joseph gets me back to the table where I sit and quietly fume in their direction. Renee is heaving, nearly hyperventilating when they get up and walk out. Malcolm shoots a glare in my direction as they pass through my line of sight. He guides Renee out with his arm still around her shoulder.

I inhale a cleansing breath. I need to stop shaking. Joseph is across from me, unusually interested in his dinner plate. He hasn't said a word since we sat down again.

"I need to explain—"

"No, you don't." He slices his steak methodically into pieces and systematically shovels them into his mouth.

"I want to explain my reaction, just then."

"No need. I get the picture." He keeps chewing, swallowing, sipping water. "We'll be late for the movie. Are you going to finish your dinner?"

"You still care about that dumb ass movie?"

He sets his fork down next to his plate. Picks up his napkin, wipes his mouth. Lowers his arms to the table where they rest on either side of his plate.

"Since you put it that way... no. I don't care about the dumb ass movie. I care about a woman that I thought cared about me, who I thought I might be building something with. I care about not being the man that you call 'your man'. In fact, I care so much that I don't want to see the dumb ass movie now. I care about taking you home."

He pushes his chair back from the table and leans to the right to pull his wallet from his back pocket. He plucks our ticket from under his plate and stands. "I'm going to pay our tab. You might want to get a to-go box."

I can hardly breathe as I watch him walk away from the table. I brush a shaky hand against my forehead and push my plate of food away. As much as I love Ruby's. I'm not interested in eating anymore.

I used to have so much control where men were concerned. I could juggle multiple men, keep feelings at bay, and get everything I wanted from a veritable stable of eligible bachelors. These days, I can't even juggle two men without things falling apart. It's like I don't know myself anymore.

I hear my name over the din of the dinner rush. It's Joseph, standing up front near the register, keys in hand. "Let's go," he mouths to me. I sigh, push my chair back and make my way to the front of the restaurant.

The walk from the car was romantic on the way in—arm in arm, snuggled into each other against the breeze. The walk back is another story. Joseph stalks with long strides, the hard rubber soles of his boots striking loudly against the pavement. I have to almost run to keep up with him. By the time we make it to his car, I'm out of breath. I'm also ticked off. I do not sweat in my wool sweaters.

Joseph doesn't stop to unlock the passenger door to his Chevy Impala and let me get in and settled, like he usually does. He marches to the driver's side door, presses the button on his key chain to unlock it, and drops into the driver's seat. Only when he is in the car and in the seat does he press the button on the door panel to unlock my door.

"That was rude," I snap as soon as I get in the car. I yank the seatbelt from its casing; the buckle flies, nearly taking a chunk out of my forehead. "Ouch!" I screech, grabbing the metal and pulling the belt forward.

"If you weren't pulling on it like a madwoman, it wouldn't do that." Joseph grabs the belt, gently tugs it a few times and clicks it into the buckle. "Sometimes things will go the way you want them to go with a little push."

"Is that your attempt at being deep?"

Joseph glares at me, then turns his attention to the view outside the windshield while he inserts his key into the ignition and starts the car. He adjusts the knobs on the dashboard until I feel heat coming from the vents. I'm mentally thankful; it's freezing out since the sun has set.

"I'm not trying to be anything, Maxine. And you know, I think that's your problem with me. I'm not rich or brilliant. I'm not on anybody's best dressed list, and I only got invited to that party at Brent's because I know someone that knows him. You're looking for someone to upgrade you, and that can't be me. Not in the way that you're looking for."

"Look... I know you don't want to hear it, but I'm saying it anyway because I mean it. I am sorry. I didn't mean for you to hear all of that nonsense between me and Renee. I should have saved that for another time when she and I could talk one-on-one. I embarrassed you and I ruined our evening, and I'm really very sorry. If you still want to see the movie, we have time. We can go."

He doesn't say a word, utter a peep, twitch a muscle for almost a full minute. A minute is a long time when you're waiting for a response, for someone to let you off the hook, to pull you out of the doghouse. I feel the seconds tick past by each of their parts—millisecond, nanosecond... and then he laughs.

While I love his laugh—so deep and chesty and masculine, paired with his great smile and emotive eyes, his laughter doesn't feel like it's cheery and full of mirth. He's mocking me.

"What?"

He only laughs harder, to which I have no response but cross my arms tightly over my chest and glare in his direction. "What?" I demand, again.

The chuckles die down. He sniffs, then turns to me. I can just barely see his face through the thin beams of moonlight shining into the car. "You wanna know what's funny? What's funny is that you think I'm like you."

"I do not think you're like me."

"Oh, yeah, you do. You're apologizing because you think I'm embarrassed by what happened back there? That's what you think I'm upset about?"

He shakes his head, hacks out a few more puffs of laughter.

"You are an intelligent, business savvy, beautiful woman that I have enjoyed getting to know. But right now, I feel like I've wasted my time. I feel like you don't know me, and you don't care to. I'm just here for entertainment—apparently until your man realizes that he's your man. And I'm sorry, baby. I can't be that man for you. I'm first string."

"Joseph—"

"Max. Don't." He shakes his head, then turns back to the windshield and puts the car in gear. He backs out of the space smoothly but quickly and sets a course for my condo. We ride in silence; no music, no talk radio, no speaking, just the sound of tires against the pavement.

In minutes he is pulling into the circular driveway of Buckhead Vista, my high rise community. I'm reluctant to get out of the car. Where Joseph would normally get out and open my door, he sits in the driver's seat, staring through the windshield into the night. Fuming.

"So. Should I call you?"

He sighs. Breathes. Swallows. Then says, "Why don't I call you?"

I nod. So it's like that. "Great. It's been nice knowing you."

"So you're blowing me off? Right to my face?"

"You just blew me off with your 'why don't I call you' line. I know what that means."

"You know what it means to you. When I tell you I'm going to call you, what does it mean?"

My eyes roll involuntarily. "So you're going to call."

"I wish you knew me, Maxine," he says quietly. "I wish you knew that when I say I'm going to call, come hell or high water, I'm going to pick up that phone. When I say I'm going to be somewhere, I don't care if I have to wade through waist high shit, I'll be there. And when I say I'm falling—"

He stops short, wedges his elbow up against the window and covers his eyes with his palm. "Just go."

I don't hesitate to unbuckle the seatbelt, open the door and climb out of the car. Joseph slams the gear into drive and guns the engine. I watch the red taillights wind around the driveway and out onto Peachtree, tires squealing.

Why do I feel like that man just tore right out of my life?

And why do I care so much?

CHAPTER TWENTY-SEVEN

enee

In the cab of Malcolm's truck, I'm having a nervous breakdown.

"You said she knew! You said she knew you weren't interested!"

"She knows, Renee. I can't help it that she's in denial but she knows."

"Why did she call you her man? Are you dating her, too? Are you sleeping with her?"

"No, Renee. I'm not. I'm not interested in Maxine and I promise you, she knows that."

"How do you know that she knows that? Did you tell her?"

Malcolm is quiet for one second too long. He sighs, and I sense his eyes rolling in the darkness of the Denali.

"Oh. My God. You didn't, did you? You just ignored her and thought she'd pick up on it, right?"

"I mean... how many times does a guy have to turn down a date invite before she gets the picture?"

"She doesn't take hints!"

I toss my head against the headrest and throw a small temper tantrum, kicking my arms and legs. "I don't understand how I could explain to you that I absolutely didn't want to hurt her, that she's my oldest friend, and how you can respond with how I shouldn't worry about it, because she knew nothing was there."

"I thought she knew that Renee. I never responded to any of her advances. I have never accepted a date invitation and I don't chat on the phone with her, no matter how many times she calls just to talk. If that doesn't spell disinterest, I don't know what does. And besides, she was with a guy that didn't seem to understand that he wasn't her boyfriend."

My frustration mounting, I can think of no other place I'd rather be than home. I need all of my comforts right now and unfortunately he is not one of them. "Malcolm… just, let's go. Take me to my car. Please."

"You're not going home already? You have Jessie another couple of hours. We've been looking forward to tonight all week."

We've been able to steal snippets of time—an hour here, a lunch there, a quick dinner, a walk down the street on a quiet evening, but we've been planning on spending this time together for weeks. The bookstore was busy, even for right after the holiday season. The shop hadn't been empty all day and since it was just Lexie and I until our part-time clerk came in at 4 o'clock, I'd skipped lunch, opting for a cup of coffee and a slice of banana bread from Mona's shop.

By the time Malcolm showed up for our date, I was starving. And since Ruby's was close, we dropped in for a quick bite before heading to his place to watch a movie, snuggle on the couch and hope it led to something a little more naked.

It wouldn't be the first time. We took care of that on our third date and it was everything I imagined it would be—a beautiful evening illuminated by a full moon; a cool wind blowing over us from the open patio doors; a full bottle of robust red wine and an entire box of chocolate-covered fruit to share. My first man-made orgasm in over four years took my breath away. I clung to Malcolm, hanging on for dear life, just trying not to float away into the atmosphere. When I came down, he was there, hovering over me. Watching my return to earth and reality.

I shooed away feelings of shyness. Malcolm had seen me, all of me, at my most vulnerable. If I couldn't be myself in that moment, I couldn't ever be myself with him.

I didn't have to worry about that. He seemed to appreciate every inch of me, dipping his head toward me and brushing those plump lips against mine. "I love being with you," he whispered against my lips. "You are an amazing woman. I can't wait to be with you again."

So I sat up, pushed against his shoulders until he was lying on his back and straddled his body. "Me either. So let's do it again."

Between his schedule and mine, we hadn't been able to revisit the experience. Tonight would have been our first opportunity… but I can't. Tonight, I feel like the worst person on the planet.

Malcolm starts the truck and drives the few blocks to his place. Instead of driving into the garage, he pulls in next to my car and puts the truck in park. "You don't have to go home, Renee. Just come up. We'll talk."

I shake my head, my lips a tight, straight line. "Not tonight."

"But maybe another night?"

I want to say yes, another night, and soon, but I know…I just know that this is already a mess. I don't see how I can keep seeing Malcolm with Maxine so angry and feeling like I stole him. And me feeling so guilty about not telling her about it.

"I'll call you," I promise, and climb out of the truck, head to my car and slip into the driver's seat. I point my car toward home much earlier than I intended to. Earlier than I want to. Feeling things I don't want to feel.

My seat pulses, a sensation I don't recognize as my phone vibrating inside my bag right away. I pick up the phone to see that I've missed a call from Maxine. Here we go.

Maxine is like an animal when she's angry, when she feels she's been wronged and lashes out. I once heard that the wolverine is the only animal that kills for pleasure. This reminds me of Max when she's angry. I swore that my first run-in with her over a man would be my last.

Decatur High School. Eleventh grade. Maxine was already popular—pretty, long silky hair, light skin tone and bourgeoisie enough that girls either wanted to be her best friend so they'd get noticed, or they wanted to scratch her eyes out, because their boyfriends noticed her.

Adrian Lewis had just transferred to Decatur. He played basketball, so he was tall, but he wasn't thin and lanky. Rather, he was muscular, powerful. He oozed charisma with a ready smile and an easy laugh. He was extremely bright, so he was in a lot of my Advanced Placement classes. Maxine decided that she wanted to sink her claws into him before any of the cheerleaders could get their hands on him.

Unfortunately, Adrian was oblivious to the chirpy, stylish girl that hung out at his locker and tried to impress him with her clothes and entice him with her sultry tone and smoky eye shadow. Instead, he spent a lot of time with me. The AP courses at Decatur were ahead of those at his old school and he needed to catch up. I offered to help, and that's where I took a wrong turn.

For half of our junior year, I was a traitorous whore because Adrian would rather spend time bent over a textbook with me. When he took me to Homecoming instead of asking Maxine, she was inconsolable. It didn't matter that she had her pick of every boy at Decatur High. Adrian was the one she wanted, and the idea of Maxine Donovan not getting something she wanted drove her out of her mind.

Max and I wouldn't make up until after Adrian and I stopped dating. It took Debra forcing us together to make that happen, and I promised myself—and Debra– that I'd never go through that with Maxine again.

I'm afraid to pick up the voicemail that eventually alerts on my phone. I know without listening that she's used up the entire allotted amount of recording time telling me exactly what she thought of me being with Malcolm.

I slide my finger across the screen and bring up the voicemail app, then put her message on speaker.

"I just want you to know that you are a lowdown, dirty bitch for what you did and I know you know it was wrong, Renee. I know you're not stupid. You know I was trying to get with Malcolm, so don't even try that innocent, big eyed, crying thing with me–"

I press the fast-forward button and skip ahead ten seconds. "—don't talk to me, don't email me, don't come to my office or my house, you hear me? I want nothing to do with you and you tell Malcolm that–"

I skip ahead another ten seconds. "—think you've made some kind of fool out of me, but y'all got another think coming, if you think I'm going to be played out in public by a weak ass bitch. We're supposed to be friends, Renee. You're supposed to have my back, not go behind my back—"

The message ends there, cutting off her diatribe. The phone vibrates in my hand and Maxine's face and phone number pop up on screen. I let it roll to voicemail. In fact, I turn the phone off, drop it into my bag and get out of the car. I'd rather sit in front of the TV with a man that doesn't know my name than deal with Maxine tonight.

The next morning, I get Daddy up and moving, showered, dressed, fed and planted in his chair with his mp3 player and some music. Big band and Southern Jazz are his favorites lately, so I leave him to enjoy the music while I clean up the kitchen and straighten up his bedroom.

When Jessie comes in, I head to the showers and get ready for work. Gladwell's New Year's sale is going to be aggressive this year, and I need to spend all day updating our system and making sure we're well stocked. I'd forgotten that I turned off my phone the night before, so I press the button on top of the device and turn it on, only to find that all hell has broken loose.

Three voicemails from Maxine. I decide not to listen to them. I need not ruin my day before 10am.

Two messages from Debra, one asking, just what in hell is going on? And one that just said, girl, call me because Maxine has lost her damn mind.

Last, a message from Malcolm with sincere apologies and a request to see me when I have time.

I slide through the missed calls and click on Debra Macklin, put the phone on speaker and listen to it ring. She sounds like she's still asleep when she picks up.

"Debra? I forgot you were on a break from school. You want me to call you back later?"

I hear her stretch, sucking in a long breath through her nose. "Mmmmm...no." She yawns but sounds slightly more alert. "It was a late night. So what happened last night? Maxine called me acting like her hair was on fire or something. And she said to tell you to go to hell."

"Hang on, I'm at Starbucks." I'll just have to put up with Mona's snide commentary all day about how they're putting shops like hers out of business. I need a caramel latte, immediately. I yell my order through the drive through microphone and pull around for my coffee. "You know how overly dramatic Maxine can be. It'll die down."

"She said she saw you with Malcolm. She made it sound like y'all were tonguing each other down in the middle of Ruby's."

"We were not tonguing each other down. See what I mean? Drama queen."

"So you were with him? How long has that been going on?"

"Not long. A few weeks."

"You've only known him a few weeks. You just met him, Renee. You moved on him that fast?"

"You make it sound like I stalked the man and had to use a stun gun to get him to have dinner with me. He came to the bookstore, we hung out, and we had dinner. Dinner led to another dinner, which led to another dinner. He's a nice man. Sue me."

I pull into the parking lot behind Ruby's but instead of entering the shop through the back; I walk around front and open the door, then close and lock it behind me. Malcolm suggested I do that. Between the neighborhood homes that are set so far back from the alley that they can't see the shop and the tall hedges that separate our lot from the others around us, if something happened to me at that door, no one would find me for hours unless they walked around the side of the building. I'd never thought about it. It was the entry I had always used, even in high school.

"She is insufferable, but you know why Max is angry. It wasn't just that you were having dinner with him. It was that you two are in a relationship and she didn't know about it. And you know you should have said something, but you didn't because you didn't want to face the wrath that you're facing now."

I walk through the shop flipping on lights, turning on machines. The old IBM shudders and grinds to life. I make a note to price out some new computers. We might be able to afford to replace the desktop in my office and the Point of Sale machine up front. Maybe I can get a laptop for myself.

I wedge the phone between my ear and shoulder as I move boxes around and adjust stacks of books. "Maxine thinks all the single, eligible men in this city belong to her. Every bachelor with dark skin, pretty eyes and a great smile is hers to choose from, and only when she tosses them away can I have my pick?"

"You know it's not like that, Renee."

"Isn't it? Apparently, I can only pick from her scraps."

"I can't believe how indignant you are. You know what the issue is. Don't act self righteous to make it better."

"I'm not acting self-righteous, okay? I was wrong. I know I was wrong. And yeah, I didn't want to say anything to her because she was all stupid over Malcolm, but he is not interested in her. Ask Maxine! She'll tell you he's never accepted an invitation, they don't hang out, he—"

"Did he say to her face he wasn't interested in her?" I heave a sigh which is all the answer Debra needs. "See, this is what men do. He's playing y'all against each other and may the best woman win."

"I don't think so, Debra."

"Oh, you don't? He's telling you he only wants to be with you, in the meantime stringing Maxine along. He hasn't said one word to her about being interested in you. He's hanging out in the middle of two women willing to fight each other for him. Ya'll are some punks."

"You know, Debra, I don't want to throw your own situation in your face, but I think you're jealous."

She cackles. "What am I jealous of? Maxine isn't angry with me. I don't envy your ass one bit. Tell me something, though. You fuck him yet?"

"None of your business."

"Mmm hmm." She snickers. "You be careful over there, little girl. These big city men know just how to get what they want from a sweet Georgia peach who doesn't know any better."

My eyes narrow. I can't believe the words coming out of the phone. "And why wouldn't I know better? If I hadn't come back here, Marcus and I would probably be married by now."

"Marcus was a pussy. And so is Malcolm, to have two women fighting over him like this."

I gasp. "Debra Macklin! What is up with you today?"

"You're just mad that I'm not on your side. It's early, and you caught me in a mad mood. Everyone is all up in my ass lately and I don't have time to deal with you two. I'm going to get some coffee. Call Maxine. Bye."

I stare at the phone after the line goes dead, huff in frustration and toss it back in my bag. I'll call Maxine when I get ready to call Maxine.

I'm not ready to call Maxine.

I pick up the phone again and tap out a text message to Malcolm.

Busy day, NYE sale, no time today, sorry. Call you later. -R

A moment later, a return text comes through. Text me when you get home tonight? I'd like to talk.–M

I don't answer. I don't have an answer. I like Malcolm, but some of what Debra said rings true to me. That a big, strong, meaty, muscle bound man couldn't pick up the phone and talk to a little woman and make things clear—especially since he was trying to start something with her friend—speaks volumes to me.

I don't have much time to commiserate about the potential demise of my budding relationship and the almost certain implosion of my oldest friendship. The foot traffic in and out of the store is nonstop. The high school and college-aged kids sprawled all over the couches and tables, using every available power outlet, talking, laughing, roughhousing loudly is maddening. I make the rounds, rushing anyone who wasn't doing anything useful—like studying or quietly reading—out the door.

"This is so unfair," whines a lanky, pale kid with fire engine red hair and freckles. His army green jacket is too big and so are his jeans with the holes in the knees. It's freezing outside, but he's wearing sandals and no socks.

"It's totally fair," I tell him, shooing him toward the door. "I own the place. You're not buying anything and you're disrupting paying customers. This isn't a hangout joint. Try the bar next door. Out you go."

The day passes quickly, with Lexie, Mona, a part timer and I running around the store. I might even describe the day as fun. Gladwell's has become less of a burden, less something to rehab into a sellable business and more of a home away from home, a place that the neighborhood has come to appreciate.

We're starting to have regulars now, people who come in once a week or so to browse the sale items, paw through the used and donated books sections. We have an author event almost weekly, and I get calls and emails all the time about local musicians and clubs that want to use the small but cozy space available for their various functions. For a low fee, they can fill the room to overflowing. Even Mona has offered to stick around for those events. I don't mind her making a bit of extra money at all. Whatever gets her rent paid is fine by me.

The Annual Gladwell New Year's sale will kick off in the morning. Extra stock has been added, prices have been programmed, and we have bundled series. The staff memo has been prepared and posted in the break room and at the register with a color coded list of what books are on sale and for how much. The setting sun reaches through the windows, coloring the air with a rosy glow. This is my cue to slip off my apron and name tag, wave goodbye to my staff and head for home. I'm eager to see Daddy and Jessie, to see how their day went.

Despite my new habit of entering and exiting via the front door, I forego it tonight and open the rear door. Parked next to my Corolla is the familiar black Denali. Malcolm's elbow juts out of the opening of the driver's side window. I hear the faint strains of a popular hip-hop song as the door opens, and he steps down from the cab.

I move toward my car, unlock it, and toss my purse inside. Malcolm slowly makes his way around the rear of my car.

"I'm on my way home. Jessie has plans with her kids tonight."

"I won't keep you. I just wanted to see you. I hope we're okay, Renee."

I shake my head, squinting into the brightness at the height of sunset. "I don't know that we are, Malcolm."

He steps back, makes a complete turnaround and faces me again. "How can I make this right? I really care about you."

"I think it might be too late. You assumed that Max would just fade away, knowing that the type of woman that she is would never let her do that. And, you know…"

I expel a breath, leaning up against the dusty exterior of the car. "I'm to blame, too. I should have said something. I should have been on the up and up with her. And I wasn't. Because… maybe deep down I knew that she'd be this pissed."

"I'm sorry. I didn't know it would be this bad. This is on me. I knew she was interested, and I didn't want to deal with it. I honestly thought she'd get the picture, eventually."

"Well, she didn't. And while she would have been upset anyway, she's ready to explode because you're not just seeing someone else. You're seeing me. Someone she should be able to trust. So… I hope you get that I just don't know how this is going to work."

"You can't be friends with her and date me?"

I laugh. Sure, if Maxine was a normal person. But she's halfway crazy. "I think the question is if Maxine can be friends with me if I date you. Right now, I think the answer is no. And I'm sorry, but she's been there for me at my roughest, lowest times. I'm not going to choose you over her. As bad as I want to, I'm not."

"So if she can't get over this, you're just going to be alone for the rest of your life?"

My gaze hardens and my brow wrinkles. "Why the hell does everyone assume I can't get a man? Either I'm naïve and I don't know what I'm doing, or I'm never going to meet anybody ever again if I walk away from this."

I push off of the car and swing the door open. "I'm not some ugly duckling. I'm not a hopeless charity case. I may be different from Maxine, but I'll tell you one way I'm like her. I don't bend to the whims of just any old dick that comes sniffing around. I do the choosing around here and I choose just fine. Now, if you'll excuse me, I have a father to take care of. Family takes care of family, right?"

I get into the car and slam the door shut, dig my key out of my purse and jam it in the ignition. With a spray of rocks and dust, I peel out of the lot, around the building and onto Broad Street.

Never mind these tears that sting at my eyes and the emotion pulling the ends of my mouth down. Never mind that I think I just threw away the best thing that has happened to me in a long time. Never mind that I think, despite not dating Malcolm, I'm not sure Maxine is going to forgive me.

CHAPTER TWENTY-EIGHT

ebra

I grope for the ringing phone, lost somewhere in the folds of bedding.

"Hello," I croak, not even bothering to open my eyes and check the display. I'm sure it's Maxine.

"Why are you still asleep?" She demands. "It's almost 8 o'clock. What's wrong with you?"

I roll over and squint against the bright sun peeking through the blinds. I'd forgotten to close the drapes last night. "I can't sleep in without getting questions?"

"No. I don't know you as a person who sleeps in. You were up at the ass crack of dawn every day that you stayed with me. And you fell asleep on me last night."

"Oh... did I?" I came to around 3am with the lamp and TV still on and three empty mini bottles of vodka in the bed with me.

"Yes, you did. It wasn't even late."

"I'm sorry, Max. I must have been tired." I sit up, which the pain in my head doesn't like. "Uhm... why are you calling me at eight in the damn morning?"

"For the same reason I called you last night. To tell you about your friend Renee. I never liked her, you know. You forced her on me and I wanted to stay friends with you so I went with it, but I never liked her."

"Bullshit, Maxine. You side with Renee on everything. Don't tell yourself any tall tales just because you're mad at her right now."

"Well, right now I feel like I never liked her. How could she do that? Just go right behind my back like she didn't know I was trying to work something out with him. We went to lunch one day, and I told her all about it."

"All about what, Max? About how he didn't pay any attention to you, how you never went out with him, how he isn't interested in you and he wants Renee, just like I told you a few weeks ago?"

She huffs. I can just see her stomping her little foot. "You are such an evil person when you're unhappy."

"I'm not evil because I'm unhappy. I'm evil because I am tired, and you called me at 8 AM on my vacation from my very stressful job. I'm evil because I am telling you things you don't want to hear and I'm sorry but someone has to say it. Malcolm isn't interested in you. You know that. Why not let Renee have her fun? Maybe he likes women like her."

"Over women like me?" I roll my eyes. Maxine is a legend in her own mind.

"It's not unreasonable that a man would be attracted to Renee. She's pretty, smart, friendly, loyal—has to be, she's been your friend for a long time and you know you don't deserve it."

"She wasn't loyal last night. She wasn't loyal when she started messing with Malcolm and didn't tell me. She should have come to me. She should have said something, but no. She let me find out when they walked into Ruby's, all cuddled up together. How long did she think she could get away with that?"

"Probably until you moved on to someone else and wouldn't be as angry to know that she'd been dating him."

"What kind of friend is that?"

I chuckle. "One who knows how you are, especially with your men. Renee ain't no dummy."

"I disagree. And what do you mean, how I am with my men? What does that mean?"

"I don't want to get into it Max. It's too early and I am too tired and I'm not getting in the middle of this, like last time. You remember?"

"That boy would have liked me just fine if she hadn't butted her four eyed nerd ass between us."

"This is why I'm not involved." In the background, I hear voices and loud noises like hammers banging and planks stacking. It's unlike Maxine to be anywhere near a construction site. "Where are you, anyway? Sounds like the Taj Mahal is being built behind you."

"I have a cocktail Open House this afternoon. The Mouth of the South can finally unload this place. We're staging and getting things ready. Hang on."

Maxine gives marching orders through the muffled microphone. She is a force, for sure. Just never get on her bad side. "Anyway," she says, coming back to our conversation. "I just called to see if you'd heard from the little wimp. She's not answering my calls."

"You know they always have a big sale at Gladwell's around the New Year."

"I've got to go. If you talk to her, tell her I said go to hell."

"I'll uh… pass the message along. Have a good day, Max."

"Mmm hmm," she hums, and the line goes dead.

I don't know what has gotten into these girls, but I don't have time or energy for middle school antics. And that's exactly what they are. So immature and unbecoming, especially of fully grown adult women.

I remember little of last night. Maxine called, and I vaguely recall the first few minutes of her rage and expletive filled narrative. I faded after a while and by the time she hung up, I was in a deep fugue.

I need to get up and get rid of the bottles. Every morning I muffle the clink of glass between newspapers and other paper trash, dump them into a bag and drop them into the bottom of the trash bins at the curb on my way to work or to run errands. I don't need to see Roberta's knowing eyes and sympathetic smile. I especially don't need to give her a reason to kick me out. It's not home, but my little room is an acceptable substitute. It's as close to home as I'm going to get right now and it's near the school, where I've had to be extra focused and on my toes lately.

Thank goodness for these three weeks of vacation, because I need it. The kids were wild and out of control, so ready for some time off. My staff... you wouldn't even know some of them were adults. Snickering, snide comments in the hallways, talking through meetings, abject disrespect without a care who sees it. They way they figure it, I broke the rules and therefore don't have any power to enforce any others, so they can do as they please. Unfortunately, some were surprised to see that I still have some power, and I'm still tasked with running the school efficiently.

Write-ups went out just before the break. I'd been documenting, taking notes, preparing my case against those that felt they could be insubordinate. I gave them an opportunity to think about whether they want to risk an entire career—an illustrious one for some who've been teaching for over twenty years—on the ability to get back at me for one infraction. I would be dealt with, for sure. Whether they joined me on the chopping block would be another question. I expect some adjusted attitudes when we're back in January.

I don't know if mine will be one of them. I feel like I've given up. I got an email from Bernice that my appointment to go before the school board is January thirteenth. I have until then to seek counsel and prepare my case, if needed. I don't even know if I have a case to prepare. I had an affair with a teacher. I can't defend that.

On the last day of school before break, I looked up to find David Loren standing in my office. I hadn't been alone with him since I left his apartment that day. He walked in and closed the door, then took a seat in one of the chairs opposite my desk.

"You shouldn't be here, David."

He tossed a folded sheet of paper on to my desk. "We need to talk about that," he said. I picked it up, unfolded it and read the few lines of typed print that states that he's to appear before the school board on the same date that I have my hearing.

"It looks like they want you to give a statement. I'll do my best to protect you."

"That's not what I'm concerned about."

I paused. "What are you concerned about?"

"I think they want to use me against you. I'm not about that. That's not how I want this to go down."

"What do you mean, use you against me? I'm the only one at risk, here. Don't put yourself where you don't have to be for my sake."

He sat forward, leaning his elbows on his knees. His eyes, even with mine, reminded me why I felt attracted to him—they're so expressive. He wears his feelings on his sleeve. Willard hides every emotion. He could be a great poker player. "I was with you because I wanted to be with you. It wasn't a power thing. I wasn't trying to sleep with my boss. I cared about you. Still do. Thing is, we both knew the rules. We were both wrong. I came in here last September because I was mad that you cut me off. I rebooted the relationship so I could break it off. I got caught up again, then I got loose and because of that, we got caught. Now you have to defend yourself and your job, and that's my fault."

He sat back, pointing to the slip of paper I was still holding. "Let's talk about what you want me to say."

I returned the page to its tri-fold and handed it back to him. He took it, opened it, read it again and folded it closed.

"I don't want you to tell them anything different than the truth. I don't want you to risk your job. I don't want you to lie. I don't want you to embellish anything to try and save me. I think they're going to assume you'd lie to save my ass, anyway."

"Not really. We broke up, remember?"

"Because we had to, remember?"

He scraped the stubble that dotted his chin and cheek with the palm of one hand, his face betraying a deep thought process. I clasped my hands together and rested my chin on my fingers.

"Don't stress about it, okay? Just tell the truth. They're going to make the decision they're going to make, regardless of what you say."

"What decision do you think they'll make?"

I hesitate to speak it because I think if I say it, it'll happen. So I don't. But it lives in my thoughts, and even that makes me nervous.

Instead of answering, I stood and walked around my desk and opened my office door. "Have a good day, Mr. Loren. Thanks for stopping by."

David nodded, his lips drawn in until his mouth was a tight, straight line. He walked out of the Administrative offices without a glance backward in my direction. I turned to walk back into my office and noticed half of the secretaries staring.

"Don't you ladies have work to do?" I didn't wait for an answer. I sensed them all jumping back on the phones and email and other tasks as I slammed my door shut.

I'm about to lose my job. I don't know what I can do about it.

Willard took Kendra up to visit his parents in Chattanooga for Christmas. I wanted to spit nails and fight him over it, but Kendra was looking forward to visiting the Macklin farm.

Willard comes from a long line of money makers and managers. His grandfather owned and sold a successful investment firm. His father was a CPA for the firm and, as partners, split the hefty profits. Free of any children or responsibilities and with no real ties to the Atlanta area, his parents moved to Tennessee and bought acres of prime real estate. They built a sprawling top of the line home, built a stable and a barn, and started buying cattle and horses and chickens. Kendra loves going up there to ride her favorite horse, milk a cow or two, gather eggs for breakfast every morning. Besides, her grandparents are rich and they dote on her.

After I knew they'd left town, there wasn't a reason to stay sober.

Every day I get up and putter around, but with nothing to do, I end up at various liquor stores around town. I'm not much for bars and this is such a small area that I feel like someone I know, or who knows me, will see me. I drop into a store, grab a few bottles of something that looks like it might taste good, and tuck them into my work bag. I slip into my room after saying hello to Roberta and hide them in the closet. Then I go about my day. Until the sun sets.

The evenings are still the hardest. I never realized how much I enjoyed waiting for Kendra to come home from band practice or visiting her friends. Around the time I would usually be settling into the couch with a book, halfway paying attention to whatever sitcom or awards show that Kendra is watching, I escape to my room and crawl into bed with a bottle.

I cry and drink. And drink and cry. And get sick and drink some more.

I didn't realize what I had. Willard and I almost never fought. He was just so damn agreeable. It's easy to be agreeable, I guess, when you're never home. They say that the sign of a failing marriage is a couple that doesn't fight. It means they don't care anymore. There's no passion. There's nothing to fight for. Willard and I were not fighters or arguers. Before now, we never even snipped at each other. That's why his behavior right now is so puzzling. I didn't think he had it in him.

Every night I gulp back some throat-burning elixir and think bitter thoughts about how good of a parent Willard is being right now. Of course he can be a good parent—he left all the raising to me. While he was at the firm, I was working and going to school and raising Kendra. She's an intelligent, responsible, beautiful girl, and that is mostly my doing. Now he wants to take over and take credit for the rest of her formative years.

Every night I've hurled a stomach full of alcohol into the toilet, brush my teeth, wash my face and fall into bed. Sad but drunk enough to sleep.

I slide back down into the bed and bunch the pillow up under my head. Maxine can be so tiring. And my head hurts. I lay there, feeling my heartbeat pulse in my temple before I drifted back to sleep. The phone rings again.

I finally roll out of bed, dig through the medicine cabinet for some pain reliever, and run a glass of tepid water from the sink. I swallow some pills while watching myself in the mirror. I've looked a mess for a long time. My twists are puffy, my skin thin, dry and sallow, and my teeth are yellowing from the drinking. And the vomiting. I'm not much in the mood to do anything about any of these issues, so I shuffle back into the bedroom and climb back in the bed.

I probably shouldn't have snapped at Renee. Or at Maxine. I'm taking all my problems and issues out on the people I love, but really, do they not realize that me losing my life and my job trumps this man they're fighting about? He's not the last handsome man on the planet. At least I hope not. I might be in the market for one, eventually.

I crawl back into bed, roll over, and flop onto my side to go back to sleep. I have no plans to get out of bed today.

For what? No friends. No husband. No daughter. No house. No lover. Soon I won't have a job, either.

What's to get out of bed, for?

CHAPTER TWENTY-NINE

$\mathcal{M}$axine

I have my fingers crossed that Braxton's place will sell this weekend. We've invited some of the city's most elite and high powered to this overblown Open House. We hope that over 500 people will walk through this elegant, golf course home and that one, or several of them, will entertain an offer before the weekend is over.

Not only do we have the Newman event, but the Stone Mountain house is back on the market, ready to sell. Jonathon will be over at that property running another Open House. Less ostentatious but I hope just as successful. The winter market has been slow. A lot of my agents, not just Vanessa, aren't selling much.

After our hallway chat, Vanessa cleaned herself up. She got her hair done, bought a small but sharp new wardrobe and a few new pairs of shoes. I gave her as much help as I could, but Virgil was the driving force behind her personal renovation. He even took her shopping, showing her a few stores around town where she could find quality pieces at great prices. I'm not surprised. Virgil is fashionable, but he's also very thrifty. I've never seen someone fight so diligently for the lowest price possible on linen paper or loose leaf tea.

Vanessa invited her entire client list to the Open House. I'm secretly hoping that one of her clients makes an offer. She seems to need the commission and though it's a split, and she has to pay back her advance, it will still put her in comfort for a while.

Today, she is at my beck and call in jeans, sneakers and a t-shirt, hair pulled back in a tight bun and a fresh clean face. There's an enormous moving truck in the driveway, stuffed with furnishings, rugs, accessories, bric-à-brac—all the things that make a house a home. We have the day to get set up before the caterers arrive. Then we rush to change and be ready to receive guests at 6PM. It's going to be a long, full day.

Thankfully, I have my work to distract me from the mess that is my personal life. I'm still seething. Renee knew how I felt about Malcolm. I should have guessed, way back at Brent's party, that this would happen. They stole away together, chattering away about books and who knows what else.

Debra is right. Malcolm has always played things low key. That's not the point. Renee knew that I hoped that would change, listening to me go on and on about him in one ear while receiving his sweet nothings in the other.

"No, no. That table doesn't go in here. It goes in the formal dining room." I point to the larger room with the arched windows. Two men in overalls and gloves, temporary help hired for today, cart a ten-foot table around the corner to the bigger room and center it under the chandelier as directed. "Now I need the chairs to this table. Dark wood, white seat cushions. Go, go, go."

They hustle out of the house and to the truck, careful to only step on the plastic and cardboard walkways I've laid down. The floors have been buffed to a brilliant shine, and I don't want anything to mar them.

I pace the house, arms crossed. Most of it is still empty and echoing at this point, but the rubber soles of my sneakers don't make a sound as I wander.

I think about Joseph more than I want to and much more than I expected to. By this time of day, I would have already talked to him, since he likes to call me in the morning on his way to the office. Then we exchange a few emails, a few text messages, sometimes we make plans to have lunch or dinner. Sometimes we meet in the shopping plaza between our offices to have a cup of coffee and chat for a minute. I can't explain how I feel with him. It's easy. I don't have to try. He's not asking to be impressed. He lets me be me.

That should be enough, right? To just be?

My life is exactly the way I want it. I have the home, the car, the job I've always dreamed of. I'm thirty-six years old, in the prime of my life, making moves I never thought I'd make twenty years ago when I got my first job at Phipps Plaza.

But I'm not happy. I thought if I found that person who filled in all the circles — stability, ambition, similar likes and desires, that I'd finally find that happiness. I could have had that with Malcolm. Only he's not interested in sharing that with me. He wants to waste it on Renee.

The venom in the pit of my stomach stirs up again. My fists tighten until my fingernails dig into my palms. Just wait until he realizes that she doesn't know the difference between a light bodied and a full-bodied red wine; that she's never been to the symphony or the opera; that she shops at Wal-Mart and thinks her Juicy Couture sweat suit is actually couture. Malcolm seems too "big city" to fall for a simple, small-town girl like Renee.

Maybe I should bide my time and let him figure that out. He'll hurt Renee, but that's what she gets. She should learn to never compete with me for a man. I'll win that race every time.

Several hours later, the house glitters, packed with well-dressed men and women, all with a glass of wine or champagne in hand. Most of the house is furnished. The wood gleams, the glass shines, the metal reflects. The smells vary between the different dishes being prepared—stuffed mushrooms with caramelized onions, freshly baked mini croissants drizzled with buttercream icing, and a variety of tartlets from bourbon pecan to lemon meringue to key lime.

The wait staff, dressed in black, wander through the main rooms with tray upon tray of delectable bites. Between the sweets, the wine and the champagne, I'm beginning to love cocktail open houses. If we don't have to stage it, it's a wonderfully high class way to show off a home.

My agents are leading tours of the home in groups, handing out slick color brochures. Even Braxton and the new Mrs. Newman are here to oversee the production and answer questions about the property. He wanders the house from one end to the other with his fiancee on his arm, smiling and nodding but looking bored.

Vanessa rounds a corner, escorting a towering young man in an expensive suit and a shock of blonde hair atop his head. His brows are blonde, and he's pale. It's all I can do to avoid staring at him as Vanessa makes an introduction.

"Clay, this is Maxine. Donovan is her firm, and this is her listing. Maxine, this Clay McBride, of McBride & Sons. His grandfather is Judge Rufus McBride, who just recently announced that he's running for a Republican seat. Clay thinks this property might be a great step up for him and his wife."

Clay extends a hand to me and I almost cringe at the clammy texture of his skin as we shake. "Pleasure to meet you ma'am," he says to me in a quiet voice that holds a slight drawl. "This is a lovely home. I was just telling Vanessa here that Brandy and I ought to look into upgrading into something nice like this. A bit more room than we need, but we can always fill it with children, right?"

"Of course," I answer with a smile. The answer is always of course. "There's plenty of room, and so much open space that can be a nursery or a play area, even a study room as your children grow. Do you have children?"

He shakes his head, taking a long sip of champagne. "Not as

DL WHITE

yet. But that is the plan." Clay steps back, takes another look around and nods. "I think I may bring the wife out tomorrow. Have her take a look."

"We'd be pleased if you and Brandy put in an offer. Give Vanessa a call and she'll take good care of you."

He gives a short, solemn nod as if the decision is already made, then hands his half full glass to Vanessa. "I've got to run. Brandy and I have a previous engagement this evening." He extends a hand to Vanessa. I grab both glasses of champagne so she can send him off properly. Also, so I don't have to shake hands with him again. "See you soon."

"That makes three!" Her voice sparkles with glee as we watch him walk out.

"Three what?"

"Three clients interested in putting in an offer. This is so exciting!"

"Let me tell you something, Vanessa." I hand both glasses of champagne back to her. "Rule number one in luxury real estate is to look the part. Rule number two? Don't get excited until you're at closing. Get me?"

Her face falls, as I knew it would. How an experienced agent still gets excited before anyone has made a sale is beyond me. "The potential gets you feeling good about yourself, but it doesn't count until the wire hits the bank. That's the bottom line. Until that moment, you've got work to do. So…"

I gently wedge my knuckle under her taut, pointy chin. "Dump that champagne. Refresh your lipstick. Grab a glass of wine, paste on a smile and sell this house."

She smiles effortlessly, then turns and heads toward the kitchen. A few moments later, my eye trails her slim figure in a simple Donna Karan dress to the dining room, where she holds a fresh glass of white wine and a bright smile. She points at some feature in the room and looks back to her captive audience. Makes a joke, I suppose, because they all laugh together. Then, as a group, they move to another room.

Virgil appears next to me in requisite Gucci pin stripe. It's unusual to see him in actual shoes, since he only wears slippers in the office. "She's a fast learner. Eager. Hungry. Reminds me a lot of you, actually."

"She seems to be doing much better lately. Looking great. I agree with you there, but never form your lips to say that fashion challenged tart reminds you of me, Virgil."

Virgil rolls his eyes while sipping from a glass of amber liquid. "Of course I don't mean fierce-in-every-way Maxine. I mean her attitude. She's a go-getter. She has that 'I don't hear no' quality. She harassed most of her mailing list to show up tonight."

He hands me a stack of cards we make available at showings and Open Houses. Interested parties supply valuable information about their home wish lists. The third rule of luxury real estate is that buyers of million dollar homes are rarely looking for them. Real estate is a nice tax write off and I often sell homes by merely suggesting that a beautiful property has opened up.

I flip through the cards and note that Vanessa's name is on the Referring Agent line on nearly one third of the stack. "Excellent." I hand the stack back to him. "Let's keep an eye on her, though. If she doesn't sell something in the next forty-five days, we'll re-evaluate her role. I like her, but I don't have room for dead weight in the field. I need agents that can close deals, not just look cute at the showing."

Virgil is nodding. We are always one mind. "Done. The clock starts today." He steps away, and I am left alone again to survey the action.

By 9pm the house is empty. While the catering staff is gathering glasses and plates, I call everyone to the foyer for a brief meeting before we head out for the night.

"I want to thank everyone for your hard work today, specifically Vanessa and Virgil, who put most of the house together." I hold up a thick stack of inquiry cards and I can't help my grin. "I could not do this without all of you, so thank you very much."

I hand the stack to Virgil, who flips through them, sorting them by agent. "Virgil will make copies of all the cards we've collected. Your stacks will be on your desks for you to make follow-up calls. I expect to see a lot offers on this place, so put on your sales hats and may the best agent win. Don't forget that there's a commission split at stake here."

With a clap of my hands, I call an end to the short meeting and the agents all file out. Vanessa hangs behind, her coat over her arm.

"Thank you for giving me a chance, Maxine. I appreciate it."

"Stop thanking me and start selling properties," I tell her. I try to make it sound friendly, but I'm sure it doesn't come out that way. I hold the door open and shoo her out of it. "You too," I tell Virgil, who is still sorting cards. "Out. I'm positive you have something better to do tonight."

He glances up at me, smirks, and goes back to sorting the cards across the table. Six stacks grow in front of him. "What, like you don't? Where's Joseph tonight?"

I close the front door and paw at a stand of silk flowers in a tall, onyx vase. "Hell if I know. Wherever men disappear to when they're not dating me anymore."

He straightens, his brows knit together in utter confusion. "I thought you and he were—"

"He was fun for a while, but I'm done with him."

"You're not still hung up on Malcolm Brooks, are you?"

I swallow the lump that arises in my throat at the mention of his name. "Why?"

"Because he's a waste of your time. You may as well not exist to him. There are so many men that would beg to spend time with you."

"Malcolm is fucking my best friend."

It just fell out. Just like that. A little too loudly. It got awfully quiet in the kitchen for a few moments before the tinkling sounds of glass against glass continued.

Virgil drops the cards, grabs my arm and leads me from the

foyer to the living room. He plucks two glasses of wine from the serving table and hands me one, then directs me to the couch where he plops down next to me and kicks off his shoes.

"Shut up and tell me everything."

CHAPTER THIRTY

enee

I pull into a space near a door standing wide open. It's one of many in a long line of glass doors, but it's the only one that allows a wide beam of yellow light to spill out onto the sidewalk and the parking lot. I thought I'd arrived early enough to not have to jump in like I belong, like I know what I'm doing, but I already see people in the room, milling about. On the window next to the open door, a sign hangs that reads: ALZConnect Decatur District Alzheimer's Support Group Meeting, 8PM.

Before I turn the key to cut the ignition, I close my eyes and suck in a breath. Do I really want to do this? Do I really need to do this?

I suppose the reason that the door is wide open is that if I had to reach out and open that door to step inside, I'd probably change my mind and run away. I walk into a room that is warm and bright and smells like freshly brewed coffee. A slight turn of my head reveals a large silver pot with a spigot, a stack of paper cups and coffee fixings. There's also a tray of sugar cookies in Christmas cut out designs, no doubt picked up on discount because the Christmas season officially ended when the New Year rolled around.

"Hi there," drawls a voice behind me that sounds familiar. I come face to face with Norma, the receptionist from Golden Rays. I am happy to see her. "I remember you," she says, her smile wide, her blue eyes friendly, her hair… so red.

"I remember you too. From Golden Rays, right?"

"Uh huh. Is this your first time?" I nod, which makes her open her arms and draw me into them. When she pulls back from the impromptu hug, she grips my shoulders and squeezes. "It's real nice to see to you. I think you'll find that you have a lot in common with some of our regular attendees. Wouldn't you agree, Nancy?"

An older woman with dishwater blond hair cut into a messy bob is setting up chairs in a circle. "Whatcha say?" She asks, unfolding a chair and straightening, adjusting the wide rimmed glasses perched at the end of her nose.

"She's a little deaf." Norma guides me into the room with an arm around my shoulder. "Pick a seat anywhere you like. You're early, but don't worry, this room will fill up. Get some coffee and a treat, if you like."

I thank her and choose a seat that's off center. I don't want to be the spectacle, smack dab in the middle. I pull my phone from my pocket to turn it off while I'm in the meeting and notice the missed texts. One from Debra, two from Malcolm — 'just saying hello' from this morning and a 'can we talk soon' from this afternoon.

I ignore them all and power down the phone, slipping it into the pocket of my purse. I'm not focusing on anyone right now but my father. He's my priority. And, by natural consequence, myself.

I found the note that Ron, the intake physician at Golden Rays, had given me, buried at the bottom of my purse. At the time, I thought a support group for caregivers was a dumb idea. I would never sit in a group and complain about having to take care of him. But day in and day out, I'm watching the man I know as my father disappear inside the shell of a man I've never met, who doesn't know me.

One afternoon I sat down at the old IBM in my office at the bookstore and typed up the website to the support group. It's a national group with local districts and chapters. The Decatur District was having a meeting, and I told myself I would go, just to see what it was about. If it really was a bunch of people complaining, I wouldn't go back.

But if it's a network of people who understand what this life is like, I think it might save my sanity. I'm hoping it's the latter, as I sit and watch the room slowly fill with people. Some are quiet and timid, inching their way into the room like me, looking around, clutching the strap of a purse or a fistful of pages that look like MapQuest directions. Norma approaches each person who comes through the door with a greeting and a hug, directs them toward the seating area and invites them to grab a cup of coffee or a snack.

A few minutes before eight o'clock, another familiar figure steps in, nearly blocking the light in the room. Dr. Ron sweeps into the room with a ready grin, greeting everyone he comes into contact with. Shaking the hand of one drawing another in for a side hug and a chuckle. His long legs carry him to the circle which is almost full.

Instead of sitting at the head of the circle, he drops into an empty seat near me. After greeting a few people on each side of him, he leans around the person sitting next to me and smiles. "Renee, right? Good to see you finally came."

"I'd have come earlier if I knew you'd be here."

"Ah. I guess I could have mentioned that part. I started this group a few years ago with just a couple of people. It's grown into a great group. I think you'll enjoy it." He leans across the chair between us to give my shoulder a reassuring rub. "You get some coffee?"

I shake my head. "No, thanks. I need to hit the bed as soon as I get home. My dad takes up all my energy lately and I need my sleep."

He laughs, nodding. "Understood," he says, then stands and claps his hands together a few times. A silence falls across the room as conversations halt. "Let's all find a seat and get started, shall we?"

Ron begins the meeting by asking for new attendees. Shyly, I raise my hand, then blush when everyone welcomes me by name. He gives a brief lecture coping with drastic changes in behavior and cognitive ability. I can't learn enough about staging since the huge change with Daddy. I want to know what to expect next. I don't want to be blindsided by the next episode, or the new thing he can't do anymore.

Ron's speech makes me whip out a pen and piece of paper and take notes on things to ask his doctor when we visit him next. After his brief lecture, Ron gives the floor to the group for open discussion, questions and emergent issues.

"What happens if they get violent?" asks one woman. Everything about her whispers her timidity. She cowers in her chair, a worn brown leather purse on her lap. "The other day, my husband threatened me with scissors. I know it's not his fault, but I don't know what to do. I can't call the police or they'll arrest him." She pauses and shakes her head, her mousy brown, shoulder length hair whipping around her face.

"Was he angry? Frustrated about something?"

"I'd laid out a shirt for him to wear. He can dress himself if I lay it out. He hates green, and the shirt was green and I forgot. I'd left the scissors out and he grabbed them and just... came at me." She clutches her throat. Her hands are shaking. She must have been terrified.

"Foremost, get to a safe place. Then remember that emotions will come and go quickly. The disease affects the brain. Violence is rooted in some kind of emotion, usually frustration, but they don't remember the appropriate method to emote. Much like a toddler, it comes out in a tantrum."

The lady nods, her eyes wide, sucking in every bit of information that Ron offers. "And you'll want to report the incident to his doctor. I know it feels like tattling, but it could be something easily addressed with medication if he's frequently feisty, as I like to call it."

Ron smiles at her; she seems to relax as she smiles back. "And if he is consistently violent and you're being hurt, you'll need to assess your care plan. That's not a situation you should be in. Let's talk after the meeting." She nods, her head bobbing quickly. I have a feeling that much more is happening in her house than she is letting on.

Ron then turns to me. "Renee. Tell us about Bernard. He's mid stage, correct? How's he doing?"

I launch into an overview of my father's condition. "It really is like taking care of a child. We keep him busy all day so he doesn't nap and he'll sleep at night, otherwise he roams the house. I've childproofed the cabinets, added an extra deadbolt to the door, and double locked the windows so he can't get out while I'm sleeping. Most nights I'm so exhausted, I fall into bed and pass out. I've got a baby monitor in the room, but I don't always hear him. My nightmare is that he'll try to cook and burn the house down, so I take the knobs off of the stove every night before I go to bed.

"He loves cards, but he can't play the same games he used to play anymore. We do puzzles and I got him some audio books because he can't read. We look at photo albums and he's always asking who's this person, who's that person... people he's known his entire life. He can just barely feed himself, he barely dresses himself. And sometimes he hates what he's wearing, so he strips naked."

The room titters with laughter, but I also see nods. Other people who see the same things going on in their homes, who 'get it, who hear me and understand. I feel relieved. "I have one nurse. I run a bookstore in town and it's crazy busy. Between the store and my dad, I don't get a life to myself. My life is him, taking care of him, cooking for him, keeping him entertained, listening to him yell about... whatever. Asking for my mother who has been dead for eight years. I've had to tell my dad every day that his wife is dead. I can't say the words anymore."

"Think of her as sort of a security blanket–something he hangs on to because it brings him comfort." Ron is a giant of a man, but his voice is the most soothing tone. "It's pretty uncomfortable to live in a world that you know you should know and remember, but you don't. You might try looking at some old photos of your mother, if you have them, when he asks for her."

A light bulb explodes in my head.

Right after Mama died, Daddy packed up every photo of her and put them away. He couldn't stand to look at pictures of her, smiling and happy and healthy, knowing that we had just buried her. Over the months and the years, I thought the pictures would be back up, but they never reappeared.

Maybe that's what he's always looking for. The pictures of Mama.

I'm eager to get out of the meeting, rush home and dig through the boxes in the garage, find every last picture of my mother and spread them around the house. Daddy wants Lorraine? He's going to get Lorraine.

An hour later we are milling about the room as Nancy and Norma stack chairs and chat with everyone. I track down Ron to make sure I say goodbye to him.

He draws me into a hug. "I hope you'll be back. Every other Tuesday, we're here, talking Alzheimer's and offering support. You're always welcome."

"Thank you so much." I step back and tip my head up to see his face. "I'll definitely be back. This is a great group of people."

"It sure is. And hey, before you go, if you wouldn't mind dropping by the table and offering up your email address. We have a little daily support email chain that goes around. You'll want to get on that, especially if you have a question or an issue on an off week. It's a great resource."

I give him one last hug goodbye, stop by the rickety card table at the front of the room and fill out the information sheet with my email address and phone number, crossing my fingers that none of the members are freaks. I also toss a few dollars in the collection basket for refreshments. I snag a cookie on my way out and head to my car.

Sliding into the driver's seat, I root through my purse for my keys and my phone. I start the car and turn the phone on, seeing that I've missed another text from Malcolm. At least he is persistent. I bring up Malcolm's number and highlight it so the phone will dial him.

"Renee." He sounds surprised, and he should. I haven't spoken to him since before the New Year, since that conversation outside the bookstore. "I wasn't expecting to hear from you."

"Hello, Malcolm."

"Are you... at home? The bookstore?"

"Support group meeting for Alzheimer's Caretakers. The meeting just broke up."

"Oh, that's great. I hope the group gives you the support you need. You do a lot for your dad; it must be nice to get recognition for it."

"It's not about recognition. It's about the best care for my dad and making sure that I'm doing everything I can to be around to take care of him."

"Sorry... that was the wrong way to say what I was thinking—"

"Was there something you needed? You keep texting me."

"Just you, Renee. I miss you. I care about you. I want to be with you and I'm serious about that."

"Mmm. I hear you, but I don't know if you hear me. I can't choose you over Maxine. I hurt her badly over this. I can't."

"I hear you, Renee. But let me ask you... have you spoken to Maxine? Have you talked to her about your feelings? Have you approached her about us at all?"

Now isn't a great time to admit that I haven't spoken to Maxine in weeks. At first I avoided her calls. She'd call morning, noon and night and leave nasty messages that I stopped listening to. I refuse to accept any messages through Debra, who finally stopped agreeing to pass them along. Then she stopped calling. And Debra stopped relaying messages.

So I called her, but she didn't pick up. I left her a message that I wanted to talk and she didn't call me back. I emailed her and got no response. I don't dare drive by her condo.

"I can't reach Max," I tell Malcolm, which is so close to the truth, even I believe it. "And besides, I don't feel like it should be up to me to plead for permission for us to date. If I knew you'd never talked to Maxine about your lack of interest in her, I never would have gone out with you again."

"I was wrong about that, and I'm sorry. I'll talk to her, but I think she'll talk to you before she'll talk to me."

"Well, the last message I got from her was 'go to hell' so we'll be waiting awhile."

He exhales a long, dejected sigh. "So, if we can't talk to her about us, then aren't you sacrificing something you want for no reason? I mean, if the friendship is the reason we can't date, but you don't have a friendship—"

"We will always have a friendship. This is what you have to understand about me and Debra and Maxine. We love like sisters, we fight like sisters, but if something happened and someone had to come to my defense? Maxine would be first in line."

"Are you sure? Because it seems like she's throwing a huge tantrum over not getting her way. It's been how long since you talked to her? That doesn't sound like a sister to me."

"You will not score points with me by talking shit about Max. That won't get you where you want to be."

"Okay," he says, his voice a low rumble over the line. "Okay. Again, I'm sorry. The words aren't coming out right tonight."

"Just give it some time. I owe it to Max to let her calm down and see things in the light of day. She holds grudges, and she's very sensitive. If I feel like things might change, I'll let you know. Until then… I think we should consider us on indefinite hiatus."

My, that sounds familiar. Sort of like when I left Philly, thinking

I'd be right back and ended up not going back at all. The first time, it was for my dad. This time, it's Maxine.

"I guess I don't have a choice but to accept that and hope that it changes. Take care of yourself. It's hard to do when your priority is someone else."

"Thanks, Malcolm. I appreciate that."

The line goes dead without another word. I feel like all the air has been pressed out of my lungs. Despite my rant the last time I saw him, I felt like I might never find another man as perfect as Malcolm. I threw that fish back in the pond, and since I'm staring at the possibility of having my dad around for a long, long time, I may as well get used to being alone.

My shoulders sag as I drop the phone back into my purse, put the car in gear and back out of the space. I head home to my dad, to find photos of my deceased mother and hope it brings him some peace.

I pull into the garage and cut the engine, but I leave the garage light on as I step into the house, dropping my purse on the kitchen counter as I move through the room. I step over the baby gate that we've started using to keep Daddy out of the kitchen. He can no longer figure out how to get past it. Jessie is on the couch, intently staring at a movie on TV. The knitting needles in her hands are a blur.

"How was your meeting?" She asks, without turning around or missing a stitch.

"It was great. I'm surprised."

She nods a few times. "Good. You figure on going back?"

"I think so. I got a lot of good information. Met a few people. It's nice to be in a room of people who get it." I glance at Daddy's chair, which is empty. "Where is he, by the way?"

"He just went down. I wore him out, today. I hope he sleeps well."

"Me too, but we both know he's old and demented and that combination means they don't sleep much."

Jessie finishes a row, then sticks her needles into the bundle of yarn and gathers her belongings to put into her bag.

"You don't have to rush off. I'm going to look through a few of the boxes in the garage. I want to find my mother's pictures. I think that's what he's been looking for, all this time."

Jessie twists her body around to look at me. "You think so?"

"It's just a guess. I'm hoping I'm right."

I watch Jessie stuff her bag full of things and push herself off of the couch. "Well, let's see what we can find. If I remember right, some boxes are labeled."

It doesn't take us long to find what we're looking for. In a sturdy cardboard banker's box, way in the back of the garage is every photo of Mama that was on the walls, in a photo album, in frames around the house. He'd sealed it well with tape and store it up off of the floor so it wouldn't be damaged.

I ripped off the tape and removed the lid. So many memories inside this little coffin that Daddy built, her likeness and image, moments with her trapped in time. The box holds an inkling of her scent. Shalimar. It wafts up from her belongings. I smile and feel warm inside, remembering how she always smelled when she hugged me. Even now, if I smell Shalimar on someone, it makes me want to hug that woman.

The photos are all there, even the one we had reproduced for her headstone with the blue dress, the waves of graying hair and the beautiful smile. I cart the box inside the house and over the baby gate and set it on the dining room table.

"So... what now? Do I leave them here and let him discover them? Do I put them up on the walls? I don't want to shock him."

"Show them to him in the morning," she says. "Help him decide where to put them. I think that would be nice for him."

I smile, feeling proud of myself. She pats my shoulder, then walks past me to the living room and picks up her bag. "I was meaning to tell you I'm looking to start my retirement paperwork from Atlanta Rehab. The business was sold and I don't like the new owners. Much as I don't want to leave Bernard, I'm just about done with those folks."

I breathe and swallow and nod my head, but inside I feel myself on the edge of hopelessness. I can't do this without Jessie. I can't put him in a home. I don't know what I'm going to do.

"I appreciate the notice," I tell her. "It'll take a lot to replace you. Daddy really loves you. I know it doesn't seem like it, but he does."

She chuckles, heaving the bag over her shoulder. "I love that old man, too." She leaves through the front door. I'm alone with a demented man and a box of photos.

I love him, too.

CHAPTER THIRTY-ONE

ebra

I awakened this morning, hoping for a calming feeling in my chest, some clarity to my thoughts, a directed path that my feet should take. Some words in my mind that might save me would be great.

So far, nothing I've hoped for has materialized. My heart feels like it's about to beat out of my chest, my thoughts are a tornado and I am direction-less. I meet with the Board of Education in a couple of hours and I'm sick about it.

I got through as much of my day as I could stand before I escaped to my office, shut and locked the door. I've no plans to open it until it's time to head to downtown Atlanta and the Services Center, where the School board meetings are held.

The letter I received said to arrive promptly at 7:30pm. I glance at the digital display on my desk phone. It's 2:45. I want to pass out when I think about time dragging on for five more hours.

My stomach rolls and I feel intense pressure in my chest. To my right sits a bottle of Pepto-Bismol, taken from the school nurse this

morning. "Just a little sour stomach," I told her. I uncap the pink
peppermint elixir and down another mouthful.

I haven't eaten since last night. Roberta has mentioned more
than once that I rarely eat and I can't seem to kindly brush off her
observations. At first I really liked my smaller shape, but now my
clothes are baggy, my pants sag in the seat, the backs of my shoes
flop off of my feet. I look a mess, gaunt and pale. I don't really care.

Last night, Roberta made dinner–Meatball Parmigiana, and it
smelled sinful. She cooked a pot of pasta, tossed a salad and baked
a loaf of garlic bread in her bread machine. I detected the scent of
garlic in the air from the driveway as parked next to her sporty
Miata.

"Debra," she called out, closing the oven door as I walked into
the kitchen. She smiled that lovely grin at me, the chandelier
glinting off her silver hair. "I cooked this evening. I hope you'll join
me. There's so much food."

I clutch my stomach and screw up my face. "It sounds delicious, Roberta. But I'm not feeling well. I have an important
meeting tomorrow evening and I really need to prepare for it."

"Is it that you're not hungry, or is your stomach upset from the
alcohol?" The way she asks is so gentle and motherly, I almost
don't notice how passive aggressive she is. "Come." She comman-
deers my arm and leads me to the eat-in kitchen table. "Set down
your bags. There's no use hiding the bottles. I see them, you
know."

I'm forced to sit at the table, at a spot set especially for me. I
tuck my bags just under the table, reach for the water and take a
few gulps.

"That's a good girl. Drink up. Lots of water will be good to
flush your system."

She retreats to the stove and starts bringing dishes to the table.
Decadent elements are arranged attractively in what must be
antique china. Roberta must have noticed my admiration of them.

"I brought these over from Italy in seventy-four when I visited
my Nonna. That's Italian for grandmother. It cost me so much to

send them home that Ludo, my husband, said we may as well have bought a brand new set."

I chuckled. "And what did you tell him?'

"He already knew he'd lost that argument I told him we could never buy a set with these memories. These dishes have been in our family for nearly a century."

"And who will you pass them on to?"

She took a seat across from me and held out her hand. When I didn't understand what she meant, she pointed to my plate. "Your plate, honey."

"Oh, I really—"

"Hand me your plate, Debra." I don't know why, but I obeyed, passing it over to her. She was nice enough not to give me a portion that would feed an army; a spoonful of everything and a small slice of bread. She handed the plate back to me and I set it back in its spot on the mat. "Try that much. And if you want more, there's plenty."

Roberta served herself, spooning up a generous portion of meatballs, pasta, bread and salad, then drizzled a generous serving of olive oil vinaigrette over the greens. I remember being able to eat like that. A home cooked meal, my family around a table, sharing the happenings in their day. The corners of my mouth pulled downward.

Not yet! I told myself. Do your crying when you're alone.

"That's an excellent question, about my dishes. One for which I have been trying to find an answer for some time." She took in a bite of meatball, a pinch of bread and chewed, gazing at some spot above my head while doing so. "I have four daughters. The oldest should get the dishes. But she's already purchased a new set. She doesn't need two full sets of China. The next two in line are the most ungrateful children I've ever had the displeasure of bearing. And my youngest…"

She let out a brief huff of laughter as she reached for a glass of wine. "She's off backpacking through Europe or volunteering at a refugee camp in the Andes Mountains… or is she mining for gold in Rio? I never know. I can't keep up with that one. She owns nothing that doesn't fit in her backpack, so..." She sighed, shrugged her slight shoulders and sipped a little more. "Dishes probably won't be her thing. Maybe I'll give them to my nephew."

"You think your nephew would want them?"

"Well, he's gay as broad daylight. He might."

I'd been slowly chewing a piece of the meatball which was delicious. Tender and flavorful, it paired well with the light salted pasta and the crisp salad. I laughed at her comment about her nephew and took another bite. Eating is not so bad. It just has to be homemade, I guess.

"Your important meeting tomorrow?" I knew what she was asking and confirmed with a nod.

"I'm nervous. I don't know what they're going to say. I don't know what I'm going to say. I should have called an attorney." I dropped my fork on my plate and anchored both elbows on the table. My face fell into my open hands and I sighed the longest, loudest sigh. I was hoping it would make me feel better, but it didn't.

"No matter what happens, honey, you gave Morningside your best."

"The PTA doesn't think so."

"Well," said Roberta, picking up her wineglass again. "Fuck the PTA."

Indeed, I think as I lean back in my office chair, close my eyes and wait for the Pepto to work.

At 7:20 pm, I pace the tile floors outside of the boardroom, not paying much attention to the strains of the Business Meeting on the other side of the door. Staff members are welcome but not required to attend the monthly meetings. Early in my career, I attended meetings like clockwork. Always present, taking notes, soaking in the atmosphere. After I got the job at Morningside,

other things in my life took priority. I haven't missed it. It's as boring as it sounds.

The elevator down the hall chimes and David steps out of the box in a pair of black slacks and a long-sleeved, collared shirt. My eyes are drawn to the broad width of his shoulders, the bulges where his biceps fill out the sleeves, the way his shirt tapers at the waist where it's tucked into belted slacks. His shoes are shiny and black and click against the tile floors as he approaches.

"Mrs. Macklin," he says, stopping in front of me. He's been growing a goatee since before the winter break.

"Mr. Loren." I respond, tearing my eyes from him and issuing a brief nod before I step away from the door.

"Didn't see you around today. I wasn't sure if you'd make it tonight."

"I didn't have a choice. I'd be here if I was on my deathbed."

He snickers and leans against the wall. "I wouldn't."

"Really? What would you do? Let them fire you? Let them take away everything you've worked for? Tell me, David Loren, Athletics Director for all of two years, what would you do?"

"I wouldn't let them make me beg for my job. You already said you know what's going to happen. I don't know why you're even here, trying to pretend like whatever you say in there will make a difference. What I would do is take my dignity and go to another school."

"You don't care if they fire you too? You're the other half of this equation."

He seems bored as he answers. "If they fire me, they fire me. I'll look for another job. I'll work at Home Depot. I'll do construction. I'll answer phones if I have to. But you want to keep this job. You need this job and that school needs you. So I'm here."

"Yeah, well, don't do me any favors." I draw my cardigan in and close it around my body. It's so big that I can practically wrap it around myself twice. "Just tell the truth, like I told you. And remember that someone saw us together, so don't go making things up."

"I wouldn't dream of it," he says, just as the double doors to the Board room open and people file out. When the pathway clears, I step in through the doors and approach the front of the room where two long tables are set with six spaces. Bernice is one of them. She smiles in my direction. I try to smile back.

I take a seat in the third row of chairs and look around. The room is dotted with people, most of them I don't know. David sits in a seat on the other side of the aisle.

Front and center, in the first chair in the first row on my side, is Charlotte Rogers, current PTA President. She's a shrew of a woman, with a dainty waist, platinum blond spiky hairdo and a ton of jewelry. Her wrists and fingers sparkle as she makes conversation with a few people. She seems, to me, to be one of those perfect moms. Time for the PTA and the kids' soccer practices and in-between makes her own baby food and fosters Corgi Puppies and volunteers at the hospital. All the while being evil and catty, deep down inside.

She stops talking when she turns far enough to see that I've arrived. Her face goes stone cold, and she whips around quickly to wait for the meeting to begin.

They call David to the front of the room. He is seated at a table and chairs directly in front of the six-member board. They pepper him with light questions before they get too deep: where did he go to school? What was his major? How did he end up at Morningside? Had he enjoyed his experience so far?

Charlotte had to muffle a smug chuckle with a cough at that question. To be honest, I mentally answered it for him. Yes. He enjoyed his experience quite a lot, thank you very much.

"How long did you and Mrs. Macklin have a relationship?" Bernice asks this question, as gently as she can.

"From start to finish, it was approximately one year."

"One continuous year?"

"No, ma'am. Over one school year. Mrs. Macklin ended the relationship when the school year ended and did not plan to rekindle—"

"We're not asking you about what Mrs. Macklin intended," interrupts an older man, balding, salt and pepper coloring the hair he had left. "Please answer from your point of view."

I detect David taking a long, deep breath. "We broke up at the end of that school year. I restarted the relationship shortly after the new school year began."

"Why?"

"It upset me that she broke it off. She was acting like we'd never been together. Extra professional, calling me Mr. Loren. I went to her office and restarted the relationship. I knew what I had to say and do and it worked."

"And you kept this relationship going... again, for how long?"

"A week or two. Until we got caught. Then we were completely done." Except for that time I went to his apartment, and we had sex.

"So the relationship ended when—and because someone saw you?"

"Yes, ma'am."

"Thank you, Mr. Loren," says another board member, after a few more questions. "You're excused. You're welcome to stay if you like, but you won't be called back. Please take a seat or exit quietly."

David stands, and without looking right or left, heads straight out of the room. The door closes softly behind him.

I pass Charlotte on my way to the front of the room. I'd been hoping she'd get bored and leave, but she'd never give me that satisfaction. She wouldn't miss a front-row seat to my execution.

I hope my legs don't give out on me as I make my way to the seat up front, settle in and try not to look at Bernice. The board member in the middle begins with the straightforward questions.

"Mrs. Macklin, where did you begin your teaching career?"

"Tucker Elementary, fifteen years ago. I taught Language Arts and Social Studies."

"And when did you move into Administration?"

"Five years ago. I was an Assistant Principal at Tucker. When

Morningside was built, I started working part time as an Assistant Principal and I was a substitute teacher."

"When did you work full time, administratively, at Morningside?"

"I was formally promoted two years ago."

"How was your first year as a full time Principal?"

I smile, remembering the rush of excitement. "Exhilarating. Stressful. Lots of work. Never ending work, but I'm happy to be at Morningside."

"Last year, you began a... shall we say, non-sanctioned relationship with a teacher. We've already heard from him — Mr. Loren."

"Yes, I did."

She holds up a bound book that I know well, forward and backward. The Rule Book. "Does this manual look familiar, Mrs. Macklin?"

"It's the Rules and Regulations Guide for the staff at Gwinnett County Public Schools."

"Would it be safe to say that you've read this manual and know it well?"

"Yes, ma'am."

"Then you should recognize this passage I've bookmarked." She opens the book to a previously marked page and holds it up to show me the highlighted section. "Regulation 14, Part 12, Section A, under Conduct, it reads that no senior member of staff shall fraternize or otherwise become romantically involved with a junior member of staff. Should this occur, one member of the staff must transfer to another school so as not to be under direct command or undue influence."

She looks up from the passage, her eyes full of questions. "Mr. Loren stated that the relationship between you and he went on for one school year. Then ceased and began again. Is this your statement as well?"

"Yes ma'am," I answer with a nod.

"Knowing the regulations, as you say you do, why was this

relationship allowed to continue? Why was Mr. Loren not transferred to a different school in the county?"

"I didn't really think about it. I knew that we shouldn't be together. But it took us a while to hire David. I wasn't willing to lose him. The school year was ending before things got to any degree of... inappropriate. As Mr. Loren submitted, I'd ended the relationship after that year."

"But then allowed it to rekindle the following school year."

I sigh. "Yes, ma'am."

Bernice takes over, flipping through her notes again. "Tell us what happened the afternoon of August ninth."

I fidget in my chair, pulling my cardigan around me again. I don't like telling this story anymore. "Mr. Loren and I were in my office. He'd stopped in to drop off a form that I require before school begins. We had restarted our relationship the week before, so the rekindle was very, very new—"

"And still very against regulations," interrupts the older man again. I nod in agreement. I won't get anywhere fighting what's true.

"Mr. Loren and I were talking. I asked if he needed anything else, since I was heading home. He... he leaned in to kiss me. The kiss was... long—"

"You were in your office? On school grounds? Kissing a teacher, who isn't your husband, Mrs. Macklin?"

"Yes, sir, but—"

"Did you make a habit of kissing Mr. Loren in your office? On school grounds?"

"No sir, I did not."

"And what happened?" Bernice picks up the questioning again, eyeing her colleague.

"I heard something at the door. I saw the shadow of a person run past the window. It was late in the day, so no one would have been at the school. Mr. Loren ran to catch them, but couldn't find the person."

"So, someone at the school saw you together, and that's what started this whole thing."

"Yes, ma'am," I concede with a nod.

"And when did you know that this relationship seemed to be common, public knowledge?"

"When you — Superintendent Johnson called me to tell me that someone had lodged a complaint and she was looking into it."

"What would be your best-case scenario for an outcome of these proceedings?"

I shrug, nearly speechless. "I... expect that all sides will be taken into consideration and dealt with fairly. I expect to be disciplined. I hope I can expect to still have a job."

I catch myself before I tear up, before my voice quivers and I break down in front of six people who hold my fate in their hands. Maybe crying wouldn't be such a bad idea.

"Thank you, Mrs. Macklin. The board will discuss these proceedings and make our determination as to disciplinary action. Until such time, I hereby place you on Administrative Leave. I advise you to be present at Morningside tomorrow to pass along any duties or responsibilities to your most qualified Assistant Principal. After that, please refrain from visiting school grounds—"

"Byron, she's got a daughter at that school," says Bernice. "I don't think that's workable. You want her daughter to meet her around the corner?"

He sighs, irritated with the subject and objection to his ruling. "Fine. Except for morning drop off and afternoon pickup, you will not enter the grounds at Morningside for any purpose that does not involve your child. Understood?"

I'm numb, so I hope I'm nodding as they continue to ramble. I'm handed a sheet of paper and asked to sign to acknowledge my Administrative Leave. I scribble my name on the line indicated and am told I'm free to go. On wobbly legs, I make my way to the door.

Bernice calls out to me but I feel like if I stop, I'll collapse, so I keep going through the double doors, down the hall to the elevator, to the parking garage, to my car.

Inside the car, I sit in the darkness, in the shadows. I lean my head against the steering wheel, lower that big stone wall I'd been building all day, and I cry. I cry so hard, so violently, so thoroughly. The very last thread I was holding onto has just been cut.

Tap tap tap. My head shoots up to find Bernice at my passenger window, bending over to peer inside. I insert my key into the ignition and push the button to roll down the windows.

"Are you okay?"

I sniffle and swipe a hand at my wet cheeks and runny nose. "No. If I'm honest, I'm just trying to get far enough above shitty to drive home."

"You want me to give you a ride?"

I shake my head, wiping more tears. I just know I'm smearing mascara and lipstick everywhere. Maxine would have a fit. Then hand me a handkerchief. Dab, dab, dab.

"I'll be fine. I just need a minute. Thanks."

"For what it's worth, I'm sorry that had to happen. I did my best to paint you in a good light — a great principal who made a mistake and owns up to it."

"I know. And thank you for that. I'll talk to you soon." I roll up the window rather rudely, but at the moment I don't care. I just want to get home. Get in the bed. Drink myself stupid.

I pull out of my parking space, leaving Bernice standing in the same spot.

"It's not a suspension, Debra. It's just a leave of absence."

Renee sounds tired, and I'm sorry to have to bother her at night, but I can't talk to Willard and my family is so standoffish since I came clean about the reason I'm not living at home. Maxine turns every conversation into something about her. So Renee it is.

"They can dress it up anyway they want. Call it any fancy thing. It's a suspension."

"Did they suspend David?"

"No. But I didn't think they would. They don't want him, they want me." I warble into the phone, holding it to my ear with one hand, steering with the other, shooting up the Interstate like a bat out of hell.

"You thought they'd discipline you, right?"

I flick my turn signal and exit the interstate, then turn right at the light. "I was either fired or they were going to give me a slap on the wrist. It's the not knowing that's pissing me off. I can't work past tomorrow. I have to sit at home until they decide. I don't even live at home!"

I hear sheets rustling as Renee shifts. She yawns and I feel bad again for calling her at night. "Maybe you can concentrate a little on the home stuff. Are you going to sign those papers Willard sent over?"

"I don't know. I don't want to sign them without talking to him."

"What do you think he's going to say? What's he going to tell you that you haven't imagined, or that you haven't already told yourself?"

"I just want him to talk to me. Tell me he's mad, instead of acting like a three-year-old. He's so angry and so determined that this one... thing... caused me to throw our entire marriage away. Trust me, if I wanted to throw my marriage away, I could have."

"But you didn't."

"I didn't."

"Because.... why?"

"Because..." I pause, scrambling for an answer. Why didn't I throw it away? Why can't I let it go? Is it that I can't admit defeat? I won't let this be entirely my fault? Or do I really want this marriage? "I don't know, Renee. Don't ask me hard questions when I just got suspended. Now's not the time for intellectual queries."

She laughs. "Sorry. I'm tired. You know how I get when I'm tired."

I turn onto Roberta's street and pull into the driveway, then put the car in park. "How is Bernard?"

"He had a long day," she says, stifling yawn. "Doctor's appointment, we went to lunch, had a little walk. I took him up to the cemetery again to put some flowers on Mama's grave. Then we came home and had some dinner, did a puzzle together, watched a movie. It's like having a big old kid, you know?"

"It sounds like it. So he's not doing too badly, then?"

"He's stable for right now. He's doing alright."

"And you? Have you talked to Malcolm? Maxine?"

"Nope, and nope."

"Oh. Are you going to?"

"I broke it off with Malcolm. Maxine won't talk to me. I'm trying to give her some space, but I chose my friendship with her over a gorgeous man who cares about me and she doesn't have a word to say about it. I could be cuddled up with him right now. I could be having sex right this minute. So she can call me when she's done acting we're still in high school fighting over Adrian Lewis."

"I haven't talked to her either. Every conversation turns into some bitching about Malcolm. But if she's not going to talk to you, call Malcolm back. No sense in being miserable on all fronts. Maybe you could work out some of that angst under him."

"Or on top of him, even," she quips, her dry sense of humor coming through. We laugh together until she sighs. "Seriously, I wish I could have both. Maybe she'll come around."

"Maybe."

"And maybe he'll still be available when she does."

"A girl can dream."

"Yeah. So listen, I know it's not that late, but I've been up since early this morning and I need to get some sleep."

I gather my purse and belongings from the car so I can get into the house. "Alright, hon. Sleep tight."

"Hey, you too. You don't seem like you're well lately. Get some sleep. Eat some food. Take care of yourself. For me?"

"Yes ma'am," I tell her, smiling into the phone. "Thanks, Renee. Love you, girl."

"Love you, too, Deb. And if you talk to Maxine, tell her I love her immature ass."

"That's a message I can pass along. Goodnight."

I toss the phone inside my bag, on top of the bottles, and head inside. I tip toe to my room, through the scent of residual pasta, meatballs and garlic bread. Roberta's TV blares the Golden Girls, as usual.

I drop my bags in my room and head back to the kitchen. Maybe I feel like having a small plate before I go to bed. I just promised I'd start taking care of myself. No time like the present.

I rustle around in the kitchen, pulling out leftovers, a plate and some silverware. I hear Roberta's door open and her slippers sliding along the carpet. She peeks around the corner in a long robe that zips up the front, all the way to the chin.

She takes a seat at the table. "Dish up another plate of that, will you? Nothing like a bit of pasta and meatball before bed, hmm?"

I pull down another plate and serve us two small helpings of meatballs, pasta and garlic bread. I put one plate into the microwave and press the buttons to warm it up for a few minutes. While waiting, I lean against the counter and cross my arms over my chest.

"I didn't mean to interrupt your show."

She waves her hand through the air. "It's a DVD. The Girls will wait for me when I get back. I just love that little Sicilian Sophia. She's a little spitfire. I like to think she reminds me of myself."

I laugh. And nod. "Well, they suspended me. I know you're waiting for the update."

"Suspended? But not fired."

I shake my head. "Not yet. I go in tomorrow and turn over a few things to my Assistants and…" I glance at her and shrug a shoulder. The microwave beeps. I pull the plate out and set it in front of her, along with some silverware. I put my plate in the microwave, press more buttons, and lean against the counter again.

"What are you going to do with your forced time off?"

"I hadn't gotten that far yet. My friend suggested that I work on my personal life." I bark out a short laugh.

"It's not a bad idea," she muses, then spoons food into her mouth. She chews and watches me. I watch her watching me. The microwave beeps. I sit across from her with my plate and start eating. "I don't mean to offend, Debra. I care about you."

"I know. But you don't know everything that's going on. I know you disapprove of the drinking. It's how I cope right now."

Roberta is quietly eating. Half of her plate disappears before she says, "I watched Ludo drink himself to death."

My eyes shoot up to meet hers. I find them full of compassion and the shine of tears. "I didn't know. I've been so flippant. I'm sorry."

"It's alright. I know it's tough. And it's a way to deal. But… don't let your coping mechanism kill you."

I can't think of a response. None of the excuses I've cooked up for getting around her scrutiny seem appropriate. We eat in silence under the glaring light of the lamp above the table.

She slides her fork onto her plate and stands, taking it to the sink. "Just leave the plates. I'll take care of them in the morning."

She shuffles back down the hall to her bedroom and a few moments later, canned laughter seeps through the door.

I finish my plate, surprised at how hungry I am. I wash both plates and all the silverware, set them in the drainboard to dry, put away the pans of leftovers and wipe down the counters

In my room I peel off my clothes, remove my jewelry and my shoes. In the closet, my collection of bottles sits in their hiding place. I eye them… then turn around and go to the bathroom.

Not tonight.

CHAPTER THIRTY-TWO

enee

I set my phone on the charging dock, turn up Daddy's monitor and snap off the bedside lamp. Just as I'm on my way to sleep, the phone vibrates against the wood of the nightstand. I groan, sliding to the edge of the bed to read the text I've just received.

Guess who'll be in Atlanta tomorrow?

Marcus. I haven't seen him since a few months after I left Philly. I'm not really in the mood to be reminded of what I left behind but I roll over, phone in hand, and tap out a text.

Let me guess… he's about six two, two twenty, answers to the name Marcus. Why are you coming to Atlanta?

Conference. Remember those?

I chuckle. I remembered them well. Meetings all day, parties all night. Marcus is about to have a good time.

Yeah, I remember. Be careful. Atlanta isn't like Philly.

I don't plan to party too hard. I was hoping to see you, actually.

I place a hand over my fluttering heart, trying to stop it from flip-flopping out of my chest.

Let me know when. I have to make sure I have care for my dad.

Oh yeah? You gotta hook him up with a sitter or something?

A nurse. He can't be alone.

I gotcha. Okay, yeah. I'll let you know. Can't wait to see you. I bet you look good.

It takes everything in me not to bite that apple, tempting though it is.

See you soon. It'll be fun to catch up.

Sure will.

I know Marcus. I know his lines and how he phrases things. It's been years since I saw him but he hasn't changed. I know he's looking to hook up when he's in town. It's as if he doesn't remember how we ended and then he made it out to be my fault.

I replace the phone on the dock, then snuggle back under the covers, but now I'm wide awake, mind racing.

At Daddy's assessment appointment, I reviewed the changes I've seen over the last few months with his doctor. I was sure that he'd made gigantic leaps in staging. His decline and impairment-measured in seven levels, comes in at a low five. He was a three when I first moved back to Atlanta.

It disappointed me, of course. A change in staging would give me more hours from the state. I'm stuck with the same hours I've always had for a man that now requires constant care. I can't afford to pay Jessie out of pocket and she can't keep donating hours. I'm between a rock and a hard place.

Daddy's Ford Pension could cover the cost of care in an approved facility, the best of which is Golden Rays. I've been thinking it might be the best situation for everyone to move forward with placing him. This time, I don't feel guilty because I'm trying to get away from him. I feel guilty that I can't do more.

Jessie is retiring. Gladwell's is doing better. Maxine hates me, and Debra is too involved in her own life to be invested in mine. Malcolm is on indefinite hiatus.

And doors that lead back to Philly seem to be opening.

Is this a sign?

Thursday morning, on my way to the shop, my phone buzzes with a text message.

Free tonight for dinner?

I pull into my usual spot at Gladwell's and sit in the car to text him back. Let me check, but it should work as long as it's not too late, like 6?

While I wait for him to answer, I unlock the doors and start opening up the place. Blame the cold weather or the resurgence of reading because of all the weird new movies coming out that were books first, but a season that's usually slow has kept this little spot hopping for a while. Lexie scheduled a poetry reading this evening, so she'll be in early to set up merchandising and the performance area. If she and a part timer can cover the store, I can join Marcus for a quick dinner and come back and close up.

By the time I check my phone for a response, it's past ten am. Sounds great. Convention is at Marriott Marquis. Maybe we can eat around here somewhere.

At 5:15, I wave to Lexie as she's setting the stage with her guest. Even with traffic, the hotel is easy enough to find. I swing my car through the circular drive and leave it with the valet, then push through the double revolving doors to the plush lobby of the Marquis. I hadn't been at the Marquis since the last Pharma conference that I'd attended, when we both worked for SimCore, a Statin manufacturer. Marcus and I had just started dating and being in the hotel brought back some steamy memories that put a smile on my face.

I mill around the lobby since I'm a few minutes early. The building is decorated in lush greens and deep purples from the plush carpeting to the colors on the walls. There are signs posted on every flat surface or pole directing patrons to an exhibit or a fashion show or a round table meeting, where professionals gather to discuss industry practices or issues, but usually turns into a bitch session about supervisors, systems and clients. I stopped going to them after the second conference.

"Hey you," says a voice behind me. Smooth, not deep but not

high pitched, easy going. I'd know that tone anywhere. I whirl around and come face to face with Marcus and it hits me in one fell swoop how much I've missed that face. He opens his arms and I step into them, wrapping my arms around his torso and squeezing tight. He feels the same. He smells the same.

I pull out of the hug before I get too comfortable, grip him by his forearms and get a good look at my ex-boyfriend. "You look great," I tell him, then squeeze his biceps, since I've got them in my hands. "You've been working out."

His smile grows wider, and he gives me a deep, chesty chuckle while pushing the long sleeves of a gray thermal knit shirt over his elbows.

"I put in a little work."

"You put in a lot of work, from what I felt there. It's good to see you."

He laughs again. "So uh…" He glances around, then angles his thumb down the hall. "There's a restaurant right here, if you want to stay in the hotel. Food's good. Or we can take a walk down the street and grab something."

"No, no. Here's fine if you're okay with that. It's just great to see you." I've got to stop saying that. Get ahold of yourself, Renee.

We are seated at a table near a window. I remember that Marcus never liked to have his back to a room. Almost by habit, I choose that seat. He chuckles when he notices, then unwraps his silverware from the napkin wrapped around it and spreads the napkin over his lap.

Marcus asks about Daddy. I give him the usual report. "That's got to be tiring. Taking care of him all day, all night. Is it?"

I nod. I'm incapable of lying about what an effort it is to care for my father. I'm not trying to be a hero anymore. I'm just trying to get through the day. "It is. And I want to say it's rewarding, but…" I shrug, spreading my napkin across my lap and reaching for the water that the waiter sets on the table. He hands us two menus, reviews the daily special and steps away to let us decide what we're eating. "I have help. I couldn't do it without his nurse. I'd have to put him in a home without her."

"Wouldn't a home be the best thing for him, though? He could get round-the-clock care. And you could sleep at night."

"I haven't had a full night's sleep in four years."

"It seems like a lot for one person to take on, you know?"

I open the menu, scanning the options. "I want him someplace familiar while he still knows where he is. There'll be time enough for him to not know what the hell is going on."

He laughs at my wry, sarcastic joke, but I'm serious. I want to wait until he's late stage, but I may not have a choice.

"So what else is happening in your life? How's the shop? Your friends, those girls you were always talking to? Are you seeing anybody down here?"

I grin. "You really only care about the answer to that last question, right?"

"No, no," he protests, though lightly. "I care about all aspects of your life, Renee. But yeah, I want an answer to that last question right away."

I laugh, realizing that the ease with which I can fall back into ribbing and playful banter with Marcus is amazing. And telling.

"Gladwell is great, my girlfriends are okay. We're going through the usual challenges that life sends our way." It's the most politically correct answer I can think of to replace the term 'hot mess', which would more appropriately describe our current friendship. "And uh... I'm not seeing anyone. I was, but we're... on a break."

"On a break?"

"On a break."

"Okay." He nods, slowly, perusing the menu. "So, on this break... he can see other people? And so can you?"

"That's what a break is, right?" I reach for my water and sip, then grin and add, "Not like our break, where I thought we were trying to work things out and then I found out you were dating someone else through a mutual friend. Not that kind of break."

Marcus rolls his eyes. Just the reaction that I expected. "There you go, again. I thought we squashed that beef."

I laugh. "We did. I like bringing it up to make you uncomfortable."

"It's working. So what do you want to eat?"

We place orders for burgers, his with cheese and a side of fries. No cheese on mine and a side salad.

"You don't look like you need to be dieting," he comments, tipping out of his chair to glance at my physique in jeans and a fitted sweater.

"I know I don't. That's because I've been dieting." If running around at all hours of the night after Daddy and all hours of the day after my bookstore staff while sucking down coffee and the occasional brownie, cookie or, if I get lucky, a sandwich counts as dieting. Maxine would be so proud of me. I've lost twenty pounds. That Juicy Couture sweat suit she hates doesn't even fit anymore.

"Well, you look good. Really good." He leans forward, resting a forearm onto the table. "So, tell me about this guy you're on a break from. What does he do? What does he look like?"

"Why do you want to know about him? We're on a break. And it's more like a hiatus. An indefinite hiatus."

"Okay. So…"

"So, he's not someone that you need to be worried about, Marcus. Tell me about you. Are you seeing anyone? How's work?"

He pauses, then sits back in his seat and folds his arms. "I get it. You don't want to talk about your man."

"I don't have a man." I cross my arms to match his pose. "Talk. About you."

"Me." He sighs while glancing at the darkening view of downtown Atlanta. "I'm cool. Work is good. I told you about my promotion. I'm leading a sales team, now. That's a challenge, but I'm making it. Family is good. Kenny says hey."

The mention of our mutual friend warms my heart and makes me smile. I haven't seen or spoken to Kenny since I last visited Philly to close my apartment and turn in my work property —

laptop, keys, badge. He's funny to the extreme; he even moonlights as a standup comedian. He was always writing new material and making Marcus and I listen to different iterations of the same joke.

"Tell him I said hey. So, dating."

"Dating... uh..." Marcus fidgets, reaching around to rub the back of his neck. "I'm not. I haven't dated since Lise, honestly."

My eyebrows lift in surprise. "Nuh uh. That was over a year ago!"

"Yeah. It was." He rubs his palms up and down his thighs, his face bearing a sheepish grin. "It's been awhile."

"I'd say so. Too busy with work? No one piques your interest?"

"Couple of reasons. Most of them shallow." He shrugs. "One big one, though."

I know Marcus, so I know what's coming, but I ask anyway. "That one being?"

"That I miss you. When I found out they moved this conference from Chicago to Atlanta, I jumped on board. I knew I could see you if I came to town."

"You could have seen me anytime. Book a flight and come on down. You wanted SimCore to pay for it, you cheapskate."

"I never met a dollar I didn't like. I'll agree to that. But I wanted a reason to be here, not just hanging around hoping you'd find a minute. I could come down to this conference and plan to meet up with you. Dinner, some talking, whatever else comes up."

I open my mouth to respond, but our dinners arrive at that serendipitous moment. His eyes don't leave my face while the waiter is arranging our plates and condiments. When the waiter finally leaves, I can't avoid his stare any longer.

"Well, it's not that I'm not flattered. I... am really flattered." He smiles, his eyes sparkling. I know that look. "Marcus, I don't want you to get the wrong impression. I know you and I know how you operate. I know that look in your eye." I point at him with the tip of my knife. "Don't get any ideas about me going up to your room tonight. Besides, I'm sure there are some fine young ladies wandering this hotel looking for a good time."

I return to dressing my burger with mustard instead of mayo. Debra is always railing about mayonnaise and how it's fattening.

He takes a bite of his burger, chews, and swallows. "I know that look in your eye, too. When you talk about Mr. Hiatus, you try to pretend he's not important to you, but I think he is."

I take another bite of my half burger. "It's complicated."

"So, uncomplicate it. Who's complicating it?"

Over the rest of our dinner, I relay the entire story — Maxine's crush, Malcolm's disinterest, our budding romance and both of our failings where Maxine is concerned. "It's just that... she has men everywhere. All the time. She goes out on dates like some women change underwear. I didn't think he mattered all that much to her. I can't have just one man?"

"It's not really about that, Renee. I know you know that. Bras before Bros. Bros before Hoes. Friends are supposed to have a code." He picks up a fry and bites down on it. "If he doesn't really want her, there's not much she can do about it. Why not just let him go, let you be happy?"

"This is my exact question!" I'm so excited and yet frustrated that I fling a piece of lettuce to the table next to us. Thankfully, it's empty. I get up and retrieve the errant leaf and tuck it away while Marcus tries not to laugh. "She's mad that he wants me and not her. Any other woman and she'd say good riddance, like always. Since it's me..." I shrug, spearing more leaves of lettuce and a wedge of tomato and pop them into my mouth.

"So you like this guy and he likes you. She's mad, but she won't talk to either of you. Meanwhile, y'all are on indefinite hiatus because of her spoiled ass throwing a tantrum." He shakes his head, bites the end off of another fry. "If I'm this guy, I'm coming to get you. What's his deal?"

"I told him to back off."

Wrinkles form across his forehead. "Renee. Why?"

"Because... Maxine... she... we just..."

He points with the rest of the fry he bit off. "Lifelong friend, blah blah blah. Do you think she's thinking about that friendship right now? Let me answer for you. No. She's not thinking of you or him. She's thinking of herself and I don't mean to talk ugly about your friend, but she ain't no friend right now."

"I know… it's just…"

"Look, Renee, she can get hip or get out. She can't make him want her. Might as well give it up and let him be with who he wants to be."

"But isn't that shady and petty and… I mean, shouldn't I choose the friendship over the man? Because I feel like that's the right thing to do here."

"The right thing to do should make you happy. To quote a great modern day rapper, is you happy?"

I laugh harder and longer than I should have. The joke wasn't even that funny, but I felt somewhat relieved. Instead of suffering and keeping everything to myself and playing the martyr, I could have just talked to Marcus all along.

"So I should call this guy, you think."

He gives me a nod with a single bob of his head. "Come off of indefinite hiatus. Get you some."

"I will if you will." He lifts his hand, curled into a fist. I bump it with mine.

"Do it. And don't do the Renee thing where you give up everything you want and everyone's happy but you." He lifts both hands in surrender. "I get that you're stuck. That doesn't mean you never get joy. And especially don't give up things that make you happy for people who don't show you the same courtesy. When's the last time Maxine gave up something because it made you happy?"

"It's not even about that. I want to be with him. But I don't want her to hate me because I'm with him."

"You might not have your cake and eat it too."

I suck my teeth and frown. "But I sure want that cake."

Marcus and I stroll out of the hotel restaurant side by side and wait at the valet stand for my car. I have a small to-go container holding the second half of the hamburger from dinner. I saved it for Daddy, but I'm still hungry. I might eat it in the car on the way back to Gladwell's.

"I've got to head back to the shop to help my manager close up. I wish you could see the place while you're here."

Marcus shoves his hands into his pockets. I see the balled up fists protruding from the denim. "Next time. It was nice to see you. And I do hope things work out with the guy. What's his name, anyway?"

"Malcolm." I try not to smile, but I can't help it. "I hope he hasn't moved on already."

"Nah," says Marcus. "He's waiting for you. Trust me on that." He nods toward my car, which has appeared in front of us. The valet hops out, leaving the car running and the door open. "The Corolla is still rolling, huh?"

"Yup. Ask my Daddy where his American made Ford Mustang is." I cackle as I dip into the driver's seat and let Marcus close the door. I press the button to roll down the window. "It was great seeing you. And really, just book a flight. Come down anytime."

"Yeah. I'll just come on down and hang with my ex-girlfriend and her big hunky boyfriend Malcolm."

"How do you know he's big and hunky?"

He smiles. "You have a type." He taps the top of the car with his palm and steps back. "Tell your Pops I said hey."

"He doesn't know who you are."

"That's okay. It'll be like a little mystery."

I laugh and pull away from the curb, round the other side of the circular drive, and hit Peachtree Road still laughing.

The bookstore is hopping when I pull into my spot. People are milling around, books in hand, chatting amongst themselves. The couches are full and the makeshift stage is occupied by a group of people standing in a semi-circle. I recognize Lexie's guest, a local poet from her Creative Writing MFA program who self-published a book of poems as her final project. I make a note to pick up a copy and not even use my discount.

I wave at Lexie as I pass through, straightening chairs and

stacking books, checking in with the counter clerk before I escape to my office. I close the door, dig my phone out of my bag and unlock it. And then sit there, staring at it. Breathing. Psyching myself up.

I scroll through my contacts until I come to the B's. Brooks, Malcolm. I argue with myself for a few minutes before I click on his name and watch the screen change as the phone dials out. I listen to the line ring and ring and ring, and just before I think it's clicking over to voice mail, the line picks up.

"Renee? Is everything okay? Should I come down?"

"Everything's... everything is fine. I just uh..." I pause. Clear my throat, sit back in my chair. "I had a good talk with a friend of mine tonight — actually an ex-boyfriend."

I hear him take a quick breath, then push out, "Okay."

"Do you remember our second date? I wanted to stay but I wouldn't, because I thought it was selfish to want to be with you instead of going home to my dad. And you said you learned that you didn't have to sacrifice happiness to be a good person?"

"I remember something like that."

"You know, I just... I love Maxine and I'm so sorry she's upset and I would do anything to make everything all better between her and me. I really care about you, Malcolm. More than I've cared for anyone in a long time, in a way I didn't think I could feel about someone again. And I miss you. And I'm tired of suffering and sacrificing what I want to be a good person. Max is either going to let it go, or she's a childish person I don't want to be friends with."

I pause, inhale a breath, then finish. "What I'm saying is that I think we should talk."

I hear what I think is a sigh of relief come from the other end of the phone line. Tell me about it. "I'm all for talking. What are you doing right now?"

"Uh... hiding from the crowd of people in my bookstore. Lexie booked a poet, and the shop is full of people standing around stroking each other's egos."

"You mean like a poetry slam? I didn't know they did those in Atlanta."

I laugh. "I don't think this was quite a slam."

"Oh. Well, do they snap their fingers when they're done?"

"I think that might be a stereotype."

He chuckles. It's good to hear his laugh again. "Are you hungry?"

"Starving."

"Why don't I roll by, pick you up, we'll go by Ruby's before they close—"

"But the last time…"

"Maxine is not your mama. And she's not mine. She doesn't tell me where I can eat with you. So, ten minutes?"

"Five. I'll be waiting out front."

CHAPTER THIRTY-THREE

$\mathcal{M}$axine

It's unusually warm for a late January evening. I'm taking advantage of the mild Atlanta winter weather to enjoy a glass of sparkling beverage on my patio. The city is never more beautiful than when basking in the glow of the deep pinks and oranges of sunset. Sipping a crisp rose', I lean over the decorative scrolls that top the wrought-iron balcony. I have a corner unit that wraps around the side of the building with balcony access from my bedroom and living room.

It's been an exciting but tiring few weeks at Donovan. Just as I'd hoped, there was a bidding war over the Newman property. When Braxton called to review the offers and the top bids, I pushed Vanessa's client Clay and his wife Brandy to the top of the list. Coupled with a discount on my commission, the entire package was appealing and they went for it. The deal closes next week, which boosted Vanessa's confidence, and she sold another house the very next week. The week after she sold a sprawling estate to an up-and-coming record producer who needed an Atlanta home with plenty for room for a personal studio.

The Stone Mountain property finally sold. In fact, in the post holiday season, we have been able to clear several properties off of the trouble list. If all goes well, February will be a banner month for us.

Other areas of my life haven't sailed so smoothly. I've met a few men in the last few weeks, but they were too boring, too old, too young, or too nervous. If you can't carry yourself with confidence, don't bother. Maxine Donovan doesn't shrink in anyone's presence. Joseph has the quiet confidence I like. Sure of himself without being arrogant.

I don't indulge my thoughts about him much. He's called, as he promised he would. I don't answer the phone. The flowers he sent me have long since died. My email, text and voice mail boxes are still full of messages I've heard and seen but have gone unanswered.

I miss him. I miss his smile and his laugh and his silly sense of humor; how he made me feel more deserving of things I want than men who could provide those things without a second thought; his quick wit and depth of knowledge on current events and world issues. We once spent an hour conversing about the 2008 Economic Collapse. I've never been so riveted.

Maybe Debra was right. Maybe I don't think he's good enough. Maybe I am stuck up and judgmental. Perhaps I chase money and the men who make a lot. I choose men with the means to provide the things I want, the life I want to live. Growing up the way I did — destitute, on welfare and food stamps, with Inell exposing me to the underbelly of south Atlanta in the process— taught me how to be self sufficient, how to provide for myself. I turn to glance over my condo and its pristine whiteness and pat myself on the back. I think of what a success Donovan is, and I feel pride.

Inell also taught me to be with a man above my station in life. "Aim high, Maxine," she'd preach. "Pursue the man that doesn't need your money."

I've lived by that rule my whole life.

Renee's been leaving messages, too. She called weeks ago to tell me she and Malcolm were no longer dating. She wanted me to call because she was ready to make up. Well, good for her. I plan on being angry for a while. This can't be fixed with backtracking. She should have never been with him.

I promised Virgil that I would give the situation some space and time, let it settle and see what shakes out. Under no circumstances was I to call, email, or pursue Malcolm, even though he and Renee are no longer dating. "If he'd sneak around with her, who knows what he'd do if he was with you. You're better than him," said Virgil.

I try to keep that speech in an endless loop running through my head. It helps, especially when my finger is hovering over his name in my phone and I'm itching to call him.

"Screw this." I step back from the patio and inside the condo, pulling the glass doors shut. I lock them, grab my keys and purse, and head toward the front door. I've spent the last five evenings alone on the couch, watching reality soap operas. I've seen so much diva attitude, catty in-fighting and unrealistic drama that my real life squabbles seem elementary. I need a change of scenery and some comfort food, and I only know one place that will give me that.

The dinner rush is over by the time I get to Ruby's. I'm shown to a cozy booth right away, close to the front of the restaurant. I prefer the back but decide not to make a fuss.

The waitress slides a menu across the table along with some silverware. I request my usual Perrier and a glass of ice. She nods and bounces away to retrieve them. The corners of my mouth turn down as I remember the last time I was here with Joseph, and he laughed about the Perrier habit.

"Don't you come here a lot?" The waitress asks, bringing my water, ice and a straw. "With two other ladies?"

I nod. "We've been coming here a long time." I don't know when that'll be happening again. Debra stopped calling and started sending me to voice mail. When I have talked to her, she sounds drunk, but Debra's not much of a drinker. I chalked it up to her being tired. And I'm not speaking to Renee.

"One of 'em, one of your friends, is here. She's around the way, to the left." I thank her, then give her my order. As soon as she walks away, I slide out of the booth and make my way through the restaurant and turn the corner.

Malcolm and Renee are enjoying yet another cozy dinner at Ruby's. Just the two of them. They aren't as cuddled up as before. Renee, in fact, looks a little tense and withdrawn. Malcolm sits across from her, his arms on the table, leaning forward. They are deep in conversation.

I don't mind interrupting.

Full steam ahead, I march toward them and slam my palms onto the surface of the table. Both shoot straight up and nearly jump out of their seats.

"Max!" Shouts Renee, her voice ringing out in the quiet restaurant.

I look from one to the other with what I hope is a menacing grin. "Renee! Crazy how you told me that you weren't dating Malcolm and even crazier how I keep running into two people who shouldn't have been dating in the first place, who say they aren't dating now, but always seem to be together. Isn't that crazy, Renee?"

"Why would you care? I've left you I don't know how many messages and you've not had the decency to return one phone call."

"I didn't realize there was an appropriate span of time to return a call from a backstabbing bitch."

Renee puffs a sharp breath and raises both hands, palms out. "You know what, Maxine? I'm not doing this with you. I tried to apologize, I tried to talk to you, and you've ignored me—"

"I tried, too," Malcolm offers. "No return calls, no email, nothing."

I barely feign interest in what that hunk of meat is saying to me and give him a sad face. "Aw, poor Malcolm. I see you talked her into going behind my back again. Did your bed get cold?"

Renee starts to stand. I stop her with a hand on her shoulder. "No, no. You two stay. Eat. Enjoy your meal. Enjoy each other. Enjoy knowing that you put a good fuck over one of your best friends." I turn to Malcolm, then. "She's probably not even that interested in you. She's just happy when she can take a man from me."

I turn on a heel and stomp back to my table, slide into the booth and suck down half a glass of water. I should have stayed home with a nice glass of wine and the city skyline. Instead, I'm fuming at an old diner.

Renee storms around the corner and stops at my table, balled fists propped on her hips. "I need to know what exactly your problem is. And is it possible for you to be a bigger, more spoiled brat? You just can't stand that he doesn't want you, can you?"

"I'm not interested in speaking to you. Date him. I don't care anymore, because our friendship is over. I hope he makes you happy, and that he was worth throwing away a great friendship."

"The friendship wasn't all that great," she spits, hovering over me. Goading. Looking for a response. I ignore her until she grunts, fists clenched, and stomps away. When the waitress brings my plate, I hand it back to her.

"Can you pack this up to go? I'm not staying."

Not with those two under the same roof, probably consoling each other. I feel like going home, settling in on the couch and cracking open something that will have me sliding off the couch in a drunken stupor in a few hours.

"Oh and waitress?" She turns, my plate in her hands. Her expression tells me what she thinks of me. I don't really care, but I don't want her to spit in my food. "Add a slice of sweet potato pie to that?"

The waitress turns around again without a word and marches back to the kitchen.

I sniff and suck down more water. "Guess I'm not the only one with an attitude."

CHAPTER THIRTY-FOUR

enee

"I told you," Malcolm says. The look on my face and the speed with which I returned must have told him everything he needed to know. I slide into the chair across from him.

"I should know better, by now. I should."

"You want me to go talk to her?"

"No." I shake my head and lean forward, propping my elbows on the table. "I don't want you to do anything. She just informed me that our friendship is over."

"Over me." Malcolm seems horrified.

"No. Over me. I'm supposed to be loyal to her."

"There was nothing to be loyal about. I wasn't interested in her. Trust me... maybe I didn't look her in the eye and spell it out, but she knew it. Otherwise she wouldn't have worked so hard. She bought me a table."

"Well, when she wants someone, she lets them know."

"I had no illusions about how she felt. I know her type. I used to be married to her type."

At this, I freeze. And glare at the man across the table from me. "How… did I never know you were divorced? You are divorced, right?"

"Yes. For a few years." He leans forward so our heads nearly meet, his arms crossed and resting on the table. "You didn't know because I didn't tell you. Because she's not important."

"Not important? An ex-wife is important." His gaze doesn't lift from the surface of the table, so I prod. "Malcolm?"

He sits up and glances around, as if he expects someone to be eavesdropping. "Can we get out of here? I'll tell you everything. Just not here."

I'm already standing. This, I've got to hear.

"I can't stay long," I tell him as I follow him through the door of his condo. "Jessie can stay for a little while since Daddy's sleeping."

"You want anything? Wine, water?"

"Nah. I'm good." We settle in on his couch, in plain view of the behemoth table that takes up so much of the dining room. "You should get rid of that thing."

"Why? Because Maxine bought it?"

"Because it doesn't fit your place."

"I might have it cut down and painted. I could make it fit."

I shrug. I'd be happier if it went away, but it's not my place to decorate. "So? Your ex wife… what's her name?"

"Charlene," he answers quietly, with a wistful tone. "Charlene Tillman. She never took my name. Had to keep her independence."

"So, your next wife has to change her name?"

"Up to her," he says easily. "But I'd like it if she did. I want to feel like we're truly one. With Charlene, she was her, and I was me. We were never… us. She had her own money, her own business — IT consulting. Smart, savvy, confident. Very beautiful."

"Like Max."

He nods, once. "Charlene chased me until I gave in. Never took no for an answer. She ran the relationship pretty much. Moved in with me, told me we were getting married, then planned an elaborate production of a wedding. I think her parents were happy to get rid of her.

"I wasn't sure what I was doing with my life. My agency was just getting off the ground. I felt like a hunk of meat, most of the time a sitting duck between potential harm and some guy who probably doesn't even need a bodyguard.

"Once I found my niche and enjoy my work and assert myself, Charlene didn't take to that. She didn't like me having an opinion about where we were spending a long weekend or what house we were buying. She was in charge. She made that clear. And I didn't like that."

I'm intrigued by how much his ex sounds like Maxine. No wonder he wasn't interested in her.

"Then my mother and my father started getting sick. We'd bought this huge house in Baltimore. You know how I say, family takes care of family?"

I nod.

"Charlene had never heard of that. She wanted nothing to do with my parents staying with us, but I put my foot down. My sister and I figured that each of us could care for one of them. Since I had the most room and more money, I took mom. Charlene had a fit. She couldn't imagine that I'd defy her, but I would not put my mother in a home and have strangers taking care of her.

"My mom and her hospital bed and her machines and monitors all moved in. Charlene acted like she wasn't there. Wouldn't bring her a glass of water or a bowl of soup." His lips curl in disgust. His eyes seem far away, as if he is reliving the experience all over again. "That was it for me. I told her to leave. It was over."

"Good for you."

He chuckles. "I wish it was that easy. It'd be cool if she left on her own terms, but me telling her to go? Would never fly. She moved out of our bedroom, but she refused to leave the house. I started working at home to take care of my mom, but also to make sure she wasn't disturbing my mother. I'd walk into my mom's room and Charlene would stand there, in the corner. Those two would stare each other down."

"She sounds crazy."

"The day I buried my mother, I packed up my clothes, my equipment and my files and moved in with a buddy. Left her and the house and everything in it. Filed for separation. It was a year before the divorce was final. The only reason she agreed to it is because she found someone else to control. One of my best guys, too."

"Wait. She cheated on you while your mother was dying with one of your employees?"

He nods, his bottom lip wedged between his teeth. "She moved him into the house that we bought together. He's sleeping in my bed, eating at my kitchen table, parking his car in my garage. Dude thought he was me. Then he took my job. They started up a firm in DC, directly competing with my agency."

Malcolm slides a palm over his closely cropped hair and runs his tongue along his bottom lip. "I didn't want to be in the middle of that. I'd just lost my mother and my marriage. I was grieving. I wanted a fresh start, and I needed to get out of DC. I called up Brent, and we started talking about expanding."

"And then you came here and immediately met Charlene the Second."

Malcolm barks a hearty laugh. "On day two of living in Atlanta. The last thing I wanted was to get involved with another domineering woman, so I tried to steer clear. I didn't know if she was crazy like Charlene, but I wasn't interested in finding out."

"I see. I would have done the same thing, I guess. But still—"

"I should have said something. I know. Especially when I met her friend who was sweet and funny and the exact opposite of Charlene." He shrugs, then exhales a soft breath. "I felt like there was going to be a scene. And I wasn't into that. After I heard she was dating somebody, I thought we were in the clear. I didn't mean to come between the two of you."

"You're not anymore."

He reaches out to stroke my face, then cups my chin and brings me to him. His lips press against mine, softly at first but then with more pressure, until I open my mouth and our tongues dance together for the first time in what has felt like a very, very long time.

We moan in unison, then laugh mid-kiss. Reluctantly, I pull back.

"I should have said something to her. I thought we were in the clear, too. I didn't know she held a claim on all single men in this city."

"She doesn't have a claim on me. That yours, if you want it."

I smile and heave a long breath of relief. "I want it. I want you. I want to be with you. I'll deal with Maxine. But I'm not giving you up for her."

"I hate to be the source of strife between you. That's why I tried to let go when you told me you needed a break."

"It's not about you." I kiss him again, cupping his cheek in my hand. His stubble pricks my skin, but I don't mind.

"I wish you didn't have to go, tonight. We could spend the entire night apologizing to each other."

My brows rise as an idea strikes. "Well... you could come over. My dad's asleep by now. We could watch a movie, have some popcorn. Snuggle up on the couch together."

"Doesn't he wander around at night?"

I grin. "You've gotta meet him sometime."

He laughs. "I don't think I want to meet him while I'm wrapped up with his daughter on his couch."

"He doesn't remember that I'm his daughter. Hell, he doesn't remember that he owns the couch." I don't mean it to sound as sad as it does. But I guess it is sad. He drops a kiss on my cheek and pulls me to him.

"That's got to hurt, right in the heart."

My forehead rubs against his shirt when I nod. "It's like I've already lost him. It's a weird place to be."

"You're doing a good job. You know that, right? You're doing a good job."

"I feel like I'm failing. I want to take care of him, but I can't do it by myself."

"You'll think of something. It'll all work out."

"I wish I could feel comforted by that."

"So choose to be."

He tucks a finger under my chin and tips my face up. "I've been down this road before. There's nothing wrong with planning for the future, but the best thing to do right now is take things one day at a time. Enjoy the time you have with him. It's finite. You'll never get it back. When you're ready to take the next step, you take it. And you have faith that everything is going to work out."

I press my lips to his chin and sit up. "If I don't leave now, I'm going to have to pay Jessie to stay all night."

He flicks his wrist to check his watch. "I'll stop by. Keep you company."

I grin and stand, pulling my sweater down over the band of my jeans. I reach for the handle of my purse and slide it over my shoulder. "I'll text you when Jessie leaves."

"I don't get to meet the famous Jessie?" His teasing smile and playful, low tone tugs at my heart, sends shivers down my spine.

"She's a nosy, middle-aged woman who would never, ever shut up about you. Asking questions, looking for details, living vicariously." I shake my head, the endless litany of questions flying through my head. "The less she knows, the better."

"I'll see you in a little while. I'll bring some popcorn."

I stretch up onto my toes to snake an arm around his neck, then to drop a kiss on his lips. "And some wine. That red that you give me every time I come over."

"You got it." He kisses me again, squeezing his arms around me. I've missed that feeling. "I'm glad you're back, Renee."

"I'm glad to be back." I disengage myself and walk out of the door. "See you soon."

CHAPTER THIRTY-FIVE

ebra

The caller ID on my phone reads Atlanta Journal Constitution. Kendra tells me they've been calling the house, too.

It's been over a month since they suspended me and I'm frustrated. Fire me. Slap my wrist. Fine me. Reprimand me. Do something besides leave me in limbo!

All I've heard from Bernice is that they're weighing all of their options and reviewing the case thoroughly. I've also heard that my case isn't top of mind or a top priority. Morningside has sufficient staff to run the school, and the board is more concerned about rolling out Spring Assessment tests.

I heard that David resigned, effective at the end of the school year. I don't know if they forced him to resign or if it was his idea. I haven't seen or spoken to him. I'm afraid if I go to his apartment we'll end up in bed again, so I haven't stopped by. It breaks my heart to see him give up. I would have liked to save him, talk him into staying, but I don't see how he could ever regain the respect of the rest of the staff. Not that David cares about that.

Reports from the school are that things are fine, normal as everything. Nothing is out of place, everyone knows their job, and the school is running well in my absence. I'm proud of my people, but I'm worried, too. What if they don't really need me?

I suppose I should check the messages and see what these calls are about, although I can guess. The cheating scandal rocked Atlanta Public Schools. There's still fallout and endless reporting on how teachers changed answers on tests so their students wouldn't fail. Now, every blip on the horizon about a school related scandal hits the news wires. I guess they've discovered my indiscretion and resulting suspension. Or maybe they were tipped off. The very thought of Charlotte Rodgers stirring up attention gives me indigestion.

The phone rings again. I pick it up.

"What do you want?"

"Is this Debra Macklin?"

"Don't you know who you're calling?"

"I know the number I'm supposed to have." The voice on the other end of the line is high and squeaky. He sounds young, like newspaper intern young. Maybe he's trying to get his first break. Maybe it's his job to collect quotes. He sounds a little cocky, but not at all commanding. "I need to confirm that I'm speaking to Debra Macklin."

"This is she."

"Okay, great. So, uh, my name is Matt—"

"Hello, Matt. What can I do for you?"

"Uh, well I'm calling today for a comment from you on a story we're running on Morningside. You know what I'm talking about?"

"I'm smack in the middle of it."

"Right, so that's a yes?"

"That's a yes."

"And uh... so do you have any comment?"

"On... what?"

"On the situation?"

"The situation?" I admit I'm having fun with him. I'm not sure he knows what he's calling about. A cup of coffee with cream and Kahlua sits to my right. I pick up the mug and take a sip. "Elaborate."

"Uh, well you said you were in the middle of it, so do I really have to explain to you what's going on there?"

"Do you even know what you're calling about, or do I have to give you the story, too?"

I hear an agitated sigh, then rustling in the background. Maybe he's looking at some notes. "Ma'am, I'm just trying to do my job."

"Then do it. What story?"

More rustling of paper. "Okay. They have suspended you from your duties as Principal of Morningside because of a relationship with a teacher. They brought you before the school board for disciplinary action last month."

"That sounds like a story."

"So it's accurate, then. Did you have a comment?"

"I have no comment on your story."

"How about on the fact that the teacher you had an affair with has been fired?"

He wasn't fired. He quit. Right?

"I have no comment except that you may want to check your facts on that one."

"Well, Charlotte Rogers has a lot of details that make sense. She said you probably wouldn't comment." My blood boils at the mention of her name. Hasn't she done enough?

"I have no comment on her assumptions about me."

"Okay…" He pauses. I hear a swift intake of breath and he comes back, quieter this time. "You know, this story is going to run in Sunday's paper and given the Atlanta cheating scandal, people are definitely going to pick up this edition and read it. If you have anything to say to defend yourself, now is the time to bring it up. We can print your words and your perspective, or we can spin this with whatever angle sells papers. It's up to you."

The Sunday paper. I've been keeping a low profile, but this is going to blow the lid off of everything. "I hear you. I understand your point. I still don't have any comment."

He sighs. "Suit yourself."

"And sir? If you could please stop calling my residence? My twelve-year-old lives there. I don't want her to be a part of this."

"No problem. We've already spoken to her."

"What? What did you—" The call drops before I can finish my question. What in the world would they have said to Kendra?

My next call is to the house, but it's the middle of the day on Friday. No one is home. I call Willard at his office.

"Macklin."

"Willard, it's Debra."

My greeting is met with silence. He must have picked up the line, not realizing who was calling. Any other time, he ignores my calls. Specifically, since he dumped those separation papers on me.

"Are you there?"

"Yeah. I'm here." His voice is gruff and low. "What do you want?"

"I just got a phone call from the paper. They're digging for a story about the goings on at Morningside."

"Yeah. We got a few messages at the house. I haven't spoken to them."

"Well, this guy… Matt. He says he talked to Kendra."

"What?" Now he's loud, his voice a higher pitch. "When? I don't want her in this, Debra."

"Neither do I, which is what I told Matt when I told him to stop calling the house. He said it was no problem because he'd already spoken to Kendra."

He wheezes loudly, like he's having a panic attack. "I don't know what else to do, Debra. I've been trying to pull us away from you, from this situation to protect Kendra, and no matter what I do, you seem to rope us back in."

"Rope you back into what? How? I'm the one that moved out. I'm the one that went before the school board and let them judge me. I'm the one suspended from a job I love. Your life hasn't changed a single bit except it's made you become the father you should have always been."

"So that's a dig at me, right? That's a dig at the life I built for you and for Kendra and for how hard I work to maintain that life. You think you carried our entire household on your shoulders, Debra."

"Didn't I? And wasn't that the problem? It takes both of us to make it work, Willard. But it wasn't both of us carrying our household. Sometimes I don't think you remember that you're married. You get up and go to work and come home and go to sleep. I might see you on a Sunday, but you spend that day in your office or out doing whatever you want to do."

"At least I wasn't out having an affair."

"Yeah. At least you weren't having an affair. Like me. But did you ever stop to ask yourself why I had an affair, Willard? Ever?"

"Nope. 'Cause I know it wasn't about me. I'm a good man and a good husband and a good father. And I was providing for my family's future while you were out doing your PE Teacher or whatever this punk's job is."

"You know what, Willard… what you are not is a suitable partner. What you are not is a good lover."

"Aw, Debra—"

"Ask yourself when was the last time you and I had sex. Try to remember."

"It was before you told me I wasn't the only man you've been with, that's for sure."

"Don't skirt the question. When? Do you even remember?"

"I'm not having this conversation, Debra. I'm at work—"

"You'll never have the conversation any other time, either. You've decided this is completely my fault and there's absolutely nothing you could have done, or not done or said to play a part."

"That's right. That's why you need to go on and sign those papers so we can get this over with."

I sigh, closing my eyes and cradling my forehead in the palm of one hand. "Don't you even love me? Isn't there anything worth saving, Willard? Twenty-two years... there's nothing you want back?"

Willard doesn't answer for a long moment. But when he does, it shoots right through my heart. "These are questions I ask myself about you. What I think has nothing to do with this. I'm not the one that did this, Debra. You're looking to place blame on me, and I get that we had our problems. I didn't look for the answer in the arms of someone else."

He pauses for a moment, inhales a breath. "I've got to go. It's tax season, so..."

"Yeah. Yeah, I know. It's busy. I'll see Kendra tomorrow."

"No, you won't. She's at my sister's with her cousins this weekend. I told you that."

That's right. I forgot. I remember when I used to love for her to go off and see her grandparents or her cousins. I'd have a weekend alone at home to read or clean or organize. Willard would come home and we'd have a nice dinner and watch a movie together. I miss that more than I miss having a job. More than I miss being with David. More than I miss sex.

I hang up without another word and slouch into the hardback wooden chair. Roberta is gone, visiting one of her children, either the oldest or one of the ungrateful daughters in the middle.

I cut back on drinking out of respect for Roberta and the memory of her husband. I don't think I'll drink myself to death but I hate to worry her, so I've been trying to do without most nights.

Tonight won't be one of those nights.

CHAPTER THIRTY-SIX

$\mathcal{M}$axine

I only see Inell a few times a year.

It's not that I don't love her; it's that we get along better when I stretch time between visits. She got married this summer to a gentleman she's been seeing for a few years. He's a salesman of some sort that she met through work. Since her wedding, she's been too preoccupied to bother me, but the honeymoon must be over, because she's been calling, asking when she's going to see her daughter.

When I first went into real estate, my goal was to get us out of that ramshackle house in Decatur. She still owns it, the house and the land it sits on, a quarter of an acre but it's all hers. I pay a landscaper to keep the yard looking tidy, but the house is so old, there's no interest in it.

Over the years, gentrification made its way to Decatur. Land was snapped up, homes renovated and rebuilt. I figured it would only be a matter of time before someone would get around to inquiring about the tiny two bedroom, one bath shack on an empty plot of land.

She called me a few days ago because she wants to review an offer she received from an investment company. She's had that place for a long time, since just after I was born, so I'm skeptical that she's going to let it go, but I've agreed to come for lunch and look.

My father Isaac, who never married nor had any other children, died in a construction accident about ten years ago. He and Inell had a twenty-year relationship, a more off than on love affair. Imagine her shock when she was informed that he added her as a beneficiary to his life insurance policy. I had the Brookhaven house put in her name and with the check from Isaac's policy, paid off the mortgage and has been happy to live there.

The two-story colonial home holds some great memories for me. We felt like we were living in a palace for the first few months. Real hardwood floors, new carpeting, fresh paint. We painstakingly decorated, going from room to room, front to back. While Inell isn't as picky as I am, she has excellent taste. The house always looks warm and inviting whenever I visit.

I pull into the driveway and park next to a powder blue BMW. I know this is Inell's car because blue is her favorite color. It's a cute, sporty little thing. I take the sidewalk to the front door, pull the iron screen open and test the knob. It turns.

"Hello!" I call out, as I step into the house. The place smells heavenly, like fresh bread baking. "Inell? Where are you?"

"In the kitchen!" I hear the oven door close as I round the corner into the open space of the kitchen, dining room and living room. I get my love of clean, white spaces from Inell, but she also loves to dress up the white with splashes of bright solids — fuchsia, orange, purple and indigo blue give the room a light, springy feel.

"There's my girl." She smiles at me and I see myself in her. It's the same smile that stares back at me every morning. I get my height from Isaac, who was over six feet tall. Inell has always been short, but she's getting more miniature in her golden years. I have to bend just to wrap my arms around her. She hugs me tightly, then pulls back to look me up and down. She does this every time I see her, though I look exactly the same.

"Would you like some tea? I just made some this morning. Randolph enjoys sun tea with lemon."

I take a seat at one of the bar stools on the other side of the island. "Tea sounds great. You got anything to give it a kick, though?"

She chuckles and opens a cabinet that reveals a lazy Susan packed with bottles of alcohol. "Pick your poison."

I pick out a small bottle and pour a few splashes into a tall glass of tea brimming with ice cubes. I take a few sips and lick my lips. "What did you make? I smell bread."

"Oh, I baked up a loaf to go with some stuffed chicken breast and I've steamed some vegetables. Randolph and I have gained so much weight since the honeymoon I've been cooking lighter."

"Are you trying to make me ask about Randolph, Inell?"

She turns from the stove where she is moving chicken breasts from a baking pan to individual plates. "Why would I make you ask about Randolph? I tell you everything you need to know about him."

My phone buzzes inside my bag. I pull it out, check it and slide it back inside. Joseph. I'm going to have to do something about him. "Just checking. Every sentence is Randolph this and we're doing that."

"You've got some kind of chip on your shoulder, girl."

I sip my drink and try not to roll my eyes at Inell. "I don't have a chip. I'm just not annoying."

"It's not annoying. It's happy. You could do with a little happy."

"I'm plenty happy."

Inell slides a plate of food across the island to me. It looks and smells delicious. Before I can ask, she hands me a knife and fork. I use both to dig in, slice off a piece of stuffed chicken.

"You're rude these days. I haven't even sat down." She sets a plate at the spot next to me and hops up into the chair.

"Sorry. It's been so busy at Donovan that I've learned to eat while I can." Joseph hated so much that I'd skip meals, he used to send care packages to the office. Protein bars, nuts, raisins, things to stash away that can be eaten quickly. I've long since finished the last of the last box he sent me.

"You work too hard, Max. Donovan will run just fine without you micromanaging everything. I can just imagine how you are in a relationship."

"I'm fine in a relationship," I argue, albeit with a mouth full of food.

"Well, are you seeing anyone?"

"Not right now."

"Mmmm. Mmmhmmm."

"Don't think you know everything. I was seeing someone, and I was fine in that relationship." I slice more chicken, chew, then add, "I just haven't decided if I want to be with him."

"What's stopping you from deciding?"

I poke at a hunk of steamed squash, spear it with a fork tine. "You know, the usual…"

"Not tall enough?"

"No."

"Bad in bed?"

"Mother…" I take a long sip of my infused tea. I feel it kicking a little.

"Ah." She nods with that irritating, knowing smile. "He doesn't make enough, then. Those are your usual reasons."

"He makes okay money. Not more than I do, though."

"That's not the point."

"Isn't it? Didn't you always tell me to go after men who make more than me?"

" I taught you to be self-sufficient—"

"And I am."

"And I'm proud of that. But before you so rudely interrupted me, I was going to add that I also taught you to seek men that don't need your money to survive. Do you know what I mean?"

"I heard it all my life. Don't date a poor man. Shop for a man who lives above my station in life."

"Oh, Maxine. Sweetheart." Inell sets her fork on her plate, pausing to wipe her mouth. "That isn't the end of that sentence."

"Inell…" I drop my fork and turn to face her. "Why do I feel like this lecture has changed since you found love? You never dated men that didn't fit your standard. If he couldn't provide for you, he wasn't an option. You're not about to tell me I should lower my standard and settle."

"No, I'm not about to tell you that. But I think you maybe took my words too literally. If he's doing well for himself and he has the potential to earn more, that's wonderful. More than that, he should provide for you in ways that money can't buy. He should make you smile. You should catch yourself daydreaming about him. He should make you look forward to time with him. He should make your heart happy. He should make you like yourself. He should make you forget your troubles, however temporarily.

"You're out there looking for rich men and I understand why. I know how we lived for all those years and I'd do anything to never go back. But Maxine… we don't live in that little house in Decatur anymore. We're not on assistance anymore. I don't turn tricks and sell drugs anymore."

I suddenly feel sick to my stomach, but I know it isn't the food. I don't like thinking about how we used to live, about the things Inell used to do to make ends meet.

"The secret to a happy life is not a rich man. It's great if you can find love and money, but if you haven't found what you're looking for in his pockets, maybe you should try looking in his heart. I know my daughter, and I know her stubbornness will cause her to lose out on someone wonderful, just on principle."

With that, Inell picks up her fork again and digs into the steamed vegetables.

I see her point, but I've been this way for almost thirty-seven years. At her encouragement, I might add. Suddenly I'm supposed to stop considering a man's bank account and earning power? Date regular, average, nine to five, clock punching, boots wearing, Wal-Mart shopping, coupon clipping, polo shirt owning men?

I shudder, feeling even sicker. I don't think I can back down quite that far. But... when I think about a man that makes me smile, that makes me look forward to our time together, Joseph is the only face I see.

Inell is right about another thing. I am stubborn enough to miss out on a great man because I need to be right.

"Alright, fine. Message heard, loud and clear. Can we change the subject, please? What about this investment company that wants to buy the house?"

"After lunch," she says, flapping a palm as she digs into her meal. "Tell me more about how busy Donovan is. I own one percent of that company — a status report would be nice."

I'm roped into cleaning up after lunch. "There aren't even that many dishes, she chides, standing at the sink. I'll wash, you dry."

"You know they make these things called dishwashers," I grumble, tying on one of her aprons. If I get dirty dishwater on my new Prada sport blouse, I'll be inconsolable.

"I own one. It makes little sense to waste the water." Her hands dip into a sink full of sudsy water and she scrubs each dish with a thin, striped, rough piece of cloth. She's always used one. I thought every mother did until I went to Debra's house and her mother used a sponge. Renee's mother loved her dishwasher.

Inell washes, then rinses, then hands me every dish, glass and piece of silverware. I use a soft microfiber cloth to dry them and stack them in the drainboard. She is picky about where her dishes are set in the cabinets, so I let her do that herself.

"So, what do you think about the offer?" I ask her, setting the last fork in the silverware caddy. "Does it seem reasonable?"

"I don't know. That's why I called my daughter, the real estate expert, to look at it."

She drains the sink, wrings out her dishcloth and arranges it on the divide between the two sinks to dry. We remove our aprons and, with fresh glasses of iced tea, I follow her to her office.

Inell has worked in telephone sales for years, winning awards and accolades from her peers. If they only knew the young Inell, the woman that did whatever she had to do to make sure she and her daughter had food on the table. She rounds her desk, a behemoth piece that takes up most of the room. It's cherry wood with lots of doors and drawers and is covered in mounds of paper, manila folders and dust.

She rifles through a few stacks before she comes upon an envelope, torn open with pages protruding from it. I take it and pull out the pages, unfolding them as my eyes scan the letter.

"The offer is interesting, about four hundred thousand. I know the house isn't worth that much, but the land could be."

I take a seat and flip through the pages. "Looks straightforward, but I'd like to have my attorney look at it. And it might be worth it to have the offer evaluated independently. They could cheat you out of property value."

She nods, her chin cradled in one palm, her index finger tapping her cheek. "I had the same thought. They must think the land is worth something, if they're willing to offer anything for it. And it's been abandoned so long, they must think we'll let it go for a steal." She clicks her tongue and shakes her head, moving back into her chair. "They're about to get a rude awakening if that property values at more than they're offering."

"So here's my question... do I even waste my time on this?"

She perks at my question. "What do you mean, waste your time?"

"Think about it. This is Grandma Elise's house. It's been in our family for ages. You're really considering letting them buy the land and everything on it? Bulldoze the house and every memory we have in it? Let them build something new on it, without feeling like you sold out?"

I fold the pages together and stuff them back into the envelope. "I'll have my lawyer look at the offer and have the land evaluated.

If you have any doubt at all, it's a waste of time. You'll never let that house go."

Inell won't look at me. She's gazing out through the door in her office that leads to the patio and pool. She's silent, for Inell. "If I ever had a reason to get rid of that house, I figured I would. Maybe I wanted you to look at the paperwork, in case there was any reason to refuse the offer. Maybe I'm looking for a reason to say no."

"Or maybe you need a reason to say yes. To let go of that house, of the way we used to live. You just told me we don't live there anymore."

She turns her face to me, and I see every second of her fifty-seven years on this planet, from the deep grooves around her mouth to the eyes that seem to sink into her face. "I guess you can see what the lawyer and the city say about the land. That's worth the time. I'll think on it, and depending on how those things turn out, I'll decide if I'm going to let it go."

"If it comes out that the land is worth much more than they're offering—"

"Then we counteroffer, baby. I know you know how to do that."

I grin at her. She knows how to stroke my ego. "Yes, ma'am. I do."

She pushes her chair back from her desk and waves me along as she leaves her office. "Let's sit in the sunroom and enjoy our tea."

Inell's sun room is an addition, built a few years ago when she got a sizable salary increase after completing her MBA. She's been after me to do the same thing, but aside from continuing education courses in real estate, I haven't stepped foot in a learning environment since high school. I'm not in a hurry to feel like the old lady in the room, so there's no rush in my mind.

We each settle into a black resin wicker chair with powder blue cushions. The windows span wall to wall, floor to ceiling, allowing the sun to stream in and bring warmth and a natural brightness to the room. I set my glass of tea down on a coaster and scoot back while Inell fills me in the latest gossip with her friends, our family and her husband.

"Now, what else have you been doing besides working? You mentioned one man that you're not seeing... is he the only interest, or is there a line, as usual?"

"I've been out with a few men lately. Not really the cream of the crop. And before you roll your eyes at me, it's not about money."

"Then what is it?"

I shrug a shoulder, frowning. Outside the bank of windows, the well-groomed bushes are flowering. Let it get warm for half a day in Atlanta and things grow. "No juice. No spark." I avert my gaze to her small, round face. I notice jowls beginning to form. I avoid the compulsion to feel around my chin and make sure I'm not growing any. "You know what I mean?"

She nods a deep bend from the neck, eyes closed. "Mm-hmm. I do. To me, it was the difference between Randolph and every other man before him. I could have been with anyone. Same as you. You could have had the one that owned the car dealerships. The banker. The investor. Remember the millionaire from Macon? He seemed very attracted to you."

"I remember them all. In the end, it just didn't work out for a lot of reasons." I reach for my tea and sip, lick my lips and set the glass back down again.

"So tell me about the man you're not seeing. Is there a spark with him?"

After a few moments of thought, I nod. "Yes. There's a spark."

"And the only reason you're not with him is that he doesn't make enough money for you."

"No, that's not it. I mean, it's part of the list of reasons. It's a long story..."

"I have all afternoon."

So I tell Inell the story. The whole story: meeting Malcolm, trying to rope him in. How I knew he wasn't really into me, but there are few men that say no and mean it, and I hadn't intended on giving up on him. How I'd introduced him to Renee and how the next thing I knew, I was seeing them together. The embarrassing scene I caused that night.

Inell has been frowning throughout my entire story. This is the reason I don't tell her anything about my life. She's the only person with any kind of influence over me.

"So you were with Joseph, feeling the spark, smiling, laughing, being loved. Everything was alright everywhere, but you fly into a jealous rage because the other man likes Renee? I didn't teach you any better than that, girl?"

"It's not about him. It's Renee. I feel like she should have left him alone."

"You just told me he wasn't interested in you."

"But I was interested in him."

"So what, Maxine? You're not hurting for male attention. There's spark and a man that wants you and you want him, but you're caught up in his pockets and worried about a man that doesn't want you." She clicks her tongue at me, a gesture I hate.

"You'd better straighten out your life, young lady. I didn't raise you to fight over men. You have too much to offer to be running after someone who's not running after you."

I sulk, sitting in the chair next to Inell, feeling appropriately chastised. One side of me wants to keep arguing. The other side knows she's right, but doesn't want to admit it.

"What has Renee said? Is she sorry for going around you?"

"Of course she is. You know Renee." I fidget with my bracelet for a few moments. I know Inell is going to flip her lid when I tell her the latest development. "I kind of told her I didn't want to be friends with her anymore."

She scowls, as I knew she would. "Maxine Elise. You didn't tell that girl that. You've known her—"

"Since we were kids, I know. I told her to go on and date Malcolm. What do I care? He doesn't even want me."

"So you threw a tantrum."

"She called me a brat."

"This reminds me of when y'all was fighting over that boy your junior year. We're supposed to grow out of childish ways, Maxine. You make up with that girl and let her be happy. And pray that the man with the spark wants you back. His pockets don't matter if his heart is rich. You hear me?"

"Yes, mother," I answer, quietly.

I walk past the powder blue BMW again on my way out. Sometimes she really riles me up, but she's the only person that can tell me things I don't want to hear, even things I've been telling myself.

I slide my thumb across the handle of the Maserati to unlock it and climb in, exhaling into the warm, stale air. My bag buzzes. Again. This time I pull out the phone and, seeing Joseph's name and photo on-screen, press the green button to pick up the call.

"Hello."

"Hello? Max?"

"Yes. Hello, Joseph."

"Oh. Hey. I thought I was going to get your voice mail again."

"No. You've got me. It's good to hear your voice."

"Yours too. I've missed it. I didn't think I'd ever hear it again."

"I know. I apologize for that. I'm at my mother's, where I've learned that I'm immature and I still act like I'm in high school. She told me not to let a good man slip through my fingers. So… I'm trying not to do that."

"By good man, you mean me, right? Not a rich man. Not Malcolm."

I smile into the phone. "Yes, I mean you, silly."

"Me, silly? Woman…" He chuckles. How I have missed that sound. I close my eyes and smile into the phone upon hearing it. "So… can we talk?"

"Do you want to meet me at my place?"

"I'm on my way right now. Should I bring anything?"

"Just you. I have everything I need but you."

. . .

Joseph is waiting for me in the lobby of Buckhead Vista when I step off of the elevator from the parking garage. A strange flutter moves through my chest when I see him. He's wearing one of the sweaters I bought for him, a beautiful charcoal v neck.

He approaches me slowly, his steps deliberately plodding as he makes his way across the marble-floored lobby. When he's in front of me, he stops. And stares, like his eyes can do all the talking for him. And maybe they can, because I like what I'm reading in them.

"Maxine." His tone melts me. He opens his arms. I only hesitate for a second before I step forward and into a tight embrace.

I've missed this man, the way his arms feel around me. The tone of his voice when he laughs or when he's picking on me about something. Him. I've missed him.

"It's really good to see you," he says, angling his head to whisper into my ear. "I couldn't stop thinking about you."

I step back and almost regret the move because it means I'm not wrapped up in him anymore. I reach for the elevator and press the call button. "Let's go upstairs and talk."

Two steel doors slide open and we step inside, ride to the twelfth floor and get off again. Joseph remains quiet as he follows me down the hallway. Our footsteps are muted by thick pile carpeting and every few feet, there's an artful object on the wall, on a table, flowers in a vase.

I insert my key into both locks and let us in. The place looks the same as always, but it seems so much brighter with Joseph there. I drop my bag at the foyer table, kick off my shoes and carry them into the living room.

"Can I offer you anything? Some wine, something stronger? A cup of coffee, maybe?"

"I'm great right now, thanks."

He gestures toward the couch and waits for me to sit before he joins me, then scoots over so he is close. So close I can see the stubble growing in on his cheek and smell the spicy fragrance of his cologne. So close I can hear his breathing changing and see his pulse at the base of his neck.

"So—" I begin.

"Well, I—" he started, at the same time. "Go ahead."

"No, no, no. You go ahead."

"Maxine..." He eyes me playfully, which makes me laugh. "What did you want to say?"

"I uh..." I shift sideways, tucking one leg up under me. "I just... wanted to apologize. For everything."

"What constitutes everything?"

"I mean... everything. From using you in the beginning and not really being serious about seeing you, to harboring feelings for Malcolm that I knew good and well weren't being reciprocated. For wasting your time and your money, for being shallow and selfish with someone that just wanted me to be happy. And for not realizing what I had when I had it."

He pauses for a moment, then asks, "Is that everything?"

I shrug. "I mean... there are some micro-aggressions like the tantrum I threw at Ruby's and when I called Malcolm 'my man'—"

"You call that a micro-aggression?"

"It was... aggression on a small scale—"

"A small scale? Maxine, you cussed your friend and that guy out in the middle of Ruby's without a care in the world who heard you."

Still ashamed from my tongue lashing from Inell, I dip my head and pout. "I know. I'm sorry. I'm sorry for that night, I'm sorry for all the nights I sat here and looked at the messages you sent me and said nothing. I'm stubborn, according to my mother. I'm impressed that you kept trying."

"I was sure I could wear you down," he says, with a cocky grin. "Sounds like I need to meet your mother. I like the things she has to say about you. I just wanted you to talk to me, to say something to me. Anything. Go away, forget my name."

He stares and adds, "Or... let's try again. Let's have something real."

"I'd like that. Something real. With you."

I've definitely never been here before, asking for a relationship with a man. It's… humbling.

"You would, huh?"

"I would. I know I don't deserve another chance—"

He presses a finger against my lips, halting my words, then dips his head toward mine and replaces his fingers with his lips. The kiss is sweet and light, but it sends shivers down my spine all the same, awakening my body from a long sleep.

When he pulls back, his eyes seek mine, his fingertips stroke my face. "There's no such thing as not deserving. We all get every chance to be happy, no matter how many chances it takes."

"How'd you get to be so wise, Mr. Glass?"

"Years and years of being stupid, Ms. Donovan." He laughs, slouching into the supple leather of the couch. "So, you've been doing okay?"

I nod. "Business wise, yes. I thought it was going to be a rough winter, but my team pulled it out at the last minute. February is going to be crazy, and our spring market is right around the corner. It's an exciting season in real estate."

"I bet," he says, nodding along. "And personally?"

My eyes slip from his face and focus on the carpet. "Not the best, lately. I still haven't made up with Renee. I saw them the other night and… it wasn't pretty."

He tucks his finger under my chin and tips my head up so I can see him. "I didn't come all the way over here to still compete with Malcolm. You're not still hung up on that guy. Right?"

"I'm not," I promise, almost laughing. "I'm really not. It's just Renee, and this stupid feeling I get when someone prefers her to me."

"You like to win the fight."

"It shouldn't be a fight, I know that. And if he makes her happy—"

"You think she should have come to you, to let you know you were out of the running."

I nod, vigorously. "Instead, I had to find out in a really bad way, and I don't react well to finding things out in a bad way."

"Me either. Like how I had to find out I wasn't your man."

"I'm so sorry for that. It was childish, and you didn't deserve that. Please forgive me?"

Joseph pauses, lifting a hand to study perfectly shaped, buffed and shiny fingernails. After a few moments of silence, he quietly responds. "Was I your man?"

"Yes. I didn't want you to be. But you were."

He nods, his lips pursed together. "But you want me to be your man, now?"

My smile is tentative. I'm hoping his reluctance is just teasing. "If you want the job."

"Oh, I want the job." His stare is intense, passion filled. I want nothing more right now than him. "You know why?"

I can guess what he's about to say. At least I hope he's about to say it. Because if he does, I'll say it too.

He reaches for my hand and winds his fingers between mine. "Because... Maxine... you need me."

I laugh. Serves me right.

"What?" He grins, almost laughing aloud at himself. "You don't think you need me?"

"I know I do. I just... I thought..."

"Just..." He prods, then pauses, his eyes narrowing, his head tilted toward me, as if we are in secret collusion. "What did you expect to hear?"

"Nothing, Joseph." I stop myself before I let myself say anymore. It'll come. And when it does, I'll be ready. "I'm just happy right now. How about some wine?"

"To celebrate you coming to your senses? We can start there, but you know I'm hoping to make up for lost time."

I feel the most enormous sigh of relief cross my lips. "I can't tell you how much I'm looking forward to making up for lost time."

CHAPTER THIRTY-SEVEN

enee

I was at the shop when I got the call. Malcolm had stopped by with dinner, a sandwich and chips. We spread out our meal at a Bistro table and I enjoyed the first food I've had all day. The shop is packed with what has become the usual crowd– students from area colleges using a few tables and the couches, every available plug taken up by a laptop or charging an electronic device.

Lexie brings my phone to me, its melodic tone chiming away. I'd left it in my office. "It's been ringing off the hook." She hands it to me. "I thought it might be about your dad."

"I'm sorry. Guess I forgot to turn the ringer off." I scroll through the call history, past messages from Grady Hospital. I glance up at Malcolm, confused. "Who's calling me from Grady? Jessie would have called here if something was going on with my dad."

"Listen to the messages," he says, wiping his mouth with a napkin.

I pull up the last message left and let it play on speaker. "This message is for a Renee Gladwell. This is the last dialed number from a mobile phone belonging to Debra Macklin. There's been an accident. If you could please return my call at this number, I would appreciate it. Thank you."

Already up and out of my chair, I press a number to return the call and listen to it ring while rushing back to my office.

"Grady Hospital. Can I help you?"

"Hi," I yell into the phone. "I got a phone call, because one of my friends was in an accident. They asked me to call—"

"Name, please?"

"Debra Macklin."

Rapid typing. "Are you a relative?"

"No. Someone called me and said—"

"I can't release patient information to anyone who isn't a relative."

"Then why did someone call me and ask me to call them?"

"I'm not sure, ma'am. Is there anything else I can help you with?"

"So you can't tell me if Debra Macklin is there?"

"No, ma'am." I hang up before I throw the phone across the room, grunting in sheer frustration.

"Do you want me to drive?" Malcolm stands in the doorway of my office, keys in hand, Lexie behind him.

"No. I don't know how long I'll be. They can't even tell me she's there. Excuse me."

I push past him and down the hall, out the back door. I unlock the car, fall into the seat and shove the key into the ignition. A tap tap tap sounds at the passenger side window. Malcolm is hunched over, staring at me from the passenger side window and poised to open the door as soon as I unlock it.

I roll down the window and lean over the passenger seat. "I'm sorry. It's Debra. I have to go."

"I know. I'm going with you. Open the door."

There's no time to argue, so I unlock the door. Malcolm ducks inside and snaps his seatbelt in place. Sending gravel flying, I back out of my spot and dart out into the street, headed for Grady Hospital.

CHAPTER THIRTY-EIGHT

$\mathcal{M}$axine

My eyes open and slowly adjust to the semidarkness. The clock next to my bed reflects the time onto the ceiling–7:54 PM. I yawn and try to flip to my back but I'm pleasantly bound by Joseph's arms. His breathing is light and steady, whispers on my neck and back.

The phone lights up the room with notification of a message. I stretch one arm as far as it will go and tip the phone and the dock over. Joseph stirs behind me, sucking in a long deep breath and mumbling something incoherently. His grip on me loosens, so I reach further and grab the phone and scoot back to my spot.

I have several voicemails from Renee and a few text messages, which surprises me, considering we're not talking. I pull up the first voice mail and listen. Renee sounds like she's been crying.

"Maxine!" She pants into the phone, breathless. "Please call me when you get this message. Debra's been in an accident."

My brows furrow in confusion. What? Accident? I listen to the rest of the messages, which are all a variation of the first. I sit up and scroll through the history. Renee has been calling for an hour, in between sending texts.

MAX! Please don't ignore this! Debra was in a car accident. She's at Grady. Call me!

Maxine, please call me. Bad accident.

Call me call me call me! Where are you?

I am up, and out of the bed in seconds, flying through the dark room. I snap on a lamp. Joseph stirs and sits up, pulling the sheet up over his naked hips. "What's going on?"

Frantic, I rifle through my drawers. "I have to get to Grady. Debra's been in an accident." I toss the phone on the bed and dash to the closet, reaching for the first pair of jeans and a shirt to pull on.

Joseph is already out of the bed, picking up his clothes from the floor where he'd left them earlier. Rather, where I left them when I undressed him. "I'll drive."

"You don't need to—"

"Maxine." He glares, pulling his sweater down over his chest. He pulls on his jeans, locates one sock and then the other while I get dressed. "I'll go get the car. Meet you down front."

He bends toward me as I'm sitting on the side of the bed, slipping on a pair of socks. I tip my head up to him and let him kiss me, just like it was a natural, habitual thing for us to do and not something we'd just fallen back into hours ago.

"Don't forget your phone," he reminds me before he ducks out of my bedroom, keys jingling in his hands.

After the front door closes, I process what's going on.

Debra. Accident.

I suck my teeth as I slip my feet into a pair of loafers, pick up my purse from where I dropped it when I came in, sweep out of the door and to the elevator. My heart is thumping so hard, I hear it in my ears. I hope it's not bad.

What if it's bad?

I slide my thumb across the screen and scroll to the last missed call. Renee picks up right away. "Hey. I'm on my way. Anything new?"

Renee can barely speak, but she fills me in. "They won't tell me anything."

"Did you call Willard?"

"I tried. He didn't pick up at work or on his cell." She hiccups. "I don't want to call Kendra..."

"No, no. She shouldn't find out that way. I'm on my way. Just... just hold on, okay?"

"I'm trying," she sobs.

I hang up as I reach the first floor; I walk through the lobby and outside where the taillights of Joseph's car glow in the shadows just beyond the building entrance. He pulls away as soon as I get inside and snap my seatbelt on, then hangs a right onto Peachtree Road.

I can hardly think. Debra could be seriously, fatally hurt. We could lose her. I'm shaken.

I've never been so scared.

CHAPTER THIRTY-NINE

enee

My shoes squeak as I pace from one end of the dull, wax coated tile floors of the waiting room to the other. The waiting, the not knowing, the helplessness is killing me.

I try Willard again, and I finally get him.

"Renee? What's going on?"

I hate to be the one to break the news to him, that his soon to be ex-wife is laying in a hospital bed somewhere at Grady, but someone's got to do it. "Check your messages," I tell him, after sharing what I know. "And please let me know what's happening. They won't tell me anything."

"I'll call you back," he promises. The line goes dead.

I'm so stressed out, I can't stop crying. Malcolm is handing me Kleenex from a small plastic pack. My phone buzzes. It's Willard.

"I just talked to the police. She ran into a median on the interstate. Head on. They said she was drunk. What's she doing drinking? Debra doesn't drink, maybe a glass or two a year."

"Maybe she wasn't a drinker before, but she seems to be one now."

"They have moved her to the Trauma Unit up there. She's unconscious. Broken arm, broken leg. The car is probably totaled. Renee, I... I just don't even know what to think."

"There's no time to think, Willard. Just move. Get here. I know it's tax season, but it's your wife. Bring her daughter. You know she's going to want to see Kendra when she comes out."

"I don't know if Kendra should be—"

"Willard, please!" I'm nearly hysterical in his ear. He must think I'm crazy, but I don't care. "She's going to want to see Kendra. Please, just get her and bring her here."

"Okay, alright. I'll meet you guys up there. Did you call Maxine?"

"Yeah, I finally heard from her. She's on the way."

"You know Debra. She's going to want all of her girls."

Limp with worry, I sink against Malcolm as he puts an arm around me and pulls me in. I cling to him, moving as close as I can get in uncomfortable plastic hospital chairs.

"She's up in Trauma," I tell Malcolm. "She'd been drinking. Debra's not a drinker. She must have been so sad."

Debra had called me earlier in the day but I hadn't had time to talk to her. I had told myself I'd call her on my lunch break but I worked through that and my dinner break. I didn't end up talking to her at all. Who knows how long she was out wandering the city, weaving through traffic, drunk off her behind?

"We should go upstairs and wait for her husband." Malcolm grips my inner elbow as we stand and head for the elevator.

The Trauma ward is on the fourth floor. We step out of the elevator into what seems like ordered chaos. Gurneys and wheel-chairs line the hallways outside exam rooms. Nurses dash past us in a rapid walk going one way, doctors in baggy scrubs going the other. I'm looking around for any sign of Debra.

We find a few seats together in a waiting room. I keep an eye out for Willard, but I don't expect to see him soon, since he has to get Kendra before coming.

I feel relieved knowing Maxine will be here soon. That she's here for Debra is all I care about.

A few moments later, Maxine and a familiar man step off of the elevator and wander down the hall. I wave, directing her toward us. Despite our argument the other night, I get up and hug her, squeezing her tight. Surprisingly, she hugs me back and nods at Malcolm before she takes a seat next to me.

"How long have you been here?"

"A few hours," I tell her, pulling a fresh Kleenex from the pack and handing it to her. She uses it to dab under her eyes. "Willard is on the way."

"So we don't know anything else?"

"She'd been drinking. Hit a median, head on. Her car is probably totaled."

Maxine sighs heavily. "She loves that car."

"If she'll be ok, though, I'd rather have her than the car."

Her top lip curls, as it always does when she's irritated. "I wasn't insinuating otherwise, Renee."

I tip my head up to glare at her, shaking my head. Not here. Not now.

Maxine sits, her posture stiff against the cushion of the chairs. "I guess we just wait."

Willard rushes in, his long legs covering multiple square feet per second. He's dragging Kendra behind him. Maxine and I stand and open our arms to Kendra. She folds herself into us, wrapping her arms around my waist.

"Is my mom going to be okay, Aunt Renee?"

I hug her, tight and close to me. Maxine wraps her arms around the both of us. "Let's just pray that she will be. We'll just pray."

Willard is at the Nurse's station, then follows a nurse down the hall. A few minutes later he comes back to the waiting room, the corners of his mouth draw down almost to his chin. I'm afraid to ask.

He lowers into a chair near us, the slump of his body betraying his worry. He's dressed in work clothes— a long sleeved collared shirt, tie, gray slacks, and dress shoes. When we were in high school, Willard wore slacks and a collared shirt to school. Debra liked that about him.

"They're keeping her sedated. She took a hit to the head. There's some swelling so they want her to rest. It'll be awhile 'til she comes out."

"But she's... she'll make it?" I ask.

"They think so. We just wait and see right now."

He rubs a palm down his face and exhales a long, hard breath. The air is charged with so much tension. "I talked to her yesterday, something about an article in the paper. We had an argument." Willard bends forward and rests his elbows on his knees. His head twists toward Maxine and me. "When did she start drinking?"

Max and I are twins as we shrug our shoulders. "I've never known Debra to drink." I shake my head. "It's not like her at all."

"I talked to her a few nights ago. She sounded... her words slurred a little," Maxine says. "I thought she was tired. I didn't really think she was getting drunk."

"Cop said her blood alcohol was over the limit. Not by much, but enough." Willard clasps his hands together between his knees and shakes his head.

"I learned in science class that people in comas can hear folks talking to them," says Kendra. "Can I talk to her?"

Willard hesitates before answering, searching my eyes, then Maxine's before returning to Kendra's face. "She looks bad, baby. You sure you want to see her?"

"I want to talk to her. I want to tell her we're here." Kendra stands and pulls at Willard. "Take me to her room."

CHAPTER FORTY

ebra

I have a colossal headache. My entire head hurts. My body pulses with pain. Must have been a doozy of a binge. I don't even know how I made it back home.

A voice calls to me. It's not Roberta, thank goodness. I'd be so embarrassed to be passed out drunk in front of her. When I can get my eyes to open, I'm almost blinded by an overhead light. I groan and turn my head but that brings more pain.

"What the—" I force my eyes open and take in the scene. I'm not at home. One arm and one leg are in a cast. My mouth feels gritty and my head throbs. I hear beeping. I'm obviously in a hospital bed. I don't know how I got to a hospital.

"What happened?" I can't feel my lips. I can only see out of one eye.

"You had an accident. You versus a median. The median won."

That sounds like Maxine, but I can't see her. I try to turn my head but a lightning bolt of pain shoots down my neck.

"I can't see you, Max. Where are you?" I hear footsteps and

shuffling and Maxine, Renee and Kendra all come into view. "Hey... hey, baby." I reach for Kendra with my free hand and notice the IV for the first time. "My sweet angel, I'm so sorry you have to see me this way."

She bends to drop a kiss on my cheek and smiles as she cups my face. "I'm glad you're awake, Ma. We were worried. Daddy was here. He went to get some coffee. He'll be back."

My eyes fill with tears. "Daddy came?"

"Aunt Renee called him." She steps back and waves Renee over. My sweet friend is already blubbering, dripping her tears all over my face. Maxine comes around the other side and covers us both. All three of us are sniffling and whimpering, then wiping away tears.

"You scared us, Debra," says Renee, grabbing the nearest hand. "I'm so glad you made it. Do you remember anything? Where were you going?"

My memory exists in bits and pieces, flashes and large pockets of blackness, like one of those old films, on the filmstrip. I lick my lips — my entire mouth is so dry. "The last thing I remember is getting in the car... what day is it?"

"Saturday," Renee answers. "Late Saturday."

Saturday? I don't even remember the rest of Friday.

"I guess I've been out of it for a while. My landlord is out of town and Kendra was visiting her cousins. I... I don't know..." My brain feels foggy, like thick clouds slowly clearing. "I hit a median? Where was I going?"

"Honey, I don't know. The police are going to want to talk to you, but not right now. Just rest and heal."

The police? "I didn't mean to worry you all. I don't know what I was thinking."

"Shhhh," Renee soothes, stroking my arm, being careful not to mess with the IV. "Don't worry about that right now. Get well enough to meet us for brunch, soon. Okay?"

I'm getting teary thinking how long it could be until I can be with them again. "You guys have to come visit me at Roberta's.

She's a lovely woman but she'll smother me to death. And—oh my car! Has anyone seen it?"

"Debra, would you relax?" Maxine leans over me, her face close to mine. "Willard said the car is toast, that you were lucky to make it out without more injuries. And you can stay with me if you need to. You're not such a bad roommate, you know."

Kendra moves around Renee and works her way into the circle. "Aunt Maxine, my mom is coming home. She's going to live in her own house and sleep in her own bed and I'm going to take care of her."

"Kendra, I think your dad and I need to talk—"

"I already told him," she says. "I told him everything, that I'm tired of my parents living apart and that maybe this accident is some kind of sign. Maybe it's God pushing you guys back together. Maybe it's nothing. All I know is that when you get out of here, you are coming home."

She turns to Renee. "I have to get her clothes and stuff from Roberta's house. Can you help me?"

Dumbfounded, Renee glances at me, then at Maxine, then at Kendra. "Well, who put you in charge of anything, little girl?"

Surly, she curls her neck and switches her glare between me and Renee. "I am not a little girl. Besides, my dad already said it was fine."

Renee surrenders, shrugging her shoulders. "I'll help however I can."

The door opens behind Maxine. A doctor and nurse stride into the room. He seems surprised to see my eyes open.

"Looks like our patient is awake." He leans over me, shines a penlight into my eyes, presses certain points around my head and body and asks if they hurt. They all hurt.

"I'm concerned about your concussion," he says, after rattling off some numbers to the nurse, who notes them in a chart. "We'll keep you for a few days to make sure you're stable. You've got a broken arm—" He gently touches my arm, but I'm expecting pain so I flinch. "And you have a hairline fracture in your left leg. I put casts on. Expect it take about six weeks to heal though your arm may take longer.

"I'm watching your head injury, but all signs point to a narrow miss as far as brain damage. You have great vitals right now and I see nothing to be alarmed about. You might find that you'll suffer a bit of memory loss and some nausea, but you should be no worse for the wear in no time at all."

"My head is killing me."

He nods to the nurse, who makes another notation on the chart, then pokes at one of the bags connected to one of the IVs that dripping fluid into my body. "We'll adjust your pain dosage. It'll make you sleepy, but the pain will subside." He slips the stethoscope around his neck and pockets the penlight. "Any questions?"

"When can I go home?"

He shakes his head, his lips a tight line across his face. "Monday, maybe Tuesday. You had a severe hit to the head. I want to make sure you're okay before we let you go." He steps back and he and his nurse and their squeaky shoes walk out.

"I could bring you some books. Maybe some magazines," offers Renee.

I nod, though it makes my head hurt. "That would be nice. It seems I'm going to be laid up for a while."

The door opens again, and Willard walks in. It's been so long since I saw him, face to face, in the flesh. He's holding a cup of coffee and he looks dead tired. His shirt is wrinkled, his pants look slept in. He looks around the room before his gaze lands on me.

"Debra. You're up. I mean, you're awake."

"I just woke up a bit ago."

Maxine and Renee corral Kendra and usher her out the door, leaving Willard and I alone. For the first time in months, I'm alone in a room with my husband.

"I know you have a long lecture that you've been writing in your head. May as well pile it on now."

"I don't... ah..." He shakes his head and takes a seat in the chair next to my bed. "Believe it or not, I don't have a lecture. I'm

glad you're here. I mean, here with us. I thought we'd lost you. Seems like you're going to be okay."

I smile, though it makes my lip hurt. "Well, I'm alive. It'll be awhile until I'm okay."

Willard pauses for a long moment. Then asks, "Are you glad to be here? To be alive?"

"Of course I am. Why would you ask me that?"

"Because I didn't know if..." He scratches his head. He does that when he's nervous. "Because of our conversation, and the newspaper article, and... the suspension. And the separation. Maybe it was just too much for you. I thought..." Willard doesn't finish his sentence, but I pick up his meaning.

"You thought I was trying to kill myself?" I let out a short, coarse laugh, which makes my head throb and my throat feel like I'd swallowed several knives. "I was drunk, not suicidal."

He sips his coffee and grips the tall Styrofoam cup with two hands. "Kendra tells me that you're coming home and that I don't have a choice in the matter."

"Do you want me home? I don't want to make things uncomfortable or difficult—"

"Kendra says—"

"What does Willard say? Does Willard care? Will Willard be angry to see his wife back in the house? Would it be easier for Willard if I stayed someplace else?"

He pushes up from the chair and shoves a hand in his pocket, then paces the small room. I can sense him mentally counting the tiles.

"Willard is tired. You know? Willard has been Super Dad and tax accountant and estranged husband for the last nine months. Willard has been alone and lonely and angry. Willard doesn't know what he wants, except he wants Kendra to be happy, so... if she wants her mama at home, her mama will be at home."

He sighs, ambling toward the door. "I've got to go up to the office and grab a few things. I'll take Kendra home for a little bit. She didn't sleep all night, and she needs to get some rest. I'll bring her back later. We uh... we'll get your room ready. Doc say when you'll be released?"

"Monday or Tuesday."

He nods, sucking his bottom lip in between his teeth. "Okay. I'll plan to work at home next week, then."

"Willard, you don't—"

"Just let me do what I need to do, okay? I'll see you later."

Willard walks out and I stare at the closed door for a few seconds. That was the longest, most civil conversation I've had with my husband in months. Since the summer. I think my accident scared him. Scared him badly enough to envision a life without me.

Well, good.

Kendra comes in for a quick minute before her dad takes her home. She's a bossy little thing, telling Willard and me everything that's going to happen when I come home. Her excitement is palpable. And a little contagious.

I can't deny that I'm excited to be at home. My home. In my own bed, with my own TV and my daughter right down the hall and my husband.... Somewhere. I don't know where Willard fits into this new picture.

One step at a time.

Tuesday morning, I am released with two casts. It's almost comedic how I get into Willard's car, but I finally fit in the front seat. The Lexus is roomy and comfortable. I lean back against the leather seats and breathe a sigh of relief to be out of the hospital. Hell, to be alive. And to be going home.

Kendra begged to come and pick me up, but he wouldn't let her miss her classes. "She'll be excited to see you when she gets out of school. I might go pick her up so she can get home faster."

"Oh, she'd like that. She's so excited."

"Yeah," is his response. He pulls away and weaves through the parking lot to the exit. Grady Hospital grows smaller and smaller in the distance.

"I appreciate everything you're doing for me, Willard. You don't have to."

"I don't?" He scoffs. "Let's not pretend this is more than what it is."

"I'm not pretending anything is more than it is. You could have let my friends take care of me and gone on with your life, but you're here. It's not a sign of weakness if you just accept my gratitude."

"I don't want you thinking that—"

"I don't think anything!" I snap. "I was thanking you for your damn help. Can't we even be civil?"

He grunts and keeps driving, hits the Interstate and speeds up. After a few beats of tense silence, he says, "You're welcome. Anything you need… you let me or Kendra know. We'll take care of it."

Willard pulls up to the house and parks in the garage so I have room to get out. I already miss my Benz coupe. I still haven't seen the car. I'm sure I'll cry when I do.

The doctor put a walking boot on my cast and my arm in a sling, hoping they would help me be more mobile. Willard is outside my door, offering a hand to help me out of the car.

"You ready?" He grips one hand; I leverage my good foot on the ground before I let him pull me out of the car. I hop backward a few times, with Willard holding me under my arms. I steady myself, putting pressure on the fractured leg. A shard of pain shoots through my leg and it nearly gives out.

"Okay, maybe we need to–"

"Just… just give me a minute. Let me just…." I lean against Willard and put as little weight as possible on the broken leg.

We hop-shuffle around the car to the inside entrance that opens into the kitchen. Willard fumbles with his keys with one hand while holding me up with the other.

"Maybe I should have let Kendra stay home to help," he grumbles, fitting the key into the lock. The door swings open and the sight of my kitchen is the most beautiful thing I've seen in a long time. It's cleaner than I expected it to be. Everything is in its place, as if I just left yesterday.

"We've been taking care of the place," Willard says, watching my eyes float from the colorful burst of silk flowers on the table to the place mats to the counters. "Kendra does a lot, actually. Always telling me how her mother does things."

I allow myself a smile as we limp through the kitchen. "The back steps are shorter, but the stairwell is narrower. I think I want to try just leaning on the banister and I'll just hop up, step by step, if you'll come up behind me?"

"Whatever you want to do," says Willard, and follows me to the staircase behind the kitchen, the one I used to hide from Willard and escape to my bedroom.

One by one, I hop up the set of stairs from the main floor to the second floor landing. With only one arm, it's harder than I thought it would be. I end up half crawling the last few steps, with Willard doing his best to keep me from falling backward. I'm sweating and heaving deep breaths by the time I get to the landing.

My bedroom is bright with midmorning sun. It smells fresh, the furniture free of dust, the carpet patterned with fresh vacuum stripes. A bouquet of daisies in a clear glass vase sits atop the bureau, and a handmade card leans against it. I recognize Kendra's distinctive artist's hand and her chicken scratch signature. The bedspread is unfamiliar to me — a deep chocolate brown with cream striping across the top, middle and bottom. The pillows look new, plump, with new pillowcases.

Renee's book shipment has arrived. There are piles of romance novels and a stack of magazines on the nightstand next to my bed.

"Y'all went all out. I love it."

"Kendra worked hard on it last night."

Willard helps me remove my coat and I sit on the bed while he takes off the one shoe I can wear. I do a one armed, one leg scoot across the bed and finally collapse against the pillows.

"Do you want to get in the bed, under the covers, or just sit this way for a while?"

"I'm hot from all that hopping around. I'll just sit here."

Willard stands next to the bed, scratching his head and glancing around. He doesn't know what to do with himself. I try not to laugh.

"I could use a glass of ice water, if you don't mind."

His footsteps pound down the stairs, then plod back up. He carries a tall glass of water with cubes still bobbing to the surface and sets it on the nightstand.

"I need to get to some work," he says, stepping back. "But I'll just be downstairs, so yell if you need me. Or call me from your cell phone." He picks up my bag, rifles through it, and pulls out the prescriptions he had filled for me. "I think it's time for your pain killer."

He sets the bottles on the nightstand next to the glass of water. "I'll be back up in a while to see if you feel like some lunch."

I nod, giving him a tight smile. "Thanks. That'd be nice."

He backs away, then out of the room and down the stairs. I exhale with relief.

Finally. I'm home.

CHAPTER FORTY-ONE

ℳaxine

My heels sound a dull tap against the tile as I pace. I wander past a bank of mailboxes, then turn and march back again. I'm waiting for Malcolm to come down to the lobby of his building so we can talk. My visit is a surprise, sprung on him at the last minute. I called from the car as I was sure he'd already be awake, but his voice was thick with sleep. He agreed to meet me, however, if I would give him a few minutes to freshen up.

"No problem," I'd told him. "I'll wait for you downstairs."

A black Denali slides in to the space next to my car. I recognize it as Malcolm's truck, but why... I understand as Renee climbs out of the passenger seat. I still haven't made up with her. Not officially. We've both been over at Debra's, each taking a few nights a week to sit with her, take her to therapy, do things for her she can't do herself, like cook or clean. Between Kendra, Willard, Renee and I, Debra is doing really well and gaining weight.

But Renee and I are still cold to each other, barely speaking, ships passing in the night. She can't stand tension, so if we argue, she is the first to come forward and make things right. She's standing her ground this time. I don't blame her.

They walk from the truck to the building, hand in hand. Malcolm laughs at something. Their steps are leisurely, unhurried. It makes me smile.

For a while now, I have felt no tinges about Malcolm and Renee. No ribbons of anger or jealousy winding through me. No hurt that they're together. I have no interest in Malcolm or who he dates, but since he's dating one of my oldest friends, I'm only concerned that she's happy.

Malcolm pulls open the front door and lets Renee walk in ahead of him. The smile on her face when she walks through that door tells me everything I need to know. She's happy. They are in love.

"Hey, Max." Renee walks right up to me and hugs me like we've been the best of friends all this time. "Malcolm said you two had an appointment, so I'll leave you to it." She glances back at Malcolm, grabs his hand and squeezes. "I'll be upstairs, sweetie."

He nods at her and reluctantly releases her hand from his. "Okay, babe. I'll be up in a minute."

"Renee..." I grab her arm, clutching the inside of her elbow. "I want you to be here for this. What I have to say, I should say to you both. I wanted to do it in person. Today. Before I lost my nerve."

I notice a slight hitch in Renee's smile. "We're doing this here? Now?"

"I don't want to take up your time together and Joseph is waiting for me to meet him for breakfast."

"Oh?" Her smile returns. It's less bright, but it's back. "You're still with him?"

I don't like to show my excitement over men, because you just never know what might happen, but I am excited about Joseph and I let it show. "He's wonderful. I'm happy. He's made me realize that I needed to talk to you. Both of you," I add, halfway turning toward Malcolm.

I'm nervous. Maybe because I'm about to own up to a lot of ugly and hope I get forgiveness. "I don't even know what to say," I start. "I've said some terrible things to you, Renee. I mean, for a long time–since the day we met, practically. And you're still my friend and I don't know why, but I'm thankful. I don't deserve your friendship, especially lately."

She starts to cry, of course. You can't say good morning to Renee without her bursting into tears.

"There's no reason that you shouldn't be happy every day of your life and if Malcolm makes you happy then I have no right, nor would I ever want to stand in the way of that. True friends are happy when the other finds love. I need to work on being a true friend to you. Debra, too."

"Oh, Max..." Renee grabs me and pulls me to her. I feel the mid-cry hiccups jolting her body while she's squeezing me. "I'm so sorry," she says when she lets me go.

Her face is beet red, her cheeks shiny with tears. I zip open my purse and hand her a handkerchief. She uses it to dab her face and wipe her nose. "There was a right way for this to happen. I had so many opportunities to tell you about Malcolm and I didn't, and I'm sorry. I never meant to hurt you."

"I know. I said some wrong things and did some wrong things, too. I just want it to be in the past." Renee nods and sniffles, swiping her nose with the handkerchief.

"I wanted to apologize to you for being so overbearing," I tell Malcolm. "You made your interest — or lack thereof more than clear. When I knew you were interested in Renee, I should have stepped aside. I acted immaturely."

Malcolm nods, but doesn't offer an apology for not telling me about dating my best friend behind my back. I let it go. My relationship is with Renee. As long as she and I are okay, I can deal with Malcolm.

"Let me tell you something, though, Mr. Brooks. Renee is happy today. If she doesn't stay that way, I'm coming after you.

And if you think I'm playing, think again. Maxine Donovan does not mess around. You know that, right?"

Malcolm laughs, as does Renee, while sniffling and dabbing her cheeks. He slips his arm around her waist and pulls her to him. She leans into him, fitting her head in that perfect spot between his chin and his chest. That's my favorite spot on Joseph.

"I'll let you guys get on with your day. Renee, I'll see you tomorrow at Debra's?"

"See you tomorrow. Have a good day, Max. And thank you."

I leave the building without looking back, get into my car and slip on a pair of Chanel wrap around shades. As if on cue, my phone buzzes.

How'd it go?

I reply, *Went great. That girl is a championship crier, though.*

You made her cry?

This makes me laugh. *Happy tears, baby.*

I got us a table. There's a little old woman in here bossing the staff around…

I grin and squeal with excitement. I haven't seen Ruby in ages. She and Grandma Elise were close. When I was a girl, she'd tell me stories about how they used to play Bingo down at Decatur Square Baptist Church.

I'm on my way, I text him. *Tell her Maxine is coming!*

CHAPTER FORTY-TWO

enee

"So uh… Renee…"

Lexie has that look and that tone of voice that says she's about to be nosy. I glance over at her while roving the stacks, placing the books I lent Debra back into circulation. She's going through them like wildfire, so I'm also pulling anything else I think she'd like to read. It's already warm outside and the pollen in the air is driving me crazy. The sun, high in the sky, beats down on us through the plate-glass window.

"Yes, Lexie?"

"That big ole hunk of a dude that's been hanging around here lately…"

I laugh at 'big ole hunk of a dude'. That is my favorite thing about Malcolm. He's been coming by in the evenings after work. I'm finally revamping the security system at the bookstore, so he's been checking on the daily progress. He also likes to sit and read a book or a magazine and wait for me to take a dinner break. If it's

slow, we leave for the night and catch a movie or get something to eat.

"I know I introduced you to Malcolm." I slide a book into an empty spot in the stacks and move down the line.

"Well, yeah, but I mean… you know…"

"You work in a bookstore and can't come up with a better sentence than yeah, I mean, you know?" I chuckle and slide another book into the stacks.

"Is that man your boyfriend, or what?"

"Yes." I grin over at her and slide another book in its place. "See how easy that was? I don't know even know why you asked."

"What happened to Marcus?"

"Marcus lives in Philly."

"Right, but…"

"And when he was here, he hinted at getting together, but…" I shrug, moving to the next aisle. "I guess I'm over him." I shudder at the thought of what I almost gave up to go back to what I thought was a better life.

"I should hope so, considering the big ole hunk of man. So then you're not looking at selling the bookstore anymore?"

I almost answer but I take in my view of a place that has brought me such a feeling of accomplishment. I still sense my mother here. I've hung a few photos of her from Daddy's stash and I'm even thinking of changing the name to Lorraine Gladwell Books. I think Daddy would like it. And she would, too.

"Not soon."

Lexie heaves an audible sigh of what I can only assume is relief and turns to walk away. "Lex?" She stops in her tracks and turns back around. "Were you worried about that?"

She meanders back over to me. "A little. I was thinking about getting a loan to buy it, if you were going to sell it."

Surprised, I stop stocking and turn to Lexie. "I didn't know the place meant so much to you."

"This place is like home to me. I spend so much time here. I even bring my son here sometimes, to do his homework." Lexie's son is a cute little boy with deep brown skin, big eyes and a serious mind for other worlds. I often find him burrowed in a corner of a couch, his head deep in a science fiction novel.

"That makes me happy. I think that's what my mother would have wanted."

Lexie grins and tugs at her new Gladwell's apron. "I didn't know her, but I think she'd be proud of this place, Renee." She turns her back to me but twists around again. "Oh, and if that big old hunk of man has a brother or something..."

I laugh and wave her off. "I'm serious!" She giggles as she walks away.

The phone in my apron pocket buzzes. I dig it out with my free hand and check the display.

Took your dad for a walk. He talked about your mom.

I smile at the message and text back a smiley face.

Malcolm met Daddy a few weeks ago, thankfully not when we were tangled up together on the couch. Daddy was uninterested at first, but the more Malcolm came around, the faster friends they became. Daddy even knows his name. Malcolm will sit with him if I have to run to the grocery store or take a shift at the bookstore. They play card games, watch movies and listen to music, so many things I don't have time or patience for. Malcolm has even been talking about spending the summer getting the Mustang running. I've never ridden in Lorraine. It would be nice to take a spin, just once.

Most nights, Malcolm stays with me. In our house. In my bed, which I felt guilty about, with the sounds of my father snoring and mumbling coming over the monitor. I quickly got used to waking up next to him, though. When I get up to get Daddy moving, he heads to his apartment to shower and dress for work. I love having him around all the time.

I love him. I just love him. And he loves me.

My shift at the bookstore goes quickly. Once the midday crowd thins, I pack up my newly plucked selection of books and head up to Debra's. When I pull up into the driveway, Debra is kneeling in front of the flower bed that runs along the porch and around the side of the house. She's bent over a mound of dirt, her behind on full display to the neighborhood. Several trays of blooming flowers line the sidewalk next to her.

I park and cut the ignition, then step out of the car. "Debra Marie Macklin," I call to her. "Just what are you doing?"

She twists around, a grin plastered across her face. "Planting flowers! What does it look like?"

I grab my bag and the box of books from the backseat and walk up the sidewalk. I dump my things on a step and take a seat on the porch.

"I can see that you're planting flowers. Why you're doing it with one arm and a bum leg, though…"

"I have two arms. This cast is a formality." She lifts her arm and shows me the worn cast that's supposed to be in a sling and immobile, but is dirty from digging in the garden. She wields a shovel in the fingers of that hand and with the other, pats around a freshly planted blob of dirt and roots with bright flowers protruding from it. "I said I wanted to plant the garden before it got too late in the year. Willard brought me these this morning."

As if he was listening for the mention of his name, the front door opens and Willard steps outside, in jeans, a t-shirt and a pair of sandals with socks. So close, Willard. So close.

"Hey, Renee. Good to see you."

"Don't you hey, Renee me. How do you have Debra out here planting flowers with two broken limbs? What's wrong with you, man?"

Willard chuckles, lowering himself to the step next to me. He's holding a glass of tea. "You know she doesn't like to sit still. I come out here every few minutes to make sure she hasn't passed out." He sips his tea, the ice clinking against the side of the glass. "You need something, Deb? Water?"

"I'm okay. Thanks." She picks up another plant and inserting into the freshly dug hole she created minutes ago. After patting down the dirt around it, she sits back and wipes her forehead with her palm, which just smudges dirt across her face.

"Looking a little tired. Isn't it time for your meds?"

Debra checks her watch and frowns. "Okay, I get the hint. Come help me up?"

Both of us hop up to grab an arm and help her stand. She limps up the steps to the swing. "Renee, come sit by me. And bring that box. I want to see what goodies you brought me."

"I'll get your pills," offers Willard, already halfway back in the house. "Renee, you want some tea?"

"Sure," I tell him, and he ducks into the house. I set the box between Debra and I and she digs through the books. "Willard is nice, lately."

"We decided to be civil. Neither of us wants to suffer the wrath of Kendra." She squints at a book, flips it over, flips it back and adds it back to the stack it came from. "We're starting counseling soon."

"Yeah?"

"Uh huh." She nods, while reading the blurb from the back of a book. "I need my bifocals. I can't see a thing."

"Is that a good thing or something you're just doing to hold off on separation?"

"We figure it can't hurt."

"I meant to tell you, I read that article. The one in the paper. They called it Scandal at Morningside. It was pretty lame."

She grimaces. "By the time I remembered it, I couldn't bring myself to look at it. I've heard that it wasn't that bad. Might as well have been about Charlotte Rogers. She's the only person who offered a comment." She clicks her tongue. "That, coupled with the accident, made things clear for me."

"What things? What's clear?"

"I can't go back to Morningside. Not this year, maybe not at all. I don't even know if I want to be a Principal anymore. The politics makes me sick. And that some... tart like Charlotte Rogers who didn't dedicate her life to those students..."

She goes back to sorting books.

"Well, she sure messed my life up, didn't she? David's too. He quit, I heard. Effective the end of the school year. No assignment for next year, so far. No one should have that kind of power."

"What about next year?"

"The District offered me a Sabbatical. A year of unpaid leave. I'm going to take it and decide what I want to do. I might get another school. I might go back to teaching."

"For Gwinnett?"

"Bernice would like that. I think she wants to keep an eye on me. I could go to Atlanta."

"Like they don't have enough problems right now."

She laughs. "I'd fit right in. Scandal city over there. They need teachers, though. And the new Superintendent seems like she's going to be great. All business. All about the kids. I like that."

"Isn't that step backward, though?"

"Not if it saves my marriage and my career."

The screen door opens and Willard steps out with two glasses of tea. Cupped in the palm of his hand are a few pills, which he drops into Debra's palm.

"Thank you, dear," says Debra. Willard grunts something that sounds affirmative and walks back into the house. "He's coming around." She laughs and practically throws her pills down her throat, takes a sip of tea and yanks her head back. I watch her swallow the entire mouthful, then suck down a few more gulps.

I sip mine, entirely more dainty.

"Maxine said she finally made up with you."

"I wasn't expecting to hear from her for a while. I figured maybe around summer—"

"In time for her birthday." Debra snorts a laugh. "I love that woman but she is stone cold nuts."

"She is crazy, but she is ours."

"So how is Malcolm? No one tells me anything anymore. I have to ask, and it's getting annoying."

"If you would behave so you can get your casts off and come to brunch, we'll tell you everything you need to know."

"Renee, just spill, dammit. The only romance I have right now are these books."

"Malcolm is fine. Daddy really likes him, too."

"Yeah? That's big. Bernard doesn't like anyone."

I sip more tea. "He wants to move in. I don't know if I'm ready for that."

Debra's brows shoot toward her hairline. I've been waiting to spring that on her... she would be the first person I told. She's the first person I tell everything. "Move in," she repeats. "With you and your dad, move in?"

"He took care of his mom until she died, but I don't think Malcolm realizes how bad things are going to get with my dad."

"Or maybe he does, and he wants to be there for you when it happens."

I shrug. Hadn't thought of that. "Maybe. I'm holding him off. Thinking about it, though."

"Don't think too hard."

"I won't. So, how are you doing? I mean... with everything?"

"I'm... awake." She nods, resolute. "Like the accident woke me up. Maybe that bump on the head did me some good. This whole experience has shown me a lot about my life. Turns out what I thought was wrong with it, was just fine. Needed some work, is all."

She taps me on the leg with a smile. "Remember when we used to have slumber parties and talk about what life was going to be like when we got older?"

I stretch my legs and give the swing a light push while we reminisce. "We were going to drive fancy cars and have big houses and rich, handsome husbands and important jobs and lots of kids and be perfect wives and mommies. We were going to prove women could have it all."

"And then we grew up and life happened. Hell, the only one of

355

us to halfway make those dreams come true is Maxine and look at how much work it takes to be her."

"Here I am with no kids and no husband, raising my father. This is not where I thought I'd be in my mid-thirties." I give Debra a sidelong glance. "You made out okay. Kind of."

She shakes her head, wistful. "I thought I was living a fairy tale, but the fairy tale was not all it was cracked up to be. But that's just it. It's just stories, a wish from some time in the past when I didn't even know what I was talking about. I want my real marriage, my real life. My real husband, with all his flaws. My real daughter and her teenage attitude. I just want everything back the way it was before. But better. And I have to believe that's possible. I have to believe in second chances, otherwise…"

She shrugs, her gazed fixed on me. I've never seen her so serious. "Otherwise, what am I even doing here?"

CHAPTER FORTY-THREE

ebra

I take a seat in the waiting room and drop my bag at my feet, pick up a magazine and mindlessly flip through it. Willard, who'd dropped me off to park the car, arrives a few minutes later, taking the seat next to me.

"Hello," I say to him, still flipping through the magazine. We are working on pleasantries, like me saying hello and Willard responding with words, not grunting.

"Hey. Aren't we on at four? Are we early?" He checks his watch, I check mine.

"Right on time. She's still in session, running a little late."

"She runs two-hour sessions. You'd think she could wrap it up on time."

I eye him, slapping the magazine closed. "You have somewhere more important to be?"

He glances at me, anger flashing in his eyes. "Work is stacked to my eyeballs. I have business returns due at month end."

"Yeah, yeah. You're important."

"I just want my whole two hours, Debra. We're paying for the time, I want the whole time. That's all."

He's right. I know it. I relent, laying a hand on his arm. "I apologize. You're working hard and making time for this. Thank you."

He shakes my hand off and stands, stalking to the reception desk. "Is Janet ready, or should we reschedule? I took off work for this appointment."

"She's just finishing up with a couple. She'll be right out."

"No, five minutes ago she was finishing up. Now she's running into our time. We're paying four hundred dollars an hour for her to give some other couple our time. Buzz her and let her know we're here."

The frosted glass door opens and a couple comes out, followed by our marriage therapist, Dr. Janet Wilson. I let Willard pick her, and she's supposed to be really good. She's tall, thin and the antithesis of style. Her brown curls are dull but plentiful, spilling down her back and barely contained by the headband she always wears. Her belted dress falls to her knees and her large feet are encased in misshapen flats. Maxine would have a field day with her.

"Is there a problem?" Janet asks, eying Willard, then me.

"The Macklin's are ready for you, Doctor."

Janet smiles and waves us back. I follow Willard and the doctor down the hall to her office where we take our usual spots, next to each other on a leather couch. Janet settles into a chair and begins with her usual question: "So. How was the week?"

I look to Willard; he looks at me. We decide between each other to answer, "Fine."

Janet nods, tucking her fist under her chin, propping her elbow on the arm of the chair. "So there were no challenges, this week? No arguments? Everything's… fine?"

I shrug. "Yeah, it was fine. Before today, we had had no arguments in a few—"

"Today. What happened today?"

Willard rolls his eyes. "I flew off the handle because we'd been waiting when it was time for our appointment, that's all. It was nothing."

"That's not what I'm talking about. I'm talking about when I touched you, and you acted like my hands were made of acid. Whenever I touch you, or I say anything to you, you roll your eyes. You act like my words are ridiculous and my touch is poisonous."

He petulantly crosses his arms. "You need to stop being so damn grateful."

"Let's go with that," says Janet. "Why shouldn't she be grateful? You let her move back in, you're working on the marriage, you're doing so much for her. She's expressing gratitude and that pisses you off. Why?"

I'm curious to know the answer.

"Because I don't deserve it. I don't need a thank you after I do every little thing."

"Why don't you deserve that, Willard?"

"Because I let it happen," he blurts. "I let her get unhappy, and she strayed. I told her she had to leave, and I let her pack her things and move out. I let her get depressed and start drinking and get in a car accident. I let my daughter almost lose her mother. She was inconsolable. I just... thought..."

Willard relaxes and clasps his hands together. I realize that his hands are shaking. So is his voice. The only time Willard ever cried was when Kendra was born. "What if everything that's happened since last summer resulted in Debra being killed?"

"What if, Willard? What does life look like, without your wife?"

He shakes his head, over and over. "I've never known anyone but Debra. I've never wanted to know anyone but Debra. I was angry that she wanted to know someone besides me like that. I wanted her to feel as unwanted as I felt." He sniffles. "I feel like I made it happen. I feel like I wanted that to happen to her."

"Did you really, though? Did you really want her to get drunk, have an accident and almost die?" Janet looks to me. "Do you think your husband wanted you to die?"

"No." I make sure Willard sees me saying, "I don't think that."

"What do you think? Tell Willard, Debra."

I twist my body toward him and slide a hand into his. He doesn't pull away; his fingers instinctively wind around mine. "You're angry and you have every right to be. But you're not an emotional person. You don't talk about your feelings, so you didn't talk to me about how angry you were. We would have gone on not talking until…"

My shoulders bunch up in a shrug. "Who knows? We could have separated and divorced and never said another word to each other. I think you planned on staying mad for a long time. Being mad was going to get you through, but my accident scared you and stunted your anger. Now you don't know what emotion to replace the anger with. You're frustrated, both with yourself and with me."

Willard sniffles and relaxes against the leather backing of the couch. Janet reaches toward the table for a box of Kleenex and hands it to him. He snaps a few tissues from the box and sets it back down on the table.

"Let's talk about our progress in healing this marriage. There's been no sex since you've been back, Debra. Correct? And that's been, what… eight, ten weeks?"

"Ten weeks."

"Willard, you're still not sleeping in the bedroom?" He shakes his head. "Well, how do you expect sex to happen if you're not in the same bed?"

Willard lets out a chuckle. He doesn't want to laugh, but I do.

"I'd like you to set a deadline for when you're going to move back into the bedroom. It doesn't have to be right away. It doesn't even have to be soon. I want to focus on strengthening this marriage and not just being two people living in a house together. You're not spending four hundred an hour to live like roommates, right?"

I nod in full agreement. Janet's next statement makes me giddy.

"I also want you to plan some sex. It doesn't have to be romantic, candlelight and wine and sweet utterings. Just do it. Sex says things that words can't or won't. In fact, you don't even have to speak to each other, if you don't want to. But work on it. At least once a week."

Janet looks to me, then Willard. "Any issue with that?"

His expression seems pained. He glances around the room before his gaze comes back to Janet. "I don't know if… I mean, she was with someone else."

"That's true. That's the whole reason you're here. And if you want this marriage to work, you're going to have to figure out how to forgive her for that. You'll always punish her if you can't do that."

Willard mumbles something while shredding the Kleenex in his hands. I tap his thigh with our joined hands. "Alright." He glances at me, his bottom lip between his teeth. "Sex, huh?"

I hope my expression is plain when I repeat, "Sex."

He scratches his head — his nervous tell. "We'll work on it, Janet."

"Great," she says, clapping her hands together, then pauses. "I don't need to know about the sex. Trust me, I'll know."

On the way home, Willard is quiet. Suddenly, the car pulls to the side of the road and comes to a stop. Willard moves the gearshift to park. I look around us. The highway is empty. The car seems fine.

"Something wrong?"

Willard stares out of the windshield. He licks his lips and asks, "Do you love me?"

"Yes," I answer without hesitation. "I think the question is… do you love me?"

"No," he says, his head shaking in a slow, deliberate rhythm. "That's not the question. That was never the question. Here's what I don't understand. I don't understand how you love me but…" He hesitates, his voice trailing off. He can't even say the words.

"But I stepped out on you?"

"I can't get my mind around it." His forehead creases. His eyes narrow as his eyes direct their focus to mine. "I want to get it. I want to get it, so I know how to stop it from happening again, because I can't do this again, Debra."

"In the ninth grade, when Jerome Hawkins snapped my bra and ran away, but you clotheslined him in the hallway? He landed right on the back of his big head and you leaned over him and said, 'shouldn'ta been doin' that.' You remember?"

Willard chuckles. He remembers.

"You've always been there for me. But over the years, that's sort of… faded away. You care more about your job than anything else. And when I needed someone to protect me, even if it was from my own unrealistic ideals of what our marriage should be, I had no one. I felt alone."

"But you weren't alone."

"I didn't say I was alone. I said I felt alone. You were there, but not really."

Willard frowns and moves to put the car in drive again. I stop him with a gentle touch.

"I'm not trying to beat up on you, and this isn't the blame game. If it was, the majority would fall on me. But you asked me. You said you wanted to get it, and I'm sorry if you don't like my answer. This is the nitty gritty right here. The truth. The stuff you didn't want to hear because you thought you'd done nothing wrong. That's what was going on and why I was tempted by someone. David was paying attention. David told me things I wanted to hear. He showed me things I needed to see."

"So why didn't you stay with him, if he gave you so much and told you so much and showed you so much? Why not call us done and move on with this man that was doing so much for you?"

I smile. "Because he isn't you. He's not the boy I fell in love with in high school. He's not the man I married. He's not the father of my baby girl. He's not the man I dream about growing old with."

Willard fiddles with the keys in the ignition, then the buttons on the dashboard. He turns the navigation system off and back on. He scratches a patch of hair at the crown of his head.

"What uh... what are these things. You know? That you want me to tell you? And show you?"

"That you love me, for starters. Do you know how long it's been since you told me you loved me? That you need me for more than cooking and doing your laundry and raising your daughter. Maybe that I excite you, that you enjoy being with me and you think of me as more than the maid and the cook and the caregiver. That you like being married to me. That I'm the love of your life. Am I?"

He nods. I don't know if he means to, but his head bobs up and down in agreement. "I get that I work a lot and it takes a toll. Maybe I could try working from home some days, but it's not like I'm out there doing nothing, being nothing. I'm building something for us, Debra. That's what I didn't understand, what made me angry the most."

"You were working hard for us and I was thinking about myself."

He sighs and I know I've done it again, taken the wind from his sails. He wants to be angry, but I keep dismantling any reason to be.

The interior of the Lexus is quiet, the sounds of passing traffic muffled by the thick windows. Willard says nothing for a long while. Then, quite to my surprise, he turns to me and says, "I want my marriage. I haven't spent fourteen–well twenty-two years with you to throw them away. I'm not making a lot of promises about how everything's going to be perfect but... I want to try."

He pauses, gesturing to me with the lift of his head. "Do you, Debra? Do you want us back? Do you want this marriage?"

"Yes," I answer with relief. "More than anything... yes. And it's we. We'll try. We've got a long life ahead of us. We're young and Kendra will be out of our hair before we know it. We could spice things up some. I mean, I don't want to swing from a chandelier or anything—"

"Aw, Debra, come on!"

I try not to laugh at Willard as he turns his gaze toward the driver's side window and props his arm up on the door. He's biting his thumb, out of nervousness or shyness, I can't tell. Willard's way of asking for sex is to nod his head toward the bedroom and say 'come on.'

"I just think any thoughts or desires that you might have, that you push to the back of your mind and think 'Debra wouldn't do that'...I want you to tell me those things. Because I might do them for you."

"Did you do them for him?"

"Willard..."

"Alright, I'm just playin'."

He drops a hand to my thigh—the first time he's willingly touched me in months. His eyes meet mine and we gaze at each other for a few moments. If Willard could blush, he'd be beet red.

"So, if I said I wanted to have sex tonight, with my wife, in our bed... is that good? Is that what you're looking for?"

I'm grinning like a fool at Willard pushing himself to be forward. "That's good, baby." I reach over and stroke his cheek, then tickle him behind his ear, like he likes it. He reaches for the gearshift and puts the car in drive.

"Maybe Kendra can go someplace later."

"I'll find a place for her to go."

CHAPTER FORTY-FOUR

$\mathcal{M}$axine

My office is awash with a mixture of the purple glow of dusk beaming through the window blinds and the harsh overhead fluorescent bulbs shining down on me from above. I'm not paying attention to the sunset, which is my favorite time of day. I'm not annoyingly glaring at the reflection of the overhead lights in my monitor. My mind is hovering somewhere in the great unknown, trying to think about how I got there, how I live there, and how I can never go back.

I caught a terrible cold a month ago, the worst I've ever had. Donovan was busting at the seams and I felt I couldn't take the time off. My cold grew into something nasty and debilitating. I was down for the count, confined to the bed until Joseph, tired of my stubbornness, dragged me to a doctor. Three straight days of sleep and antibiotics and I was feeling somewhere near myself again. I even had enough energy to get dressed and go to dinner, and later, I felt good enough for a short but blissful bout of sex.

And that's all it took to take life as I know it and shoot it out into the realm of who-knows-what's-going-to-happen-now?

I don't know if stressed the word is for how I'm feeling about what I suspect is true. I should be out of my mind over it. This is not what I planned for my life. This is a detour I had no intention of taking. I should be angry that I let it happen.

But I'm not. I'm apprehensive. The smallest bit excited. And nervous, mostly about hiding it from everyone, including Debra and Renee until I know for sure that I am pregnant.

I've spent most of the day staring out of the window, rubbing my still flat belly and letting my mind wander. I had to stay an hour later to get a few contracts out of the door and now I'm about to be late for dinner.

I cannot be late for this dinner. It's important.

I pack up my desk, slip a Hermes bag over my shoulder and leave my office, locking the door behind me. I step to Virgil's desk and clear my throat, interrupting his session of mumbling while staring at printouts.

"Do I look ready to meet Joseph's parents?"

Virgil spins in his chair, his critical eye flowing from the form-fitting Burberry dress and Zanotti pumps to the glittering gems in my ears and around my neck.

He nods. "Maxine, you're flawless as ever. Where to, tonight?"

I roll my eyes. "Some steak place his parents like. Longhorn."

"How... rustic."

"This is how I know I love this man. I'm willing to eat at some-place called Longhorn. That's not the kind of place where people throw peanut shells on the floor, is it?"

I glance down at my new pumps. Joseph rolled his eyes at them, saying they looked exactly like every other pair of black shoes in my closet. But he makes me happy, which is why I'm willing to eat at a regular, non-elite steak house for dinner. Not Chops. Not Bones. Longhorn.

"You're thinking of Texas Roadhouse," Virgil says. "Longhorn has good steak." He wrinkles his nose. "No seafood."

My hurriedly eaten lunch almost comes up. "Definitely, no seafood. Wish me luck."

"Don't need it. They'll love you."

I pass an open, lit office and think nothing of it. It's not unheard of for an agent to be working past six o'clock. I'm still in, as is Virgil. A sniffle and half of a sob makes me stop in my tracks. I'm late. I don't have time, but I double back anyway and stick my head into Vanessa's office. She's at her desk, which faces the door, but she's turned away, her head in her hands. She sniffles again.

"Hey. Vanessa. What's up?"

Her head pops up, and she nearly jumps out of her chair. "Maxine! I didn't know you were still here."

"I was just leaving. Are you alright?"

Her face falls like she's going to cry again. "I just got some bad news."

"Is there anything I can do?"

I've loved hearing her laughter waft down the hall into my office, but the chuckle she gives me isn't her usual fun and bubbly quality. It's sardonic and gritty.

"Unless you can work some kind of miracle? I'm fucked." She gulps, her eyes flying up to my face to see if I've frowned at her utterance. "Sorry."

I ease into her office and take one of the seats across from her desk. Her office is simple and tasteful, minimal without being plain. She's orderly and likes clean surfaces. Except for her computer, a file organizer, a three-line office phone and a few framed photos, her desk and credenza are clear of clutter.

"You've been quiet, I've noticed. Is there something going on?"

She shakes her head, moaning. "My husband. Soon to be ex-husband, rather. He's been living... what do they call it? A double life?"

"What's that? A double life?"

"He's having an affair. Well, it's more than an affair. It's like he's with me and her. And here I thought I was his one and only."

She sniffles, leans over to grab the handles of her purse and rummages around in it until she produces a packet of Kleenex. She pulls one cloth from the plastic case and dabs at her eyes and nose.

"He's a salesman. Technology, cloud computing, all those buzz words. Business is booming, he says. He has all these business trips he needs to go on. Clients to schmooze. Deals to close. He's gone for weeks at a time and he's always on the phone, it seems like. I never even thought to question him. Everything was always taken care of."

Her lip quivers and her nose flares and tears fill her eyes again. "They have a house together, Maxine. They take vacations together–vacations he and I planned but he could never get the time off of work. Meanwhile, our mortgage and our family and the life we built together–he left it all behind. I don't know which life is fake and which is real."

"How did you find out about this? About her?"

She sighs, wiping away the streaks of mascara from under her eyes and down her cheeks. "He always handled the finances. He opened the mail and paid the bills. He's just always taken care of everything. I never had to worry. I never thought to save any money. That was for me and the kids and fun things.

"Anyway, a few months ago, one of the kids picked up the mail. I flipped through it and some envelopes looked serious."

With bated breath, I wait for the dramatic reveal. Paternity results? A welfare check? STD Test?

"We were in foreclosure," she answers, her affect suddenly flat and void of emotion. "Thousands in arrears, plus late fees and interest. I almost passed out." She pauses and sniffles, taking another swipe with the wad of Kleenex clutched in her palm.

I'm almost afraid to ask. "And the others? What were they?"

"Notices from the IRS for back taxes. We file separately. He said that made more sense because of his business expenses. It turns out it's because he doesn't like to pay taxes. He hadn't paid them in years. He's into the government for almost fifty grand. That's where I lost it. What if they come after me? I don't have fifty thousand dollars!

"I confronted him and he swore on the bible, on our kids, on his mother's grave that it was a mistake. He'd take care of it. Well, I started snooping and finding things, stuff I hoped I wouldn't find and didn't want to believe, but it was right there in my face. He always said he didn't believe in Facebook, but he has a profile where he's connected to her. This woman. Jasmine. They have friends and a social life. Barbecues and couples nights and last spring, when our youngest had her kindergarten graduation and he said he had a conference he couldn't miss because he was the Keynote Speaker?"

She huffs. "He was at happy hour with her and their friends at Davio's."

I'm floored. Jaw on the floor, limbs numb, speechlessly floored. "Wow. So bold."

"He was always too busy to do anything with me or our kids. He always had to work. Now I know what he was working on. How does he even live with himself?"

"His day planner must be serious." I instantly want to take back my snide comment, but Vanessa laughs.

"He's mega organized, obsessive about planning. That's why I couldn't believe he hadn't paid the mortgage. You don't forget to pay the mortgage six months in a row."

"So today you got some bad news?"

She sniffles, the corners of her mouth pointing toward her chin. "Our house is scheduled to be sold at auction. I was hoping I could save it, but after the bank kicked me and the kids out, I've had a hard time getting back on my feet."

Vanessa sucks her teeth and sighs. "I love that house," she moans. My heart almost breaks. "It was the first piece of property I owned. We bought it together."

"The first piece of property you bought with this man and he let it go under? For some other hot thing? That's we call a sign. Now you get to find a place that's all your own, that you will love just as much or more because it's yours. And that will happen in no time at all because your listings are selling—"

She snickers. "None of that matters with this foreclosure on my credit. He shut off our cards, drained our accounts, and he's gone... everything's gone. I sold everything I could, pawned my jewelry, put my nice clothes into consignment. The kids and I are in my aunt's basement. I don't know what to do."

She warbles again, but I reach across the desk and lift her chin so she can see me. "What's this bastard's name?"

"Warren."

"Is Warren Jackson sitting crying because the house got sold and his marriage is over and his credit is bad?"

She shakes her head. "I know you want to drown your sorrows and feel sorry for yourself, but you don't have time for that. Good riddance to bad rubbish, Grandma Elise used to say. You get yourself together and get back on your feet. Show Warren he might bring you down, but he didn't take you out. You have children?"

She nods. "Two girls."

"They're going to need you to be strong and press on. You can do this. I might not know exactly what you're going through, but I've been through some things in my life. Tomorrow, we'll do lunch and I'll tell you all about it. And we'll work on a plan to get you where you need to be."

I stand and hook the strap of my bag over my arm. "For now, go wash your face and gather your things. Go be with those girls. There's more to life than work, and they need you more than Donovan does right now."

I give her a nod and step out of her office. Now I'm late so I pull out my phone to text Joseph to let him know I'm on my way.

As soon as I use the bathroom.

⁓

"Are you nervous?"

Right this second, as I gauge my feelings, I'm miraculously calm as we wait in the masterfully appointed private office of Dr. Tracy Lewis, Obstetrician. I got a recommendation from Debra without her asking what it was for. Dr. Lewis is supposed to be really good, thorough and caring and willing to answer questions from frantic, nervous first-time mothers.

Though, I am neither frantic nor nervous. We already know what the blood test will say. We're waiting on confirmation so we can both know with all certainty that we have created a new life, one that will eventually become autonomous and take everything we taught him or her into the world.

Now that? That scares me.

"I'm okay." I stretch an arm across the space between our chairs. He grabs my hand, scooting his chair over a few inches, closing the space. "Are you nervous?"

"Nah." Joseph gives off an air of supreme confidence. It's faux, and I know it. And he knows I know it. But it's cute. "Just... I don't like waiting."

"You are naturally impatient."

"You would know. The speed of light moves too slow for you."

"Why wait for something I can have right now?"

Joseph chuckles, wrapping his other hand around our inter-twined fingers. "We probably need to talk about what we're going to do when she comes back in here and tells us we're going to be parents."

"I was thinking about that, too." I glance over at him, my eyebrows raised. "Suggestions?"

"Why even ask me? We're going to do what you want to do."

"It's polite to pretend I am going to consider your opinion."

"Well, I say we move into my condo and sell yours."

I click my tongue and look away quickly, before rolling my head back toward him. "Would you be serious?"

"I am serious! Your place will sell for more and my place is cheaper—"

"In a less developed neighborhood with fewer amenities and no view. The carpet in your condo is ten years old—"

"Like we can't renovate?"

"And I think there's something growing in your freezer."

"Okay. Well, your place is bright white even with the lights off and it's nowhere near child proof."

"Like we can't childproof? The baby won't even move for the first six months."

"Your furniture is Italian leather. White Italian leather. Expensive, white–"

"My furniture was an investment that has stood the test of time. It's sturdy, and it's held up well. It can survive an infant. Or a toddler."

"I think you need to listen to reason, Maxine."

"And you are the voice of reason."

"I think I make more sense."

"Hi, have you met me? Maxine Donovan, Donovan Realty. I know what I am talking about and no way would I live in that building."

"So much for listening to my suggestions."

He blows a puff of air toward the ceiling and lets his gaze drift to the construction scene outside of the window. Piedmont Hospital is adding on or tearing down, but they're making a lot of noise doing it.

"So… maybe we meet in the middle," I suggest.

"Meaning?"

"Meaning… we move into something new together."

"Hi, have you met me? Joseph Glass, Investment Banker. Three mortgages is crazy."

"I meant that we'd both sell and move to someplace new."

Joseph starts to respond, but the door opens and Dr. Lewis walks in and softly closes the door behind her. She's plain Jane, short with a choppy asymmetrical haircut. She wears baby blue scrubs under a white lab coat. Her smile is warm and her blue eyes are sparkling. She has a cheery disposition and a pleasant voice. I liked her right away when I called for an appointment.

Dr. Lewis takes a seat in the monstrous chair behind the desk. She's so short she looks like a child playing in her father's office. "Well, I won't belabor this, mom and dad. You're definitely pregnant. Based on your last cycle, I'd estimate that we're very early on."

She looks up from the page she's reading and gives me a wink and a smile, then stands and plucks a few books and a folder from a stack on her desk. "Let me assure you you're fine. You're healthy, you're young, and right now everything is perfect. I'd like you to take some information with you. I've found that new mothers enjoy them and they aren't as alarmist as the Internet can be."

Dr. Lewis hands the stack to Joseph. He takes them and begins flipping through the folder full of information. "Looks like we've got homework," he mumbles.

"There's a directory of resources for everything from Introduction to Baby and Lamaze classes, information on Doulas and Midwives—"

"Doo what? Wife what?" I giggle and elbow Joseph. He chuckles because he finds himself funny.

"You'll figure it out eventually, I promise. And what you don't figure out, you'll wing it with the best of them."

Dr. Lewis turns to focus on me. I know I'm about to get a lecture, but the blows hit softly. "The most important thing is to relax. Make sure you're getting in good nutrition, not junk. Stay active. Get your rest. And don't let this one—" she angles her head toward Joseph, " — drive you crazy. You're about to go on the ride of your lives. Enjoy it."

Joseph and I stand, and she walks us to the door. "See my nurse on the way out and set an appointment for four weeks from now. We'll do your first sonogram and make sure everything is on schedule and going okay. In the meantime…"

"I know, I know. Rest and don't stress."

After I set my next appointment, Joseph and I walk through the office complex and parking lot like we have nowhere to be. We have plans to go to lunch, something I've been looking forward to all day. I've been ravenous for the last week.

Joseph clutches the books and the folder in the crook of an arm. "I guess we can look through some of this stuff over lunch."

I give a small pout. We have plenty of time to 'do our homework'. "I'd rather talk about us picking out a place to live."

"Together?" I glance up at him and catch the corner of his mouth tipping up. "I know you're a real estate professional and everything, but I have to live there too. I get a vote."

"Yes, of course. Together." I sigh as we stroll. My car is in sight, sitting in wait for us.

"What's that sigh about?"

"Just thinking. About everything."

"Everything like what?"

We reach my car and I pause at the passenger side, leaning against the door. "You and me and this baby. And moving. And my friends and Inell and your parents. And work..."

"We're not five minutes out of the doctor's office and you're already stressing."

"I'm not stressing. Just thinking. Taking it all in."

I glance up at him, the father of the baby I'm carrying. For a fleeting moment, I think about how it could have been Malcolm, and the thought makes me sad.

I wouldn't have wanted a baby with Malcolm. I want a baby with Joseph.

He moves in and slides his arms around me. I am surrounded by him — arms, scent, the sound of his voice. "We'll take everything one day at a time, one step at a time, alright?"

"Together?"

"I'm not going anywhere, Max. I love you. I'm right here with you. We're going to do this together."

I've never had a man tell me he loved me–not like Joseph tells me. I love hearing it. He loves saying it. I love saying it back and having someone to speak those words to. And mean it.

"I love you too."

I let him hold me for a few moments until my stomach rumbles. Joseph laughs and digs the key fob out of his pocket to unlock the car. I get in on the passenger side, indulging Joseph in his latest affinity — driving a Maserati. A year ago, no one else had ever driven her. Today, I'd let him drive me to the ends of the earth and back.

Joseph presses the ignition button, and she roars to life, then adjusts for the heat and humidity. The fan blows cool air across my forehead. I relax against the headrest and close my eyes. And smile.

"You go to Ruby's all the time. You sure you want to go there today?"

I nod and keep smiling, eyes still closed. "Today is special. Special days call for Ruby's."

CHAPTER FORTY-FIVE

ebra

A loud tweet blasts from the whistle hanging around my neck, gaining the attention of two girls having a slap fight in the middle of the basketball court. "Ladies, I know you know better! To the sidelines and give me twenty push-ups!"

The girls grumble but stomp out of bounds and lazily, slowly do their exercises.

"Those are the sorriest push-ups I have ever seen. I ought to make you do them over." I snap my fingers and direct them to the bench where their teammates sit. They're already not happy that I'm making them play basketball, but they're not at the community center to sit around and text boys.

I'm not supposed to enjoy my punishment, but I do. A judge whose grandson had attended Morningside presided over my plea to reckless driving. I was sentenced to pay a fine and serve community service. Two Saturdays and one Friday a month, I volunteer at the West Atlanta Community Center. Two days a week, I help run a tutoring service at another center. It fills up the time I'm taking off from Morningside and I'm enjoying it so much, I might consider a new career.

"Lawrence. Patrick."

I call out two boys standing in a corner, having a quiet conversation. "If you're going to talk, fine. But move while you do it. How about some ping pong?" They frown and shake their heads. "Foosball?" More frowning. "Well, find something besides standing and exercising your jaws, or I'll find something for you. Get me?"

The kids hate it when I come on Saturdays. Or so they say, but when I'm not here, they ask when I'm coming back. They don't care about things like scandals, suspensions or a DUI. All they care about is this cool lady that seems to care about them. And brings her cute, just-turned-thirteen-year-old daughter sometimes.

Two short blasts on the whistle means activity time is up. I pull the lanyard from around my neck and hand it to my replacement, Monique. "They're your problem now."

"Gee, thanks," she says, jumping into action, heading to the basketball court where two boys are play wrestling. At least I hope they're playing. "I know I told y'all last week about that rough housing! Get off of him!"

I laugh, picking up my bag from under the desk and walk out the front door into the blazing sun. I check my watch and hurry toward my car.

It's been a few months at least since we had our regular brunch, what with my accident, Maxine and Renee fighting, then things getting busy with both of them. I'm excited to see my girls.

I hop into my new Benz coupe, the replacement for the totaled car. It's a newer model than I had before, loaded with bells and whistles. Maxine helped me pick it out. Willard rolled his eyes when I showed it to him in the catalog, then said he didn't care as long as it was within budget.

I disarm the security system, a necessary evil for the neighborhood, get in the car and press the ignition button. I can't get used to not needing a key to start the car. She purrs to life, and I put her in gear, ease her out of the parking lot and onto the street.

Willard is slowly making his way around. He hasn't moved back into our bedroom, but frequently sleeps in our bed. Janet prescribed weekly sex and in the beginning it was barely once a week. Now we're having sex a couple of times a week which is more than we'd had in the year before our separation. Who knew that all I had to do was drag him to a therapist to tell him to have sex with me?

I expected our first time together to be awkward. And it was. Clunky and quiet, with Willard just going through the motions. Over time though, it's done wonders. It's brought back tenderness between us. We can sit in the same room and talk and laugh about things. Share the couch, watch a movie with Kendra. Take a drive or pick up a few things from the grocery together. Willard is trying and I appreciate every stride.

Sex isn't a quick fix, though it has helped. We're still in therapy. We'll be in therapy until we don't need it anymore and who knows how long that will be? We have a lot to work out, Willard and I. He's still a little angry, but right now he loves me more than he hates me. It's a delicate dance, but we're learning the steps.

I officially resigned as Principal at Morningside. Not because of the scandal, not even because of the accident. I was prepared to ride out the storm but the longer I was away from the job, the less it mattered that I go back. The school didn't burn to the ground. The kids still arrive and go to class and eat lunch and depart. The world keeps turning, even though I'm not there.

In some ways I think maybe Charlotte was right. Maybe I wasn't ready for the job. Not mature or seasoned enough; not hardened enough. It takes more than loving the students and the staff and the building to be a good Principal. I didn't fail at my job but I wasn't a raging success either. I don't know if I'll go back to Administration, but I have a year to figure it out.

I haven't heard from David. Or about David. It's not that I don't care about what happens to him. I have a marriage that I'm trying to put back together and caring about David is what tore it apart. I wonder where he'll end up when his job at Morningside ends. I'm not going to find out.

I pull into the freshly paved parking lot at Ruby's. I can still smell the tar and the lines that mark the spaces are bright white. I park next to Maxine, press the key fob to lock the car and rush across the parking lot.

A Denali screeches to a halt in front of the entrance to Ruby's. The windows in the front are down and I hear laughter. I look back and see that it's Malcolm. Renee is fussing—laughing but fussing. She hops down from the cab, pushes the door closed and walks around the front of the truck.

"Have a good time. Call me when you're ready."

"Roll down Daddy's window a second?" The rear window rolls down to reveal Bernard in the back seat, wearing a Braves cap pulled low on his head. "Have fun today, okay, Daddy?"

"Where am I going?"

"You're going to the park to fish. Remember?" His face scrunches up and Renee steps back. "Don't forget his sunblock."

"Stop worrying," says Malcolm. "We'll be fine. Look, there's one of 'em behind you." He points to me; Renee turns and grins. Malcolm pulls away, performs a three-point turn in the parking lot and heads back onto the street.

"Seems like Malcolm is fitting into the family just fine," I comment, walking arm in arm up the sidewalk to Ruby's entrance.

"Yeah. I think Daddy likes him more than he likes me."

We laugh as we step inside, the bell over the door clanging to announce our entrance. Maxine gets up from the bench, looking irritated. Fortunately, I'm used to that face.

"Which of your arms was broken?" I gesture with the right arm. She grabs the left one and pulls me and Renee to the hostess stand. "We're all here. Can we sit now?"

The waitress shows us to our usual table, which has likely been standing in wait for an hour. The new policy at Ruby's, Maxine informs us, is that we can't seat ourselves anymore. "Even if you have a reserved table and have known the owner your entire life."

Renee laughs, playfully tapping her with a napkin as we all take our usual seats. "Why are you so pissy today?"

"Because I'm hungry."

The waitress brings water and sets a glass in front of Maxine. Before Max can even start, Renee stops her. "Perrier, a glass of ice and a straw for her. Please, before her head explodes."

Maxine grabs a package of crackers from the iron basket on the table, rips it open and shoves one into her mouth. Renee and I stare as she chews one, then the other cracker, crumples the wrapper and tosses it to the center of the table. She lifts her eyes to greet our stares.

"What? I had a light dinner last night, and I didn't eat this morning."

The waitress returns with the iconic green bottle, a glass of ice and a straw. Then, Maxine asks for a menu. Renee and I stare at her, again, as the waitress hands it to her.

"Okay, what is going on with you today, Maxine?" I ask.

"I can't change my mind every once in a while?"

"Sure you can. But you can't act crazy while you do it." I unwrap my straw and dunk it into my water glass, taking a few sips before setting it back on the table. "The omelet is good, if you're looking for something light."

Maxine visibly retches. "Ugh, no eggs. I think I'm having pancakes. Maybe some bacon. And some fruit. I've never had the fruit here."

She uncaps her Perrier, pours it into her glass, dunks her straw and takes several long drags. "So, how's everyone? What's new?"

"Nothing much over here," I answer. "Still volunteering and tutoring. The kids are cool. School ends next week and Willard is taking us on vacation."

"To where?" Maxine asks. "And if it's Chattanooga, I will wring your neck."

I laugh. "I'd wring my own neck. Getting up at five am to feed some goats is not a vacation. His parents have a beach house in Destin, so we're going to spend a couple of weeks out there. I'm looking forward to it."

"I think that's nice," says Renee. "You and Willard could really use the time away."

"I think it'll be good for us. Good for all of us. Even Willard is excited and Willard does not get excited."

"How are things, Willard-wise?" Renee asks.

"Things are okay. Really. Not perfect, but the counseling is working, and he's making an effort. That's all I can ask. We might just make it." I tap Renee on the arm, eager to change the subject. "And your world? How's Gladwell?"

"We're great. I hired a full-time clerk to help Lexie out. Unless things slow down–and pray they don't, it'll be a great summer. Which will be nice because it's the last summer I'll have Jessie."

"So she's really done this year?" Max asks. "Bernard must have worn her out."

"I don't think she's ready to be done with Daddy, but she's ready to be done with Atlanta Rehabilitation Center. She's been there for thirty years, so I guess she figures it's time. She's going to have to move in with her daughter, though. She lives about ten minutes away so Jessie can drop in to see Daddy any time."

"Does she want to live with her daughter?" I ask.

Renee hesitates, screwing her lips to the right before answering. "From what I can tell, I don't think so. But she doesn't really have a choice. Social security doesn't go very far these days."

"Couldn't you just hire her right out?" asks Maxine.

"Not at the rate she gets paid through Atlanta Rehab. Daddy's pension helps a lot, but I'm still stretching every dollar I can. I'm hoping I can find someone who's as good as she is that Daddy gets along with, and that's going to be hard."

"Good luck with that," I offer. "Maybe you can pay room and board as part of her compensation and work out a wage you can afford? Jessie knows Bernard. She's there all the time and you have the space. Then she doesn't have to live with her daughter and you keep the best nurse your father has ever had. And I'm betting that you can still apply for help through the state. They don't care if Jessie is working for an agency, just that someone's working the hours."

Renee sits up straight, her brows knit tightly together. I watch the wheels turn, albeit slowly, through her mind. "But… even if I could get her to agree to it, wouldn't that be like a twenty-four-seven gig? How is that better? At least now she gets to go home."

"You give her a couple of days a week to do whatever she wants to do. Live-in care doesn't have to be servitude. Let her define what will work for her. You want to keep her, right?" Renee nods, vigorously. "Then it's worth a shot."

"Exactly," agrees Max. "If she says no, you move on to the next option. You should look into it though, and I bet she'll do it."

"I'll think about that. I promise I will. But speaking of houses and moving…"

Renee turns to Maxine, hands propped on her hips. "Why are there bulldozers and a construction crew crawling all over Castle-rock? There's nothing there but a pile of dirt now."

I perk up at the mention of Maxine and Inell's old place. That little house held a lot of memories for us. "What? The house is gone?"

Maxine plucks another pack of crackers from the container on the table. "Inell got a letter from an investment firm offering her some number out of the blue for the house and the land. Seemed shady, so we looked into it. The house is worth nothing. But the land…"

Her lips form a smug grin. "The land has really appreciated, based on how revitalized the neighborhood has become. This builder is running through, snapping up properties and building these mini mansions. All of that renovation is bringing up property values. I'm sad to say I wasn't even paying attention. I could have some investment property."

Maxine pouts, but only briefly. "Anyway, they wanted to give Inell just under half a million for it. It's worth almost twice that."

My jaw drops. "Inell was sitting on million dollar property and didn't know it?"

Max crunches into another cracker and talks while she chews. "It settled out at around eight hundred thousand–more than we ever thought a pile of dirt and wood would be worth. She borrowed against it, razed the old house and we're building a new one in its place. Craftsman, brick exterior, updated finishes. Nothing big, but a far cry from the shack that used to be there. It should turn out nice."

"So Inell is moving back to Decatur? What about the Brookhaven house?"

"She was planning to build the new house and sell it, but those plans have changed recently. The crew is moving pretty quickly and uh..."

She bites her bottom lip in what I think is an attempt not to smile. "Inell wants to gift the house to Joseph and me. We're hoping to move in before the baby gets here."

She stops talking right there. Then smiles that big, brilliant Maxine smile like she hasn't just dropped the biggest bomb of her life on us.

I stare at Maxine. Hard. Renee stares at Maxine. I guess she's not sure she just heard that, either. Maxine is eating crackers and giving us the stupidest of grins.

"Maxine..." Gently, I tell myself. "Before whose baby gets here?"

Maxine chews and gulps down a mouthful of Saltines. "Mine," she answers, quiet as a church mouse. "Mine and Joseph's baby."

"So..." Renee takes the same approach as I do. Calm and quiet. "You're pregnant."

Maxine nods.

"Well."

I pause and try to breathe. But I can't. Maxine is pregnant. These are words I never thought would fly through my brain. "That's why you're crazier than usual today. But honey, do you want to be pregnant? Can I jump up and hug you, or is this not a good thing?"

Maxine sighs, her eyes rolling hard. "I said we wanted to be in the house before the baby comes. What did you think I meant by that? I've got to spell everything out for you?"

So I scream. Then Renee screams. And starts crying, because that's Renee. Maxine cries, probably because she's pregnant, and I cry because Maxine is crying. We get in our usual huddle — one of us in the middle, the other two alongside, and cry together.

When we surface, the waitress is standing near us, one eyebrow cocked, giving an uncomfortable stare to the three crazy ladies crying in the booth in the back. We laugh like it's not unusual at all and hurry to place our orders.

Maxine sniffles, plucking a Kleenex from a plastic pack. "I've been dying to tell you, but I wanted you to be together and I couldn't do it over the phone. I was going to tell you as soon as we sat down, but I was so hungry."

Renee frowns. "Where's your handkerchief? Maxine Donovan doesn't use Kleenex."

"Oh, I cry at the drop of a hat these days," she says, dabbing under each eye. "I got tired of washing the things. I'm going to have to give in to a lot of modern conveniences in the coming months."

"You mean like shopping at department stores?" I smirk at Renee across the table.

"Oh, stop."

Renee giggles. "Let's register her at Sears."

"Don't even think about it."

"Does Prada even make maternity clothes?"

"Of course they do," says Max, throwing me her exasperated look. "I've already bookmarked some cute things. I can't wait until I start to show."

"And Joseph? Is he okay about it? How'd he take it?"

"Like he's the only man that ever made a baby. He's already told everyone. I told him not to, because... you know." She shrugs.

"He said that was silly, and he was happy and he couldn't keep it to himself."

"Are you happy, Max?"

She's trying not to, but she beams when she smiles. "I am. This isn't how I thought it was going to go, but... I'm up for it. I kind of have to be though, don't I? It's going to happen. And Inell is more than ready to be a grandmother. She thought that wasn't ever going to happen."

"So, Maxine," says Renee, grinning like a fool. "Do you remember when you used to pick on me because I was fat?"

She scoffs, ripping open another packet of crackers. "Why are you bringing up old shit, Renee? We are so far past that."

"I'm just saying... you're going to gain some weight. I'm here for you."

"Shut up, Renee."

Between loud giggles, I suggest, "Maybe Maxine would like to borrow your Juicy Couture sweat suit? She loves that thing."

"I do not. It says Juicy across the ass!"

"It's comfortable. And roomy." Renee's eyes flick down Maxine's still slim physique. "You'll need it, eventually."

Maxine punches the air with the middle finger of both hands, but she's laughing. "Neither of you get to be Godmother. How about that?"

"You'll change your mind when we throw you a baby shower sponsored by Wal-Mart."

"At Wal-Mart," Renee adds.

"Why are we still friends?"

The waitress arrives right on time. I get the omelet and Renee gets the shrimp and grits. Maxine can't look at either of our plates. Head down, she cuts her pancakes and sausage into bite-sized pieces and drowns the plate in syrup.

"Is Malcolm still moving in with you, Renee?"

Renee blanches, by reflex, glancing at Maxine, who is elbow deep in syrup, moaning with every bite. I could say the building was on fire and I don't think she'd hear us.

"We're still talking about it. It's not that I don't want to live with him. I don't want him to give up his freedom. He's hell bent, though, and he's always at the house, anyway."

"What are his plans for his condo? I just sold that place to him, not even a year ago. It's a nice unit in a great space."

"He's thinking of subletting. Maybe to a student in the fall."

"I might have a tenant for him. One of my agents. Her husband dipped out on her. They lost the house, and she's staying with some relatives, but I know she'd like to get back out on her own. I'll connect the two of them, if he's interested."

"I'll let him know, Max. Thanks."

"And you know…" Bashful, Maxine's eyes lower to her plate, where half of a pancake sits soaking in thick syrup. "I think it's great that Malcolm has worked out for you. I'm thrilled for you."

"Don't make me cry again, Maxine."

"I won't. Then I'll start."

"And then I'll start." I pipe in. "And I'm done crying."

"Amen," says Maxine. "You know what girls? We've been friends for thirty years this year. Can you believe that?"

I look at Maxine, then Renee. Renee looks at me, then Maxine. Maxine's head swivels from me to Renee and back.

"Thirty years with you? Yes, I believe that."

We laugh together, like we always do. Then I lift my water glass. Renee lifts hers, and Maxine lifts her pretentious glass of Perrier.

"No matter what happens with us — kids, marriages, breakups, whatever…we're always going to have brunch at Ruby's."

"Hear, hear!"

Our glasses clink together, and we seal it with a sip.

We have to roll Maxine out of Ruby's. She's sleepy and silly, giggling as she wanders out of the front door. Her phone warbles from inside her bag. She digs for it and slides her thumb across the screen to pick up the call.

"Hey… we just finished eating," she says, watching Renee and

I bask in the warmth of the spring sun. "Yeah, I told them. We all cried. Yes, even me."

Renee and I crowd her and shout congratulations into the phone. Maxine laughs like I've never heard her laugh before and wiggles a few fingers before she bounces off to her car. I gawk at the flat, sensible shoes I didn't notice before and laugh out loud. I've never seen Maxine so happy. All those years, when she thought she had everything she needed, she had no idea.

I'd say I hope she knows that, but the glow on her face tells me she does.

The Denali slides into a parking space, its engine rumbling loudly. Through the windshield, I see Jessie in the backseat, talking Malcolm's ear off. Behind Malcolm, Bernard is slumped against the window with his hat over his face, fast asleep.

I offer a hug to Renee. "I'll call you this week. I want to order some books for the community center. I'm starting up a reading program."

"Sounds good," Renee says, her voice muffled by my shoulder. I pull back, but she hangs on for a few seconds longer than usual. "Thanks for your advice."

"Of course. I'm full of excellent advice for everyone else." My brave smile falters.

"You don't fool me, Debra Marie. We'll have some coffee or something when you pick up the books. Maybe you need to talk to someone that doesn't charge four hundred an hour."

"Yeah." I nod and bring out a genuine smile. "That would be nice. Now go. Hang out with your hot man."

"And my dad. And his nurse." She jokes, but her grin is wide as she backs away. "Love you, girl."

"Love you, too. Have fun and good luck." Renee climbs into the passenger seat of the truck and leans across the center console to kiss Malcolm. He backs out of the spot and rolls out of the parking lot, headed toward the Gladwell house.

I realize that I am still smiling. My smile must really be genuine. My bag vibrates as I walk to the car. I pull out my phone and see that Willard is calling. My heart skips a beat as I pick up the call.

"Willard? Is everything okay?"

"Everything's fine. I cut out early."

"Oh?" This is unheard of. Willard almost always works a full day on Saturday.

"Yeah. I thought we could do something easy for dinner. Maybe drop Kendra off at a movie and uh... you know."

I press the button on the key fob to unlock the car and dip inside. "Sounds good to me," I tell him, pressing the ignition button. Cool air blows through the car's interior. "What's your idea of easy?"

"Well, Kendra wants to order a pizza. I'm all for it."

"Why am I not surprised?"

While I was gone, my husband and daughter got themselves accustomed to delivery pizza. Willard mentioned in therapy that it drives him crazy how I never feed them anything that tastes good, that low fat pizza and light beer seem like a punishment. So, every once in a while, I ease up on my healthy eating rules and indulge them.

"I guess we could have a salad to go with the pizza."

I chuckle and give in. "That sounds good. I'll stop and pick up a few vegetables. Would you like me to get you something to drink?"

Willard hasn't had a drink since I've been home. He feels like he might tempt me and no matter how many times I tell him it doesn't work that way, he's sensitive to drinking around me. I almost hear the waiver in his voice, but he stands firm. "Nah," he says. "I'll be okay with what we've got here."

"I'll see you soon. Tell Kendra to find out what other kids are doing tonight, so she can go. And then... you know."

Willard's low laughter sounds seductive. "I'm on it. Drive safely."

"I will." And, because I haven't said it in a while, I tell him, "I love you, Willard."

It takes him a few beats, but he answers back. "I love you too, Debra. See you soon."

I end the call and stare at the phone for a second, blinking back tears. I hadn't heard those words from Willard in so long. Though they were said over the phone and not face to face, I am happy.

I wouldn't wish the last year of my life on my worst enemy. No, not even Charlotte Rogers. But I'm grateful for the lessons they forced me to learn.

I spent a long time looking for something to fill a void in my life. I didn't find it.

What I found was a renewed love for my husband, a new career and a stronger friendship with two wonderful women that I'll love for the rest of my life

I don't Have It All. Not by a long shot. But I want what I have. It's more than enough.

ABOUT THE AUTHOR

Atlanta based women's fiction and romance author DL White began seriously pursuing a writing career in 2011. She harbors a love for coffee and brunch, especially on a patio, but her true obsession is water— lakes, rivers, oceans, waterfalls! On the weekend, you'll probably find her near water and if she's lucky, on an ocean beach.

When not writing books, she devours them. She blogs reviews and thoughts on writing and books at BooksbyDLWhite.com. Grab a book by DL White and #Putitinyourface.

For more information about me/my books:

BooksbyDLWhite.com
authordl@booksbydlwhite.com

facebook.com/BooksbyDlWhite
twitter.com/author_dlwhite
instagram.com/author_dlwhite

ACKNOWLEDGMENTS

First to my "seasoned" readers... Thank You. I would not be here were it not for your interest in my work, so I am eternally grateful for your loyalty and encouragement!

To my new readers– thanks for taking a chance on this writer and this book. I truly hope you enjoyed reading Brunch at Ruby's and that you'll be on the lookout for more books and novellas in the near future.

I owe so much to people who've held me up when I wanted to quit. My long suffering Critique Partner/Beta/Circle of Truth And Things Like That Believer **Vicki M**– I wouldn't be here if it wasn't for you. Thank you from the bottom of my heart!

My Girl Time gals Paige and Jamie, **My NF gals**, **The PDubs**, **The Brunch Divas** (whose solidarity and beautiful friendship gave me the foundation for Ruby's), and **The Improperly Coiffured Trollops**– you are all my heart. I love you to the end of the earth and back. #14Hours, y'all.

No acknowledgement would be complete without thanking the best Bestie that ever Bestied, Ms. **Kimberly Flonnoy**, my countless (for serious, I had three rounds) Beta Readers (thanks **Vera!**), Critique Partners, writing pals and my ever supportive ring of friends and family. I like to say that writing is a solitary art, performed in concert. Thanks for joining my band.

~

ALSO BY DL WHITE

BOOKS
BY DL WHITE

Select titles available in ebook, paperback, and audio at
booksbydlwhite.com/books

FULL LENGTH NOVELS

Brunch at Ruby's

Dinner at Sam's

Beach Thing

Leslie's Curl & Dye

The Guy Next Door

A Thin Line

The Never List

SHORTS

Unexpected, A Holiday Short

Second Time Around, A Potter Lake Holiday Novella

The Kwanzaa Brunch, A Holiday Novella

Still I Rise (Coming Winter 2020)

CPSIA information can be obtained
at www.ICGtesting.com
Printed in the USA
BVHW032006110721
611678BV00006B/256

9 781735 968179